P9-CRC-748

"STEAMY."
—*Kirkus Reviews*

"WELL-POLISHED."
—*Seattle Post-Intelligencer*

"SATISFYING."
—*Publishers Weekly*

SOFT FOCUS

Jayne Ann Krentz

JOVE BOOKS, NEW YORK

SOFT FOCUS

A Jove Book / published by arrangement with
the author

PRINTING HISTORY
G. P. Putnam's Sons edition / December 1999
Jove edition / October 2000

The Penguin Putnam Inc. World Wide Web site address is
http://www.penguinputnam.com

ISBN: 0-515-12922-4

A JOVE BOOK ®
Jove Books are published by The Berkley Publishing Group,
a division of Penguin Putnam Inc.,
375 Hudson Street, New York, New York 10014.
JOVE and the "J" design
are trademarks belonging to Penguin Putnam Inc.

PRINTED IN THE UNITED STATES OF AMERICA

10 9 8 7 6 5 4 3 2 1

PROLOGUE

Six months earlier...

HE SAW HER COMING TOWARD HIM, AN AVENGING warrior princess in a crisp black business suit and high heels. Her dark hair was swept up into a stern knot at the back of her head. The little scarf at her throat matched the diamond-bright fire in her blue-green eyes. One look at her and the white-jacketed waiters leaped out of her path. She strode through the maze of linen-and-crystal-set tables, her gaze never wavering from her target.

The movers and shakers of Seattle's business community sensed disaster, or, at the very least, excellent gossip, in the making. A hush fell across the club's formal dining room.

Seated in the leather-cushioned booth, Jack watched her approach.

"Oh, shit." He spoke very, very softly. It was obviously too late to pray.

One look at the fury that etched Elizabeth Cabot's intelligent face told him that he had lost his gamble. She knew everything this morning. What had happened between them last night clearly made no difference to her now.

A heavy cloud of stoicism settled on him. He waited for

her with the patience of a man who knows he is facing an inescapable fate.

She was almost upon him now, and he knew that he was doomed. It was not his whole life that flashed before his eyes in those final moments, however. It was the memory of last night. He recalled the sweet, hot anticipation and the hungry rush of desire that had flashed between them. Unfortunately, that was all they had shared. The concentrated excitement had taken him by surprise, probably because he had worked so hard to contain it for the past month. In the end it had swept away his self-control and the lessons of experience that any man his age was expected to know. He was well aware of his mistakes. Elizabeth did not believe in faking her orgasms.

She had been very nice about it last night. Polite as hell. As if her failure to climax was her fault and hers alone. Actually, she had seemed quite unsurprised, as far as he could tell. It was as if she had not expected anything more from the encounter and had, therefore, not been disappointed. He had apologized and vowed to make amends just as soon as physically possible. But she had explained that she had to go home. Something about an early-morning meeting for which she had to prepare.

Reluctantly, he had driven her back to the gothic monstrosity she called home on Queen Anne Hill. When he had kissed her goodnight at the door of the mansion he had assured himself that he would get a second chance. Next time he would get it right.

But now he knew there wasn't going to be a next time.

Elizabeth arrived at the booth, vibrating with a degree of passion that had been noticeably missing in the final scenes last night.

"You conniving, two-faced, egg-sucking son of a bitch,"

she said between her teeth. "What made you think you'd get away with it, Jack Fairfax?"

"Don't be shy, Elizabeth. Tell me what you really think of me."

"Did you actually believe that I wouldn't find out who you are? Did you think that you could treat me like a mushroom? Keep me in the dark and feed me manure?"

There was no hope of defending himself. He could see that. But he had to try. "I never lied to you."

"The hell you didn't. You never told me the truth. Not once during the past month did you give me any hint that you were the bastard who engineered the Galloway takeover."

"That was a two-year-old business deal. It had nothing to do with us."

"It had *everything* to do with us, and you knew it. That's why you lied to me."

In spite of the hopelessness of the situation, or perhaps because of it, he started to get mad. "It's not my fault the Galloway deal never came up between us. You never asked me about it."

"Why would I do that?" Her voice rose. "How was I supposed to guess that you were involved in it?"

"You didn't work at Galloway. How was I supposed to guess that you had a connection to the company?" he countered.

"It doesn't matter. Don't you understand? That takeover was as ruthless, as cold-blooded, as anything I've ever seen in business. The fact that you were the hired gun who tore that company apart tells me exactly what kind of scum you really are."

"Elizabeth—"

"People got hurt in that takeover." Her hand clenched very

tightly around the strap of her elegant shoulder bag. "Badly hurt. I don't do business with men like you."

Jack saw Hugo, the maître d', hovering uneasily at a nearby table, obviously at a loss to decide how to quell the escalating scene. The waiter who had been on the way to the booth with ice water and bread halted, unmoving, a short distance away. Everyone in the dining room was listening now, but Elizabeth was oblivious to her audience.

Jack was morbidly fascinated himself, even though he was at ground zero. He would never have guessed that Elizabeth was capable of such drama. For the past month she had seemed so calm, so composed, so controlled.

"I think you'd better cool down," he said quietly.

"Give me one good reason."

"I'll give you two. Number one, we've got an audience. Number two, when you finally do cool off you are going to regret this scene a lot more than I will."

She smiled at him with such freezing disdain that he was amazed there were no icicles in her hair. She waved one hand in a wide arc that encompassed the entire dining room. He took that as a very bad sign.

"I don't give a damn about our audience," she said in ringing accents that no doubt carried all the way into the kitchen. "The way I look at it, I'm doing everyone here a public service by telling them that you are a lying SOB. I won't regret a single thing about this scene."

"You will when you finally remember that we've got a signed, sealed contract for the Excalibur deal. Like it or not, we're stuck with each other."

She blinked once. He saw the jolt of shock in her eyes. In the heat of her outrage, she had apparently forgotten the contract they had both signed yesterday morning.

She rallied swiftly. "I'll call the Fund's lawyers as soon as

I get back to the office. Consider our contract null and void as of today."

"Don't bother trying to bluff. You can't get out of our deal just because you've decided I'm an SOB. You signed that damned contract, and I'm going to hold you to it."

"We'll see about that."

He shrugged. "If you want to tie both of us up in court for the next ten or twelve months, be my guest. But I'll fight you all the way, and I'll win in the end. We both know it."

She was trapped, and he was pretty sure that she was too smart not to recognize that simple fact.

There was a tense moment while he watched her come to terms with the realization that he had won.

Frustrated rage flared once more in her face.

"You will pay for this, Jack Fairfax." She reached out and swept the pitcher of ice water off the tray held by the motionless waiter. "Sooner or later, I swear you will pay for what you did."

She dashed the contents of the water pitcher straight at him. He did not even try to duck. The only escape route was under the table, and somehow that option seemed more ignominious than staying in his seat.

The icy water splashing in his face ignited the temper that he had been struggling to control. He looked at Elizabeth. She was staring at him, the first signs of shock and horror lighting her eyes. He knew that it was just beginning to dawn on her that she had made an almighty fool of herself.

"This isn't about the Galloway deal, is it?" he said softly. "This is about last night."

Clutching her purse, she took a step back as if he had struck her. "Don't you dare bring up last night. This is not about last night, damn you."

"Sure it is." He swiped a chunk of ice off the shoulder of

his jacket. "I take full responsibility, of course. It's the gentlemanly thing to do, isn't it?"

She sucked in her breath in a stunned gasp. "Don't try to reduce this to sex. What happened last night is the least important aspect of this entire affair. In fact, what happened last night was so unimportant and so unmemorable that it doesn't even register on the scale."

Last night had meant nothing to her. He lost what little remained of the control he had been exerting over his anger. His hands closed around the edge of the table. He rose deliberately to his feet, heedless of the fact that he was still dripping ice water. He smiled slowly at Elizabeth.

"On my own behalf," he said with grave politeness, "I would like to say that I didn't know going in that I was dealing with the original Ice Princess. You should have warned me that you've got a little problem in that department. Who knows? With some extra time and effort, I might have been able to thaw you out."

As soon as the words were uttered, he regretted them. But they hung there in the air above the table, frozen, glittering shards of ice. He knew they would never melt.

Elizabeth fell back another step. Her face was flushed. Her eyes narrowed. "You really are a bastard, aren't you?" Her voice was low and much too even now. "You don't care a damn about what happened in the aftermath of the Galloway deal, do you?"

He ran a hand through his hair to get rid of some of the cold water. "No, I don't. Business is business, as far as I'm concerned. I don't believe in getting emotionally involved."

"I understand," she said. "That's precisely how I feel about last night."

She turned on one needle-sharp heel and walked out of the restaurant without a backward glance.

Jack watched her leave. He did not take his eyes off her until she disappeared through the door.

The twinges of impending fate that he had experienced when she had entered the dining room grew stronger. He knew that she must be feeling them, too.

They both knew the truth.

She could walk away from what had happened between them last night, but she could not walk away from the business contract they had signed. For better for worse, for richer for poorer, it bound them together more securely than any wedding license could have done.

CHAPTER ONE

SEATTLE
*Between midnight and dawn,
Wednesday morning*

HE WAITED FOR HER AT THE REAR OF THE PARK-
ing lot, huddled against the brick wall, shivering in the light
windbreaker. The streetlamp wasn't working right. It cast a
faltering, sickly glow that did little to dispel the shadows.
There were only a handful of cars left in the lot. Pioneer
Square was quiet at this hour. The nightclubs and the taverns
were closed. Other than the drunk he'd tripped over in the
alley, he'd seen no one else. That was a good thing, because
the kind of folks who did show up in this part of town at this
time of night were usually quite scary.

It was raining, a relentless mist that drove the predawn
chill deeper into his bones. But he knew it wasn't just the
night air that made him feel so cold. It was the fact that he
hadn't kept his twice-daily date with Madam Lola this
evening. He hadn't been able to afford her tonight, and now
he was paying the price.

He'd first met Madam L. back in grad school. He had
been a good student in those days. Everyone had said he had
a bright future in chemical engineering. Probably would
have held a few patents by now if he hadn't met Madam
Lola. It was a woman, a student in one of his classes, who'd

introduced him to Lola. She'd assured him that sex was great after just one dose. She'd been right. But Lola soon became more interesting than sex. More interesting than getting a Ph.D. in chemical engineering. More interesting than the successful future he'd once planned for himself.

Lola had taken over his life, and the lady was a harsh mistress. She demanded his obedient attendance twice a day. If he missed even one dose, he felt like that stuff on the parking lot pavement that he'd stepped in a few minutes ago. And he also felt cold. Very, very cold.

But *she* would be here soon, and she would bring the money she had promised to pay him and he would buy some more time with Madam L. and everything would be okay again. He could maintain pretty good when he kept up with his twice-daily appointments. Good enough to hold a job. For a while, at any rate. Balancing work and Lola was never easy. He could usually get by for a few months, and then something always went wrong. Either he failed a drug test or he started taking too many sick days. Or something.

He hoped he could last a while longer in his present job. He sort of liked it. Sometimes when he was working at Excalibur he pretended that he really had finished that doctorate; that he was a respected member of the research team like Dr. Page, maybe, not just a lowly lab tech. He felt bad about what he'd done tonight. But he hadn't had a choice. His salary at Excalibur was good, but it wasn't good enough to pay for the amount of time he had to spend with Lola these days. His other employer was very generous, though.

And *she* would be here soon. With lots of cash for Lola.

He heard her footsteps first, high heels echoing lightly on the wet pavement. He straightened away from the damp bricks, anticipation driving out some of the chill. Not long now and he would have what he needed to warm him once more.

"Hello, Ryan."

"About time you got here," he muttered.

She walked toward him through the thick shadows. The hood of a long, black raincoat concealed her face. "Everything went well tonight, I assume?"

"No problem. Lab's a mess. It'll take 'em days to clean up."

"Excellent. It was probably unnecessary. Just a precaution in the unlikely event that Fairfax or Excalibur security calls in the police. It will send them off in the wrong direction."

"Companies never call in the cops on this kind of thing if they can help it. Bad public relations. Freaks out the investors and clients."

"Yes. And that is the one thing that Excalibur can't afford to do right now." She moved her hand, reaching into her purse. "Well, I think that takes care of everything. You've been a fine employee, Ryan. I shall be sorry to let you go."

"Huh?"

"I'm afraid I don't need you anymore. In fact, you've become a liability." She removed her hand from her purse. There was just enough light from the dying streetlamp to reveal the glint of dark metal.

A gun.

He struggled to come to grips with the reality of what was happening. But by the time he understood, it was too late. She was like one of those women in the old black-and-white films that Dr. Page loved, he thought. A femme fatale.

She pulled the trigger twice. The second shot was unnecessary, but she wanted to be quite certain. There was a line in the script that summed up her philosophy on details.

A lady with a past has nothing to lose. But a woman with a future can't be too careful.

CHAPTER TWO

SOME CEOS HAD BAD DAYS.

Some got stuck with entire weeks that went so far south a map and compass were required to avoid the dreaded Sea of Red Ink.

He was now officially in that unfortunate latter group of corporate mariners, Jack concluded. He could even read the small printed warning at the edge of the map. *Beyond these shores there be dragons.*

It was enough to make a man superstitious. Apparently disasters really did occur in threes.

"We'll need damage control," Jack said. "Lots of it."

He surveyed the chaotic wreckage of what was left of Lab Two B. Broken glass and smashed equipment littered the workbenches. Sensitive instruments lay in pieces on the floor. One of the vandals had used a can of bloodred spray paint to scrawl the words "Vanguard of Tomorrow" on the east wall.

"This is too much," Milo moaned. "It's just too much on top of everything else. Excalibur will be ruined."

The monotonous litany was starting to get on Jack's nerves. But then, his store of patience had already been badly frayed.

The vandalism of Lab Two B was only the latest in a series of ominous incidents that had struck tiny Excalibur Advanced Materials Research in the past few hours. In the grand scheme of things, it was not even the worst incident that had occurred. The murdered lab tech topped the list.

"We'll deal with it, Milo," Jack said. He was paid to say things like that, he reminded himself. Today he was going to earn every cent of his salary.

"Deal with it?" Milo snapped around to face Jack, his thin face working furiously. There was a feverish light in his eyes. "How do you deal with the end of everything we've worked for for so long? How do you deal with a disaster? We're not going to get a second chance. The Veltran presentation can't be canceled. You know that."

"I said we can handle it."

"How are we supposed to do that?" Milo bounced wildly. "Getting Grady Veltran's attention in the first place was an incredible stroke of luck. You know his reputation. If we start making excuses and try to postpone the presentation even a day, he'll cross us off his list."

Jack suppressed a groan. He did not need this. He had enough problems on his hands. But Milo Ingersoll was his client. Clients needed to be handled with kid gloves at times like this. It was part of the job.

Milo was barely twenty-five, but as the only member of the eccentric Ingersoll clan who displayed any potential for leadership and management, he had assumed a heavy burden. Following the death of his great-aunt, Patricia Ingersoll, the founder of Excalibur, he had left engineering graduate school and taken the helm of the small, family-held company. Within days he had realized that he was in over his head. Patricia had been bedridden during the last year of her life. Without her guidance, the company had floundered.

When Milo took charge he realized at once that the firm was on the brink of bankruptcy. He also understood that he lacked the management skills and experience to pull it back from the brink.

He'd known that he needed help, and he'd known that he needed it fast.

Displaying the foresight, determination, and raw passion that Jack figured would one day make Milo a formidable executive, he had sought out a turnaround specialist, a consultant who might be able to save the faltering little high-tech company.

Jack would never forget the day the intense young man had burst into his office and alternately demanded and pleaded for assistance. Milo had been passionate, frenzied, willing to do anything, promise anything, sign anything, to save the family firm.

The Excalibur situation presented just the kind of problem that intrigued Jack. Saving small, closely held companies in dire straits was his specialty. Training his replacement, in this case Milo, was part of the package deal. He had long ago understood that teaching and mentoring the next generation of leadership was crucial to real long-term success. There wasn't much point salvaging a small company if it went under the day after the turnaround specialist walked out the door because no one left behind could manage it.

Milo had all the qualities needed for his future job. He was enthusiastic, intelligent, hardworking, and, most important, wholly devoted to Excalibur. During the past six months he had begun to imitate Jack in a variety of ways, not the least of which was his choice of attire. He now routinely eschewed the casual look that was endemic throughout the high-tech industry in favor of a classic suit and tie. Unfortunately, his taste still tended toward green and brown.

Jack had made a mental note to take Milo to a good tailor before he finished the Excalibur project.

But this morning Milo was not a model of the conservative business style. He had still been in bed when Jack had phoned him to tell him about the vandalism. Milo had apparently been so shaken by the news that he had not bothered to finish dressing before he left the house. He had managed to pull on a pair of jeans, but he was still wearing the top half of what looked like very old, very faded, striped pajamas. His bony bare feet were encased in worn, scuffed slippers. His red hair stood up in jagged little tufts. Behind the thick lenses of his heavy, black-framed glasses, his sharp hazel eyes glittered with a combination of outrage and frantic despair.

Jack took pity on him.

"This isn't a disaster, Milo," he said quietly. "It's a setback, but it's not a disaster."

"I don't see how you can tell the difference."

"Trust me, I can tell." Jack glanced at the thick-bellied man hovering uneasily in the doorway. "All right, Ron, let's get this lab cleaned up."

"Yes, sir." Ron Attwell, the head of what passed for Excalibur's small security department, was sweating. There were dark stains under the arms of his khaki uniform shirt. Perspiration beaded his forehead.

Jack didn't blame him. He wasn't feeling real cool himself, in spite of the fact that, like everything else in Lab Two B, the HVAC system was state-of-the-art. The air-conditioning was the only thing that was still working in the trashed research wing.

Milo was right, the ruined lab definitely qualified as a disaster, but damned if he was going to admit it out loud, Jack thought. He was the guy in charge. It was his job to pretend

that there were no problems that could not be dealt with here
at Excalibur.

"I want full security maintained," Jack continued quietly.
"Use only janitorial staff who have been authorized to work
in this building and make certain no one throws anything
away, not even a broken bottle, until someone on the Soft
Focus team has looked at it first. Got that?"

"Yes, sir."

Milo twisted his long-fingered hands in a gesture that
would have done credit to a character in the last act of *Car-
men*. "What's the point of employing full security measures
now? Talk about closing the barn door after the horse has
gone."

"Milo," Jack said very softly.

Milo jerked at the tone of voice. He blinked quickly and
broke off abruptly.

Jack held Ron's gaze. "Box up all the debris and leave it
here in the lab. Make sure nothing gets hauled away."

"Yes, sir." Ron wiped his forehead on the back of his
khaki sleeve. "I'll get right on it, Mr. Fairfax."

"Make sure everyone involved in the cleanup keeps his or
her mouth shut. Understood?"

"Yes, sir."

"Anyone who discusses the situation outside the company
will receive an automatic pink slip."

"Yes, sir." Ron dug a notepad out of his left pocket and
fumbled for a pen. "I'll do my best, sir, but you know what
rumors are like in this business."

"I know," Jack said. "But our official stance is that no serious damage was done."

Milo scowled. "Is that why we're not calling the cops?"

"Yes."

"But why bother trying to keep this a secret? We're not

the only place that's been hit by those damned Vanguard of Tomorrow crazies. They ransacked one of the labs at the UW last month. It was in the papers."

"And there was that software-design firm they tore up a few weeks ago," Ron volunteered. "Tried to torch the place."

Jack gave each man a level look. "We don't need this kind of publicity. The last thing we want to do is call attention to Excalibur's security problems."

Ron blanched. "Yes, sir."

Milo scowled. "It's not as if—"

Jack quirked a brow in Ron's direction. Preoccupied with making notes on his pad, Attwell did not notice the small gesture. Milo, however, finally seemed to get the point. He shut his mouth, tightened his lips into a thin, disgruntled line, and reluctantly subsided.

"Any kind of publicity which implies a weakness in our internal security measures is bad for the company," Jack said with a patience he was far from feeling. "That type of news tends to make potential clients and customers very, very nervous. I doubt if we'll be able to keep a complete lid on this, because the Vanguard of Tomorrow crowd will probably go straight to the media to take the credit. But we're going to try to minimize the story on our end. Understood?"

"Yes, sir." Ron snapped his notepad closed.

"It's your job to limit the in-house leaks, Ron," Jack said. "Langley in PR will handle the press."

"Right." Attwell shoved his fingers through his thinning gray hair. He drew himself up with a visible effort and straightened his slumped shoulders. "I'm sorry, sir. This shouldn't have happened. Those thugs never should have gotten in like that." He made a disgusted sound. "We've never had any kind of trouble like this before. Who'd have figured?"

"Yes," Jack said. "Who'd have figured?" Obviously no one in Excalibur's creaky, painfully old-fashioned security department, he thought. But he refrained from pointing that out.

Updating security at Excalibur had been on the list of priorities he had made six months ago when he had agreed to take the CEO position. But retooling a low-tech group of night watchmen, most of whom were nearing retirement, into a modern, streamlined, security team required time and money. There had been so many other priorities, he reflected, none of them cheap. Excalibur's financial resources were limited. It had been his decision to pour everything into the Soft Focus project.

But sometime during the past twenty-four hours, Tyler Page, the researcher scientist who had finally made Soft Focus work, had disappeared together with the only existing specimen of the newly developed, high-tech crystal. It was enough to give even a sane, logical, reasonable executive a case of paranoia.

He turned on his heel and walked toward the swinging doors. "I'm going back to my office. Keep the area clear of unauthorized personnel during cleanup, Ron. Report to me when you're finished."

"Yes, sir." Ron cleared his throat. "Sir, I'd like to tell you again how damned sorry I am about all this."

"If you apologize one more time," Jack warned, "I'll fire you."

Ron flinched. "Yes, sir."

Jack planted a hand against one of the heavy doors, shoved it open, and went out into the hall.

"Wait," Milo called. "Hold up there a minute, Jack. I want to talk to you."

"Later, Milo. Right now I've got to get hold of Langley. I want to brief him before the press starts calling."

"I know, I know." Milo trotted into the hall behind Jack. "But we've got to talk about the other situation."

"Later." Jack kept moving toward the elevators.

"No. Now." Milo bustled along beside him. "What if this business with the murder and the trashed lab brings that . . . that *woman* here? She'll start asking questions."

"Don't worry, if Elizabeth Cabot shows up, I'll handle her." Talk about wild, outrageous promises. If his recent track record was any indicator, he'd be lucky not to get impaled on the heel of one of her expensive, made-in-Italy, leather pumps.

Milo snorted. "But you know what she's like at the monthly board meetings. Always wanting details and demanding information. If she gets wind of the fact that Page and the specimen are missing, there's no telling what will happen."

"You're wrong."

Hope flared in Milo's eyes. "I am?"

"Sure." Jack smiled grimly. "I know exactly what she'll do. She'll cut off our funding before we can finish sweeping up Lab Two B."

He was pretty sure Elizabeth had been looking for an excuse to rip up their contract for the past six months. The destruction of the lab and the disappearance of Soft Focus would give the Aurora Fund lawyers grounds to claim that the company was no longer financially viable. As the major creditor, the Fund could force Excalibur into bankruptcy.

"I knew it," Milo whispered. "We haven't got a prayer."

"Get a grip. If Elizabeth Cabot calls about the vandalism, I'll deal with her. There's no reason for her to suspect that we've got a problem with the Soft Focus project."

"But what if she does suspect something?" Milo quivered in agitation. "What if she starts nosing around? Asking questions? You know how pushy she can get."

"If she asks any questions, I'll answer them."

"But *how*?"

"Dunno. Maybe I'll try a nice, bald-faced lie."

Milo stared at him. "How can you make jokes at a time like this?"

"I wasn't joking. Like I said, I'll deal with Elizabeth Cabot. You concentrate on handling your family. We don't want any of them to get word of this, either."

Milo blinked several times and then grunted. "Aunt Dolores would have hysterics. Uncle Ivo would probably collapse. God only knows what my cousins would do. Especially Angela."

"You know damn well what Angela would do. She'd start demanding that Excalibur be sold or merged. She's been pushing for that since your aunt died."

Milo's hand closed into a fist. His head came up. "Never. This is my company. Aunt Patricia left it to me because she knew I would take care of it for the family."

Jack smiled slightly in spite of his foul mood. "That's the spirit, Milo. Don't worry, we'll recover Soft Focus."

"But how are we going to do that?"

"Leave it to me." Jack stopped in front of the elevators and punched the call button. "I'll get it back. But it will take some time. I'm going to have to turn everything else over to you for the next ten days or so."

"Ten days? But the Veltran demonstration is scheduled for two weeks from today. We have to have the crystal back in the lab by then or everything goes right down the toilet."

"As you just pointed out, we've got two weeks," Jack said quietly. "You haven't had as much experience as I'd like yet, but we don't have any choice. You're going to have to handle your family and the press and day-to-day operations here at Excalibur all by yourself while I'm gone. Think you can do it?"

"Of course I can do it. That's not the issue. The issue is the crystal."

"I'm aware of that."

The elevator doors finally opened. Mercifully, something was working right today. Jack got into the car and stabbed the button that would take him to the third floor. He looked out at Milo's haunted face and dredged up another dose of reassurance. "I'll find it, Milo."

"How the hell are you going to do that?" Milo wailed.

Jack smiled humorlessly. "Thought I'd start by taking a vacation."

The elevator doors finally closed, cutting off Milo's keening cry in mid-shriek.

Alone in the cab, Jack propped one shoulder against the paneled wall and gazed unseeingly at the lights on the control panel. The bottom line was that Milo was right. The loss of Soft Focus was a major catastrophe for Excalibur.

With its unique optical properties the hybrid colloidal crystal had the potential to play a critical role in the development of the next wave of computer development, a generation of systems founded on light-based technology. Optical computers worked by encoding information into light pulses. Soft Focus was designed to control and transmit light in highly specific ways on a microscopic level.

Patricia Ingersoll, a brilliant researcher with a host of patents, had developed the concept, but she had become ill and died before she could make it a reality in her labs. Tyler Page, an equally brilliant, but extremely eccentric member of Excalibur's R & D team, had worked closely with her for years. Page had been certain that he could complete the work on the crystal.

When Jack had taken on the task of saving Excalibur, he had made the decision to base the entire future of the company on the development of Soft Focus. In retrospect, it was possible that he had made a monumental mistake, he thought as he got off the elevator. But it was not as if there had been anything else to go with. Without the crystal, there was no way to salvage Excalibur.

He had sought funding from all the usual sources and had been rejected by all of them, in spite of his personal track record. The bottom line was that no one was willing to back Excalibur now that Patricia Ingersoll was gone.

Late one night, while going through a pile of the company's old financial records with the assistance of a medicinal glass of scotch, Jack had made the discovery that once, several years ago, the Aurora Fund had backed an Excalibur project. From what he could discern, it looked as if the deal had been some kind of personal arrangement between Patricia Ingersoll and the Fund's previous manager, Sybil Cabot. The contract had been nothing more than a paragraph-long agreement. It would have meant little in court.

He had soon learned that Sybil had died two years before. She had left the Fund in the hands of her niece.

Without a lot of hope but seriously short of alternatives, he had contacted the Fund's new manager, Elizabeth Cabot, and proposed a renewed financial commitment. To his amazement, she had agreed to discuss it.

The morning he walked into her office, located on the first floor of the old mansion, he had known he was in very serious trouble. After an hour in Elizabeth's company, he had finally acknowledged to himself that he was going to consign all his ironclad rules against mixing business and pleasure to hell.

She had gone for the Excalibur pitch. She had also accepted his invitation to dinner.

Two weeks later, he had discovered her connection to the Galloway deal and he had known that he was walking a tightrope.

He forced aside thoughts of the past as the elevator doors opened. He went down the carpeted hall to the executive suite. It was early, not yet eight o'clock. This floor was still quiet.

In his mind, he quickly made his list of priorities. The first item on the agenda was to ask his secretary to check with HR to get a phone number for Ryan Kendle's next of kin. Durand, the detective in charge of the murder investigation, had said he would take care of notifying the man's relatives. But as the CEO of Excalibur and Ryan Kendle's employer, Jack knew he had a responsibility in the matter. He did not look forward to the task.

According to Kendle's personnel file he had no family here in the Seattle area. He had been hired a few months ago to work as a lab technician. He had been a loner with no close friends at Excalibur. And now the man was dead.

Durand's working theory was that Kendle had been into the drug scene. He'd explained that the lab tech had been shot when a drug transaction apparently went sour sometime between midnight and dawn in a deserted parking lot in Pioneer Square.

Jack walked into the outer room of the executive suite. A wave of relief went through him when he saw that his secretary had come in early. Marion was on her feet behind her desk, making coffee.

She turned quickly, a strained expression on her round

face. Behind the lenses of her oversize glasses, her eyes were wide with anxiety. The coffee scoop clattered on the table.

"Mr. Fairfax."

"I can't tell you how glad I am to see you, Marion. We've got a hell of a day ahead of us. Remind me of this when we do your next performance review."

"Mr. Fairfax, there's something you should—"

"Later. The only way we're going to get through this morning is one step at a time."

Jack slung his black windbreaker over a hook on the aging brass coatrack in the corner. When he had assumed the CEO position at Excalibur six months ago he had discovered that the company had taken the concept of dress-down Fridays to the outer limits. All the way to Thursday, in fact. Flannel shirts, jeans, and running shoes were the norm for most of the staff.

From the start, however, he had routinely come to work in a suit and tie, even on Fridays. He was an old-fashioned kind of guy in some ways. This morning, however, when the three A.M. phone call informing him of Excalibur's newest disaster had come, he had yanked on the first items of clothing he had found in his closet, a long-sleeved black pullover and a pair of jeans.

The call had not awakened him. At three this morning he had been sitting in the darkness in his living room, staring at the lights on Queen Anne Hill, a glass of scotch in his hand, contemplating the loss of Soft Focus. He had discovered only hours earlier that it had vanished from the lab vault.

He glanced at Marion as he went past her desk toward the door of his office. "I take it you've heard what happened in Lab Two B, Marion?"

"Yes, sir. The security guard told me when I arrived."

"The media will be on the phone soon. The Vanguard of

Tomorrow bunch won't waste any time crowing about their latest strike against the evils of technology." Jack paused, his hand on the doorknob. "Call Langley. I want to see him immediately."

"Yes, sir."

"No one except Langley or me talks to the press. Got that?"

"I understand, sir." Marion gazed at him with an odd expression. She lowered her voice. "But that's not what I wanted to tell you, sir. When I got here a few minutes ago, I found someone waiting in your office."

"That homicide detective? Durand? Is he back?" Jack looked at Marion over his shoulder as he pushed open the door. "What's he want now? I've already instructed HR to give him a copy of everything we've got in Kendle's files."

"No, sir." Marion cleared her throat in a very pointed manner. "Not the detective."

"Who the hell would have the nerve to go into my office without—" He stopped when he saw the woman who stood in front of the floor-to-ceiling window.

Damn. He had been wrong earlier when he had concluded that disasters came in threes. Today his came in fours.

CHAPTER THREE

SHE HAD SWEATED OUT THIS CONFRONTATION for most of the night. Now that the inevitable was upon her, she was surprised by her own reaction. She was cool.

True, she could feel the telltale tingling on the nape of her neck, but she always got that disturbing sensation when Jack was in the vicinity. And she was definitely a little tense. No, make that very tense. But she could handle some tension. She was accustomed to it after having attended six monthly meetings of the Excalibur board of directors.

The important thing was that she was in total command of herself. Her hands were not waving in the air. She was not shivering with anger. She had her back to him as she studied the view of the Excalibur parking lot and the broad expanse of Lake Washington in the distance.

Definitely cool.

She'd dressed for battle this morning. Her hair was pulled into a severe, sleek twist. She wore a silver-gray suit with a very fine stripe woven into the expensive fabric. The fitted jacket was padded a bit to give her shoulders a strong line. The cuffs of the trousers broke across the instep of a pair of high-heeled leather pumps. Gold gleamed discreetly in her ears.

All she lacked was a riding crop to complete the image. It was a depressing thought.

"Good morning, Elizabeth. Always nice to have you drop in for a visit."

Whatever happened, she would not lose her temper and start yelling at him.

She was cool.

That was good to know, because she was furious with him. And ever since the disaster in the Pacific Rim Club dining room, she had harbored the deep, abiding fear that one day she would again lose her self-control with Jack and make a fool of herself a second time.

She turned slowly away from the view of the mist-shrouded lake and the ghostly monoliths of the Seattle office towers that lay beyond.

She made certain that her coolest, coldest smile was firmly fixed in place. It was not easy. She wondered how long it would take before she could look at him without feeling that little rush of excitement that made her insides tighten and her breath catch in her throat. It had been six months now. The situation was not improving.

She sought refuge in the business that had brought her here today.

"Good morning," she said crisply. "I understand you've got a problem here at Excalibur."

"Nothing we can't handle." He closed the door and motioned her to a chair. "Have a seat. I'll ask Marion to bring in some coffee."

"Thank you." She walked to the nearest padded leather chair and sat down. Very deliberately she twitched the fine wool fabric of her hand-tailored trousers and crossed her legs.

She was cool and she was in control, all right, but she was breathing a little too fast and she could feel her own pulse. All she had done was walk across the office, but her body was reacting as though she were thirty-five minutes into her forty-five-minute daily workout routine.

She watched Jack go to his desk and sink down into the black leather chair. He leaned forward, punched a button, and spoke briefly to his secretary.

With a small sense of shock, Elizabeth noticed that his thick, dark hair was a little tousled looking, as if he had combed it with his fingers. Either that or someone else's fingers had recently been running through it. Very firmly she suppressed the twinge of dismay that thought induced.

Still, it was odd to see him looking so casual, she thought. On the handful of occasions they had been in each other's presence during the past few months, Jack had always been dressed in full executive battle dress: expensively cut suit, a crisp shirt, and a conservative tie.

This morning his black pullover and jeans made him look even more dangerous than usual, she thought. Probably because the snug-fitting clothes made it obvious that the power in his shoulders and the lean, graceful strength of his body were for real, not a product of good tailoring.

At some point during the course of those first, heady few weeks together, she had discovered that he worked out regularly, too. But instead of pursuing a standard physical fitness program at his athletic club, he studied one of the more obscure martial arts.

At the time she had taken his interest in the exotic exercise and philosophy as an indication of a deeply buried

romantic streak. Which only went to show what lust had
done to the analytical side of her brain, she decided. It was
perfectly clear now that Jack studied the ancient theories of
strategy and defense because he was endowed with a ruthless, not a romantic, streak. The bastard was a born predator.

The door opened. Marion appeared with two cups of coffee. She glanced uneasily at Jack, as though seeking guidance. Then she plastered a smile on her face and handed one
of the cups to Elizabeth.

"Thank you," Elizabeth said.

"You're welcome, Miss Cabot." Marion put the second
cup on Jack's desk and fled.

Elizabeth pretended not to notice. She was well aware
that here at Excalibur she was viewed with great wariness.
Everyone knew that she held the reins of the Aurora Fund
and that the Fund controlled the fate of Excalibur.

She wouldn't be surprised if all of the employees had
heard the tale of the disastrous scene in the Pacific Rim Club
dining room, too. Gossip like that had a way of getting
around town.

Jack took a deep swallow from his cup, lounged back in
his chair, and looked at Elizabeth. "So you heard about our
little problems already? I'm surprised the news reached you
so quickly."

She raised her brows. "Yes, I'm sure you are. How long
did you intend to keep it quiet?"

He shrugged. "Just found out about it, myself, a few hours
ago. Haven't even heard from the press yet."

She frowned. "You're going to talk to the media about
this?"

"Probably won't be able to avoid it."

"I see. And just what, exactly, do you plan to tell the
reporters when they do get here?"

"Not much to tell, is there?" Jack took another swallow of coffee and set down his cup. "We got hit by the same crowd that trashed the university and the Ecto-Design labs. The cleanup will take a few days, but Two B should be functioning at full capacity again by the middle of next week. In the meantime, we're strengthening our security measures."

She stared at him, momentarily thrown off stride. "What in the world are you talking about?"

He gave her a politely inquiring look. "I beg your pardon, Miss Cabot. I assumed we were discussing the incident we had here at Excalibur early this morning."

"What incident?"

"Last night one of our labs was hit by the Vanguard of Tomorrow group. You've heard of them?"

"Yes, of course." His air of excessively civil patience made her want to toss her coffee cup at his head. She reminded herself of what had happened the last time she had given in to the temptation to throw stuff at Jack Fairfax. "A bunch of antitechnology nuts. How much damage was done?"

He shrugged. "The lab is a mess. We lost some expensive electronic equipment. Insurance should take care of most of it. Like I said, we'll have things back in operation in a few days."

"I see." She drummed her fingers on the arm of her chair. "Excalibur seems to have hit a run of bad luck lately."

Jack's brow climbed. "You know about Kendle, too?"

"Kendle?"

"The lab tech who got killed in Pioneer Square sometime early this morning. The cops say he was into the drug scene. Someone pulled a gun on him in a parking lot."

"No, I hadn't heard about Mr. Kendle's death. I'm sorry."

"So are we all, Miss Cabot." Jack sat forward and clasped

his hands on his desk. "But rest assured neither Kendle's death nor the VT break-in will have any impact on the Soft Focus project. The Veltran presentation will take place on schedule. There was no need for you to come running all the way over here from Seattle to check on the status of your investment."

He had gall, she thought, trying to make her sound like a coldhearted Scrooge. As if she were mean-spirited to worry about the sizable amount of cash he had tricked the Aurora Fund into pouring into Excalibur.

She met his eyes. "I appreciate your assurances, Jack. And I believe you when you say that your employee's death and the trashing of the lab will not affect the Soft Focus project."

"Good. Now, then, if you're satisfied with the situation, I've got a full calendar today. I'm going to have to ask you to leave so that I can do my job."

"But I'm not satisfied," she said smoothly. "I merely said I understood that the murder and the break-in had no impact on the project. How could they?" She paused for a beat. "According to my information, Soft Focus has disappeared."

She had to give him credit, she thought. He did not even flinch.

"Where the hell did you get that idea?" he asked.

She took her time recrossing her legs. "I had dinner with Hayden Shaw last night."

"How nice for you." Jack gave her a politely inquiring look. "His divorce is final, then?"

She stiffened. "I didn't ask. It was a business dinner."

"Right. A business dinner. So Shaw is courting investors to help him get his new generation of fiber-optic networking devices off the ground, huh? I wondered when he'd finally get that project moving. It's been stalled for nearly a year."

Hayden would have been stunned to know that word of his top-secret development plans had already reached his archrival, Elizabeth thought. She reminded herself to proceed with caution. Jack and Hayden had a history. She knew nothing about the origins of the feud between the two men, but she was well aware that it went far beyond the scope of any reasonable business competition.

"You're aware of the Frontrunner project?" she asked.

"Sure. Shaw's going to throw a lot of money down that rat hole before he's finished, but that's his problem, not mine."

She ignored the amused disdain in his voice. "Hayden said he'd heard rumors that the only existing specimen of a newly developed material had been stolen from an Excalibur lab."

Jack steepled his fingers. "I've got some free advice for you, Miss Cabot."

"That's a very kind offer, especially in view of the fact that nothing else in our association has been even remotely inexpensive, let alone free," she murmured. "However, I'm not in the market for advice."

"That doesn't surprise me. But out of the goodness of my heart, I'm going to give it to you anyway." Jack met her eyes. "Don't trust Hayden Shaw any farther than you can throw him."

"Funny, he gave me some very similar advice concerning you."

"I'll bet he did."

She picked up her coffee again. "I suggest we get back to the subject of the rumors."

"You know as well as I do that in this business rumors are as common as stock options in new start-up companies, and even less likely to pay off."

"Are you telling me that the rumor Hayden heard has no basis in fact? Soft Focus is not in trouble?"

"I'm telling you that everything is under control here at Excalibur."

In spite of all the promises that she had made to herself on the way here this morning, she lost her temper. "Damn it, Jack, don't lie to me. I've sunk several hundred thousand dollars of Aurora Fund cash into this venture. I've got a seat on your board."

He winced. "You don't have to remind me about your position on my board."

"I've got a right to know what's going on."

He said nothing for a moment, just studied her intently, as if she were an interesting lab specimen. Then he shrugged. "What, exactly, did Shaw say?"

With an effort of will she regained her self-control. "I just told you, he said he'd heard that a new R & D specimen was stolen from your labs. We both know that the only secret Excalibur has is Soft Focus. Has the crystal disappeared, Jack? I want the truth. Yes or no?"

He gazed at her for a very long time, a dark, brooding expression in his honey and gold eyes. Her heart sank. He was going to lie to her, after all, she thought. What had ever made her think that he would tell her the truth? He had his list of priorities. If she was on it at all, her position was no doubt very near the bottom with a little notation next to her name: Ignore whenever possible; stonewall when cornered.

"True," Jack said. "The crystal is gone, and so is Tyler Page."

She stared at him, more stunned by the unexpected honesty than by the news that Soft Focus really had disappeared. She got her mouth closed and regrouped quickly.

"You weren't going to tell me, were you?" she asked.

"Not if I could avoid it." He unclasped his hands and spread them slightly. "I had a plan, you see."

"Yes, I'm sure you did. You always seem to have a plan, Jack. But it's a bit late to come up with one now, isn't it? Speaking as a member of the board, I think it would have been smarter to tighten your security *before* Soft Focus disappeared."

"The plan, Miss Cabot, was to find Tyler Page and the crystal before you or anyone else learned that they were missing."

"When, exactly, did they disappear?"

"I'm not sure. I worked late last night. On a whim, I performed an unscheduled security check at about nine o'clock. That's when I found out that the crystal was gone. An empty, duplicate container had been left in its place. If I hadn't checked the contents, I still wouldn't know that Soft Focus was gone."

She frowned. "A duplicate container was left behind?"

"Yes. It's still there in the vault. I've told no one else except Milo. As far as everyone else is concerned, the crystal is still safe in the lab. The research team has been instructed not to touch it until Dr. Page returns."

"You must have some idea of when it disappeared?"

His mouth twisted slightly. "Tyler Page went home sick yesterday afternoon. I think he took the specimen with him when he left Excalibur."

"Are you telling me that he just walked out of here with Soft Focus?"

"Tyler Page is the most respected member of the research team. Security had no reason to search him."

A fresh wave of outrage shot through her. "Why wasn't I told immediately?"

"Primarily because I knew you'd go ballistic and start threatening to yank our funding."

She smiled coldly. "You were wrong."

"Was I?"

"On one count, at least." She shot to her feet. "I'm not going to go ballistic. But I certainly intend to speak with my lawyers as soon as I get back to the office. Without the crystal, Excalibur is dead in the water, and we both know it. The Fund has a right to terminate the contract."

"That's a little shortsighted, don't you think? You and your precious Fund stand to lose a fortune in future profits. Soft Focus will be worth millions in the long term."

"You'll have to find it first, won't you?"

"I'll find it, Miss Cabot." His eyes were brilliant, unwavering. "Don't doubt that for even a second."

The relentless certainty in his voice sent an electric chill across her nerve endings. He meant every word he said. He would do whatever it took to recover the crystal.

Slowly she sank back down into the chair. "So, what's this plan of yours?"

He studied her thoughtfully for a long time. Then he got to his feet and dug a set of car keys out of the pocket of his jeans. "Come with me. I want to show you something."

She hesitated.

He glanced back at her over his shoulder as he went toward the door. "Don't worry. I'm not planning to invite you to view my etchings again. I learned my lesson six months ago."

CHAPTER FOUR

SHE WAS STILL SEETHING WITH RESENTMENT fifteen minutes later when Jack brought the car to a halt in front of the nondescript little house. She hated the fact that he could put her on the defensive so easily. Just a single, pointed reminder of their one-night stand, that's all it had taken. How was it possible that he could still have this effect on her? He was the one who should have been mortified by the reference to the short-lived affair, not her.

She studied the dirty windows, the unkempt, overgrown front yard, and the chipped and flaking paint on the porch.

"This is Dr. Page's home?"

"Yes. As you can see, he's not big on the details of household maintenance." Jack shut off the engine, removed the keys from the ignition, and climbed out. He leaned down to speak to her through the opening. "I came here looking for him last night as soon as I realized that Soft Focus was missing. He was already long gone."

She slowly got out of the car. Jack walked around the hood to join her. Together they went up the cracked sidewalk. She watched him remove a key from his wallet.

"Where did you get that?" she demanded.

"You are a suspicious woman, Miss Cabot."

"Some things I learn the hard way, but I do, eventually, learn them. I've come to understand, for instance, that it pays to ask questions first where you're concerned."

He acknowledged the unsubtle accusation with a slight inclination of his head. "I know what you mean about learning things the hard way. Take me, for instance. I haven't ordered ice water in a restaurant in six months."

She eyed him sharply. This was the second nasty crack he had made concerning lessons learned. Surely he was not hinting that he considered himself the injured party in that debacle six months ago? Talk about raw nerve.

"It sounds as if you may have developed some type of phobia," she said with saccharine-sweet concern. "Perhaps you should see a therapist."

"Haven't got the time." He inserted the key into the lock and twisted the doorknob. "Besides, bottled water is cheaper than therapy."

"Are you going to tell me how you came by Page's house key?" She cringed inwardly when she heard the prim edge in her own voice. It was Jack's fault, she thought. He had a way of bringing out her least endearing qualities.

He shrugged and opened the door. "Page keeps a second set of keys in his office desk. He's the classic absentminded scientist. Always locking himself out of his own house and car."

"So you just helped yourself?"

"Yes, ma'am. In the same spirit in which he helped himself to my Soft Focus specimen."

"*Our* Soft Focus specimen," she corrected automatically. "You're going on the assumption that Page stole it?"

"That's my current working hypothesis, yeah." Jack stood aside to allow her to enter the heavily shadowed living room.

"Given the fact that he's missing and that he's the only one who had motive, opportunity, and the technological know-how it would take to remove it from the lab, I'm going with it for now. Unless, of course, you've got a better one."

"No, I don't." She came to an abrupt halt as her eyes adjusted to the gloom. "Good grief. You're right. Page isn't much of a housekeeper, is he?"

The room had a shabby, neglected air. Faded cushions adorned a sagging sofa covered in cheap orange fabric. There was a film of dust on virtually every surface. The threadbare carpet looked as if it hadn't been vacuumed in at least a decade. There were crumbs on a plate that had been left balanced precariously on the arm of the plump, over-stuffed sofa. A cup with dried brown residue in the bottom sat on the coffee table. Something green was growing in it.

The room didn't just feel cluttered, Elizabeth thought. It felt old. As if it were in a time warp. There was an oddly familiar look about it, she realized. Something about the way light slanted through the blinds creating bars on the floor reminded her of a scene from an old film. The sleazy detective's office, she thought. Just before the mysterious lady client walks through the glass-paned door.

And then she noticed the movie posters on the walls. Cold-eyed men with guns, sultry, dangerous femme fatales, lots of screaming yellow and red ink. Lots of shadows.

She glanced at some of the titles. *The Blue Dahlia. Mildred Pierce. Stranger on the Third Floor.*

"Page is into film noir," she said.

Jack closed the door. "You don't know the half of it."

She walked slowly through the room. "On the face of it, it looks like he just walked out the door and might be back any minute."

"Don't think so," Jack said. "His closet is empty and his

personal stuff has been cleaned out of the bathroom. He's gone, and I'm damn sure he took the crystal with him."

"But why would he steal it? What can he hope to do with it on his own?"

"Sell it," Jack said succinctly.

"But Excalibur holds several patents on the crystal. No competitor would touch it, because you could tie him up in court for years."

Jack's mouth twisted in a humorless smile. "That leaves a whole lot of other potential buyers, including several foreign business interests and the governments of a half-dozen countries, who don't give a damn about patent rights."

She sighed. "Yes, it does."

"It also leaves us," Jack said quietly.

"What?" She spun around to look at him. "You think Tyler Page might try to sell it back to Excalibur?"

"Why not? Page knows exactly how important that crystal is to the company. He also knows that we're under a tight time crunch. If we don't have Soft Focus available for the Veltran presentation, we're dead. It will take months to produce another sample of the crystal large enough to use for a demonstration."

"But that's equivalent to taking it hostage and holding us up for ransom."

"Yeah."

"Why, that little—" She broke off as a depressing thought struck her. "I don't think he'll try to sell it back to us. Excalibur doesn't have any extra cash. And even if I dig into the Aurora Fund reserves, we couldn't possibly compete with bids from foreign business consortiums or governments. Tyler Page must know that."

"Sure." Jack paused. "But there are two reasons why I think we might be in the running."

"Go on."

"First, Page is brilliant in his field, but he's a man of limited horizons in other respects. He's spent most of his life in a lab. I doubt that he knows how to go about contacting foreign business interests, let alone foreign governments. That kind of thing takes a certain amount of sophistication and experience."

"Maybe some foreign interest contacted him first and offered to buy it from him."

"It's possible, but if he'd sold us out already, I think he would have been smart enough to leave the country. He's got to know that I'll be looking for him and I won't stop until I find him."

She frowned at the cold determination in his voice. "You'd use your own time and money to look for Page, even if it was too late to save Excalibur?"

"I wouldn't have any other choice," he said simply.

"What do you mean, you wouldn't have any other choice? Of course you'd have another choice. You can cut your losses at Excalibur and find a new client."

"I don't do business that way." He looked around the room, as though the conversation had begun to bore him.

"Wait a second," she said. "Are you saying this is about your reputation?"

"I'm a consultant, Elizabeth. My reputation is all I have to sell. I always fulfill my contracts. No client of mine has ever been burned this badly on my watch. I sure as hell don't intend to set any new precedents with Excalibur."

"For heaven's sake, you sound like a hired gun who makes his living shooting down your clients' enemies for them."

He shrugged. "Whatever."

"You're talking revenge here, not your professional reputation."

He managed to appear even less interested in the direction the conversation had taken than he had a moment ago. "Call it what you want. The bottom line is that I'll do whatever it takes to find Page, and I have a hunch he knows that."

She eyed him warily. "All right, I get the point. You said the first reason you think Page is still in the country is because he lacks the know-how to sell Soft Focus abroad. What's the second reason you think he's still hanging around?"

He angled his head toward the nearest of the film posters hung on the wall. "That's the second reason."

She followed his gaze. "I don't get it."

"When you know a man's secret passion, you know his greatest weakness."

Baffled, Elizabeth studied the poster more closely. An enigmatic Humphrey Bogart and a sultry Lauren Bacall were posed in a tense scene. The title, *Dark Passage,* was scrawled in red across the bottom.

She looked back at Jack. "So Tyler Page likes film noir. How does that help you find him?"

"He isn't just a fan of old movies," Jack said. "He actually produced a new one. "

"I don't understand."

Jack went to the table and hefted a book from an untidy stack. It had a black and white cover. Elizabeth noticed the word *noir* in the title.

Jack opened the book and removed a glossy little brochure that had been carelessly stuck between the pages. "I found this last night when I came looking for Page." He handed the pamphlet to her.

The picture on the front featured a seedy-looking private eye, complete with trench coat and gun in hand, standing in a dark alley. The cold light from a neon sign above a nearby tavern cast his profile into sharp chiaroscuro. The words "Mirror Springs Annual Neo Noir Festival" were printed down one side of the picture in yellow ink.

Elizabeth looked up. "What's this all about?"

"Like I said, Tyler Page made a movie." Jack jerked a thumb at one of the posters. "That one over there, to be specific."

"You're kidding." Elizabeth walked toward the poster to get a closer look.

Although the artwork paid homage to classic poster design, she saw now that it was a contemporary image. It featured a sultry blond actress with fine, sculpted features and eyes that had seen far too much of the dark side of the world. The woman wore a figure-hugging, low-cut gown and held a gun at her side. She gripped the weapon with casual ease, as though accustomed to its weight.

The phrase "Once you start running in Fast Company you can't stop" was written in slashing red script across the top of the poster.

Elizabeth read the rest of the poster quickly. *Fast Company*. Starring Victoria Bellamy. Produced by Tyler Page.

She glanced up. "So?"

"Take a look inside the brochure," Jack said. "One of the movies scheduled to be premiered at the Mirror Springs festival is *Fast Company*."

She opened the brochure and flipped through the list of films until she saw the title: "*Fast Company*. Produced by Tyler Page."

She raised her eyes to meet Jack's. "It takes money to produce a film, even a small, independent one like this. Did Page have that kind of cash?"

"Good question." He gave her an approving smile. "I happen to know someone who is very good with computers. I

asked him to see if he could get a look at Page's bank trans-
actions during the past year."

"That doesn't sound real legal."

"Stealing the results of his employer's secret research
project wasn't real legal, either. At any rate, it looks like
Page went through a lot of money in recent months. Mostly
for expenses associated with the film. But judging from the
amount, I doubt that he could have underwritten all the costs
of *Fast Company*. I'm guessing there were other investors."

She frowned. "But Page got the credit as producer?"

"Yes. Who knows? Maybe he was the biggest investor. My
computer whiz also picked up on the fact that, in addition to
funding *Fast Company* during the past year, Page cleaned out
his bank account two days ago. Furthermore, wherever he is
at the moment, he did not use his credit cards to get there."

"You had your whiz check Page's credit-card records,
too?"

"Figured I might as well make a thorough job of it."

Elizabeth grimaced. "Leaving the pesky little legal issues
aside, I have to admit that it does look as if Page planned his
recent disappearance."

"Damn right he did." Jack's eyes gleamed with brooding
anticipation. "But I think I know where he's going to turn up
next."

She realized he was looking at the brochure in her hand.
She waved it once. "This film festival?"

"Yes. Page poured everything he had into *Fast Company*.
I doubt if it's much of a film. Just a small, independent production. We're not talking big-budget Hollywood block-
buster here. Probably won't ever be screened anywhere else
in the world except at the Mirror Springs festival. But I've
done a lot of research into Tyler Page during the past few
hours, and I can tell you one thing for sure."

"What's that?"

"No matter what else is going on in his life, Page will find a way to attend the premiere of *Fast Company*. That film is the culmination of all his fantasies. He sees himself as a player. For one week, at the Neo Noir Festival, he'll get to live his dream. Who could resist an opportunity like that?"

Understanding dawned. Elizabeth hurriedly checked the dates on the brochure. "It says the festival starts this Saturday. This is Wednesday."

"I'm leaving for Mirror Springs on Friday morning," Jack said. "That little SOB is going to show up there. I can feel it. And when he does, I'm going to be there waiting for him."

The grim promise in his words sent a chill down her spine. "Jack, maybe we should call the police in on this."

"You know as well as I do that calling in the cops wouldn't do any good. This is white-collar crime. Nobody calls the cops in on this kind of thing. The goal is to recover Soft Focus, not send Page to jail. One whiff of the police and we'll never find him in time to get the crystal back for the Veltran presentation."

"I hate to admit it, but you're probably right."

She was only too well aware that nine times out of ten, businesses did not call in the police in situations such as this. The fear of bad publicity, alarmed clients, and panicked investors was more than enough to make any corporation think twice before going to the authorities.

"The way I figure it, we've got two shots at finding Page," Jack said. "Either he'll contact me to let me make an offer to buy back Soft Focus, or else he'll show up at the film festival. I'm betting he'll do both."

"I'm not so sure, Jack. For heaven's sake, you're a business executive, not a private investigator. What makes you think you can find Page?"

"Go easy on the boundless admiration and unqualified support, will you? I'm not sure I can handle so much wide-eyed flattery from my client's biggest creditor."

She told herself she would not respond to that. She hated it when he made her sound like a brass-brassiered Valkyrie. She was never more acutely aware of her own femininity than when she was in Jack's vicinity. He, on the other hand, had as much as made a public announcement to the effect that he thought she was capable of sinking the *Titanic*.

Very deliberately, very carefully, she refolded the brochure and dropped it into her shoulder bag. She gave him a steely smile. "You make an excellent point, Jack. I am your biggest creditor. As such, I've got a vested interest in the recovery of the specimen. I'm going to go to Mirror Springs with you."

His eyes narrowed. "I don't think so."

"If Page does offer to let you ransom the crystal, you're going to need cash. Lots of it. No bank will loan you the money. Excalibur doesn't have the reserves, and I seriously doubt that you possess those kinds of personal financial resources. Face it. You're going to need the Aurora Fund."

"I can handle Page on my own."

"Maybe. But I don't intend to let you do that. Think of me as your credit card. You're not leaving home without me."

He studied her for a moment. "There are some serious logistical problems involved here."

His air of forced patience set her teeth on edge. "Such as?"

"Mirror Springs is one of those exclusive little boutique resort towns in the Colorado Rockies. Every hotel and motel in the area has been booked for months for the festival. You won't be able to get a room at this late date."

"Really?" She smiled blandly. "How did you find a room?"

He made a casual movement with his hand. "Called a friend of mine who's a vice president with one of the big hotels here in town. He pulled some strings with his second ex-wife. She manages a hotel in Denver. She pulled some strings with the concierge at a place called the Mirror Springs Resort. But even with all that, I had to pay triple the usual rate."

"I'm sure I can turn up something."

He gave her a wolfish smile that set all the hairs on the back of her neck on end.

"If you insist on going to Mirror Springs with me, I might let you talk me into sharing my room," he said much too politely. His eyes gleamed with challenge. "But you'd have to ask real nice."

"Thanks, but that price is a bit too steep for me." She forced another brittle little smile. "I'm sure I can find something a little less expensive."

She turned on her heel and walked out the door.

Oh, now, that was really mature, Elizabeth. You do have a way with men, don't you?

CHAPTER FIVE

JACK HEARD THE SOFT GRUNT OF BREATH released, sensed the faint, indescribable disturbance in the air that telegraphed the slashing kick, and glided to the side, turning smoothly away from the blow. The striking foot missed his thigh by inches. If it had landed he would have gone down.

He whirled, seeking an opening in the split second it would take for his opponent to recover from the move. He caught an arm and drew it toward him, taking advantage of the other's forward momentum.

His half brother lost his balance, tumbled lightly to the mat, and grimaced. He got to his feet with easy grace and returned Jack's formal bow.

"That makes three in a row," Larry growled as they walked off the practice floor. "You've been practicing too much lately. No fair."

It was true, Jack thought. He had been spending a lot of what little spare time he possessed these days here at the dojo. The hard physical and mental exercise provided a badly needed outlet. It wasn't as if he had a lot of other ways to work off the stress. Sex, for example, at least with another consenting adult, was out. He'd been living like a monk for six months.

"You almost took me down with that last kick," he said.

"No, I didn't." Larry's dark brows scrunched together. "It's not good for my self-esteem to always lose to my big brother, you know."

"Is that right?" Jack watched a pair of students working at the other end of the dojo. "Who told you that?"

"Read it somewhere in a magazine, I think."

"Larry, I've warned you before about reading those men's magazines."

"I only read the articles," Larry said piously.

"That's what worries me."

Larry grinned. "You think maybe I should concentrate more on the pictures?"

"Nah. Save your energy. I've tried the pictures. Hard work getting anything of a stimulating nature out of them."

"Well, they sure as hell won't substitute for a social life, which is what you've been using them for during the past six months."

"I've been busy." He realized he was feeling defensive. It irritated him to know that he was making excuses.

He also knew they wouldn't go over. Not with Larry. For all his techie qualities, and they were legion, his half brother had a surprising degree of insight and intuition when it came to people.

They had been raised apart and they had little in common except a father. Physically they shared very few traits except the color of their eyes. Larry was a couple of inches taller, with light-colored hair and a face that could have come straight off the silver screen. They had not even met until a few years ago. But the bond between them had been immediate and it had proved to be solid. Larry and Megan and their new infant daughter provided Jack with whatever semblance of a family life he possessed.

Larry gave him a knowing look. "You've had, what? Three dates? And one of those was with Megan's cousin Sandra, so it doesn't count."

"Why doesn't it count?" Jack frowned, trying to recall the details of the date he'd had with his sister-in-law's cousin. They were vague. He thought he could remember a pretty face and a cute, rounded little body. He was pretty sure he had bored her half to death. He knew for a fact that he'd been thoroughly bored that night. His mind had been on other things— namely, whether or not Elizabeth had had a date that evening.

"It doesn't count," Larry said patiently, "because Megan told me later that all you talked about for two hours straight at dinner was the state of the Northwest's economy, after which inspiring conversation, you took her cousin home, left her at her door, and never called again."

"I've been busy," Jack said again.

"Bullshit. You're still carrying a torch for that woman who runs the Aurora Fund, and you know it."

"Larry, modern men do not carry torches. Remember that. It's important. Torch-carrying belongs to another era. It comes from a time when people did stupid things and got away with it because they said that they had done them for love. That excuse doesn't fly anymore."

"You know, one of these days you're going to have to stop lecturing me. I realize you think you have to make up for lost time, but it's not necessary. Really." Larry glanced at him. "So what did you want to talk to me about?"

"Think you could play wizard again and go on the Net to

get me some financial background on a man named Dawson Holland?"

The familiar gleam of maniacal curiosity leaped in Larry's dark eyes. "Probably. Why are you interested in him?"

"I'm not sure that I am. But it's a place to start. You know what they say about following the money. Holland put together the investment package that bankrolled a little independent film called *Fast Company*. I want whatever I can get relating to the movie, and that means that I want something on Holland."

"I can tell you one thing without even going online," Larry said. "Whoever this Holland guy is, if he's the one who arranged the financing, he's probably the only one who didn't put any of his own money into the movie. And he'll be the only one who actually comes out ahead. The real investors, the ones who coughed up hard cash, will never see a dime. The only people who make money in films, large or small, are the guys who move other people's money around."

"I've heard that for years." Jack thought about the shrine to filmmaking he had discovered in Tyler Page's little house. "But there never seems to be any shortage of people lining up to finance films."

Larry shrugged. "They're all starstruck. They want to pretend that they're players. Go to the opening-night parties. Hang with the stars and the directors. See their names in the credits. Filmmaking is one of the most glamorous clubs in the world. Lots of people are willing to shell out lots of money to join it."

"I know. Just get me what you can on Holland and the film. Use my cell phone number to reach me. I'll be out of town for a while."

Larry's eyes lit with amused interest. "Don't tell me you're taking a vacation?"

"Not exactly. Know anything about film noir?"

"Those old black-and-white movies from the forties? Gangsters and sleazy private eyes and femme fatales? Live fast, die hard kind of stuff? Sure. I've watched a few of the classics on late-night TV. Some great lines in those old scripts."

"You're way ahead of me, then. But I'm going to learn a whole lot during the next few days at a film noir festival."

Larry studied him. "Are you going to take in this festival alone?"

"No, as a matter of fact, a business associate will be going with me."

"Well, now, isn't that interesting. And just who is this business associate?"

Jack set his jaw. "Elizabeth Cabot."

Larry howled with laughter.

Jack narrowed his eyes. "What's so damned funny?"

"You." Larry gradually subsided to an evil chuckle. "Going to a film noir festival with your own, personal femme fatale."

CHAPTER SIX

"SINCE WHEN DID YOU DEVELOP AN INTEREST in film noir?" Louise scowled suspiciously over the rims of her reading glasses. "Hell, you don't even like to go to the movies. I'll bet you can't name the film that won Best Picture at the Academy Awards last year."

Elizabeth stopped in front of her assistant's desk. "You're the one who keeps telling me that I'm working too hard and that I need a vacation. This film festival thing caught my eye. Thought it sounded like a change of pace."

"Change of pace, my left gluteus maximus. This is Louise you're talking to. If there's one thing I know when I see it, it's a line of bull."

Elizabeth grinned in spite of herself. "Sorry. Sometimes I forget how much experience you've had with bull."

In addition to Elizabeth, Louise Luttrell was the only other member of the Aurora Fund staff. Elizabeth had inherited her when she had inherited the Fund from her aunt.

The framed front-page headlines of several yellowing tabloid newspapers arranged behind the desk testified to Louise's former career in journalism. "Woman Abducted by

UFO Marries Captors," "Man Eaten by Giant Frog," "Ancient Alien Mummy Awakens." All of the stories carried Louise's byline.

Sixty-something, big-haired, full-figured, and not at all hesitant to state her opinion, Louise functioned as secretary, receptionist, travel agent, adviser, and confidante. She arrived at the mansion promptly at nine every morning and took complete charge of the office wing. Elizabeth sometimes suspected the Aurora Fund would collapse without her.

"Damn straight. Professional bullshit detector, that's me." Louise rolled her eyes in the general direction of the framed tabloids and then peered more closely at Elizabeth. "Talk to me. Tell me what's going on here. Are you up to something stupid?"

There really was no point trying to keep secrets from Louise.

"Probably," Elizabeth said. "But I haven't got a lot of choice."

"Let's have it. I can take it. Hell, I've taken stories involving the alien mummies. I can handle your little tale."

Elizabeth got up out of the high, leather wing-back chair and crossed the antique crimson, black, and gold carpet to stand at the window. It was one of those rare, spectacularly clear early-fall days in Seattle when the local professional photographers rushed outside to grab pictures of Mount Rainier and the Space Needle to put on postcards and calendars.

From here she could see the downtown high-rises, including the one in which Jack lived. She had spent a lot of nights gazing at that particular concrete-and-steel building. Once or twice she'd dug out Sybil's old bird-watching binoculars to see if she could get a closer look at the thirtieth floor. But the tinted windows had defeated her foray into voyeurism.

She concentrated on the view of the city as she gathered her thoughts.

"Tyler Page, the researcher who developed Soft Focus for Excalibur, has disappeared," she said. "Unfortunately, it looks like he took the crystal specimen with him."

There was a short pause behind her.

"Well, shit," Louise said eventually.

"In a word."

"Just out of curiosity, what kind of potential loss are we dealing with here?"

"If the crystal actually works and Grady Veltran agrees to a licensing agreement?" Elizabeth turned back to face her. "I couldn't even guess. The upside potential is in the millions for Excalibur."

"And we get a chunk of the profits." Louise looked briefly smug. She had shares in the Aurora Fund.

"And if we don't get it back, or it doesn't work, the Fund takes a serious hit," Elizabeth added.

"But it wouldn't go under."

"No, we can certainly survive the loss of Soft Focus. Excalibur, on the other hand, can't. Right now our worst enemy is gossip. There are already a few rumors floating around. If anyone calls for background on the Aurora Fund's position with regard to our client, Excalibur, we are officially not worried. Nothing is wrong."

"Got it. Not worried. Nothing wrong." Louise narrowed her eyes. "In other words, we're in full-blown panic mode. So what's this neo noir film festival in Mirror Springs got to do with finding the specimen?"

"Jack Fairfax has reason to think that Page will show up at the festival."

"Whoa. Hang on, here." Louise's chair squeaked as she leaned back in her chair. She cleared her throat. "Let me get this straight. The egg-sucking, lower-than-a-snake's-belly, conniving, underhanded, two-faced SOB is going to this film festival, too?"

Elizabeth smiled humorlessly. "I can't imagine where you got such a low opinion of Jack Fairfax."

"I got it from you, and you know it." Louise pursed her lips and looked contemplative. "Although I have to admit, I've got a sneaking admiration for the bastard. He must have something none of your other boyfriends have ever had."

Elizabeth glared at her. "What on earth are you talking about?"

"I'm talking about whatever it was he did that made you track him down and throw ice water all over him in front of the stuffiest bunch of corporate honchos in town." Louise smiled. "I've known you since you were a little girl, and that was the first time you've ever let yourself go over the top and stage a genuine hissy-fit scene in public. Too bad Sybil wasn't around to witness it. Nothing she liked better than to see a little female empowerment in action."

"I doubt if she would have approved," Elizabeth said shortly. "Not if she knew why I had staged the scene."

She glanced at the portrait on the paneled wall opposite the desk and felt a twist of chagrin. Sybil Cabot looked down on her with the stern but not unkind intelligence that had been her signature trait. Elizabeth remembered very clearly the day her aunt had called her into her office and told her that she intended to leave the Aurora Fund in her hands.

"You're the only one in the family who has the two things required to make the Fund achieve its full potential, Elizabeth. You've got the financial know-how and you've got the instincts of a gambler. Deep down you're willing to take a few risks, and that's what's needed to make the Aurora Fund work."

She'd had her share of good fortune when it came to taking financial risks, Elizabeth thought. But when it came to her personal life, her luck had been disastrous. For some strange reason it was a lot easier to pick a good business prospect than it was to pick a good man.

Louise squinted. "So you're going to Mirror Springs with Fairfax? Are we talking close physical proximity here?"

Elizabeth steeled herself. "No, we are not talking close physical proximity. We're traveling separately, and we will be staying in separate locations."

"Is that a fact?"

"Yes, it is definitely a fact." Elizabeth paused. "That reminds me. I'm going to need reservations, and apparently the town is full because of the film festival. Think you can find me something?"

"Probably." Louise sat forward and reached for her address file. "Mirror Springs is a popular ski resort, and Lord knows we've got a ton of clients, past and present, who ski. Plus I've got plenty of contacts from the old days in the news business. I'll make some calls. Seems to me one of my editors has a vacation place in Mirror Springs."

Elizabeth looked at the glaring headlines of the framed tabloids. "He's not a space alien or a recently revived mummy, is he?"

"Well, if you're going to be picky about it—"

"You're right. I'll take what I can get."

"So you and Fairfax are going to play detectives, huh?" Louise flipped through her card file. "That should be interesting."

"I did suggest that he call in the cops, but you know how executives are about going to the police on this kind of thing."

Louise snorted. "Nobody calls the cops in on white-collar crime."

"For good reasons." Elizabeth started toward her office. "Let me know when you find a place for me in Mirror Springs. I'll also need airline reservations to Denver and a rental car on the other end."

"Right." Louise paused. "I almost forgot, your brother-in-law called again."

"Merrick?" Elizabeth groaned. "What did you tell him?"

"Same thing I told him the last four times he called. That you were busy."

"Which is the honest truth."

"You won't be able to duck him forever, you know."

"I know. But I can at least duck him for the next few days while I'm in Colorado."

A gleam of speculation appeared in Louise's eyes. "Out of idle curiosity, whose idea was it for you to go to Mirror Springs with Fairfax? His or yours?"

"Are you joking? Mine, of course. He told me he wanted to handle this thing alone, but I told him to forget it. I'm going with him whether he likes it or not."

Louise concentrated hard on her address file. "I was afraid of that."

"ARE YOU CRAZY?" Milo bounced and twitched his way back and forth across Jack's living room. "You can't take off now. We've got a disaster on our hands."

"The only way to avert disaster is to find Page and that damned crystal." Jack walked out of the bedroom, fastening his cuff links. "Mirror Springs is our best shot."

"I don't like this, Jack. I don't like it one damn bit."

"Neither do I, but it's not like we have much choice. Remember, while I'm gone your job is to keep a lid on rumors and gossip. Officially, everything is under control at Excalibur. Got that?"

"Yeah, yeah, I got it." Milo's face tightened. "Cousin Angela's going to be the tough one. I think she went to see Ms. Cabot again yesterday."

Jack glanced at him sharply. "Any particular reason?"

"How should I know?" Milo spread his hands. "Probably just her regular bimonthly attempt to convince Ms. Cabot to stop backing your every move as CEO. Angela figures if she can get Elizabeth Cabot to turn on you, she'll have enough votes on the board to get rid of you."

So far Elizabeth had backed him at every turn, Jack thought. But an alliance between Angela and Elizabeth was a grim possibility.

Milo stared at him, eyes widening. "You're in a tux."

"Very observant." Jack glanced out the window as he picked up his jacket and shrugged into it.

From here he had a good view of Queen Anne Hill. If he squinted, he could just barely make out the lights of Elizabeth's castle. He had spent more than one night during the past six months sitting alone here in his living room with a glass of scotch, staring at the distant glow. He had told himself that it would be tacky to get a telescope.

And pointless.

A purely scientific experiment with a set of binoculars had confirmed that there were too many plants and bushes on the balcony outside Elizabeth's bedroom to allow for a clear view of the interior.

He wondered if she was dressing for the reception at that very moment.

For the past few days, right up until the disappearance of Soft Focus had distracted him, the business charity function had been the high point on his calendar. Typically he avoided such events whenever possible, but he had been looking forward to this one with the same mix of perverse anticipation and foreboding that he got in the days before an Excalibur board meeting. Another chance to see Elizabeth. Another chance to torment himself with all the might-have-been possibilities. Another chance to fantasize about second chances.

And now fate had dropped a ticking bomb in his lap. The good news was that he was going to spend the next few days working very closely with Elizabeth. It was also the bad news, because they would be working together under the worst possible sort of pressure. He figured he would be lucky to survive with his sanity intact.

"Why the hell are you in a tux?" Milo demanded. "You're not going to a party tonight, are you? You're supposed to leave for Mirror Springs tomorrow morning."

"I told you about the charity reception."

Milo's jaw dropped. "You're still going to attend? After everything else that's happened?"

"I don't think it would be a good idea to skip it." Jack glanced at his watch. "Failing to show up would add fuel to the rumors that are already circulating. We can't afford that. In business, perception is all. Never forget that, Milo."

"Huh." Milo's thin face crunched into a darker frown. "I'd sure like to know how those rumors got started."

"So would I." Jack picked up his keys. "But we don't have time to investigate the leak now. We'll deal with it after we get Soft Focus back."

Milo trailed after him toward the door. "Tell me the truth, Jack. Do you really think you can find Page?"

Jack glanced at him as he opened the door. A wave of empathy went through him. Milo had a lot on his young, inexperienced shoulders.

"I'll find him, Milo."

CHAPTER SEVEN

HAYDEN SHAW LOOKED OUT ACROSS THE GLIT-tering ballroom. "Fairfax just walked in. That raises two possibilities. Either the rumors about trouble at Excalibur were wrong or . . ."

Elizabeth raised one brow. "Or?"

"Or else they were true and both of you are playing it cool tonight so that people will *think* they're wrong."

Elizabeth surprised herself with a low chuckle that she thought sounded remarkably genuine. "I can tell you this much: Jack Fairfax may be cold-blooded enough to put in an appearance tonight even if there were major problems at his company. But I certainly wouldn't be standing around drinking champagne if there were a disaster. I'd be in my office, huddled in front of my computer with a large cup of coffee, and I'd be tearing out my hair."

She had wanted very much not to attend the charity event tonight, but she knew that it would send the wrong message to those who, like Hayden, had picked up hints of trouble at Excalibur. Obviously Jack had followed the same logic. She doubted that he was enjoying himself any more than she was.

She wondered if he had noticed her standing here with

Hayden and, if he had seen her, whether or not the sight of
her chatting with his archenemy annoyed him. If it did
bother him, she knew that he would not reveal it. Jack could
play poker with the devil.

Why did she even care if he was annoyed? she wondered.
Stupid question. She was in that strange mood again, the one
she always plunged into a few days before she knew that she
was to see Jack. The days preceding a regularly scheduled
board meeting at Excalibur were always bad. The peculiar
mix of emotions was just as predictable as certain other
recurring biological functions.

She wondered what Jack would say if he knew that the
thought of being in his company triggered a severe form of
PMS in her.

An entire week together. Good grief, how could they possibly do it? She was accustomed to estimating the odds, but
she could not even begin to guess whether or not they would
throttle each other before they found Tyler Page.

Hayden surveyed her neat chignon appreciatively. "You
look lovely tonight."

"Thank you."

Hayden lowered his voice to a husky drawl. "The dress is
pretty terrific, too."

She pretended not to notice his gaze sliding appreciatively
over the long line of her spine left exposed by the backless
black gown. Hayden was interesting, very successful, and,
with his warm, brown eyes, dark hair, and good facial bones,
about ten times better looking than Jack Fairfax. He was also
a few years younger. But the last thing she wanted to do
tonight was flirt with him.

Jack's seemingly offhand question about Hayden's mari-
tal status yesterday morning had made her uneasy. Just as he
had no doubt meant it to do, she thought. Typical of Fairfax

to slip home a zinger just when she was starting to convince herself that she could get interested in Hayden.

She had told herself that she would ignore Jack's comment on the divorce, but she had known that would not be possible. Like a number of other people she knew, she had been under the distinct impression that Hayden's divorce was, indeed, final. But once Fairfax had raised the question, she was obliged to double-check the facts.

Sure enough, a discreet inquiry through her lawyer this morning had elicited the information that Hayden's divorce was still pending. There were no children involved, but apparently the battle over the division of the assets had turned extremely messy. Elizabeth did not want to get anywhere near the scene of the accident.

In all fairness, she could not accuse Hayden of having lied to her. She just hadn't asked the right question. Then again, it was a little awkward to ask a person point-blank if his divorce was officially final, especially when he had yet to ask you out on a real date. Thus far all of her encounters with Shaw had been quasi–business meetings.

But lately the atmosphere between the two of them had begun to alter quite subtly. She could not pinpoint the exact moment when she had realized that Hayden was giving off the kind of signals that said he was interested in something more than a business connection. She was still not certain that she was reading him right.

The reason she could not be sure of what was going on was that she was unwilling to ponder the depressing subject of her love life. She was still licking her wounds from the skirmish with Jack.

Things were not improving on that front, she thought. If anything, they were getting worse. Her awareness of him was preternaturally high. She had not needed Hayden to tell her that Jack had arrived in the ballroom a few minutes ago; the tingling on the nape of her neck had provided her with the same data. She was afraid the uncanny sensation was some sort of primitive prelude to a fight-or-fornicate response.

She could not seem to take her eyes off him, so she did her best to observe him without being obvious about it.

The tux did nothing to mute the edgy quality that was so much a part of him. If anything, it enhanced the air of fiercely controlled sexuality he exuded. The warmth that unfurled deep inside her at the sight of him was as irritating as it was disturbing. She watched him stop to speak to some men gathered near the buffet table. He appeared to be monumentally unaware of her.

"You know," Hayden murmured, "just because this is a business affair doesn't mean that you and I have to discuss the economy."

She flicked a glance at him. "I hadn't noticed that we were discussing the economy."

"We weren't. Just trying to get your attention." He gave her a rueful grin. "It came to my attention that you were concentrating on Fairfax, you see."

"Why is that surprising? I've got a hefty stake in Excalibur. I always keep an eye on my investments."

He gave a short, surprisingly harsh laugh. "If a woman watched me the way you're watching Fairfax, I'd like to think that she was contemplating something other than whether or not I could make a lot of money for her."

She smiled politely and set down her glass. "Now you know the awful truth about me. The bottom line is everything!"

"Maybe. Maybe not." He studied her intently. "You're not an easy woman to figure out, Elizabeth. But speaking of Excalibur, did you check out those rumors I mentioned?"

"I did, and everything is under control at Excalibur."

"Glad to hear it. Well, then, can I talk you into a dance?"

"Some other time, perhaps. I'm here to work tonight."

"All work and no play . . ."

"I'm afraid you're a little late with the warning. Too much work has already made me a very dull CEO."

His eyes gleamed suggestively. "Bet I could fix that little problem with a nice long weekend at the coast. What do you say to taking off on Friday and coming back very, very late on Monday?"

She had been right about the signals. She gave an inward sigh, wrenched her covert gaze off Jack, and turned to give Hayden a bland smile.

"Funny you should mention this weekend," she said. "I'm going to be out of town. A little vacation time. My secretary tells me that I need it badly."

He gave her a hopeful grin. "Any chance you might want some company for at least a couple of days of your vacation? I could do with a little time off myself."

He was going to force her into a corner, she realized. Better to deal with it now and get past it. She met his eyes. "I understand that your divorce is not yet final, Hayden. I don't do long weekends with married men."

He grimaced. "Ouch. I get the point. Would it make any difference if I told you that the divorce should have been final several months ago? That the only reason it isn't a done deal is because Gillian is the vindictive type?"

"Nope. It wouldn't make any difference at all." She transferred her small gold evening bag to her other hand and made to move off. "Excuse me. I see some Aurora Fund clients. I'd better go say hello."

"Sure." Something hard flashed in his eyes. It was gone in an instant, replaced by a wry expression. "One of these days I'll get through this damned divorce, you know. Even Ringstead's lawyers can't hold it up forever. We can talk about a long weekend then."

"We'll see," she said, deliberately vague. But something told her that there would never be any long weekends with Hayden.

She dutifully made her way through the crowd, greeting clients and potential investors in the Fund. Her invisible radar screen kept her clear of Jack. She caught glimpses of him now and again. Once she saw him lounging against the bar, a glass in one hand, chatting with an attorney she recognized.

He glanced toward her at that precise instant, as if he had known that she was looking at him. He raised his glass a couple of inches in a mocking salute and turned back to his conversation. For the next forty minutes, however, he managed not to cross her path. It occurred to her that he was going out of his way to avoid her, too.

Shortly after eleven she glanced at her watch and told herself that she had concluded the minimum of socializing the event demanded. She needed some sleep before the flight to Mirror Springs. She smiled at a portly, retired banker who was waxing enthusiastic about his new boat. The man was obviously in love with his most recent acquisition. She wished him happiness and slipped away to collect her coat.

When she emerged from the cloakroom, she turned and went down a quiet, carpeted hall, avoiding the more heavily traveled path to and from the ballroom. She sensed a presence behind her just before the woman spoke.

"If you're smart, you'll stay away from him."

Elizabeth froze at the raw venom in the voice. Then she turned slowly around. A small, elegantly made-up woman dressed in a very chic, very expensive red silk suit and stiletto heels stood in the hall. She appeared to be in her mid-thirties. Her pale blond hair was cut in a sleek line that highlighted her heart-shaped features. There were fine, tightly drawn lines at the corners of her mouth.

"Have we met?" Elizabeth asked carefully.

"Sorry. Allow me to introduce myself. I'm Gillian the Bitch."

"I beg your pardon?"

"Don't you recognize the name? I'm surprised. I understand Hayden always calls me that." Gillian's smile was so brittle, it was a wonder it did not shatter. "I'm his wife."

"I see." Great. A perfect way to end the evening.

"In spite of the impression Hayden may have given you, I am not his ex-wife. Not yet, at any rate. I won't give him that satisfaction until Daddy's lawyers have gotten back everything he took from me."

"This really isn't any of my business." Elizabeth made a show of glancing at her watch. "I'm on my way home. If you'll excuse me . . ."

Gillian's eyes narrowed. "My daddy is Osmand Ringstead."

Elizabeth needed no further details. Ringstead was the very powerful, very reclusive, very rich, and very politically connected head of Ring, Inc. From the Ringstead family compound he commanded a large, closely held business empire. He was rumored to be contemplating political office. No wonder Hayden was having problems getting his divorce to go through on his terms, she thought. Few people could go up against the Ringstead power and money and hope to win.

"Okay, I'm impressed," she said. "Now can I go?"

"I saw Hayden talking to you," Gillian said, her eyes

bleak. "I know how he operates. Has he invited you to go on a long weekend to the coast?"

Elizabeth managed to conceal her start of surprise. "I don't know what this is all about, Mrs. Shaw. But I can assure you, I have no personal interest in your husband."

"Let's hope for your sake that you're telling the truth." Gillian took a step closer. "Because I'm going to ruin him before I'm finished with him. He won't have a dime left. I'll get everything. *Everything*. Daddy promised me."

There was more than rage in Gillian's voice, Elizabeth realized. There was pain. She suddenly felt very sorry for the other woman.

"Believe me, the last thing I want to do is get caught up in your private affairs, Mrs. Shaw."

"This divorce is going to be a train wreck, I promise you. Hayden won't get away with trying to walk out on me."

"As I said, this is none of my business. If you'll excuse me, I'm going home."

"He lied to me." Hot tears appeared in Gillian's eyes and spilled down her cheeks. "The bastard lied to me right from the start. I trusted him. I loved him. Daddy liked him. But all Hayden wanted was my money and Daddy's connections. He used me."

Elizabeth longed to turn and run, not walk, in the opposite direction. But she could not bring herself to leave the woman sobbing alone in the hall. She pulled some tissues from the pocket of her coat and went toward Gillian.

"Here, take these." She thrust the tissues into Gillian's hand. "There's a women's lounge right around the corner. I just came from there. It was empty. Would you like to go inside?"

"He made a fool out of me," Gillian blurted into the tissues.

"I know the feeling." Unable to think of anything else to do, Elizabeth patted her gently on the shoulder. "Maybe a glass of cold water?"

"Stay away from him. He'll only use you."

"I have no interest in your husband, Mrs. Shaw."

"I saw the way he looked at you tonight." Gillian blotted her eyes. "I know he wants you."

"I don't want him," Elizabeth said gently.

"I don't believe you." Gillian lowered the soaked tissues. Her voice rose. "Of course you want him. Just like I did. Until I found out what he was really like, that is."

Elizabeth was about to argue the point when she felt the familiar tingling. Simultaneously a lean, dark figure appeared in the hall behind Gillian.

"Ready to go home, honey?" Jack walked toward her with assured arrogance. His tone was unmistakably intimate, bordering on the possessive. "It's getting late, and we've got a long trip ahead of us tomorrow."

At the sound of his voice, Gillian raised her head sharply and quickly blotted away the rest of her tears. "Oh, damn. This is so embarrassing."

Elizabeth looked past her at Jack. Unseen by Gillian, he raised his brows and smiled with cool, knowing amusement. He was coming to her rescue, and he knew she didn't like it. He also knew full well that she was in no position to refuse his help.

"I'm ready, Jack." She managed a bright little smile. "I was just having a word with Mrs. Shaw. Have you met her? Gillian, this is Jack Fairfax."

"Gillian and I know each other," Jack said with surprising gentleness.

"Hello, Jack." Gillian blinked away the rest of her tears and gave him a watery smile. "Sorry about the scene."

"Forget it."

"I heard you took over Excalibur a few months ago. How are things going there?"

"We've been busy." Jack took Elizabeth's arm, casually proprietary. "But Elizabeth and I finally managed to clear our calendars for the same week. We're going on vacation tomorrow. I think we both need one, don't we, honey?"

Elizabeth kept her smile fixed in place, but it wasn't easy. "We certainly do."

"I don't understand." Watery confusion glittered in Gillian's eyes. She glanced from Jack's face to Elizabeth's and then back again. "You're going away together?"

"That's right," Jack said. "Been looking forward to it for weeks."

"I see." Gillian looked as if she was having a problem assimilating the data. "I hadn't realized that you two were seeing each other."

"We've kept it quiet." Elizabeth gave Jack a warning smile. "For business reasons."

"Are you going to the coast?" Gillian asked.

"No." Jack tightened his fingers on Elizabeth's arm. "We're going to a resort in the Rockies. No fax, no phones, no E-mail. Just the two of us alone in the woods. But we've got an early plane to catch, so I'm afraid you're going to have to excuse us."

"Yes, of course," Gillian murmured. She blotted her eyes one last time and gave Jack a warm, tremulous smile. "Have a good time."

"Thanks. We intend to do just that."

He turned Elizabeth and steered her down the hall toward the lobby.

Neither spoke until they walked outside and came to a

halt beneath the bright lights that illuminated the hotel's front entrance.

"Don't look back. She followed us into the lobby," Jack said.

"I'm not surprised. She's very upset."

"It will look better if we share a cab," Jack said.

Elizabeth said nothing, just gave a clipped nod, acknowledging the suggestion. He was right. If Gillian was watching them, it would be better if they left together.

Jack signaled the doorman, who raised a whistle to summon the next cab in line. When the door opened, Elizabeth slipped quickly into the rear seat. Jack got in beside her. The door closed.

The back of the cab suddenly seemed like a very small, very intimate space.

Elizabeth gazed straight ahead through the window as the taxi pulled out onto the street.

"I suppose I should thank you," she said stiffly.

"Don't worry, I'm not expecting you to go overboard."

She groaned and settled back into the seat. "Thank you."

"You're welcome," Jack said.

"What happened back there was a little awkward."

"I sort of figured that," he said.

"You were right. The divorce is not final."

Jack slanted her an enigmatic glance. "Told you so."

She controlled her temper with an effort of will. "Yes. You did, didn't you?"

He did not respond immediately. She glanced warily in his direction and saw that he was looking out the side window of the cab into the night. The weak glare of a streetlight glanced off the strong line of his cheekbones and jaw, leaving his eyes in deep shadows.

"I heard Angela paid you a visit this week," he said after a while.

The change in topic surprised her. "Angela generally comes to my office twice a month. What about it?"

"What did she want this time?"

Elizabeth thought about the unpleasant scene that had taken place three days earlier. Angela Ingersoll Burrows was a tall, striking, formidable woman. Her marriage of fifteen years had ended abruptly when her fifty-three-year-old, mild-mannered husband had stunned everyone by running off with his twenty-two-year-old secretary. Left with a teenage son to raise, Angela now focused most of her time and attention on making certain that her only offspring received what she considered his fair share of the family inheritance. The family inheritance consisted solely of the assets of Excalibur.

"We talked about her usual concerns," Elizabeth said as diplomatically as possible. "She wants to see Excalibur sold or merged. She's convinced it's the only way her son will ever see a dime out of Excalibur."

"What did you tell her?"

"The same thing I tell her every time she comes to see me."

Jack watched her from the shadows. "Which is?"

She flexed her fingers around the edge of her evening bag and kept her voice very flat. "Which is that you are Excalibur's best hope and that, therefore, her son's best chance of coming into a significant inheritance from Excalibur rests with you."

There was another short, heavy silence. Jack shifted slightly in the seat, seeming to settle deeper into the shadows.

"You backed me," he said.

"Yes."

"You always do. Not just when it comes to dealing with Angela but on the board, as well." He sounded as if he were making an observation about rain in Seattle. It was expected, it was routine, it was predictable. Still, it warranted comment. "Why?"

She was almost amused by the question. "You and I have our differences, but I've never quarreled with the fact that you are very good at what you do. If Excalibur has any chance at all, it lies with you."

"In other words, your decision to back my decisions as CEO is just a business move on your part," he said neutrally.

"What else could it be except a business move?"

"Damned if I know," he said. He looked at her. "We've both got a mutual interest in recovering Soft Focus. Since you insist on coming along for the ride—"

"I'm not along for the ride," she said tightly. "I'm a full-fledged partner in this thing."

"All right, partner, what do you say we try to cooperate until we get our hands on that damned crystal?"

"Define cooperate."

"I figure it's like porn," Jack said. "You know it when you see it."

CHAPTER EIGHT

THE TIMBERED HOUSE WAS DESIGNER RUSTIC. With its burnished wooden walls, steeply sloped roofline, and expansive windows angled to capture the view, it looked like something off the cover of a high-end resort-and-travel magazine. Night had fallen, but there was sufficient golden light pouring through the windows onto the deck to illuminate a hot tub. It looked large enough to hold half a dozen people, provided they were feeling friendly. There was a massive, high-tech, state-of-the-art stainless steel outdoor grill next to the tub. Thickly padded loungers and a table completed the outdoor furnishings.

And this was just the outside.

Trust Elizabeth to land digs like these on short notice in a sold-out town.

Jack glanced again at the covered hot tub. An image of Elizabeth sitting naked in the bubbling water flashed across his brain. He took a deep breath of the very crisp, impossibly pure mountain air and counted backward from ten. When he got to zero he realized he was still semi-erect. He was also a little light-headed. He reminded himself that it took a while to adjust to the altitude.

He forced his attention away from the hot-tub fantasy and concentrated on the problem at hand. No matter how he played it, he was going to look less than brilliant. He dropped his duffel bag in front of the door and banged the brass, bird-headed knocker. This was not going to be easy.

He planted one hand against the wall while he waited for Elizabeth to respond and studied the view. The lights of the expensive condos and homes that climbed the hillsides above the village of Mirror Springs twinkled in the night. Down below he could see the glow of the shops and restaurants housed in the carefully restored Victorian-era business district. The brightest lights of all were those that marked the entrance of the Silver Empire Theater, one of the focal points of the film festival activities.

"Who is it?" Elizabeth's voice was muffled by the heavy wooden door.

He steeled himself. "Jack."

There was a short pause. He made the mistake of holding his breath again. Then he heard the sound of the dead bolt being disengaged. The door opened.

Elizabeth stood in the cozy glow of the fire. She was dressed in a black cowl-necked sweater made of some soft, cuddly-looking material. It fell to a point just below her hips. In addition to the sweater she wore a pair of snug black velvet leggings. Her dark hair was brushed straight back and secured at the nape with a silver clasp.

She gazed at him with that cautious, watchful expression that made him want to grind his teeth.

"What are you doing here?" she asked. "I thought we agreed that we would meet for dinner somewhere in the village after we each got unpacked. You said we could go over our game plan then."

"A problem has arisen."

The caution in her eyes turned to suspicion. "What kind of problem?"

"When I tried to check in at the resort I was told that there were no rooms available."

"So?"

"So," he said very deliberately, "I haven't got a place to stay."

Suspicion congealed into accusation in her gaze. "You said you knew some people who could pull some strings to get you a room."

"The strings broke."

"I see." She propped one shoulder against the doorjamb and folded her arms beneath her breasts. "What do you expect me to do about it?"

He glanced through the doorway at the high, vaulted ceiling and the expansive, warmly furnished great room behind her. A cheerful-looking fire burned in a handsome stone fireplace. He could see a staircase that led to two sleeping lofts that overlooked the central room.

He cleared his throat. "I thought maybe you could let me share this place."

"Now, why would I do that?"

"Because we're supposed to be cooperating." He switched his gaze back to her. "Look, I'm sorry about this, but the whole damn town is filled to capacity. The people at the hotel said there was absolutely nothing else available anywhere nearby. I promise I won't leave my socks lying around on the floor, and I'll try to remember to put the seat down in the john."

She deliberated a moment longer, her eyes cool and enigmatic. Then, with a small, resigned groan, she straightened away from the jamb. "I should have known something like this would happen. Okay, you can share this place. There are two bathrooms. You can do whatever you want with the seat in yours."

"Thanks." A heady sense of relief and anticipation swept through him. Probably just the altitude again. He'd get acclimated soon. "I owe you."

"You certainly do." She stepped back to allow him to enter.

She made him feel the way Dracula must have felt when he wangled the invitation to cross the threshold, he thought. He picked up the duffel and went through the doorway.

He glanced around at the gleaming wooden floors, the deep-pile rug in front of the fire, and the plush, leather furnishings. "I don't see a stuffed moose head mounted on the wall. Shouldn't there be a moose head?"

"If you want a moose head, you'll have to supply it yourself."

"That's okay, I'm adaptable. I can make do without the moose head."

She gave him a brief, reluctant smile that hit him straight in the gut because it brought back memories of all the radiant smiles he'd received from her B.D. Before the Disaster.

She gestured toward the stairs. "I've already settled into the loft on the left. You can have the one on the right."

"No problem." He crossed the room to the stairs before she could change her mind. "Just give me a few minutes to unpack. Then we can drive into the village to grab a bite to eat. I may have screwed up with my hotel arrangements, but I think I can redeem myself."

"Really?" She sounded distinctly skeptical. "How?"

He glanced back over his shoulder as he started up the stairs. "I've kept Larry busy for the past couple of days gathering background info on the other people involved in *Fast Company*."

"Who's Larry?"

"The computer whiz I told you about. He's also my half brother."

She looked surprised. "I didn't know you had a half brother."

"I've got two of them. It's sort of complicated." He reached the landing, turned right, and set the duffel on the bench at the foot of the bed. "Anyhow, I told Larry to concentrate on the money people, but I also had him give me anything else he could dig up on the writer, the actors, the director, and everyone else involved in the film."

"And?"

"And, not surprisingly, they're all scheduled to be here in Mirror Springs this week." He unzipped the duffel. "I figure we should be able to track down some of them. Maybe one of them can give us a lead on Page."

"The town is crammed with people. How are we going to find the people involved in *Fast Company*?"

He dropped a folded shirt on the bed, walked to the railing, and looked down at her. "Thought we'd start by attending a party scheduled for tomorrow night."

"A party?"

"The guy who's throwing it is the film's real moneyman. His name doesn't appear in the credits, but he's the one who structured the financing package for *Fast Company*. His name is Dawson Holland."

She was starting to look intrigued. "Interesting."

"There's more." He folded his arms on the railing. "Holland's wife is Victoria Bellamy."

Elizabeth frowned. "The star of the film?"

"Right. What do you want to bet she's the reason he backed the picture in the first place?"

"So that she could star in it?"

"Why not?" Jack straightened and went back to the duffel

bag. "He wouldn't be the first man to finance a film in order to give the woman he loved a role in it."

"No, I guess not." Another pause. "How do you suggest we get into this party without an invitation?"

"Easy. If anyone questions us, we'll just tell them the truth."

"Which is?"

"We know the producer," Jack said. "Tyler Page."

THE INTERIOR OF the Reflections café exuded a chic, contemporary ambience in spite of its Victorian-era bones. Elizabeth glanced around as she took her seat. Like virtually everything else in Mirror Springs, the restaurant glowed with the expensive, golden aura associated with glossy travel-magazine ads.

A fire crackled on the huge hearth. The light gleamed on a lot of wooden surfaces and cast intimate shadows. The diners all looked as if they had just flown in from L.A. or New York. Pleated black trousers, slouchy linen jackets, and black shirts unbuttoned far enough to show off a lot of chest hair were prevalent. So were sleek little black dresses. Those who weren't wearing black were in denim.

This wasn't the Hollywood studio crowd, Elizabeth reminded herself. These were the independent and fringe filmmakers and their fans; people devoted to the kind of small, arty films that would never appear at the mall multiplexes. She knew enough about the independent film business to know that festivals such as the Neo Noir event here in Mirror Springs constituted the only venues for the vast majority of the small, low-budget pictures made by this group.

There was something oddly touching about the passion and enthusiasm she heard in the conversations taking place at nearby tables.

". . . incredible imagery in her stuff. She uses the language of film to create a completely separate reality . . ."

"Very Chandleresque, of course. Great visual style. No real narrative closure . . ."

". . . couldn't get away with letting the killer live in the old days. The Production Code was very strict. The murderer always had to die in the end . . ."

Elizabeth looked across the table at Jack. She had probably made a huge mistake when she had agreed to let him share the house with her. But what was she supposed to do, given the circumstances? She watched him wrap a strong, long-fingered hand around the glass of zinfandel that had just been placed in front of him. Machiavellian fingers, she reminded herself. She must not forget that.

He noticed her staring at his hands and cocked an inquisitive brow. "Something wrong?"

"No." She picked up her menu.

"You notice anything strange about this town?" he asked.

She tried a sip of her Chardonnay and then carefully set down the glass. "You mean like the fact that the sidewalks are spotless and there are no signs of any homeless people and every other business in town is either a cute restaurant or an art gallery?"

"Yeah. Like that."

She shrugged. "Best zoning ordinances money can buy, I imagine."

Jack nodded. He watched her for a moment over the rim of his glass. "So you want to talk about it?"

"The Mirror Springs zoning laws?"

"No." He paused very deliberately. "Us."

She felt as if all the air had just been sucked out of the room. A direct confrontation was the last thing she had

expected. But then, this was Jack Fairfax. Expect the unexpected.

"No," she said very carefully.

He held her eyes. "We're going to have to work closely
together for the next few days. Might help if we clear the
air."

What was going on here? In her experience men generally
avoided this kind of conversation. She took a couple of deep
breaths and told herself to stay focused.

"What's to clear?" She was pleased with the way that came
out. Casual. Cool. Uncaring. Downright heartless. "There's
no reason to dig up the past. I prefer to let it stay buried."

She must have got the tone right, because Jack's eyes
hardened. His voice, however, was steady. Relentless.

"Let's get one thing straight," he said coldly. "What happened at Galloway, Inc., was not personal. Morgan hired me
to design the acquisition strategy, and that's what I did. I'm
a consultant, Elizabeth. I do stuff like that all the time."

Just like that, all her good intentions went out the window.
The outrage, anger, and raw hurt that she thought she had
successfully suppressed suddenly threatened to erupt like
lava through ice. She had to fight to keep her voice from
shaking.

"No, you do not do stuff like that all the time, Jack. I did
some checking after I found out who you really are."

"Who I really am?" He gave her a derisive look. "You
make it sound like I've got a secret identity."

"As far as I'm concerned, that's what it amounted to. As I
said, I did some research and I discovered that the Galloway
deal was definitely not your usual kind of job. You went after
that company like a shark. Don't you dare sit there and tell
me it wasn't personal."

"It was business."

"You destroyed Galloway. A lot of people got hurt in that takeover, including the nice old lady who had given them all jobs in her firm."

"People lose jobs in a takeover," he said, still doggedly patient. "It's a fact of life. Look, I know that Camille Galloway was an old Aurora Fund client, and I know that your brother-in-law worked for her. I'm sorry about that. It was just one of those things."

"It wasn't just one of those things. Camille Galloway was more than just another client. She was an old and very good friend of the family. She used to feed me cookies and milk when I was a kid. She gave my brother-in-law, Merrick, a job when he needed one badly."

"You make her sound like Saint Camille."

"She was a very nice old lady who had worked hard all of her life to build something to leave to her only son, Garth. When you ripped her life's work to shreds, you tore the heart out of her. And I mean that almost literally. In case you don't know it, Camille died of a heart attack a few months after you savaged her company."

"I know." His voice was low and grim.

She clutched her glass very tightly. "What happened at Galloway was personal and it was damned scary."

"Scary? That does it." He leaned forward abruptly, folding his arms on the table. "You know what? You're right about what happened at Galloway. It was personal. I did go after the company."

"I knew it." But there was no satisfaction in the confirmation, she discovered. If anything, she only felt more glum.

"I went to Morgan, told him I could give him his competition on a silver platter, and he agreed to hire me to handle the takeover."

"Why? What did Camille Galloway ever do to you?"

"Listen up, Pollyanna. You think I'm a shark? Sweet, kindly, Mrs. Galloway could have given me lessons."

"What are you talking about?"

"Five years ago she ripped off a nineteen-year-old kid who happened to have developed a brand-new and extremely clever software program. It was designed to make very sophisticated financial projections based on very limited data. Within one year of application, Galloway's profits nearly doubled. The kid never saw a penny more than the measly five thousand dollars Camille Galloway paid him for the software. I wanted her to pay for ripping off the kid, and I made sure she did. That's what the Galloway deal was all about."

Something in his tone gave her pause. Jack was dead serious. "Can you prove that she ripped off this kid?"

"Nope. The contract she got him to sign was one hundred percent legal. Couldn't take her to court. I approached her, asked her to set up a royalty or licensing agreement with the kid. She laughed in my face." Jack shrugged. "So I destroyed her company."

A chill went through her, all the way to her toes. "Where did you get your facts? How do you happen to know this so-called kid you say Galloway cheated, and why do you care that he got ripped off in the first place?"

"The kid was my half brother Larry."

She absorbed that in stunned silence while she searched his eyes for the truth. After a while, she slumped back in her chair. "Your brother."

"Yeah."

"The one you told me about? The one who pulled up the information on Dawson Holland and the other people involved in *Fast Company*?"

"Uh-huh."

She stared at him. "You brought down an entire company for the sake of revenge?"

"I prefer to think of it as justice."

"I'll bet you do. Sounds a heck of a lot more civilized, doesn't it?"

"Part of my deal with Morgan was a licensing contract with Larry on the software. He now gets royalties."

"I see." She took a fortifying sip of wine. "It was a family thing."

Jack looked slightly taken aback. Then he frowned. "I guess you could say that."

"And it *was* personal."

"Yes, it was personal."

She remembered what he had said about going after Tyler Page, even if it turned out to be too late to retrieve Soft Focus. "Words like *revenge* and *reputation* figure rather strongly in your vocabulary, don't they?"

He said nothing; just looked at her.

She sat forward again. "You knew who I was when you came to me for the funding for Excalibur, didn't you?"

"Of course I knew who you were. You were the head of the Aurora Fund."

"Don't try to slide around this. I meant that you knew the Fund had connections to Camille Galloway and that I was highly unlikely to provide financial backing to the . . . the . . ." Unable to summon a suitable epithet, she waved a hand.

"Egg-sucking SOB?" Jack supplied helpfully.

"To the *person* who had destroyed my former client and family friend."

He drummed his fingers on the table once and then exhaled slowly. "I make it a point to research the people I do business with. I knew that Galloway had once been one of your Fund's clients. I knew there was a personal as well as a professional relationship between your aunt and Camille Galloway. I didn't know your brother-in-law worked there, though. Does that count?"

"Don't you dare try to make a joke out of this. The point is that you knew all about the Fund's connection to Galloway but you never bothered to bring up the subject, did you?"

"It had no bearing on our deal," he said quietly.

"You can tell yourself that, if it makes you feel any better. But don't waste your time trying to convince me. The truth is, you didn't tell me who you were because you knew that if I found out that you were the consultant who engineered the takeover of Galloway, I would never have agreed to sign a contract with you. Admit it."

"Like I said, what happened at Galloway had nothing to do with us."

"How would you have felt if you had been in my shoes and discovered that I had omitted a few piddling little details concerning the destruction of one of your former clients?"

"Elizabeth—"

"Don't bother. We both know the answer." She smiled grimly. "You know something, Jack? Maybe I could be convinced that you felt you had a right to even the score with Galloway because of what happened to your brother. I've got family, too. I understand how your sense of loyalty to Larry could make you do something that dramatic. And I accept the fact that you didn't know that your actions cost my brother-in-law another job—"

"Another job?"

"Never mind. The point is, maybe I could have been talked into making some allowance for the fact that you were bent on avenging your brother, although I could never approve of the way you went about it."

He raised his eyebrows in mockingly polite encouragement. "But?"

She hated it when he gave her that superior, all-knowing look. "But you can't expect me to ignore the fact that you didn't tell me that you were the man behind the Galloway takeover before you asked me to back your plans at Excalibur."

"You mean before we went to bed together, don't you?" He looked at her. "That's what you can't get past. The fact that we had sex before you found out I was behind the Galloway deal."

She lifted her chin. "That was a factor, yes."

He contemplated her in silence for a while.

"Know what I think?" he finally asked.

"What?"

"I don't think this is just about me. I think you're equally pissed at yourself. Maybe even more than you are at me."

"What on earth are you talking about?"

"You're mad at yourself because you think you got suckered. You think I used sex to get what I wanted from you, and you blame yourself because you think you fell for a line." He turned one hand, palm up. "You feel like a fool. So naturally, you blame me. Simple psychology."

She stared at him in openmouthed amazement. "When did you take up the study of psychology?"

"I've had a lot of time to think about what went wrong between us. Six whole months, to be exact."

She felt as if she'd just been blindsided. "I'm surprised you bothered to try to analyze our relationship."

"We didn't have a relationship. We had a very short-lived affair."

"A one-night stand."

"Could have been an affair," he said. "You're the one who ended it after one night."

"Because I found out who you were. Lord only knows how long things would have gone on if Hayden Shaw hadn't told me—" She broke off abruptly, but it was too late. The damage was done.

"Figures." Jack just nodded once, as if she had confirmed something he'd already concluded. "I've been meaning to ask you who told you that I was the consultant behind the Galloway deal. Had to be Hayden."

"Don't blame the messenger."

"I'll blame whoever I damn well want to blame." He turned his attention to the menu. "Let's order and then let's change the subject. This has turned out to be one of those conversations I wish I'd never started."

She picked up her menu and opened it with a snap. "Nothing like clearing the air to improve interpersonal communications."

"Yeah, that's what I always say, too." He looked at her over the top of the menu. "Just one more thing before we put this topic to bed. So to speak."

She eyed him warily. "What now?"

"I would like to state for the record that I do not now, nor have I ever, sucked an egg."

CHAPTER NINE

"WOW. VICTORIA BELLAMY LOOKS EXACTLY LIKE she does on that poster of *Fast Company*." Elizabeth sounded awed.

Jack was surprised. The thought of Elizabeth being starstruck was almost funny. He followed her gaze across the room and spotted Victoria.

The blonde moved between clusters of guests with the languid elegance of a mermaid gliding among small schools of dull, ordinary fish. It was eleven o'clock and the large house was thronged, but it was easy to keep track of Victoria in the crowd. For one thing, she was one of the few who weren't wearing black. She was dressed in a pale, ice-blue, liquid satin dress with a low, draped neckline that could have come straight out of a late-1940s couturier's salon. Her platinum hair fell in a series of waves that framed her fine-boned features. Her mouth was full and heavy with lipstick. Her lashes were weighted down with mascara. Diamonds glittered in her ears and around her throat.

"So she looks like she does on the poster." He paused, taking a closer look. "Except that I don't think she's wearing a gun tonight. What did you expect?"

He took stock of the crowd as he spoke. The glass-walled room in which they stood was crammed with people. It looked like everyone who was anyone at the film festival was here tonight. Dawson Holland obviously was a player in this backwater niche of the film industry.

The decor was simple. It consisted largely of huge movie posters—most of which were black-and-white scenes from *Fast Company*—hung from the ceiling. The majority of the strikingly lit shots featured Victoria Bellamy. There was a lot of cute, clever-looking food around, and a bar had been set up near the entrance to the deck. When he had picked up the drinks earlier, Jack had noticed that the labels being poured were all first class.

"I don't know." Elizabeth paused, frowning slightly, as though trying to sort out her thoughts. "I guess I wasn't expecting her to be quite so beautiful or so glamorous in person. This isn't Hollywood, after all. But she looks like she really could be a star."

"The fact that she looks like a star doesn't mean that she can act."

"That's true," Elizabeth admitted.

Jack leaned a little closer to her under the pretext of reaching for a handful of nuts. He was very conscious of her standing next to him. He caught the faint whiff of a spice-and-flower-scented perfume and felt his insides tighten.

When she had come downstairs earlier dressed in a sexy little slip of a dress, her hair caught up in an elegant twist, he had wanted to break something, anything to relieve the frustration. Sharing the house with her for a week was going to be hard. Maybe the hardest thing he'd ever done. *Stay focused,* he thought. *Get the job done.*

"Look at the way heads turn when she walks through the room," Elizabeth said.

Jack glanced back at Victoria, who had stopped to talk to a thin, intense young man with short, curly hair and horn-rimmed glasses. "She's beautiful. Beautiful people get looked at. Fact of life."

"You don't appear to be as impressed as most of the other men in this room," Elizabeth mused.

"I'm impressed." He munched nuts. "But I'm not interested."

"There's a difference?"

"Big difference."

Elizabeth eyed him thoughtfully. "Explain."

He stopped chewing nuts while he grappled with that.

"I don't know if I can," he said eventually. "All I can tell you is that she looks great but she also looks like she knows she looks great. Whatever she's got doesn't translate into sexy. Not for me, at any rate."

"Hmm."

He groped for another way to explain. "She looks cold. Like she's got ice water in—" He stopped in midsentence.

Elizabeth's smile could have frozen a tropical sea. "You were saying something about Victoria Bellamy looking cold, I believe. Would you care to elaborate on that point?"

"Don't think so." He seized another handful of nuts.

"Would you describe her as an ice princess, the way you did me?" Elizabeth assumed an expression of gentle concentration, as if trying to clarify a point. "Or would that be overstating the case? After all, you don't really know the woman that well. It might be too soon to categorize her as an ice princess."

"Damn." Why did this kind of thing always happen to him whenever he tried to conduct a civilized conversation with her? he wondered glumly.

"Tell me, Jack, do you think the problem is that there

really are a lot of ice princesses in the world? Or is it just something about you that affects women that way?"

"We're here for a reason," he said very evenly. "Maybe we better get to work."

"You're changing the subject."

"Damn right." He took her arm and steered her toward another buffet table. "We'll work the room the same way we did at that charity function the other night."

"It would be too much to expect Page to show up here at the party, wouldn't it?"

"Given my luck lately, yes. But it's not beyond the realm of possibility. From what I can tell, Page loved the idea of being in the film business and everything that went with it. Being here tonight might be important to him."

"If you spot him, you might want to make sure I don't strangle him," Elizabeth said.

THE WRITER SAID his name was Spencer West, and Elizabeth could tell immediately that he'd had one too many tequila sunrises.

"High concept," he announced, slurring the second c in concept. "That's what it's all about. You gotta have high concept or you're dead in Hollywood. "

"I see." Elizabeth did her best to infuse acute interest and admiration into her voice.

Spencer was very slender and painfully intense. He had curly hair, and he wore horn-rimmed glasses. His unconstructed linen jacket hung from his thin, slightly hunched shoulders. He seemed nice enough, she thought. But after an hour of trying to cultivate conversations of this nature with people who were total strangers, her patience was starting to shred.

"You gotta be able to state the whole concept in a single

sentence." Spencer gulped more of his tequila sunrise. "One goddamned lousy little sentence."

"Sort of like an advertising slogan."

"Exactly." He looked morosely pleased at her perception.

"Must be tough."

"Hollywood scriptwriting is for morons who don't have any vision and who don't care that everything they do is going to get turned over to some committee to rewrite. I've got vision. That's why I do independent stuff."

"What was your vision for *Fast Company*?"

Spencer paused for dramatic effect. " 'Once you start running in fast company, you can't stop.' It became the tag line for the film."

Elizabeth nodded. "An unhappy ending, I take it?"

Spencer frowned. "A *realistic* ending."

"Right. Realistic. There must be a lot of pressure on a scriptwriter like yourself."

"Awesome pressure."

"I imagine everyone involved with a film has an idea or two he or she wants to contribute," Elizabeth said delicately.

Spencer snorted in disgust. "More than an idea or two. You wouldn't believe what I went through with the script for *Fast Company*. Everyone tried to get into the act. Shit, I had to completely rewrite the female lead for Vicky."

"Vicky?"

Spencer gave her a quizzical scowl. "Vicky Bellamy. Dawson's wife."

"Oh, sure. Vicky." Elizabeth smiled brightly. "Why did you have to rewrite the part?"

Spencer gave her a look that told her she had just asked either an incredibly stupid or an astonishingly naive question.

"I had to rewrite it because her husband is Dawson Holland," he said with extravagant patience. "Holland held the purse strings on *Fast Company*. He put together the finance package that bankrolled the film just so his wife could star in it. Naturally, he got whatever he wanted. Or, in this case, whatever Vicky wanted."

"I see." Elizabeth smiled weakly. "Actually, the only reason I'm here tonight is because I'm a friend of one of the investors."

Spencer contrived to look both cynical and knowing. "The money guys."

"Yes." Elizabeth searched for an opening. "Did any of them try to influence the script the way Vicky and Holland did?"

Spencer made a face. "Some of 'em hung out on the set a lot. Made nuisances of themselves. One tried to put his two cents in a couple of times, but I ignored him. I mean, what does a guy like that know? He was just some little nerd from Seattle who wanted to pretend he was a player."

Elizabeth choked on a swallow of her mineral water. She sputtered wildly. "From Seattle, you say?"

Spencer took another swallow of his tequila sunrise. "Guy named Page. Tyler Page."

"Oh, yes, the producer."

Spencer rolled his eyes. "Page got the credit, but Dawson Holland was the one who put the deal together. Takes a lot of cash to make a film, you know, even a small one. There are usually several investors."

"But Page got sole credit on *Fast Company*. I wonder why."

Spencer looked bored. "Probably put up the biggest chunk of cash. Or maybe he did a deal with Holland. Who knows? Some of those investors will do anything to get their name in the credits."

Without warning, Victoria Bellamy swam out of a nearby shoal of guests.

"Spencer."

Her voice was as glamorous as the rest of her, Elizabeth thought. Husky, low, throaty. Lauren Bacall in *The Big Sleep*. She watched Victoria exchange air kisses with Spencer.

"Nice party, Vicky," Spencer said.

"So glad you could make it." Victoria turned to Elizabeth with an inquiring look. "Introduce me to your friend."

Spencer's eyes glazed for the moment. It had probably just occurred to him that he didn't know her name, Elizabeth thought. She smiled at Victoria and extended her hand.

"I'm Elizabeth. A business associate of one of the money people. I hope you don't mind, Ms. Bellamy."

"Please, call me Vicky. Everyone else does." Vicky's laugh was low and rich. "Of course I don't mind. I just love money people. And their business associates. Are you here for the entire festival?"

"Yes. I'm very excited about the whole event." Vicky didn't seem to care that she hadn't gotten a last name to go with the first name. Elizabeth recalled the book she had scanned on the plane from Seattle. "Noir is such a fascinating genre. The way light and shadow is used as a visual metaphor is so distinctive. And the classic films did such an incredible job of catching the essence of modern moral ambiguity. And the use of the dark urban landscape—" She broke off. "Well, it's *the* quintessentially American style, isn't it?"

Vicky smiled. "Don't forget the Western."

"You're absolutely right. Westerns and noir film are both uniquely American."

"Amazing," Vicky mused.

Elizabeth wondered if she'd overdone it. "What's amazing?"

"Most money people don't talk about film like that."

"I'm just a friend of one of the investors," Elizabeth said smoothly. "I'm attending the festival because I'm a film buff."

"Who's your friend? The one you said was an investor?" Vicky asked.

Elizabeth took a breath. "Tyler Page. You probably met him in the course of making *Fast Company*."

"Yes, of course I met Tyler." Vicky smiled. "He was a rather sweet little man. He liked to hang around the set whenever possible. I think he had stars in his eyes. Didn't he, Spencer?"

Spencer gave an elaborate shrug. "All the money guys have stars in their eyes."

Vicky gave a husky laugh. "Given the fact that most of them will never see a dime in profits, I think it's only fair to allow them a few dreams. Don't you agree, Elizabeth?"

"Dreams are important," Elizabeth said. "Sometimes that's all you get."

Vicky smiled. "That sounds like a line from one of Spencer's scripts. Maybe you'd like to read the script for *Fast Company*?"

"I'd love to read it," Elizabeth said quickly.

"I'm sure Spencer could get you a copy." Vicky looked at him expectantly.

Spencer looked up from his tequila sunrise. "What? Oh, sure. Copy of the script. Got one with me. I'll get it for you before you leave, Elizabeth."

"Thanks," Elizabeth said. "I'd appreciate that."

Spencer rocked precariously on his heels and looked at Vicky. "How's it going on the stalker front? I heard about the incident at the spa the other day."

Vicky grimaced. "I wound up with a lot of red paint on my clothes, as usual. It's the third time the bastard has struck in the past month. I think Dawson is getting worried."

Elizabeth stared at her. "You're being *stalked*?"

"Some idiot has decided that I'm the incarnation of a bib-

lical harlot. He started stalking me about a month ago."
Vicky made a circular motion with her finger near her ear.
"A real loony."

"Good grief," Elizabeth whispered. "I can't imagine anything more terrifying than being stalked."

Vicky's jaw tightened. "It is a little scary, I admit. Dawson
is more concerned than I am."

"What are the police doing about it?" Elizabeth demanded.

"There's not much they can do. The police chief here in
town is a man named Gresham. He's very nice and very
earnest, but the fact is, he's got a very small force and it's not
exactly high-tech or state of the art. This week it's probably
overwhelmed with the crowd that's in town for the festival."

"Maybe Dawson should hire a bodyguard for you,"
Spencer suggested with an odd look. "He can afford one."

"He's mentioned it," Vicky said vaguely. "But I've asked
him to hold off for a while. I really hate the thought of having to have a bodyguard. I'm hoping the police will catch
him before we have to go that route."

"Good luck," Spencer mumbled into his drink.

"Thanks." Vicky stepped back. "Well, if you'll excuse me,
I'd better keep circulating. Enjoy yourselves."

Spencer watched her disappear into the crowd. Elizabeth
noticed that several other men and one or two women did the
same. She thought about what Jack had said earlier and
decided to run Spencer through a test.

"She's really beautiful, isn't she?" Elizabeth asked casually.

"Yeah," Spencer replied. "The amazing thing is that she's
not a half-bad actress. Not Hollywood material, but not bad."

"I feel sorry for her. That stalker stuff must be very
frightening."

Spencer gave a short bark that was probably meant to be a laugh. "I wouldn't worry too much about Vicky and her stalker if I were you."

"What do you mean?"

"Five will get you ten that it's all a publicity stunt. Probably dreamed up by Vicky herself."

Elizabeth felt her jaw drop. "Are you serious?"

"Sure." Spencer seemed amused by her reaction. "Hey, this may not be Hollywood, but this is still the movie business, lady. For someone like Vicky Bellamy, publicity is interchangeable with blood in her veins."

"That sounds a little cold."

"You kidding?" Spencer drained his glass. "I'll bet Vicky has to drink antifreeze in her orange juice every morning to keep herself from freezing solid."

"THE THING ABOUT noir is that it all hinges on vision and lighting," Bernard Aston declared. "You gotta have vision and lighting."

"And money," Jack said.

He glanced around the room, searching for Elizabeth. He hoped she was having better luck than he was. Thus far he had talked to a lighting technician, a member of the camera crew, and two people who claimed to have had walk-ons in *Fast Company*. None of them seemed to know or care about Tyler Page. He had finally managed to track down the director, but Aston wasn't proving any more helpful than the others.

Bernard was short and heavy, and he had left his designer denim shirt unbuttoned a little too far down his chest. The silver ankh dangling in the sparse gray hair that covered his midsection and the straggly ponytail did nothing to enhance the image Jack suspected he was trying to project.

"Lining up the money is the producer's problem. As the director, I gotta stay focused on vision and lighting," Bernard explained.

"Sure. But with Dawson Holland handling the financing, you had the luxury of staying focused, didn't you?"

"Shit. Holland was a pain in the ass right from the start. He made it clear that the main condition for financing *Fast Company* was the female lead for Vicky. It wasn't easy making her look good, I can tell you that. Woman can't act her way out of a paper bag."

Jack glanced up at one of the huge posters that dangled from the high ceiling. "She looks pretty good in that shot."

"Vision and lighting." Aston removed the olive from his martini and popped it into his mouth. "Vicky was a pain in the ass, too. Never made it in Hollywood, you know."

Jack suspected that Vicky was not the only one present tonight who had failed to make it in Hollywood.

He was formulating a question that would lead to the subject of Tyler Page, when Aston glanced past him and raised his martini in a careless salute.

"Nice party, Holland," Aston said.

"Don't thank me, thank Vicky. She handles things like this. Glad you could make it, Aston."

Jack turned very casually at the sound of the dry, cultured voice. He took in Dawson Holland with a quick glance, measuring him against the information Larry had supplied.

At fifty-seven he was more than twenty years older than his wife, but if Larry hadn't supplied the age factor, it would have been tough to guess. He had refined, ascetic features and a judicious amount of silver in his hair. "Distinguished looking" was the phrase that most people would probably come up with to describe him, Jack thought. Holland moved with the athletic ease of a man who took care of his body. He was wearing a black silk shirt and black trousers, but he somehow managed to carry off the look without appearing too painfully L.A.

He looked at Jack and smiled slightly. His gray eyes were politely quizzical. "Don't believe we've met."

"Jack Fairfax." Jack held out his hand. "And no, you didn't invite me. My date and I crashed your party. Our only excuse is that we know the producer. Or at least, the guy who got the credit in the film. Tyler Page."

"No problem, Jack." Holland's handshake was as solid as a banker's. "Business associates of people who pour money into films are always welcome here. Are you interested in getting into the game yourself?"

"I don't know." Jack glanced meaningfully at the posters. "Looks expensive. And I hear the independent film business is a real crapshoot from a financial point of view."

"Tell me about it." Dawson's chuckle was easy, unforced. "But there's nothing quite like the final product, eh, Aston?"

"No." Aston's eyes gleamed briefly. "Nothing else in the whole damn world like making pictures."

"Are you and your friend here for the festival, Jack?" Dawson asked.

"My friend likes old movies." Jack shrugged. "So we're here for the whole week."

"Your friend has good taste." Dawson winked. "Besides, it usually pays to please the ladies."

Jack glanced across the room and saw Elizabeth. She was chatting earnestly with a young man in glasses.

"Some ladies are a lot harder to please than others," he said.

CHAPTER TEN

DAWSON LOUNGED BACK AGAINST THE PILLOWS and watched Vicky come out of the turquoise and white tiled bath. She wore the robe she had brought back with her from Paris last month. It was made of heavy maroon silk decorated with elaborately stitched flowers. Her hair was piled on top of her head.

She had removed her makeup. Even without it she was still stunning. His two previous wives had both been beautiful, but neither of them could hold a candle to Vicky.

He felt the familiar heaviness between his legs. He knew that a lot of men never got past Vicky's beauty. The fools never noticed the razor-sharp brain. But he had noticed. That was why she was with him instead of some other man. Vicky traded on her beauty, but she had only disdain for men who could not see beyond it or who did not care what lay beneath the surface.

He thought fleetingly about the redhead in L.A. last month. He could not recall her name, just the nice tits. *Not nearly as nice as Vicky's.* He gave a small inward sigh and wondered again why he bothered with the one-night stands. None of the other women he had been with during the past two years since his marriage to Vicky meant anything to him. They were nameless and faceless. When he came with one of them, he usually fantasized that he was with Vicky.

Why the hell did he waste his time with the others when he had a woman like this in his bed? he wondered. It was a question that had begun to bother him more and more frequently during the past few months. Maybe he should see a shrink, he thought.

He watched Vicky sit down on the white velvet chair in front of the dressing table and cross her long legs. One high-heeled slipper dangled.

"I thought it went well tonight," he said. "You were spectacular, as always."

"Thank you." She swung one ankle absently and met his eyes in the mirror. "We may have a problem with the stalker thing, though."

"Why do you say that?"

"I think people are starting to conclude that it's just a publicity stunt. Spencer West mentioned it. I could tell that he had his doubts, and I'm pretty sure he's not the only one. Maybe it's time to end it."

"Let's let it run through the festival. The local paper gave you several column inches after the last incident. So what if a few people suspect it's a stunt? No big deal. We'll get our money's worth out of it."

She smiled. "You mean *your* money's worth."

"My pleasure, I assure you. If it helps to advance your career, I consider it a worthwhile investment."

Vicky's smiled faded. She regarded him with a somber, considering look. "You're very good to me, Dawson."

"I enjoy being good to you, my dear."

She uncrossed her legs, stood, and unbelted the silk robe. She wore nothing underneath.

Dawson felt himself grow rock hard. "Damn, but you're beautiful."

She smiled again, turned out the light, and came to him in the darkness. When she took him into her mouth he felt as though he had been swept up and roiled in a tidal wave. With the others he had to do all the work. But Vicky made love to him with the skill of a trained courtesan. All he had to do was lie back and give himself over to the thrill of the experience.

His questions about the fling with the redhead in L.A. evaporated. Vicky would never know about the others, he promised himself as she flowed across his body. He was always very careful.

He liked to think that he practiced discretion out of consideration for her. She was his wife, after all. She deserved at least that.

Just before the powerful orgasm seized him and shook him until he was limp, he thought about the way Jack Fairfax had studied one of the posters featuring Vicky in *Fast Company*. There had been a calculating look in his eyes. Probably imagining what it would be like to have Vicky in his bed.

Fairfax would never know the answer to that question, Dawson thought, because, unlike his first two wives, Vicky did not cheat.

Her priorities in life had been obvious from the outset: She craved the financial security his money provided, and she wanted to star in films. Although she could act her way through an orgasm as well as any woman he had ever known, he was almost certain that she had no great personal interest in sex. It was simply the commodity she offered in exchange for what he could give her.

She was expensive, but she was worth it. He'd had a lot of women in his bed, but never one like Vicky.

Later, just before he collapsed, exhausted, from the sex, he wondered again why he bothered with the others.

CHAPTER ELEVEN

JACK SETTLED DEEPER INTO THE SIMMERING waters of the hot tub. The steam that rose from the surface was invisible in the darkness, but he could feel the cloud of warmth that enveloped the pool.

He had not turned on any lights when he had come downstairs a few minutes ago. He had left the underwater lamps inside the tub off, too. The only illumination on the deck came from the cold glow of the moon and the stars.

He stretched his arms out along the edge of the tub on either side and leaned back to contemplate the late-night sky. It was after two in the morning. He and Elizabeth had returned to the house shortly before one.

As far as he could tell, she had gone straight to sleep, which, for some obscure reason, irritated him. How could she drop off so easily while he lay there staring through the glass at the night-shrouded mountain? The answer was all too obvious. The fact that he was in a bed a short distance away from her didn't affect her one damn bit.

He had eventually concluded that he might be able to think more clearly out here in the hot tub. He got some of his best ideas in the middle of the night, he reflected. But there was some risk involved, because he had also been known to come up with some of his dumbest ideas at night. Take the decision to start an affair with Elizabeth before he told her that he had been the man behind the Galloway takeover. Six months ago, that brilliant idea had come to him shortly after three in the morning.

He listened to the muted hum of the hot-tub motor and the soft bubbling of the churning water. The only other sound was the faint sighing of nearby tree branches.

It occurred to him that for most of his adult life he had taken for granted his ability to focus on a specific goal. His father, Sawyer Fairfax, had once told him it was a gift, like being able to write music or paint pictures. It was like anything else, Sawyer had told him. Use it or lose it. Jack had used it.

His big mistake six months ago, he decided, had been trying to concentrate on two goals simultaneously: Elizabeth and Excalibur.

He had lost the first and was precariously close to losing the second.

He heard the sliding glass door open behind him.

"Jack?" Elizabeth's voice was sharp with curiosity. "What in the world are you doing out here?"

"Thinking."

"Oh." There was a short pause. "Give me a minute. I'll join you."

"I'm not sure that would be a good idea," he said softly. Much too softly for her to hear.

She vanished back inside the house. A light came on upstairs. A short time later she reappeared. Jack watched her walk toward him through the shadows. She was enveloped in a fluffy white toweling robe.

A surge of heat went through him as she undid the sash of

the robe. She should have turned off the light before coming back down here, he thought. There was just enough glow spilling from the upstairs windows to enable him to see her.

If she expected him to simply ignore her while she climbed into a hot tub with him, she could damn well think again.

She slipped out of the robe, revealing the one-piece bathing suit she wore. So much for his fantasy of getting naked with her in a hot tub.

She frowned at him as she climbed cautiously into the tub. "Care to share the joke?"

"No."

"Why not?"

"Because it's on me."

She gave him another quick, unreadable look and then settled down on one of the benches. In the shadows he could see the water frothing around the gentle swell of her breasts, but everything beneath the surface was concealed. He would have to use his imagination, he decided. Then again, maybe that wasn't such a terrific idea, either.

"Couldn't sleep after all?" he asked.

"I did for a while. But I woke up a few minutes ago and started thinking." She tilted her head back against the edge of the tub. "We didn't make much progress tonight, did we?"

"I wouldn't say that. We identified a lot of the people who knew Tyler Page on the set of *Fast Company*. One of them might be able to give us some idea of where he is now."

"Mirror Springs is filled with people. If he's staying somewhere in town, he must have made his reservations weeks ago. Maybe we should—"

"Forget it. I had Larry check out that angle first. There's no record of a Tyler Page registered at any hotel, motel, or bed-and-breakfast in town or anywhere nearby. If he's here, he's hiding under another name. And according to Larry, he's still not using his credit cards."

Elizabeth pondered that for a moment. "If he made reservations several weeks back under an assumed name and booked them without using a credit card or check, he must have planned to steal the specimen some time ago. This wasn't a spur-of-the-moment thing."

"Nope. Looks like the little SOB planned it for quite a while."

"All this crafty, detail-oriented plotting doesn't quite fit with what you've told me about his personality. You said he was absentminded and something of a slob. Except when it came to his work."

"Maybe he considered the theft part of his research and development of the crystal," Jack said. "Gave the project the same kind of attention he gave his work."

"Or maybe he had a little help," Elizabeth suggested quietly.

Jack groaned and settled deeper into the tub. "I've been trying not to think about that possibility. If there's more than one person involved in this thing, it's going to get much more complicated."

"But it is a possibility."

"Yeah, it's a possibility. But on the positive side, there's no one else mysteriously missing from the lab where Tyler Page worked. He seems to have had no close friends or relatives."

"What about a lover?"

Jack grunted. "Everyone who knew him at Excalibur says he didn't have a love life. Didn't seem to be interested in women."

"Men?"

Jack shook his head. "Or men, either. All he cared about was Soft Focus and making movies."

She closed her eyes. "We might not find him, Jack."

He flexed his fingers around the edge of the tub. "We'll find him. He'll turn up here at the festival. He won't be able to resist."

"You're very sure of that, aren't you?"

"Like I said, when you know a man's greatest passion, you know his greatest weakness. *Fast Company* is Page's passion. Sooner or later, he'll turn up. I still think he'll try to sell the crystal back to me."

"What makes you so sure?"

"There's nothing else he can do with it except sell it. I'm his best potential buyer."

She opened her eyes and looked at him. "A couple of days ago you made some comment about not letting Tyler Page ruin your professional reputation. But what will you really do if we don't get the specimen back in time for the Veltran presentation?"

"I'm committed to saving Excalibur," he said evenly.

"And your reputation."

"And my reputation," he agreed.

"You picked a hard one this time, Jack. But most of them have been hard, haven't they?"

He glanced at her. "What are we talking about now?"

"The kind of work you do. I did some checking during the past six months. Excalibur isn't the first small, family-held company you've tried to save. Why?"

What was this all about? he wondered. Why was she getting so intense? "Turning around companies like Excalibur is what I do."

"Maybe, but I would have figured that you were too smart to waste your time with a company facing the kind of odds Excalibur is facing."

"I like the odds."

"Even if you get Soft Focus back, you can't be sure the firm will have the resources to take it to market."

"If we get it back, I can get it to market."

"Why don't you cut your losses and go find another client?"

He looked at her across the foaming water. "I don't walk away from a client after I sign the contract."

"That brings up another question. I made some calls. Asked some people I know about some of your past contracts. I noticed a pattern."

"What the hell is this? Have you spent the past six months setting up a file on me?"

"I didn't spend the *entire* time setting up the file," she said. "Just some of the time."

He was dumbfounded. She'd made a file? On him? He didn't know whether to be angry or wary or flattered.

"Well, hell," he finally said neutrally.

"I noticed that you almost always sign on with small, struggling, closely held or family-held companies. The contract you signed with Morgan to strategize the Galloway takeover was an exception to your usual pattern."

He looked up at the stars. "I needed a company the size of Morgan to make it happen. A small operation wouldn't have had the resources or the incentive to do the job."

She smiled thinly. "And you were bound and determined to have your revenge on Galloway, weren't you?"

He said nothing.

"Tell me," she said, "why do you only work for small, privately held firms? I would think that, generally speaking, the larger the company, the bigger the payoff for a turnaround consultant. Everyone knows about those golden parachutes executives in your position usually get when they take the helm of a major firm. Even if the companies go under, they routinely walk away with huge bonuses in addition to their salaries. But you don't sign contracts like those."

"You know that for a fact, huh?"

"Your business life history is in my file."

"Huh." A file. On him.

"Care to explain?" she prodded.

He chose his words with caution. "I like working with the small family-helds. I have greater control. More opportunity to affect the outcome. And there are no stockholders to appease."

She gave him a look of mingled amusement and disbelief. "You're telling me that you actually prefer dealing with squabbling family members like the ones on the Excalibur board?"

Her wry tone made him grin briefly. "I'll admit that handling the Ingersolls, especially Angela, is a challenge. Want to know a deep, dark secret?"

"What's that?"

"There have been times during the past six months when I've been damned glad you forced me to give you a seat on the board."

She gave him a knowing look. "You've used me to back you up, haven't you?"

"Yeah."

"Nice to know I haven't been a complete and unmitigated thorn in your side."

"I didn't say you weren't a thorn in my side, just that you've been a useful thorn."

She studied him for a while. "So it's the challenge and the sense of control?"

"Now what are you talking about?"

"The reasons why you almost always work for the little firms. You like the challenge and the control you have in those kinds of turnaround situations."

"Like I said, it's what I do."

"How very macho." Her mouth curved slightly. "The modern equivalent of the hired gun back in the days of the Wild West. Loyal to your employer come hell or high water. When the job is done, you ride off into the sunset."

He did not respond.

"I think there's more to it than that, Jack," she said very softly.

"Mind telling me why we're having this conversation?"

"Probably because it's after two o'clock in the morning." She paused. "Maybe I shouldn't have come out here."

"Maybe not."

She stood up abruptly in the churning water. The wet bathing suit clung, sleek and snug, to her slender waist and full hips. "This discussion appears to be deteriorating. I think I'll go back to bed."

He watched her climb out of the hot tub. "You really have a file on me?"

"A nice thick one." She pulled on her robe. "I just hope for both our sakes that you're as good as your track record says you are."

She turned and walked toward the darkened doorway.

"Yeah, me too." He stood up, strode through the frothing water to the tub steps, and climbed out.

"For heaven's sake, Jack."

He paused in the act of wrapping the towel around his waist and glanced toward the doorway. "Now what?"

She stared at him for a few seconds. Then she looked quickly away.

"Nothing." Her voice sounded oddly muffled.

"What the hell is wrong?"

"I didn't realize—" She had her back to him. "I mean, I just assumed that you were wearing a bathing suit, too."

"Why would I wear a suit? Hell, I didn't even bring one with me."

"You should have said something," she shot back on a rising note.

"Yeah, well, just make a note and put it in my file. 'Doesn't wear swim trunks in hot tubs.' "

He went to the control panel and flipped off the hot-tub switch. *Give her plenty of time to run,* he told himself.

But when he turned around he saw that she was still standing in the darkened doorway. She was facing him again, her arms crossed very tightly beneath her breasts. She watched him with brooding, unreadable eyes.

"Sorry," she said very stiffly. "I overreacted."

"Don't worry about it." He shoved his hand through his steam-dampened hair as he walked toward her, scattering a few stray drops. "We're both under a lot of pressure here."

"Yes." She frowned, as if that were a particularly new and worrisome concept, one she had not considered until now. "That's true, isn't it. We'll each have to make allowances."

"You make allowances. I'm going to bed." He started past her through the doorway.

"Jack?"

He stopped and turned to look at her. She was so close that he could have touched her. So close that he could take her into his arms. Close enough to allow him to see the haunted look in her eyes.

"What is it?" he asked softly. "Worried about how we're going to get through the week together?"

"No."

"Well, three cheers for you." He moved closer and planted one hand on the sliding glass door frame above her head. "I'm sure as hell worried about it."

"Why?" She lifted her chin, but she did not try to duck away beneath his arm. "Because you're afraid I'll freak out every time I see you sitting in the hot tub?"

"No." He leaned closer. "Because every time I see you, I want to pick up where we left off six months ago."

"Why would you want to do that? You called me the Ice Princess, remember?"

"I was pissed off at the time."

"And now you're no longer pissed off?"

"I'm still pissed," he said, thinking about it. "But that doesn't mean I don't want to pick up where we left off six months ago."

Her lashes veiled her eyes. "That would be very stupid."

"Very." He kept one hand braced against the frame and used the other one to cradle her stubborn chin. "But I've been known to do stupid things."

"Probably not this stupid."

"Don't bet on it."

"Things could never be the same," she said very distinctly. "Not now."

Images of their one night together flashed through him. He remembered his own driving urgency. He had been blindsided by his reaction to her that night. Accustomed to making love the same way he did business, with absolute control and attention to detail, he knew that he had screwed up badly. He had been utterly oblivious of the small, telltale signs that should have warned him that he was moving too quickly. Hell, if he was honest with himself, he had to admit that even if he had been aware of them, he probably could not have slowed down much. Not that first time. But he knew her failure to find satisfaction in his arms had cost him dearly. The morning after, she had learned that he was the man behind the Galloway deal. There had been no second chances in bed.

"The last thing I want," he said in a very low voice, "is for things to be the same as they were that first time between us."

"Jack—"

"You have my personal guarantee that next time things will be very, very different."

She cleared her throat. "You're missing the point here."

"Don't think so." He lowered his mouth until it was only an inch or so above hers. "I notice that you're not running, screaming, into the night."

"Should I?" she said in a hushed voice.

"Let's find out."

He covered her mouth with his own.

And the rush hit him. Just as hard and fast as it had six months ago. But he was ready for it this time; braced to withstand the high winds at the heart of the tornado. This time he would get it right. This time he would stay in control.

He held himself in check, drawing out the kiss, searching for the response he wanted. She did not pull away. But neither did she throw her arms around his neck. He leaned in closer. He could feel the firm curves of her small breasts beneath the robe. She was still a little damp from the hot tub.

Her hands went to his shoulders. She parted her lips slightly.

He suddenly got the nasty feeling that she was testing him and maybe herself as well. She was willing to dip one toe into the sea, but this time she was not about to dive in head-first the way she had six months before.

Desperation threatened to sweep through him. He realized then that he had been nurturing a fantasy. In the back of his mind, he had convinced himself that, given another chance, he could ignite the fires in her. But what if he had been wrong?

He took his hand away from the door frame, wrapped his

arms around her, and pulled her close. She made a small, muffled sound—not a protest, but not exactly a sigh of surrender. Nevertheless, he was certain that he could feel the first flicker of a genuine response.

He deepened the kiss. She leaned into him. Relief and anticipation surged through him.

"If this is a test," he whispered against her mouth, "I'm going to do whatever it takes to pass."

He knew at once that he'd lost the moment. She stiffened, and pushed herself slightly away from him. Her eyes were inscrutable in the shadows. "Thanks for the warning."

He put one hand back on the door frame above her head and gripped it hard. It was either that or pull her back into his arms again. He knew that would not be a good idea.

"What's the matter?" he asked. "Decide to run, screaming into the night, after all?"

"I'm going to walk, not run. And I don't think it will be necessary to do any screaming." She slipped under his braced arm and moved deeper into the shadows of the living room, heading toward the stairs.

She was leaving, heading back to bed. Alone. He felt cold claws close around his gut. There would be no second chances tonight.

"How long are you going to continue punishing both of us for what you think I did to you six months ago?" he asked.

She paused at the foot of the stairs and turned to glance at him over her shoulder. In the darkness he could not see the expression on her face.

"You know, I would have thought that you were busy enough this week looking for Soft Focus, Jack. But if you really feel the urge to take on yet another challenge, I suggest you try something a little more exciting than a repeat of the seduction of the Ice Princess."

"You think I want to start over because I see you as some kind of challenge?"

"Yes. That's exactly what I think."

"That's not how it is."

She did not move. "What do you want from me?"

"Another chance."

"Why?"

"Because I want you and I think that you want me. Or was I imagining what just happened during that kiss?"

She said nothing, just stood there watching him for an eternity. Then, without a word, she went up the stairs and disappeared into the darkness of the landing.

He let out the breath he had not realized he had been holding, closed his eyes, and flexed one hand into a fist. *No second chances.*

"Jack?" Her voice floated softly down from the loft.

He opened his eyes and looked up with an effort. She was leaning slightly out over the railing. He could see the pale outline of her white robe.

"What now?" he asked.

"I'll think about it."

THE PHONE BURBLED, shattering his fitful sleep. He opened his eyes and glanced at the clock. Four-thirty.

The phone squalled again.

He groped for the receiver, found it, hauled it across the pillow.

"This is Fairfax."

"It was very clever of you to come to Mirror Springs, Mr. Fairfax. But there was no cause for concern. You were on the list. You would have been notified of the location in due course."

He was suddenly very wide awake. "What list?"

"The list of people invited to the auction. I wouldn't dream of conducting the sale of Soft Focus without you."

"When? Where?"

"Relax, Mr. Fairfax. You will be notified of the time and place. Meanwhile, as long as you're in town, you may as well enjoy the film festival. Have fun."

"Who are you?"

"Me? I'm the auctioneer. Oh, by the way, there's no need to waste your time pushing *69. This call is being made from a pay phone."

There was a click and then silence.

The light came on. Jack propped himself against the pillows and watched Elizabeth hurry into his loft. Her hair was tumbled around her face. She fumbled with the sash of her robe.

"Who was it?" she asked anxiously.

"Called himself the auctioneer. Said I'm on the list of people who will be invited to bid on Soft Focus."

"*Bid* on it. You mean there's going to be an auction?"

"Sounds like it."

She grimaced. "So much for your theory that you might be able to ransom the crystal. An auction could really drive up the price."

"Yes."

She met his eyes. "Was that Tyler Page on the phone?"

He thought about the mechanically distorted voice on the other end of the line. "Could have been anyone."

CHAPTER TWELVE

EDEN SITS AT THE DRESSING TABLE AND *regards her own stunning image in the mirror. She wears silver stiletto heels and a cheap, imitation silver lamé dressing gown. The lapels and cuffs of the gown are trimmed with fake fur. Her makeup turns her face into a beautiful, enigmatic mask.*

Behind her, the cold flashing light of a neon sign is seen through the room's single window. Harry, obviously distraught, paces nervously back and forth in front of the window.

HARRY: *"The cops think I killed your husband. They're getting ready to arrest me."*

EDEN: *"That's too bad."*

HARRY: *"How can you act so goddamned casual? I'm going to go to jail for life if you don't help me."*

EDEN: *"I'm kind of busy at the moment."*

HARRY: *"For God's sake, Eden, I'm innocent. You
        know that."*

EDEN: (gazes thoughtfully into the mirror)
        *"Innocent. How do you spell that? With one
        n or two?"*

HARRY: (stops pacing and swings around to stare at
        her with an expression of mounting disbelief
        and horror)
        *"Who the hell cares how to spell 'inno-
        cent'?"*

EDEN: *"I always have to look it up, you know. Hard
        to remember how to spell a word when
        you're not exactly sure what it means."*

There was a smattering of applause as the film clip abruptly
ended. The lights came up, revealing the four panelists seated
at the long table in front of the hotel meeting room.

"Our thanks to Bernard Aston, the director of *Fast Company,* for providing us with that clip," the moderator said.
"The character of Eden is a great example of the modern
femme fatale in neo noir film. We're lucky to have the star of
the film, Victoria Bellamy, here with us on our panel today."

Under the cover of another round of light applause, Elizabeth leaned toward the young woman seated beside her.
"You did a fantastic job with the makeup. Perfect noir look."

"Thanks." Christy Barns looked first startled and then
gratified by the compliment.

Elizabeth had met the young makeup artist who had
worked on *Fast Company* at the Holland reception. Christy
was no more than twenty-three or twenty-four at the most, a

thin, sharp-featured woman with long red hair. This morning when Elizabeth had spotted her going into the workshop titled "Femme Fatale: Women in Noir Film," she had made a spur-of-the-moment decision to sit next to her.

While the rest of the panelists, which, in addition to Vicky, included the author of a book, a self-proclaimed therapist, and a film critic were introduced, Elizabeth did a quick survey of the audience. There was no sign of a short, balding little man with horn-rimmed glasses and a furtive air. It would have been too much to hope that Tyler Page would be drawn to the panel, she thought, even if it did feature some advance clips from *Fast Company* and one of the film's stars.

"The female lead of the classic noir film is the spider woman," the moderator continued. "The dangerous temptress with her own agenda, the mysterious, sexually aggressive female who threatens every man. She manipulates, seduces, and destroys. Ultimately, she is unknowable. A force of nature that both attracts and repels."

Seated at the end of the table, Vicky smiled drolly and picked up her microphone. "Speaking as an actress, I can tell you that she's also a lot of fun to play."

The audience chuckled appreciatively.

The author frowned and seized the second microphone. "The femme fatale character is at the heart of noir. In my new book, *Dark Worlds: A History of Film Noir,* I demonstrate that, in one guise or the other, the female lead subverts the patriarchal establishment. She uses the power of her sexuality to lure men to their ruin. When we think of the femme fatale archetypes, we think bitch-goddess or black widow."

Elizabeth tuned out the panelist and thought back to Jack's grim mood at the breakfast table an hour ago. Not content to wait for the auction, he had announced that he was determined to forge ahead with his plans to try to locate Tyler Page.

She knew that the thought of having to pay for the return of Excalibur's property galled him. She did not blame him.

But she was also fairly sure that his unpleasant mood owed its origins to more than just the four-thirty A.M. phone call from the auctioneer. He had not taken rejection well last night. She wondered if he now considered her a bitch-goddess or a black widow. Either one was preferable to Ice Princess, she decided. At least bitch-goddesses and black widows sounded more interesting.

One thing was certain. Jack was never going to know how difficult it had been for her to walk away from him after that scorching kiss. It had taken every ounce of willpower she possessed to climb those stairs.

Another chance? Was that really what he wanted from her? And what, in the name of heaven, had made her dangle the possibility in front of both of them? For six months she had told herself she would never trust him again. But what she had discovered in the course of checking out his business track record had made her question some of her assumptions about him. Your run-of-the-mill ruthless corporate shark who was smart enough to rescue companies on the brink concentrated on large corporations. Turnaround specialists as good at their jobs as Jack obviously was, piled up fortunes working for the big companies. They rarely wasted time trying to save small firms.

Curiosity had been plaguing her for months. That was the reason she had succumbed to the temptation to try to push Jack into explaining himself last night. She should have known better, she thought. He was not the kind of man who spilled his deepest secrets in a hot tub.

At the front of the room, the therapist grabbed the microphone. "The femme fatale is an archetype that clearly embodies the threat of the overcontrolling mother figure."

Vicky smiled again and leaned toward her microphone. "Eden is a lot of things, but she's definitely not maternally inclined."

The audience chuckled. The therapist glared at Vicky.

The author leaped into the opening. He had obviously fallen victim to the ancient publicity maxim "whenever you're interviewed, make sure that the title of your book gets mentioned at least three times."

"In my book *Dark Worlds: A History of Film Noir,* I argue that the overcontrolling mother figure is a gross simplification of the extraordinarily complex role of the femme fatale."

"Eden's not complex," Vicky drawled. "She's very simple, really. All she cares about is her own survival. Nothing else matters."

The film critic and the therapist both made desperate bids for the second mike, but the author had it in a death grip.

"In my book *Dark Worlds: A History of Film Noir,* I devote several chapters to explaining the varied roles of the femme fatale character."

Unable to get hold of a mike, the therapist raised his voice. "It's important to realize that the femme fatale comes from a seriously dysfunctional background. Obviously sexually abused as a child, she seeks to manipulate others with sex."

"No, no, no. You don't understand the role of archetypes," the critic yelled toward the microphone, which was still firmly in the grasp of the author. "They go much deeper than the limited concepts of modern psychological theory."

Elizabeth glanced at Christy. The young woman was starting to look bored.

The author gave the film critic a baleful glance. "In my book *Dark Worlds: A History of Film Noir,* I give several examples of how different actresses have portrayed the femme fatale. Claire Trevor, for instance—"

The therapist finally managed to wrestle the mike out of the author's fingers. He started to drone on about the impact of dysfunctional childhoods on the characters.

Elizabeth turned to Christy. "I think I've had about enough of this. Would you like to go somewhere and have a cup of coffee? I'd really like to talk to you about makeup techniques."

Christy brightened. "Sure. Why not?"

Forty-five minutes later, seated in the window of a small, heavily ferned coffee shop, Elizabeth discovered that she now knew far more about film makeup than she had ever intended to learn. It hadn't been hard to get Christy to talk about her craft. The hard part was finding a way to make her stop.

"I can see that a film such as *Fast Company* is completely dependent on getting the right look with makeup." Elizabeth surreptitiously glanced at her watch and wondered if Jack was having any better luck in the producers' workshop he had attended.

"Hardly anybody understands that." Christy dunked her biscotti into a mug filled with a lot of steamed milk and a shot of espresso. "Everyone thinks you get the effect just by using black-and-white film, but that's not true. I had to do a lot of research to get that edgy look for the actors. Eyebrows are absolutely key, you know."

"Vicky Bellamy appears to be a natural for that style."

Christy rolled her eyes. "In more ways than one."

"What do you mean?"

"She was always real particular about everything, including her makeup. Used to drive me nuts. Always telling me I hadn't got the arch of the eyebrows right or complaining because I didn't do her eyes the way she wanted them. Like I hadn't studied the classic films myself."

"Well, actresses are famous for being temperamental."

"Yeah, I guess." Christy grimaced. "And given the fact that her husband bankrolled the film, she got to do pretty much what she wanted on the set."

"Speaking of bankrolling the film," Elizabeth began cautiously. "Did you ever happen to meet the producer?"

"Dawson Holland? Yeah, sure."

"No, the one whose name is listed in the credits. Tyler Page."

"Oh, him. The nervous, mousy little guy who was always hanging around? Yeah, I met him."

"That sounds like Tyler," Elizabeth said. "I'm a friend of his. I've been looking for him ever since I got to Mirror Springs, but I haven't run into him."

"Hard to find anyone in this crowd right now unless you know where he's staying."

"Unfortunately, I don't know." Elizabeth paused. "I take it you haven't seen him?"

"Uh-uh."

"Did you talk to him much on the set?"

"You kidding?" Christy rolled her eyes again. "He had to be at least fifty or sixty. And he was shorter than me."

"I see."

Christy's eyes widened. "Hey, you're not Angel Face, are you? If so, I'm real sorry. I didn't mean to insult him or anything."

Elizabeth held her breath. "Angel Face?"

"That's what he called her. I heard him talking to her on his cell phone once. He went behind the makeup room to make the call. Guess he wanted to be private, but those walls are as thin as cardboard."

"You overheard the conversation?"

"Yeah. Kind of embarrassing. He really had it bad." Christy paused. "It wasn't you?"

"No. I'm a friend of Tyler's, but not his girlfriend. How could you tell he had it bad for Angel Face?"

Christy grimaced. "Just the way he talked to her and all. Sounded like he was reading lines from a low-budget script."

"What did he say?"

"Like I said, he called her Angel Face. Said she had to know that he would do anything for her. I think he promised her that they would be together forever once this was over."

"Once what was over?"

"The filming of *Fast Company,* I guess." Christy shrugged. "I forget the rest. It wasn't exactly memorable."

"So you never saw his girlfriend?"

"Nope. Just heard him talking to her that one time. Why?"

"It occurred to me that if I found her, I might be able to find him. So you don't know what she looked like, I take it?"

"Can't help you there. But I can tell you that he was crazy about her, whoever she was." Christy frowned in thought. "I remember thinking it was kinda weird, though."

"What was weird?"

"Him calling her his Angel Face."

"What's so strange about that? A little sappy maybe, but—"

"No, no, you don't get it," Christy said impatiently. "*Angel Face* is the title of a classic noir movie starring Robert Mitchum and Jean Simmons. It was one of the films I studied so that I could get the look of the makeup right for *Fast Company.*"

"What about it?"

"Well, see, Jean Simmons plays the femme fatale who ends up destroying everyone around her, including Mitchum's character. Just seemed sort of strange that a guy who was into noir the way Page is would call his girlfriend Angel Face. Not exactly a compliment, you know. I mean, the lady in the film was a psychopathic killer. He had to know that."

DAWSON HOLLAND LOOKED out at the audience. He smiled wryly. "This panel has done its best to tell you about the pitfalls of getting involved in the production of an independent film. When it comes to reliable methods of losing money, financing a film ranks right up there with walking into a casino and throwing cash into a slot machine." He paused meaningfully. "I can't help but notice that a lot of you are still here, however."

The crowd that had filled most of the seats at the producers' seminar laughed. Standing at the back of the room, one shoulder propped against the wall, arms folded, Jack watched Dawson as he summed up the comments of the panel.

"Any film is a huge financial risk. That goes double for small, independent films, because there are no studios with deep pockets to stand behind you and absorb losses," Dawson said. "Bottom line is, if you can't afford to lose your money, stay out of the business."

"But what if a major studio picks up your film and gives it national distribution?" someone asked.

Dawson shook his head. "That's the big dream, but in reality, it almost never happens. True, you might find your film on the bottom rack of a video store someday, or it may be screened at a festival such as this one. Sometimes you can make a little in the foreign market. But realistically speaking, odds are that the only payoff you'll ever see is your name in the credits."

Someone else spoke up. "But isn't there a lot of important, experimental work being done by independent film-makers these days?"

One of the panelists snorted. "Important, experimental

work and a dollar won't even buy you a cup of cappuccino. If you're going to get into the business of making movies, do it because you love film, not because you expect a return on your investment."

"My colleague speaks truth," Dawson said. "One last word of advice." He paused for effect. "On the off chance that your film actually does turn a profit, always remember the mantra of this business: Make sure your contract states that your payoff comes in the form of a percentage of the *gross* profits, not the net. For as sure as the sun will rise tomorrow morning, I can assure you that there will never be a net profit."

The audience broke into more laughter and desultory applause. As far as Jack could tell, no one looked the least discouraged by the hard facts of life concerning the independent film business. *Everyone wants to make movies,* he thought as he turned to leave the seminar room. The enthusiasm, excitement, and anticipation that animated the crowd of would-be producers was painful to behold.

Tyler Page had been gripped with this same fever, Jack reminded himself. Probably planned to use the profits from the sale of the crystal to finance another film.

Talk about stupid.

Then again, any man who could make a fool of himself the way he had last night with Elizabeth wasn't exactly in a position to scoff at another man's doomed dreams.

He walked out of the seminar room and started down the wide, windowed hall that led to the lobby of the Mirror Springs Resort. He glanced at his watch and saw that he was ten minutes late. Elizabeth had promised to meet him at noon for lunch.

"Well, Fairfax?" Dawson fell into step beside him. "Did we succeed in discouraging you?"

Jack snapped his thoughts back and glanced at Dawson. "You did a good job of laying out the downside of independent filmmaking. If it's such a great way to lose money, how come you're still involved in the business?"

Dawson put his hands into the pockets of his jacket. Comfortable. Sure of himself. "Like I said, you've got to love filmmaking. Nothing else like it on the face of the earth. And, of course, there's Vicky."

"Right. Vicky."

"My wife is very, very important to me, Jack," Dawson said. "I would do anything to make her happy. And what she likes to do is act in films."

"So you make her dreams come true, is that it?"

"It's a small price to pay for the pleasure of her company." Dawson paused. "Is the charming Miss Cabot an aspiring actress?"

"No."

"Your interest in filmmaking is personal?"

"You could say that."

"Then you have much in common with the others in that seminar. In real life they're dentists and stockbrokers and business executives."

"And research scientists."

"I beg your pardon?"

"The producer of *Fast Company,* Tyler Page, worked in a high-tech lab in Seattle."

"Ah, yes, Page." Dawson nodded absently. "I believe he did mention that he lived in Seattle. But he didn't say much about his professional life."

"He must have poured a ton of money into *Fast Company* to get his name in the credits as the producer."

"He made it clear at the outset that he did not want to share the credit. He said he wanted the film to be his movie. He was willing to put up the money to pay for the privilege."

"What about the other investors?"

Dawson shrugged. "None of them was willing to put up the same kind of money."

Jack felt his professional curiosity stir. "So tell me, how do the investment partnerships work for the guy who puts the package together?"

"Someone in my position, you mean?"

"Something tells me you don't take the same kind of risks that the other investors take, do you?"

"I do get a commission for my work," Dawson said. "It's one of the standard expenses of the partnership." He broke off as a figure suddenly loomed in his path.

The stranger scampered awkwardly backward, hands raised in front of Jack as if to ward him off. The man was of medium height. His head had been completely shaved to expose a lot of pink scalp. His clothing consisted of a black turtleneck, black trousers, and low, black boots. There was a silver ring in one ear. His eyes were concealed behind a pair of stylish sunglasses that were entirely unnecessary in the dimly lit hotel hallway. Jack wondered if the man wore the glasses in an effort to add a dramatic edge to what was otherwise a soft, round face.

"Future noir," the man intoned.

Jack did not slow his pace. "Huh?"

"Future noir." The man continued to backpedal along the corridor in front of Jack. "Gothic realism. The dark night of the soul in a dark future. Think moral ambiguity. Think murder for passion's sake. Think the eternal femme fatale. All against a black-and-white, futuristic background."

"Would you mind getting out of my way?" Jack took another look at his watch. "I'm meeting someone in the lobby."

Dawson chuckled. "Allow me to introduce you to Leonard Ledger. He's a filmmaker. Like a number of other people here, he's looking for someone to finance his next film."

"*Dark Moon Rising*," Leonard said.

Jack eyed him curiously. "*Dark Moon Rising*?"

"That's the working title," Leonard explained. "I see it as the classic noir story told against a black-and-white future. Incredible lighting effects. Minimal sets. All angles, lines, and shadows."

Jack nodded. "And you need money."

Leonard continued to walk backward. "This is very high-concept stuff. The kind of film the major studios will pick up for distribution. They'll kill for a film like this."

"I'll get back to you," Jack said. He glanced at Dawson. "That's the right phrase, isn't it? I'll get back to you?"

"Obviously you were born for this business." Dawson looked amused.

Jack turned back to Leonard. "Excuse me," he said. "I think I mentioned that I have an appointment?"

"Sure, sure." Leonard reluctantly sidled out of Jack's path. "I've got a script. I'll get it to you. You're gonna love it."

Jack kept walking. Leonard's voice gradually receded into the background.

"Get used to it," Dawson advised. "Now that you've been spotted as a potential source of money, you're going to meet a lot of Leonard Ledgers."

"I'll watch where I step," Jack said.

He was about to ask another question concerning the financing of *Fast Company* when he turned the corner and walked into the elegantly rustic lobby of the Mirror Springs Resort.

He spotted Elizabeth right off. She was standing near the massive stone fireplace. She was not alone. The man leaning intimately over her, obviously engaged in close conversation, was Hayden Shaw.

"Son of a bitch," Jack said very quietly.

CHAPTER THIRTEEN

"I'M SORRY ABOUT THE MISUNDERSTANDING."
Hayden's mouth thinned. "And on behalf of my soon-to-be
ex-wife, I apologize for whatever Gillian said to you at the
reception. She's not happy with the proposed settlement.
Her father's lawyers told her that they could get more money
out of me, but it's not going to happen."

Elizabeth tried to peek over his shoulder to see if she
could spot Jack coming out of the meeting-room hallway. "I
really do not want to discuss your divorce, Hayden."

He leaned in a little closer, very intense. There was something vaguely familiar and slightly unsettling about the way
he zeroed in on his target, she thought.

"You need to know that for all intents and purposes, I'm a
free man," he said.

"Not quite." She gave him a pointed look. "And even if
that were true, it's not important to me because it has no
bearing on this situation. You didn't come here to see me or
because you've suddenly developed a keen interest in low-
budget filmmaking."

"You underestimate yourself."

She frowned as a thought struck her. "How did you get a

room in this place? This town has been booked for months."

He made a dismissive movement with one hand. "No big deal. I know the general manager here at the resort."

"Pulled some strings, did you? Well, you wasted your time."

"What do you mean?"

She glared at him, exasperated. "Stop playing games. You're here because of those rumors you heard about Soft Focus, aren't you?"

"Is that why you're here with Fairfax?" he countered. "Keeping an eye on your number-one investment?"

"That's none of your business."

"Gillian found me in the crowd at the reception after you and Jack left." Hayden grimaced. "She was gloating. Couldn't wait to tell me that you and Fairfax were going off on a vacation together. But I know damn well that you wouldn't suddenly decide that you wanted to jump back into bed with the bastard who played you for a sucker six months ago. You're too smart to fall for his line again."

"You're right about one thing: I'm smart. Smart enough to know that you're here because of Soft Focus, not because of me." The pieces of the small puzzle clicked into place. "Damn. You were invited, weren't you?"

He gave her a politely quizzical look. "Invited to what?"

"You know what I'm talking about."

He exhaled slowly, his gaze speculative. "There's no reason we can't join forces and work together. Together we can outbid Jack. Without you, he hasn't got much in the way of resources."

Her worst fears were confirmed. Hayden had been invited to the auction. She clenched her hand around the strap of her shoulder bag.

"Give me one good reason why I would want to hurt my client by bidding against him," she said.

Hayden smiled slowly. "Revenge?"

She stared at him, mouth open, for a few seconds. He was serious, she realized. "Hurt Excalibur just for the sake of a little revenge? Good grief, Hayden, do you think I'm an idiot? I'm a businesswoman, remember? My job is to keep my clients profitable. The simple fact of life is that the Fund doesn't make money unless they do."

He glanced around with deliberate casualness and then bent his head in a seemingly intimate gesture. "If Soft Focus has even half the potential I've heard it has, there are other ways to make money with it besides leaving it in the hands of a struggling little R & D firm that will probably get swallowed up by the first big company that comes along."

A chill went through her. "I can't believe I'm hearing this. In fact, I refuse to believe it. You aren't suggesting that I sabotage my own client? Not for something as empty and meaningless as revenge?"

Hayden's eyes hardened. "There's nothing empty and meaningless about it."

She searched his face. "What did Jack ever do to you to make you hate him so much?"

Hayden did not reply. His attention had shifted to a point just behind her.

Elizabeth did not need him to tell her that Jack was coming toward her. The familiar prickle of awareness had already wafted across the back of her neck.

She turned and saw him cut through the crowded lobby with fluid, cold-blooded grace. There was no doubt that she and Hayden were his target. His face was disturbingly expressionless.

"Looks like your business associate has arrived," Hayden said. His eyes held a malicious gleam. "And he doesn't look happy to see me. Think about my offer, Elizabeth."

Jack came to a halt just behind Elizabeth's shoulder. He was close. Too close. She could feel the possessive aura that he flung around her like an invisible cloak. It was annoying, but she told herself that this was not the time or place to make an issue of his politically incorrect attitude. The last thing she wanted to do was pump up the level of testosterone in the vicinity. It was already much too thick.

Jack looked at Hayden. "I had a hunch you'd show up sooner or later."

"I always did like to go to the movies."

"Just make sure that all you do is watch," Jack said. He glanced at Elizabeth. "Let's go. We're late."

His hand closed around her arm. She considered digging in her heels and then reminded herself that the last thing she wanted was a scene.

"Where are we going?" she asked, grimly polite. "I thought we were supposed to have lunch here in town."

"We're going back to our place," he said, laying a not-so-subtle emphasis on the *our*. "I've got some work to do."

She forced herself to smile at Hayden. "See you later."

"Yeah," Hayden said coldly. "You will."

Elizabeth allowed herself to be drawn toward the front of the lobby. An attendant jumped to open one of the heavy plate-glass doors.

Outside, the snapping air and the too-bright sunlight slapped Elizabeth in the face. She pulled her sunglasses out of her purse.

Jack already had his dark glasses in his hand. When he put them on, his already stony expression became bleak and menacing.

"Where's he staying?" he asked without preamble.

That was not the question she had been expecting. "What difference does that make?"

"A lot." He turned his head. He was looking at her, but his own eyes were concealed behind the sunglasses. "Hard to get a room here in Mirror Springs, remember?"

Belatedly she realized where he was going with the question. She frowned as the implications hit her. "Hayden said he had a room here at the resort."

"Amazing." Jack's mouth twisted laconically. "Wonder how he got it on such short notice."

"He said he pulled some strings."

"Bullshit."

"Do you really think so?" She felt a stab of icy amusement. "Seems to me I recall you telling me something similar not too long ago. Guess his strings must have been better than yours, though. They didn't break."

Jack ignored that. He came to a halt on the passenger side of the car and looked at her through the dark lenses. "Be interesting to find out just when Hayden made his reservations."

"Why?"

"Because if he made them anytime before last Tuesday night, it would mean he knew in advance about the plans to steal the specimen." Jack yanked open the car door. "Maybe he even helped plan the theft."

The sharp, crisp air made Elizabeth pull her jacket more snugly around herself. "If you're thinking of wasting a lot of time investigating Hayden, I'd advise you to save your energy. I'm almost positive he didn't know about the theft until he heard the rumors late Tuesday. I think he's here because he was invited to the auction." She slid into the car seat.

Jack just stared at her for a long moment.

"Damn," he said very, very softly.

A fresh wave of unease shot through her. "What?"

"I wonder who else was invited."

The car door shut with a distinct and very final-sounding *ker-chunk*.

Elizabeth watched Jack walk around the front of the car and get in behind the wheel. Who else had been invited to the auction? It was a disturbing question.

Jack put the silver-gray rental car in gear, reversed out of the slot, and drove toward the parking lot exit.

"Look, if Hayden's here for the auction," Elizabeth said, "at least it means that he wasn't involved in the theft." She did not know just why that was important, but it was.

Jack grunted. "That make you feel better?"

"Yes."

"Why?"

She propped her elbow on the window ledge and braced her chin on her hand. "I sort of like him. I guess I just don't want to find out that I've been completely wrong about him—" She broke off quickly.

But not quickly enough.

"You don't want to discover that you were wrong about him, *too*." Jack did not take his eyes off the road. "The way you were wrong about me? Is that what you were going to say?"

"As Aunt Sybil would say, I think it's time to change the subject."

Jack's jaw tightened into a hard line. "It's possible that Hayden was involved in the theft, but now he's here for the auction because things went wrong."

"What are you talking about?"

"Think about it. Maybe Hayden orchestrated the theft

with Tyler Page's cooperation. But what if Page decided afterward that he didn't need Hayden to help him sell the crystal? What if he's got his own agenda?"

"You're suggesting that there was a falling-out among thieves? And now Hayden is trying to find Tyler Page and the crystal?"

"Just like us."

Elizabeth watched the mountain road unfurl in front of the car's hood. "I think we may have an even bigger problem on our hands."

Jack shot her a brief glance. "What's that?"

"Before I ran into Hayden at the resort, I had an interesting conversation with a young woman named Christy. She was the makeup artist on *Fast Company*."

"And?"

"And she thinks that Tyler Page was madly in love."

Jack greeted that with a short, undiplomatic snort of disgust. "Page? In love? Give me a break."

For some reason his complete disdain annoyed her. "Why is that so unbelievable? It might explain why he stole Soft Focus. He's obviously got an obsessive passion for film. Maybe he's got an obsessive passion for a woman, too. Maybe he stole the crystal for her sake."

"Are you saying you think Tyler Page stole Soft Focus so that he could sell it for a bundle of cash he could use to impress a woman?"

"Christy overheard him talking on his cell phone to someone he called Angel Face. He promised her that when this was all over they would be together forever."

Jack took his gaze off the road just long enough to throw her a quick, curious look. "You really think that there's a woman involved in this?"

"Page loves film noir. You know what they say about life

imitating art. What if he's fallen for a femme fatale type? Someone who seduced him and encouraged him to steal the specimen so that they could run off together into the sunset? It might explain his bizarre behavior."

Jack drove in silence for a while. He was concentrating again. She could almost feel him processing the data in his brain.

"Don't think so," he said eventually.

"Why not?"

"That kind of thing might work in the movies, but in real life a man doesn't throw away everything he's worked for most of his life, for the sake of a woman. For the sake of a fortune, yes. For the sake of a fortune to spend on his films, yes. But not for a woman."

Elizabeth settled deeper into her seat and folded her arms. What was the matter with her? Had she actually started to wonder if Jack had a secret romantic streak?

JACK'S CELL PHONE rang just as Elizabeth finished cutting the last of the tapanade, lettuce, and tomato sandwiches she had hastily put together for lunch. He set down the two bottles of springwater he had removed from the refrigerator and took the device out of his pocket.

"Fairfax here." Pause. "Don't worry about it, Milo. My instructions were to call with any updates. What have you got?"

Elizabeth listened absently as she carried the plate of sandwiches around the long, granite counter that separated the kitchen from the living area of the house.

"Is Durand sure?" Jack's voice was suddenly charged with intensity. "How the hell did Kendle ever get hired in the first place? No, don't answer that. I know how he got onto the Excalibur payroll. Nobody bothered to check out his ref-

erences, right? Tell Scott in HR that he's going to have some
explaining to do."

Elizabeth put the sandwiches down on the table.

"Forget it," Jack growled into the phone. "It's a little too
late for that. Did Durand say anything else about Kendle?"

There was another short pause.

"Huh." Jack walked to the window and stood looking out
at the mountains. "Interesting. No, it's nothing important.
Just . . . interesting. What about the Vanguard of Tomorrow
thing?"

There was another tense silence while he listened.

"Nothing at all in the media? Sounds like we lucked out.
Nice work, Milo. Yeah, you said all the right things to Vel-
tran's people. Good work. . . . Yeah, we're getting close.
We'll find it, Milo. Call if anything else develops."

Elizabeth almost smiled at the cool, calm, wholly unwar-
ranted assurance in Jack's voice. The man in charge, she
thought. Make everyone think you know what you're doing
and they'll follow you anywhere.

Jack ended the call and pocketed the phone. He looked
across the room and saw her watching him. "Remember that
group that trashed the Excalibur lab?"

"Vanguard of Tomorrow?" She took a seat at the table.
"What about it?"

"They haven't come forward to take the credit or responsibility or whatever it is that kind does take when it smashes
private property." Jack sat down across from her. "Apparently they didn't contact the press or go on their Web site to
brag. I find that sort of curious, don't you?"

A deep sense of foreboding went through her. "I hope
you're not going to tell me that you think the trashing of the
lab had something to do with the theft."

"I don't know. I suppose Page could have gone back to the

lab the night after he stole the crystal in an effort to conceal the loss for a while. Give himself time to get safely out of town."

"But you discovered that Soft Focus was missing a few hours before the lab got trashed. You went to see Page and found that he was already packed and gone."

"True. But it was just random chance that I checked up on the crystal when I did Tuesday night." Jack reached for a sandwich. "Page couldn't have had any way of knowing that I'd find out so quickly that it was gone. It would have been reasonable for him to assume that it wouldn't be missed until the following day or even later. For him, the biggest danger at that point was that I might call in the cops."

Elizabeth thought about it. "If you had done that, they would have been strongly inclined to blame the theft on the Vanguard of Tomorrow nuts."

"Right." Jack took a bite and chewed reflectively. "The vandalism would have sent the authorities off in the wrong direction. A nice distraction, if it had been needed. Not a bad backup strategy. There's something else."

Elizabeth's sense of premonition grew stronger. "What is it?"

"Milo said that the reason we couldn't dig up a next-of-kin on Ryan Kendle is because his résumé was fake. Phony ID, phony addresses, the works. The police are trying to find out who he really was."

Very slowly she put down her sandwich. "It happens. People often lie on résumés."

"Uh-huh." Jack took a swallow of the bottled water. "Sometimes they lie because they've got a criminal record."

"Maybe he did. You mentioned that the cops said he was involved in the drug scene. They said he was killed in a drug deal gone bad."

Jack looked at her across the table. "The homicide detective working on the case told Milo something else."

"What?"

"They scrounged up a witness. A drunk transient sleeping in a doorway. He didn't actually see the shooting, but he said he thinks he heard Kendle talking to someone just before the shots were fired."

"Someone?"

Jack hesitated briefly. "A woman."

A woman. Elizabeth thought about what Christy Barns had said about a female character named Angel Face. *The femme fatale who ends up destroying everyone around her.* She flexed her fingers to try to rid herself of the prickling sensation. "You're not thinking that Kendle was somehow connected to the theft, are you?"

"As of right now I'm leaving all options open—including the possibility that there is a woman involved."

"But, Jack, this is white-collar crime, remember? People don't get killed in white-collar crime."

"There are exceptions to every rule."

Elizabeth steeled herself against the trickle of unease. She looked at Jack and said nothing.

He frowned. "What are you thinking?"

"I'm thinking that a man like Tyler Page probably wouldn't encounter too many femme fatales in his line of work."

"Trust me, there are no femme fatales employed at Excalibur. Company policy." Jack paused, suddenly very thoughtful. "Unless . . ."

"Unless what?"

"There is one woman connected with Excalibur who has been trying to force the company to shift its course," he said deliberately. "Angela Ingersoll Burrows."

Elizabeth turned that over a few times in her mind. "I don't think so. I've talked to her a lot during the past few months. I admit that, given the right circumstances, she could qualify as a femme fatale. She's attractive enough for the part, and she's certainly obsessed with protecting her son's future, so she's got motive, but—"

"If she thinks that sabotaging the Soft Focus project might assure a sale or merger of the company—"

Elizabeth shook her head. "No. Not if we're talking violence or, God help us, murder. Besides, I can't see her setting out to seduce Tyler Page. However . . ."

"Yeah?"

She took a deep breath. "I can think of one place where Page might have met a real live femme fatale."

Jack watched her very intently. "Where?"

"On the set of *Fast Company*."

Jack was silent for a moment. "Are you talking about Victoria Bellamy?"

"The thought crossed my mind, that's all." Elizabeth shivered. "But it doesn't make sense. I mean, she's an actress, not an industrial spy. What would she know about an exotic, high-tech material, much less how to make a profit on it?"

"Probably not a lot," Jack conceded. "But Dawson Holland might. We'll know more about him when Larry finishes checking him out."

"Probably a waste of time."

"Not like we've got a lot else to do."

"I've got something else to do." Elizabeth helped herself to another sandwich. "I've got a real, live film script to read."

SHORTLY AFTER MIDNIGHT she heard him go softly down the stairs. She had finished the script for *Fast Com-*

pany a few minutes earlier and turned out her light to go to sleep.

When she heard the hushed footsteps, her first thought was that Jack was heading for the hot tub. Then she heard the front door open and close quietly.

"Oh, damn." She sat bolt upright and shoved aside the bedding. He wouldn't dare. Not without telling her.

But outside she heard the sound of one of the car engines turning over. Jack was leaving.

She knew, with a terrible certainty, exactly where he was headed. Panic shot through her. She scrambled out of bed and grabbed her jeans.

CHAPTER FOURTEEN

HE SAT IN THE DARKNESS NEAR THE WINDOW and waited. The cold moonlight slanted through the blinds, layering shadows on the hotel-room carpet. He studied the icy grid pattern and thought about the past.

After a while he opened the small bottle he had taken from the minibar. He rarely drank scotch, generally only when he was facing a brick wall.

The scotch was appropriate tonight. Not just because of the brick wall he was about to confront, but because his father had favored scotch. And this was all about his father.

The door opened. A wedge of harsh corridor light angled across the floor. Hayden stood silhouetted in the doorway.

"We need to talk," Jack said from the shadows near the window. "Come in and close the door. This won't take long."

"What the hell are you doing here? How did you get into my room?"

"Swiped a master key from housekeeping."

"Shit. You haven't changed, have you?" Hayden closed the door. He did not turn on the light. "A real chip off the old block."

"I didn't come here to talk about the past."

"No? Then why are you here?" Hayden crossed the room to the minibar. Opened it. Reached inside. Small bottles clinked. "Are you really that worried that I might get Elizabeth into bed?"

"Leave Elizabeth out of this."

"No can do." Hayden closed the minibar door, straightened, and walked to the chair opposite the one Jack occupied. He flung himself down into it. The grid of moonlight shafted across his face. He lifted his own small bottle of scotch in a mocking toast. "She's a part of it now. That's your fault, not mine."

"She's got nothing to do with what happened. Leave her alone."

Hayden looked amused. "What is it with you and Elizabeth, anyway? Can't quite figure it out."

"You don't have to figure it out. It's none of your business."

"You know, when I told her that you were the guy behind the Galloway deal, I thought sure she'd yank your funding. Didn't realize you already had her name on the contract." Hayden took a swallow from the bottle. "Your timing, as always, was damn near magical."

"I told you to leave Elizabeth out of this."

"It was too late to screw up your funding, but it wasn't all for naught, was it? Your little fling together ended kind of fast. A real blaze-of-glory thing." Hayden chuckled. "The scene at the Pacific Rim Club is legend in certain segments of the Seattle business community."

"That's enough, Hayden."

"Do you think that you maybe went a little over the top when you called her the Ice Princess, though? Not very gentlemanly to kiss and tell."

Jack was mildly amazed that the little bottle of scotch did not fracture in his hand. "Shut up."

"You might as well have written her name on the men's room wall at the club: 'For a good time you definitely do not want to call Elizabeth the Ice Princess.' "

"I said, *shut up.*"

"Word must have gotten around that she's no fun in bed. She hasn't dated much in the past six months. Tell me, just out of curiosity, is she really a frigid fuck?"

The bars of silver light on the floor were suddenly too bright. They blazed with the intensity of magnesium flares. The lines of shadows between them were as dark as the far side of the moon. Nothing in the room looked quite right.

Jack came up out of the chair, impelled by an adrenaline rush. He hurled the half-empty bottle aside, grabbed Hayden by the lapels of his jacket, and hauled him up out of the chair.

"You've pushed your luck as far as you can tonight," Jack said very softly. "One more word about Elizabeth and I will take you apart."

"Cool. I can see the headlines now. 'Excalibur Exec Jailed for Assault.' That kind of PR will certainly make future clients think twice about hiring you."

Jack shoved him up against the wall. "Do you really believe that I give a damn about the publicity?"

There was a short, brittle pause. Hayden stopped smiling.

"You're a little out of control here, Jack. Not your style."

"Yeah, but you know something? It feels sort of good."

Hayden narrowed his eyes. "If you didn't come here to talk about Elizabeth, why the hell are you here?"

The room stopped looking like a scene from a noir film. The shadows became normal again. Jack forced himself to relax his grip on Hayden's jacket. He dropped his hands and stepped back.

"The Vanguard of Tomorrow crowd," Jack said.

Hayden frowned as he removed his jacket. "The radical group that trashes high-tech facilities? What about it?"

Jack walked to the window. He looked down into the shadows that concealed the river that tumbled out of a nearby mountain canyon. "It tore up one of the Excalibur labs late Tuesday night or early Wednesday morning. But it hasn't come forward to claim the incident."

There was the smallest of hesitations before Hayden said, "So?"

"So I can't help but wonder if maybe VT had nothing to do with it, after all. But maybe you did."

There was a short silence behind him.

"Prove it," Hayden said.

"I don't have to prove it. If I decide you did it, that will be enough for me."

"What the hell do you think you can you do to me even if you do manage to jump to that totally false conclusion?" Hayden asked. He sounded mildly curious.

"You don't want to find out."

"Are you threatening me?"

"Think of it as a promise." Jack turned to look at him. "Excalibur is my client. The Ingersolls are good people. I won't allow you to hurt them just to get at me."

"I had nothing to do with the trashing of the lab." Hayden's voice sharpened. "I didn't even know about it until now. You can't pin that on me. If you're thinking of going to the cops, forget it."

"I'm not going to the cops." Jack walked toward the door. "Not yet. But if I find out that you've let your desire for revenge push you into hurting a lot of innocent people, I won't protect you."

"I don't need your goddamned protection. I've never needed it."

"One other thing." Jack twisted the doorknob. "I realize that you're in Mirror Springs because you think you can get your hands on Soft Focus. I'm not sure yet just what role you're playing in this little film script we seem to be acting out here. But I'll tell you this much: You better make damn sure that you don't try to use Elizabeth to get what you want."

Hayden gave a short, sharp, edgy laugh. "Why do I have to follow that rule? You sure as hell didn't follow it, did you?"

Jack said nothing. He opened the door and stepped out into the hall. He closed the door, went down the corridor to the elevators, and leaned wearily on the call button. While he waited for the cab to arrive, he caught a glimpse of his reflection in the mirror that decorated the opposite wall. His father's eyes looked back at him.

"It hasn't been easy cleaning up the mess you left behind, you son of a bitch," he said to the image in the mirror.

The elevator doors slid open with a soft hiss. He got into the cab, descended to the lobby, and walked out into the cold, moonlit night.

He crossed the parking lot to where he had left the car. He did not see Elizabeth bundled up in her long, black, down-filled coat until he was almost on top of her.

"I've had enough of your games, Fairfax." Her eyes glittered furiously in the shadows. "I want some answers. You owe me that much."

He looked at her and thought about what Hayden had said. *You might as well have written her name on the men's room wall at the club.*

"Yes." He ran his hand over his face once and then let it fall to his side. "I owe you that much."

SHE REPLACED THE bottle of cognac in the kitchen cupboard, picked up the two glasses she had poured, and carried them out into the firelit room. She paused near the low, square coffee table and looked at Jack.

He stood in front of the hearth, one hand braced against the mantel, and stared into the flames.

Silently, she handed him one of the glasses. He scowled at it, as if he had to concentrate hard to pull his attention back from the fire. After a moment he took the glass from her fingers.

"You went to the hotel to confront Hayden, didn't you?" she said quietly.

He shrugged and took a swallow from the glass.

"Why?" She studied his face. "What did you hope to accomplish?"

"I don't know." He slowly lowered the glass. "It's a long story."

"We've got all night."

He met her eyes. She realized that, for the first time since she had met him six months ago, he was allowing her to catch more than a fleeting glimpse of what lay beneath the surface. What she saw was daunting.

"My father was Sawyer J. Fairfax. He was a brilliant corporate strategist. Made a fortune in mergers and acquisitions during the last boom. His specialty was the hostile takeover of small, closely held companies. In his time, he destroyed countless little family businesses simply because he knew how to make a lot of money doing it."

"Go on."

"He was good at making profits and he was also very good at living a lie. He died while on a business trip to Europe. I was twenty-four at the time. Swear to God, until the day of the funeral, I assumed that I was his only son. So did my mother."

Elizabeth frowned. "You didn't know about Larry?"

"No." Jack looked at the cognac in his glass. "Turns out Larry and his mother didn't know about me, either. They lived in Boston. They were aware that my father was married and that he did a lot of traveling on business."

"That accounted for all the absences."

"Right. But none of us had a clue that there was a third son. Not until he showed up for the reading of the will."

Elizabeth drew a sharp breath. "Not—?"

"Yeah. Hayden."

"Good grief. Talk about a shock."

"Hayden didn't come to the funeral. His anger at Dad runs so deep that he blames Sawyer's lies for his mother's suicide. Unfortunately, Dad died before Hayden could get his revenge." Jack paused. "But that still leaves me."

Elizabeth closed her eyes. "I see."

"I was named executor in Dad's will. I got the job of untangling his legal, financial, and personal affairs. There were several pending lawsuits. Some incredibly arcane business deals that had to be closed out. And then there were all those people he had hurt along the way. All the small businesses he had crushed. All the families he had ruined."

Some answers clicked neatly into place. Elizabeth opened her eyes. "That's why you've committed yourself to protecting small, family businesses. You're trying to compensate for all the damage your father did."

He sipped his drink. "Don't get the wrong impression here. I'm not the altruistic type. I've carved out a market niche for myself, and it just happens to be very profitable."

She let that go. "Tell me the rest of the story."

"Like I said, unraveling my father's business affairs wasn't easy. But that wasn't the hard part."

"What was?"

"The family stuff."

"Of course." She watched him for a long moment. "The family stuff is always the hardest part."

"I will say one thing for Dad. He treated us all equally in his will. Larry is the youngest of his sons." Jack's mouth curved briefly. "We have almost nothing in common, but we get along fine."

"But you and Hayden are very much alike, aren't you? You've both got smart, savvy instincts when it comes to business. You've both got an amazing ability to focus on a goal or a problem. Good grief, now that I think about it, you've both got the same taste in clothes and food."

Jack's expression hardened. "We're not exactly twins, separated at birth."

"No," she agreed readily. "You certainly don't look anything alike."

Jack gave her a laconic look. "If that's a polite way of implying that Hayden is better looking—"

"He's not better looking," she said brusquely. "Just different looking."

"Very diplomatic." Jack shrugged. "I can't help it if I take after my father. As I was saying, Larry's mother is one of those sweet, nurturing types. I don't think she was all that surprised to learn that I existed. But Hayden's mother wasn't so understanding. She knew that Sawyer was married, but she had always believed that he would one day divorce his wife and marry her. She didn't know about me."

"Hard enough to discover that the man you loved had not only died before he got the divorce he had promised, but that he also had a son he had forgotten to mention."

Jack took another taste of the cognac. "Vivien Shaw went into a severe clinical depression after Dad died. For some reason she fixated on the idea that my existence was a bigger betrayal than the fact that Sawyer had never gotten the divorce. In the end, she took pills. A lot of them."

"And Hayden transferred his anger at Sawyer to you."

"He agrees with his mother's version of events— the one in which I was the favored child and he got the shaft." Jack downed the last of his cognac. "He hates my guts."

"There's an old saying to the effect that family feuds are the worst kind of feuds."

"I can testify to that."

"Why does Hayden use a different last name?"

"He was raised in a small town in California. His mother called herself Mrs. Shaw. He grew up with that name. He still uses it. Another way of getting back at the Fairfax family, I guess."

"I see." She hesitated. "What did Hayden have to say tonight? Did he admit he'd been invited to the auction?"

"We didn't discuss the auction," Jack said.

She stared at him. "I don't understand. What else was there to talk about?"

"I went to see him because it occurred to me that he might have been responsible for the trashing of the lab."

"What?"

Jack looked irritated by her incredulity. "I figured that he might have allowed his hostility toward me to spill over onto my clients."

"There's a term for that."

"Collateral damage," Jack said dryly.

"No." She shook her head quickly. "Impossible. I can't believe Hayden would go that far."

"How the hell would you know what he's capable of doing for the sake of revenge?"

Elizabeth turned and began to pace the room. "I can't see

him doing thousands of dollars' worth of damage to the Ingersolls' lab just to get even with you. It doesn't fit with what I know about Hayden Shaw."

"Don't be too sure how much you know about him." Jack watched her through narrowed eyes. "Why do you think he's been working so hard to get you into bed?"

"To annoy you?" Anger surged through her. She did her best to conceal it behind a mocking smile. "Now who's being undiplomatic?"

Jack's profile was all hard, inflexible planes and angles. "It's obvious that he went after you because he wanted to use you against me."

"You mean it wasn't my drop-dead gorgeous body and sexy eyes that made him fall at my feet?" She heaved a dramatic sigh. "That's right, go ahead and rip apart my little fantasy of being a femme fatale."

"Damn it, Elizabeth, I'm trying to explain—"

"Here I thought I had two men competing for my favors and it turns out that not just one, but both of them, used me to further their own agendas."

Jack watched her with steady intensity. "I didn't tell you that I was involved in the Galloway deal because I knew you would misinterpret everything."

She smiled a little too sweetly. "And your brother didn't mention that his divorce wasn't final because he was afraid I'd get the wrong impression."

"Don't," Jack said very evenly, "compare me with Hayden."

She ignored that. "You know, I really hate being caught in a war zone." She set the empty glass down very hard on the table. "It's hard on the ego."

He took a step toward her. "Elizabeth—"

"Maybe I'll just invest in a nice collection of high-class

erotica and some interesting mechanical devices designed for personal use and forget about trying to have a real relationship."

He came toward her. She refused to give in to the urge to retreat. When he was close enough for her to feel the heat of his body, he stopped. He did not touch her.

"I don't recommend that approach," he said.

She tilted her head. "You've tried it?"

He raised one hand and slid his fingers slowly around the nape of her neck. "I used a manual technique instead of mechanical devices, and the erotica wasn't exactly high-class, but, yeah, I tried it."

Whispers of awareness stirred her senses. She tried to suppress them without success. It was always like this when he touched her, she thought. Sorcery. That was the only rational explanation.

"What happened?" she asked, wishing she did not sound so breathless.

"Not much." His thumb traced a small pattern against her throat. "Not until I used my imagination."

She dampened her lower lip with the tip of her tongue and then swallowed. "What did you imagine?"

"You. With me."

A fine time to get light-headed from the altitude, she thought. The night she had opened the door and found him standing there on the deck she had known what *might* happen. Last night when she had left him with that faint, dangling promise, she had known what *would* happen. Sooner or later. But for some strange reason, she had assumed that it would be later.

"Let me get this straight," she said very carefully. "You imagined my face on the models in some porn magazine?"

"Not just your face." He bent his head and brushed his lips

lightly, invitingly, across hers. "I imagined everything else, as well."

She shuddered. "Was I wearing leather and steel studs and stiletto heels? I always wanted to wear that kind of an outfit."

"In my imagination," he said against her mouth, "you weren't wearing anything at all."

Without warning he deepened the kiss. His arms closed around her, crushing her gently. She put her hands on his shoulders and sank her fingers into the sleek strong muscles there.

"Jack."

"I've been going crazy." His lips burned against her throat. "Out of my mind."

She shut her eyes and inhaled the scent of his body, savoring the heady, indescribable essence of him. Waves of excitement swept over her. She felt his hands on the buttons of her shirt. A moment later the garment was on the floor. His palms closed around her breasts. In her haste to get dressed so that she could follow him, she had not bothered with a bra.

"I was right," he muttered against her mouth.

"About what?"

"About the feel of you." His thumbs moved across her nipples. "I spent a lot of time trying to recall exactly how soft you were."

She took her hands off his shoulders, pushed them beneath the bottom edge of his pullover, flattened them against his chest. "I wasted a lot of time thinking about how you look without a shirt."

"We both wasted six damned months."

"I'm not so sure they were wasted."

"I am."

He moved abruptly, scooped her up in his arms, and lowered her to the rug in front of the hearth. She heard the flames snap and crackle. The warmth of the fire enveloped her as Jack tugged off her jeans. But that was nothing compared to the heat of his eyes.

He put one hand on top of the triangle of curly hair at the apex of her thighs.

"Since when did you stop wearing underwear?" he asked.

"I was in a hurry tonight."

His mouth curved in a devastating grin. "So was I."

She discovered exactly what he meant a moment later when he unfastened his own jeans and removed them. He had not bothered to put on a pair of briefs. But he had thought to carry a condom in his wallet, she noticed.

He came to her at last, pinning her beneath him. She gasped when she felt his fingers slide between her legs. The deep, low-level hunger that she had learned to live with during the past few months sharpened without warning. She was suddenly ravenous. She felt herself grow moist and she knew that she had dampened his fingers. He groaned heavily and took one nipple into his mouth.

She sighed and slid her hands down the length of his spine, savoring the muscled contours of his back. His hand moved on her, exciting and at the same time maddening. He stroked gently, inside and out. Everything tingled and then tightened. She sucked in her breath as anticipation spiraled out of control. She clung to his shoulders, nibbled on his ear, and demanded more.

"I told you that this time I'd get it right," he whispered.

He moved slowly down the length of her body, leaving a trail of warm kisses along the way. But she did not realize his destination until she felt his mouth on her in an electrifyingly intimate kiss.

"Jack." She clutched at his hair.

He paid no attention, intent instead on what he was doing

to her. Nobody, she thought, could focus on a project the way Jack could. She was wound so tightly now that she was afraid she would explode. She threaded her fingers into his hair and tugged. Hard.

He did not stop.

"Jack, *please*."

The sweet tension was almost unbearable now, but he did not pause. She wanted to scream, but she could hardly catch her breath.

"Jack, so help me, if you don't—"

And then the climax hit her, wave after delicious wave of sensation. A thrill ride unlike any other she had ever taken. She could do nothing except hang on for the pulse-pounding trip.

Before it was over, Jack made his way back up her body, eased her thighs more widely apart, and used one hand to guide himself into her.

She had been so certain that she had not forgotten a single detail about their one night together six months ago. But she had been wrong. When she felt him push slowly, inevitably into her she realized that she had failed to recall precisely how hard he was and just how much of him there was when he was fully aroused.

And then, at last, he was inside. He pushed deep, filling her completely.

He lowered his head to kiss her throat. "I told you that if I ever got a chance to take this test a second time, I'd do whatever it took to pass."

CHAPTER FIFTEEN

HE PUSHED THE PAUSE BUTTON AND LEANED forward to study the frozen frame. Vicky was spectacular in this scene, he thought. It was the one in which Eden plotted with her lover, Harry, to murder her brutal husband. The lighting was exquisite. It glinted on her elegant cheekbones and deepened the shadows around her eyes. She was so beautiful. So haunted. So desperate. She absolutely had to win the festival's Best Actress Award.

He continued to study the scene with a critical eye while he munched on the hamburger he had prepared on the out-door grill. He must remember to clean up after he finished, he reminded himself. *She* had provided him with this beauti-ful house. She had also made it clear that she expected him to keep things picked up while he stayed here. She did not approve of his casual bachelor ways. He tried to please her, but it wasn't easy. She was very demanding. Very tempera-mental. Lately her mood swings seemed to be getting more dramatic. But then, she was under a lot of pressure. He understood. He was tolerant.

She was so beautiful, the most beautiful woman he had ever met. She could have had any man she wanted. He knew that she did not love him, not the way he loved her. Few could love the way he loved—with passion, conviction, total devotion. Few would throw away everything for the beloved one, as he was in the process of doing.

But she needed him. Ah, yes, she needed him. No one else could give her what he could give her, the gift she valued above all others: vengeance. His ability to bestow that prize gave him a more secure hold on her affections than any other man could ever hope to have.

He finished the hamburger and absently brushed some crumbs onto the floor. The title of a couple of classic films came to mind. He whispered them aloud to himself there in the darkness, because he thought they summed up his present situation quite nicely.

"I'm *On Dangerous Ground*. And there is *No Way Out*."

Perfect. It was the reason he loved film noir. It described his life.

After a while Tyler Page pressed another button on the remote control. The video of *Fast Company* snapped back into motion on the small screen. The voices of the actors echoed softly in the room.

> *"Some things you do for the sake of love, Harry. Some you do for the sake of revenge. Doesn't matter which reason you choose, you know. Either way, in the end, everyone thinks you're crazy."*

CHAPTER SIXTEEN

HE AWOKE WHEN THE MOONLIGHT ANGLED ACROSS his face. He opened his eyes and looked up through the high windows. The circle of silver was brilliant against the late-night sky. He was warm and comfortable. Satiated was a better word, he decided. The ideal word, in fact.

Elizabeth stirred in his arms, stretching languidly. The blanket he had snagged off the back of the sofa earlier fell to her waist. She must have noticed him gazing at her bare breasts, because she reached down to tug the large square of striped wool back to her throat.

"The rug's a little rough, isn't it?" she said.

"A little."

Common sense warned him that this would be a good time to keep his mouth shut or at least a good time not to ask questions. To ask questions would be to tempt fate. He had gotten lucky tonight. Few people got second chances. He should give thanks for his good fortune and keep his mouth shut.

Instead, he turned on his side, propped himself on his elbow, and looked down at her.

"Why?" he asked.

She gazed up at him. The only light in the room came from the fire and the moon. Her eyes were veiled by her half-lowered lashes. "Why is the rug rough?"

"You know what I'm asking. Why now? Tonight? What made you decide to give me another chance?"

"I told you I'd think about it." She shrugged. The blanket shifted again. She adjusted it. "I thought about it."

"It was because I told you about Hayden and the past, wasn't it?"

"Does it matter?"

He watched her face closely. "It matters."

"Why?"

"Because as much as I want you, I don't want any mercy fucks from you."

Her eyes widened in shock. "For heaven's sake, Jack—"

"I don't want you sleeping with me because you've decided I'm on some kind of noble quest to right the wrongs my father committed and because I've got a problem with a half brother who is out for revenge. Hell, I don't want you feeling sorry for me."

Her eyes narrowed. "If I slept with every man I've ever met who came from a dysfunctional family, I'd be an extremely busy woman."

Her tone brought him up short. Was he getting a little obsessive here?

"I guess that's true," he said.

She touched his bare shoulder, her fingers light and gentle on his skin. "I didn't sleep with you because I felt like doing you a favor. I don't do those kinds of favors."

"I know that." He was definitely showing indications of obsessive behavior, he decided. It was time to pull back, close down, put up some barriers. But he couldn't seem to stop himself. "So why did you do it?"

She wrapped her arms around his neck. Her smile was slow and sensual and filled with a hint of smug satisfaction. "I did it because I've been wanting to do it again with you for six very long months. I was pretty sure we'd get it right this time. And we did."

"You're saying this is all about sex?"

"Not just any sex." She scowled playfully and tapped an admonishing finger against his mouth. "Very, very good sex."

A wave of heat tightened his body. "I won't argue that point."

"Good. Because I don't feel like arguing." She pulled him down to her, kissing him quickly, invitingly, before he could ask any more questions.

The familiar rush went through him. He forgot about everything else except the taste and feel of her. He bent his head to kiss the curves of her breasts, but paused when he realized that she was pushing insistently at his shoulders.

He grinned and obediently rolled onto his back, curious and intrigued now. She came down astride him, circled his wrists with her fingers, and pinned him to the rug. There was a delightfully wicked, erotic challenge in her eyes.

"Is this a new game?" he asked.

"You spent the past six months reading men's magazines in your spare time. I spent the past six months reading women's magazines in my leisure time."

Holding his wrists against the rug, she began to move against him. The insides of her thighs were smooth and firm. He was already hard, but he got harder.

He looked up at her. "Does this involve little velvet whips?"

"Do you mind?"

"Not as long as we get to take turns."

"I don't know about taking turns. I think I like this position."

"Me too," he said. "Those women's magazines must have been very cutting edge, editorially speaking."

"They were." She kissed his flat nipple. "Very politically correct, too."

"Politically correct? Ah, you mean the lady on top. That's good. I can go with politically correct on occasions like this."

She smiled again and bit his ear.

He laughed softly, savoring the torment.

"My turn," he said after a while.

"Not yet," she said.

She kissed him again. Heat roared through him.

"Now," he said.

Very gently he flipped her onto her back, reversing their positions, and lowered his head to take her mouth.

"Wait," she said just before he entered her. "What about the little velvet whips?"

"We'll get to those," he promised softly.

IT WAS ONLY later, when the first gray light of dawn appeared in the high windows, that he realized that she had deliberately distracted him. It had been an effective tactic, he reflected. But the bottom line remained clear. He still did not know why she had ended the standoff that had kept them apart for six months.

He told himself it did not matter. But a part of him knew that it did matter. A lot.

He had been so sure that if he got a second chance with her in bed everything would be okay.

He was profoundly grateful that he had been given an opportunity to get the sex part of the equation right at last.

But now that that hurdle was past, he sensed the problem was not yet solved. Something was still missing.

What the hell did he want from her?

THE MIRROR COULD have served as a set for a scene from a classic film, Elizabeth thought. The atmosphere of the crowded nightclub was dark and hazy, heavy with a sense of languor and seedy decadence. Antique mirrors of all shapes and sizes hung on the walls, creating a disorienting series of cloudy reflections.

Not exactly Rick's place in *Casablanca,* but close enough.

On the small stage a sultry redhead clad in a form-fitting gown stood in the spotlight. She delivered a torchy love song in a rich, husky voice that was slightly rough around the edges.

With a little imagination one could picture Bogart sitting at a corner table, a drink in front of him, thinking about Paris.

Jack had chosen the club after making a few inquiries. Not that there were a lot of choices. Mirror Springs was trendy, but it was, nevertheless, a small town. It could sustain only a handful of night spots. The Mirror was generally acknowledged to be the hottest of the lot.

Jack had bet that it would attract the most prominent festivalgoers. He had been right, Elizabeth thought, glancing around. Everyone who was anyone was here tonight. Vicky Bellamy and Dawson Holland held court at a table near the stage. Elsewhere in the gloom, Spencer West, the writer, was downing tequila sunrises at a steady rate. He was surrounded by a group of very serious-looking people dressed in black who were also drinking heavily.

It had been Jack's decision to come here after they had attended the screening of an extremely forgettable festival entrant titled *Stranger in an Alley*. Everybody died in the end.

Elizabeth leaned partway across the small, candlelit table and pitched her voice to a level just above a whisper. "I don't want you to think that I lack faith in your executive planning ability, but are you sure you know what you're doing?"

"Trust me." He did not look away from the singer. "It has always been my experience that nothing loosens up a logjam like a little cash."

"You're not talking about a little cash. You're talking big bucks here."

"It'll be worth every cent if it gets us to Page before he pulls off his auction."

"But, Jack—"

He switched his attention from the singer to her. In the bluesy light his face was etched in shadows. She could feel the relentless determination humming through him.

"It's not like we have a lot of options here," he said. "Time is running out."

"I still say he'll show up at the awards ceremony or at the premiere of *Fast Company*. That gives us two chances to nab him."

"If this works, we won't have to depend on trying to spot him in the crowds at the ceremony or the screening." Jack broke off, eyes narrowing as his gaze shifted to someone or something behind her. "There goes Ledger. Looks like he's headed toward the men's room. If you'll excuse me, I've got an appointment."

Elizabeth winced. "Charming venue for a business conversation."

"Don't knock it." Jack was already on his feet. "I've done some of my most important deals in the men's room."

"Why in a rest room, for heaven's sake?"

"Size does matter."

She glared at him, uncomfortably aware of the heat rising in her cheeks. She silently gave thanks for the dim lighting. Jack slanted her a knowing grin and glided off through the maze of small tables. In the faint, flickering glow of the candles he was a lean, imposing figure. A man of mystery. She lost sight of him when he disappeared into a dark hallway. The sign over the entrance was done in purple neon letters that spelled out the words "Rest Rooms."

A figure moved out of the shadows and halted near the chair Jack had just vacated.

"I hate to see a lady sitting alone," Hayden said. "Mind if I join you?"

JACK FOLLOWED LEONARD Ledger into the men's room. A quick glance showed that they were alone in the facility. There were mirrors in here, too. The three antique framed squares of reflective glass that hung in a row above the washbasins appeared quite ordinary. But he couldn't say the same for the wide strip of mirrored glass set into the wall behind the urinals. The inset mirrors were positioned precisely at groin level. Any man taking a leak would find himself gazing down at the reflection of his own penis.

Which was exactly what Leonard Ledger was doing. In fact, Ledger seemed happily riveted by the scene he was viewing.

Jack took a closer look and noticed that the mirror behind the urinals had been designed to reflect a larger-than-life image. Maybe the designer should have etched a warning on the glass: "Caution: Objects in mirror may be smaller than they appear."

Jack reached back and flicked the lock on the door. At the sound of the faint but unmistakable click, Leonard glanced over his shoulder. When he saw who stood there, his slightly perplexed expression lightened instantly.

"Jack. Hey, what a coincidence," Leonard said brightly. "I was planning to catch up with you tomorrow. Got a copy of the script for *Dark Moon Rising* for you."

"Is that right?"

"You're in luck. I happen to have it with me tonight. You can take it home to read. You're gonna love it."

"How badly do you need money for your film?"

Leonard rolled his eyes, shook twice, and stuffed himself back into his pants. "Are you kidding?" He yanked on his zipper. "If money is the mother's milk of politics, it's the life's blood of filmmaking. There's never enough cash."

"Never enough?"

Obviously fearing that he had made a serious misstep, Leonard rushed into words of urgent reassurance. "Which doesn't mean I don't know how to stick to a budget. Don't worry about that angle. I guarantee I'll bring *Dark Moon Rising* in on time and under budget. No problem."

"I'll take your word for it. I'm interested in investing in your picture."

Leonard's shaved head glowed pink with enthusiasm. "Fabulous. You won't regret this, Jack. *Dark Moon Rising* is going to be big. Very, very big. And we haven't even talked about the foreign distribution possibilities. Sky's the limit there. Trust me."

"You can tell me about the distribution possibilities later. Right now I want to go over the terms of our arrangement."

Leonard blinked. "Terms?"

"I'll sign on as an investor for *Dark Moon Rising* if you help me find a man."

Leonard's mouth was already opening to accept the deal. But he closed it again very quickly and cleared his throat.

"A man?" he repeated neutrally.

"Yes."

"Well, hey. Don't get me wrong here." Leonard held up his hands, palms out. "I got no problems with your sexual orientation. Personal thing, y'know? It's just that I'm not sure I can help you out in this area. I mean, I'm not exactly Mr. Matchmaker, see? I could maybe introduce you to some people I know, but—"

Jack smiled. "Forget the matchmaking. I'm not looking for a date. I'm looking for a guy who stole something from me."

Leonard looked more wary than ever. "What did he steal?"

"That's not important. What's important is that I find him as soon as possible."

Fresh alarm blazed across Leonard's face. "We're not talking drugs or anything like that, are we? I don't want to get involved—"

"No drugs. Nothing illegal. Nothing dangerous. This was high-tech industrial theft. White-collar crime."

"Sounds like you need the cops."

"Nobody ever calls the cops on this kind of crime."

"Oh, yeah. I've heard that. Bad publicity, huh?"

"Right."

Leonard frowned. "You check the local hotels for this guy?"

"Yes. He's not registered anywhere here in town."

"But you're pretty sure he's around?"

Jack thought about the phone call he had received inviting him to attend the auction. "He's here somewhere. What I need is someone who knows who's who behind the scenes here in Mirror Springs."

Leonard looked wise. "Someone who knows the players."

"Whatever." It was hard to think of any of the low-budget

independent filmmakers he'd met here at the festival as Hollywood-style *players,* but Jack decided not to comment. He didn't want to insult Leonard. "If I give you the name of a guy who helped produce a film called *Fast Company,* think you could find him?"

Leonard's eyes narrowed. "Maybe. If he's hanging around. Is that all you want me to do?"

"There is one other small thing."

Leonard uttered a world-weary groan. "I was afraid of that."

Jack smiled slightly. "It's not so hard. I just want to be sure you keep this low-key, understand? I'm trying to find this guy, not scare him off."

Leonard relaxed, happy again. "Got it. Don't worry, I won't take out an ad in the *Mirror Springs Gazette.* What's the name of this dude you're looking for?"

"Tyler Page."

"Never heard of him." Leonard flipped one hand in a vague gesture. "He can't be very big in the business."

"He's not. But he's got ambitions."

"Doesn't everyone? Okay, I'll see what I can turn up." Leonard frowned. "How do I get in touch with you?"

"You can call me at either of these two numbers." Jack took a card out of his pocket and scrawled the number of the house where he and Elizabeth were staying and his cell phone number. He handed the card to Leonard. "Day or night. Remember, try not to make waves. He'll disappear on me if you screw up. And I will lose all interest in *Dark Moon Rising* if that happens."

Leonard glanced at the card and then looked up. Some of his initial enthusiasm had faded. "You really want to find this guy bad, don't you?"

"Yes." Jack went to the door and unlocked it. "I do."

"Hang on." Leonard hurried to follow him out of the rest room. "I'll get that script for you."

Jack paused at the door. "Mind washing your hands first?"

"I THINK I'D better make it clear that I'm a noncombatant in your little war with Jack," Elizabeth said.

"Innocent bystanders get hurt when he's in the vicinity." Hayden smiled grimly across the table. "But you already know that, don't you?"

"What is this all about, Hayden?"

"Soft Focus."

"I don't intend to discuss that subject with you again."

He ignored that. "You're here for the auction. You're Jack's checkbook. He won't be able to afford to stay in the bidding without the Aurora Fund to back him up."

"Go away, Hayden."

"I didn't get a chance to finish making my pitch yesterday. We can both make a killing on this if we work together."

"This conversation is starting to bore me."

He leaned closer, his eyes gleaming in the candlelight. "Talk to me, Elizabeth. Work with me."

"Why should I?"

"Because you can't trust Jack. You know that. Come in with me on this and I'll make it worth your while. You have my personal guarantee."

"What, exactly, do you want me to do?"

"Nothing."

"I beg your pardon?"

He grinned, a fleeting smile that reminded her of Jack. "I just want you to agree not to back him at the auction. He can't outbid me on his own."

"I thought I made it clear that as far as I'm concerned, I've got a vested interest in Excalibur. I'm not interested in taking a financial hit for the sake of revenge."

"You disappoint me, Elizabeth. I pegged you as a woman of passion and imagination."

"A lot of people make that mistake."

"If it's only the money that's standing in the way, I can take care of that. My company is worth ten times as much as Excalibur and it has its own R & D projects, remember? At least two are guaranteed to hit big. I give you my word that if you help me out here, I'll cut the Aurora Fund in for a piece of the action."

She studied him. "I know he's your half brother, Hayden. He told me the story. I don't want to get involved in a family quarrel."

Hayden stared at her. Then his eyes hardened. "Shit. What's the matter with you? He's using you. Can't you see that?"

"What I see," she said gently, "is that your need for revenge is eating you up inside. On top of the unresolved issues you've got with the past, you're going through a difficult divorce. That's undoubtedly added a lot of stress."

"Don't analyze me. You don't know a damn thing about my past except what Jack chose to tell you. And you can bet that was a pack of lies. As for my divorce, you haven't got a clue. No one does. You can't even begin to understand what it's been like dealing with a spoiled little girl who thinks her rich daddy can give her anything she wants."

The sudden gritty anger in his voice alarmed her. "Hayden—"

"Jack was smart enough to slip out of the noose before Ringstead could tighten it around his neck. I'll give him credit for that. But I got caught."

"What on earth are you talking about?"

"Didn't Jack tell you that he used to date my almost-ex-wife? Jack and Gillian. Cute, huh?"

"Oh, dear."

"She picked him because *Daddy* liked him, you see. Ringstead decided that Jack had what it took to control Ring, Inc. But fool that I was, I convinced her that Daddy would like me even better. And you know what?" Hayden's mouth twisted with savage self-mockery. "He did."

Elizabeth groaned. "You stole Gillian away from Jack?"

"It wasn't hard." He tightened one hand into a fist on top of the small table. "Now I know why."

"Why?"

"Because Jack had already figured out that the whole fucking family was poison. He probably laughed himself sick on my wedding day. And he's laughing even harder now, knowing how much it's going to cost me to squirm out of the Ringstead trap."

"You can't blame Jack for the fact that you married Gillian Ringstead. Deep down, you know that." Impulsively she touched his clenched hand. "You've obviously got issues with the past, but you won't settle them by trying to avenge yourself on your brother."

"*Half* brother." Hayden got to his feet with a quick, violent movement. "And I will destroy him, Elizabeth. The way his father destroyed my mother. For your own sake, I hope you're not standing too close when it happens. Believe it or not, I really don't want to see you get hurt."

He turned and strode off toward the entrance of the club. On stage the singer launched into another haunting ballad, a tale of love and risk. Elizabeth did not recognize the song, but she knew the wistful, melancholic feeling it produced all too well.

"Better yes than no,
Better to take the fall,
Better some kind of love than no love at all."

She let the music drift over her, feeling safe as long as it stayed on the surface. And then, without warning, it was inside her. She tightened her grip on her glass as the song stirred memories of last night.

She had made a pact with herself. She had vowed to concentrate on the physical pleasure and the satisfaction she had found in Jack's arms. *Keep it all on the surface this time.* But the singer was reaching deeper with her music, stirring more dangerous embers.

Getting beneath the surface.

In an effort to shake off the disturbing twist in the pit of her stomach, she glanced toward the purple neon sign that marked the rest rooms. There was no sign of Jack. How long did it take to make a deal in a men's room?

She glanced at her watch. When she looked back at the dark hallway again, she caught a glimpse of blond hair piled high on a gracefully held head. Vicky Bellamy was heading toward the women's room.

On impulse, Elizabeth got to her feet. She slung her small evening bag over her shoulder and made her way through the shadows toward the purple neon sign. She tried to think of a clever way to engage Vicky in a conversation in the ladies' room. *Loved your comments on the Femme Fatale panel. By the way, did you seduce Tyler Page to get him to steal a secret research specimen of a high-tech material for your husband?* Not exactly subtle. On the other hand, the approach had the virtue of being direct and to the point.

The walls of the hallway had been painted a very dark shade of purple. In the dim light they appeared almost black.

Beneath the neon sign, the corridor branched off in opposite directions. A plaque on the wall informed her that the men's room was to the left. She glanced in that direction. The door was firmly closed. Jack was apparently still engaged in his business conference. The women's room was to the right.

She went down the short hall and opened the door. There were three stalls inside, all painted purple. There were no feet showing beneath any of the stall doors. The rest room was empty.

She backed out of the small room and rechecked the configuration of the hallway. There was one other way out that did not lead back into the main room of the club. She went to the third door and twisted the knob.

She found herself standing on a small loading dock.

A draft of cold night air hit her in the face. There was a single, bare bulb glowing weakly overhead. She peered into the shadows and saw a service road and a small employee parking lot. A large metal garbage bin loomed to her right. The odor of rotting garbage and stale booze was faint but detectable.

There was no sign of Vicky Bellamy, but she caught the sound of muted voices nearby in the darkness.

She closed the door behind her, wrapped her arms around herself to ward off the crisp mountain chill, and went down the loading-dock steps. Should have brought her coat, she thought. It was freezing out here. Then again, who could have guessed that Vicky Bellamy would sneak out of the club via the rear entrance?

A sudden, jolting possibility occurred to her. What if Vicky Bellamy really was involved in the theft of Soft Focus? What if she had chosen tonight to run off with Tyler Page and the crystal while Jack was doing his deal in the men's room?

No, that made no sense, Elizabeth thought. There was supposed to be an auction. If Vicky was mixed up in this mess, she was unlikely to leave until she got her hands on the money.

She couldn't just stand here and do nothing, Elizabeth decided. Slowly, she began to prowl along the line of dark vehicles. If someone asked her what she was doing, she could always say she had just stepped outside for a breath of fresh air.

She tried to appear casual as she moved from car to car, peering into the front seats. There was enough reflected moonlight to allow her to see large, bulky shapes. If Vicky was sitting in one of the vehicles, she would be able to see the outline of her body.

The body was not behind the wheel of one of the vehicles. It was lying on the ground near the rear tire of an aging Ford.

Elizabeth stared at the outflung arms, so pale in the moonlight. She opened her mouth to scream, but no sound came out. She took an instinctive step back toward the safety of the nightclub's rear door.

Then she made herself move forward again. With a sense of great dread she crouched down and started to check for a pulse.

"Are you—?" Stupid question. Of course the woman was not all right. She looked very dead.

A brilliant light flashed on, blinding her, just as she reached out to check for a pulse.

"Don't touch her," a man yelled furiously out of the shadows. "It took me half an hour to set up this scene."

Elizabeth's nerves were already strained to the limit. The man's irate shout was too much. She shrieked in startled outrage and leaped back, fetching up hard against the fender of the car.

"What . . . what . . ." She had to force herself to take a deep breath. "What the hell do you think you're doing?"

"Making a movie." Vicky Bellamy sounded dryly amused.

Elizabeth whirled around. She still had spots in front of her eyes from the effects of the sudden bright light, but she could make out Vicky's figure. The actress stood in the darkened space between two parked cars. The moonlight turned her hair to silver.

"Sorry about that." The man who had yelled at her did not sound sorry. He sounded annoyed. He moved into the light, displaying a sophisticated handheld camera. "Didn't mean to scare you. But you almost screwed up the scene."

The body on the ground stirred. "Can we finish this? It's getting damned cold down here."

"Yeah, sure. Just don't move, okay?" The man with the camera hurried back to his post behind the lights.

Someone else adjusted the long arm of a microphone.

Vicky chuckled. "They're participating in the contest."

"What contest?" Elizabeth asked.

"The Noir on the Fly contest," Vicky explained. "It's an annual tradition at the festival. Participants get some film stock and equipment and are challenged to script, shoot, and edit a short film during the week of the festival."

"I see." Elizabeth was relieved to note that her breathing was returning to normal. "The body on the ground was awfully realistic."

"Nothing is ever what it seems in the movies," Vicky said very softly. "Or in real life. It might be a good idea if you remembered that."

Elizabeth stilled. Surely she had not imagined the note of warning embedded in the words. "Thanks, I'll keep it in mind."

"It's a little chilly out here, isn't it?" Vicky turned and

started back toward the loading dock. "You should have brought your coat."

Determined not to be left behind, Elizabeth hurried to catch up. "I wasn't planning to stay outside very long."

"What were you planning to do?" Vicky asked.

"I just wanted to get a breath of fresh air." Elizabeth groped for some plausible details to flesh out her thin story. "We're sitting in the nonsmoking section, but you know how it is. The air is never really great when there's a smoking section nearby."

"Yes," Vicky said. "I know how it is. But if I were you, I wouldn't stay out here too long. Normally, the crime rate in Mirror Springs is almost nonexistent. But this week there are a lot of strangers in town. You never know what might happen."

A shiver that had nothing to do with the chilled night air sent a trickle of alarm down Elizabeth's spine. She kept her smile in place with willpower alone. "You're certainly full of good advice tonight, Ms. Bellamy."

"I hope you'll pay attention. I don't usually waste my breath on advice, but I thought I'd make an exception in your case."

"Why?"

"I'm not sure." Vicky's smile was enigmatic. "Maybe it's the way you look at your friend, Jack Fairfax."

"Why is that important?"

"It's not important. Not really. It's just that once, a long time ago, I wanted to look at a man like that."

"What way is that?"

"As if you're wondering if you should let yourself fall in love with him." Vicky gave another throaty laugh. "My advice on that point, by the way, is don't."

Elizabeth stumbled against a small stone she had not

noticed on the pavement. She sucked in a sharp, painful breath and quickly caught her balance.

"Are you by any chance trying to warn me off?" she asked bluntly.

Vicky gave her a long, considering glance. "A lady with a past has nothing to lose. But a woman with a future can't be too careful."

Elizabeth came to a halt and said nothing. Vicky went up the three steps to the back door, opened it, and disappeared inside the club without looking back again.

Now what the heck was that all about? Elizabeth wondered. She stared at the closed door of the club for a while longer and then the cold began to penetrate. She jerked herself out of her reverie and started toward the steps. So much for her big plan to pin Vicky down on the subject of Tyler Page.

The back door of the club opened without warning.

"Elizabeth?" Jack's voice sliced through the shadows. "What the hell are you doing out here?"

"Don't snap at me like that. I've already had a major scare tonight."

"What's going on?" Jack came swiftly forward and took her arm. He glanced at the filmmaking going on in the parking lot. "What the hell are those people doing out there?"

"Making a film. Some sort of festival contest." She glanced at him. "How did you find me?"

"Vicky Bellamy stopped me in the hallway and told me that she'd seen you step outside. Something about getting some fresh air."

"That's not quite how it happened. She came out here first. I followed her."

"Followed her?" Jack swept the dark landscape with a quick, assessing gaze. "Why?"

"Well, I did have a clever little plan in mind. I was going to see if I could trick her into admitting that she was involved with Tyler Page. But things didn't quite work out."

"What happened?"

"Vicky gave me lots of sound advice instead," Elizabeth said dryly.

Jack looked blank. "Advice?"

"Yep. And then she said something really, really interesting."

"What was that?"

"'A lady with a past has nothing to lose. But a woman with a future can't be too careful.'"

"What's so interesting about that?"

"For starters," Elizabeth said, "it's a direct quote from the script for *Fast Company*."

"So?"

"So Vicky is one of a very small number of people who could possibly know that I had a copy of the script and might recognize the quote. She was the one who suggested I read it, in fact."

Jack eyed her curiously. "What's your point?"

Elizabeth turned around to watch the filmmaking in the distance. "I think she was trying to give me a warning."

Jack was silent for a long moment.

"Now why in hell would she do that?" he asked very quietly.

Maybe it's the way you look at your friend, Jack Fairfax. . . . Once, a long time ago, I wanted to look at a man like that.

"I don't know," Elizabeth said.

"Well, damn. Maybe you were right about her being Tyler Page's femme fatale. If she was trying to warn you off, then we have to assume that she's in this up to her phony blond hair."

"Yes."

"Why give herself away? And why try to get rid of you? If she knows anything about this deal, she knows you hold the purse strings for Excalibur."

"Yes," Elizabeth said. So many questions.

"And why would she think that some bad dialogue from *Fast Company* would be an effective warning?" Jack asked.

"Maybe because of what happens to the naive, not-so-bright female character who falls for the guy the femme fatale wants."

"Okay, I'll bite," Jack said. "What happens to her?"

"She gets killed."

CHAPTER SEVENTEEN

"STOP IT." ELIZABETH THREW HER HANDS UP.
"Not another word. I've had all the arguing I can take for
one night. I am not going back to Seattle, and that's final."

Jack stood motionless in the center of the rug, the very
spot where he had made love to her last night, and watched
her sweep recklessly around the room. Her anger created a
palpable if invisible wake.

When the argument had exploded into full flame a few
minutes ago, she had had her arms locked tightly beneath
her breasts. But now, as the momentum gathered, her hands
were sometimes in the air, sometimes stuffed into the back
pockets of her snug velvet jeans. Never still.

He tried for a semblance of calm, soothing logic. It was
only a facade, and he knew it. Underneath he could feel an
unholy mix of rage and tension and something that was
uncomfortably close to fear simmering. *If anything happens
to her . . .*

He paused midway through that thought, unwilling to
complete it. The truth was, he did not know how he would
react if anything happened to Elizabeth. He might go a little
crazy— make that a whole lot crazy.

He pulled himself up short with an effort of will. He would not go down that road. There was no point. It would be a clear case of overreaction. This was not some film noir script come to life. This was high-tech theft. White-collar crime. People didn't get hurt in this kind of thing. Not usually, at any rate.

But that did not mean it could not get nasty.

"She threatened you," he said for what must have been the thirtieth time. "We have to take it seriously."

"She did not threaten me." Elizabeth gave him a fulminating look. "Not exactly. She tried to warn me off. I think."

"It doesn't make sense. If she's in this, she knows who you are. She knows you've got the Aurora Fund checkbook and she knows that you can shell out big bucks for Soft Focus on behalf of your client. Why try to scare you off before the auction? Unless—" He broke off abruptly, thinking it through.

"Yes?" Elizabeth looked at him from the other side of the room. "Unless what?"

"If Vicky is involved in this, then it's probably safe to assume that Dawson Holland is also involved."

"Probably."

"Okay, for the sake of argument, let's say that assumption is true. It still leaves us with at least two possibilities. Number one: Vicky and Dawson were the strategists behind the theft of Soft Focus."

"Which fits in very nicely with my Vicky-as-Tyler-Page's-femme-fatale theory."

"Or," he continued deliberately, "possibility number two: They're here in Mirror Springs for the same reason we are. The same reason Hayden is, for that matter."

"Because they've been invited to attend the auction?"

"Right. Think about it. There aren't a lot of folks Page can risk inviting to his auction. He's a lab man, a loner. He doesn't move in the kind of circles where he'd be likely to meet high-rolling investors who would wink at the idea of bidding on a stolen item that can only be safely resold overseas. That crowd is definitely on the sophisticated side. If there's one thing Page is not, it's sophisticated."

"I take your point." She pursed her lips, eyes intent. "He would know about you and me, of course."

"Worldly sophisticates that we are," Jack muttered.

She ignored him. "He probably also knew about your long-standing rivalry with Hayden and could have guessed that your brother would be eager to bid up the price of Soft Focus."

"Right. And the one other person we know for sure he's come in contact with lately who might have enough money and few enough scruples to take part in this kind of deal is Dawson Holland."

Elizabeth frowned. "That would give us a motive for Vicky trying to warn me off tonight. She might be attempting to help Dawson by scaring off some of the competition."

"Yeah." He thought about it. "That does make some sense. I like it better than your femme fatale theory."

"That's because there is no romance in your soul." She shot him a withering glare. "You just can't envision a man taking the sort of risks Tyler Page is taking for love, can you?"

He was startled by the accusation in her voice. "I'm just trying to be realistic."

"Yeah, right." She halted abruptly. "You know what our real problem is?"

He raised his brows. "You want an annotated list?"

"I'm serious. Our problem is that we don't have enough information."

He raised his eyes to the high, vaulted ceiling and asked for patience. "No shit."

"We need to know more about Vicky Bellamy and Dawson Holland."

"I told you, I'm having Larry check out Holland."

She started toward the phone on the end table. "You asked your brother to check out Holland from a financial angle, right?"

"Far as I can see, that's the only angle that matters here."

"Maybe." She picked up the phone and punched in some numbers. "Maybe not."

He glanced at his watch. "It's after midnight. Who are you calling?"

"My assistant, Louise. She spent twenty years working for the tabloids. She has all kinds of contacts in the entertainment industry. She might know someone who—" She stopped, listening to whoever had answered the phone. Surprise flashed across her face. "I'm sorry, I must have dialed the wrong number. I'm calling for Louise Luttrell."

Jack walked to the window and looked out at the twinkling lights of Mirror Springs.

"Yes, I'll hold on a minute," Elizabeth said in muffled tones. "Louise? Who in the world was that? What do you mean, an old editor from out of town called? How old?"

Jack glanced over his shoulder, amused by the disconcerted look on Elizabeth's face.

"No, of course I didn't think you lived in a convent. I just wasn't expecting a man to answer your phone, that's all. Not at this hour, at any rate." Elizabeth glanced at Jack, saw that he was watching her, and turned her shoulder to him. "Uh, well, no, I'm not, actually. There was a slight problem with Jack's reservations at the resort, so he had to stay here and—"

She stopped speaking again and started to turn pink. Jack could hear the cackle of hysterical laughter on the other end of the line clear across the room. He smiled to himself.

Elizabeth cleared her throat and started to speak very quickly. "If you don't mind, Louise, I'm calling on a business matter. I want you to see what you can dig up on a small-time actress named Victoria Bellamy and her husband, Dawson Holland. I think they've both hung around the fringes of the film business for years and they're major figures here at this little festival."

Jack waited until she had finished her conversation with Louise and hung up the phone.

"That should get us some useful information," she said, turning back to face him. "Louise knows how to dig up the dirt on just about anybody. I should have thought of this yesterday."

"It's not a bad idea," he said.

"Gee, thanks for that glowing endorsement."

"Speaking of problems, I'd like to get back to our earlier topic."

"Which one?"

"You. Here in Mirror Springs."

She leaned against the back of the sofa, braced her arms on either side of her hips, and gave him a fierce look. "Don't even think about trying to convince me to leave."

"Elizabeth, I've got enough to worry about without having to wonder if Vicky is going to continue her little campaign to scare you out of town. It could get vicious. I don't want to take any chances."

"What you're really saying is that I've become an additional complication for you."

He spread the fingers of one hand wide. "You've been complicating my life since the day we met."

"You seem to have coped," she said a little too sweetly.

"Maybe. But this situation is getting messy."

"Well, you'll just have to deal with it, because I'm not cutting out now." Elizabeth gave him an oddly thoughtful expression. "Besides, she may come after you next."

He smiled. "You think Vicky will try to scare me off?"

"Not necessarily." Elizabeth studied him intently for a long moment. "If she's really into the role of the femme fatale, she might decide to try to seduce you instead."

He blinked. Then he gave her a wolfish grin. "That possibility worries you?"

"Yes, it does." She glowered at him. "Talk about complications. If Vicky sweeps you off your feet, we'll have real problems on our hands."

He laughed softly. "Fat chance."

Elizabeth smiled dangerously. "Are you saying you wouldn't be tempted if a woman like Vicky Bellamy came on to you?"

"Yeah, that's what I'm saying, all right. I was never good at juggling women. It's always a lot more difficult than it looks. At the moment, I've got my hands full."

"Are you talking about me?"

"Of course I'm talking about you. See any other women in the vicinity?"

She hesitated. "No."

"I thought I'd made it clear that there hasn't been anyone else for the past six months."

She turned her back to him and stood looking out into the night. "You've been busy with Excalibur."

He studied the rigid line of her graceful spine. The proud way she carried herself drew him like a magnet. "Not so busy that I couldn't have taken time to get laid if I'd wanted it or needed it badly enough. A good CEO knows how to set priorities."

"I see."

"What about you?"

"I've been pretty busy, too," she said, very offhand. "A few business dinners. That's about it."

Hayden's mocking words came back to him. *You might as well have written her name on the men's room wall at the club: "For a good time you definitely do not want to call Elizabeth the Ice Princess."*

He walked across the room and came to a halt immediately behind her. He did not touch her. "Hayden told me that it's my fault you haven't had any serious relationships for the past six months."

"Your fault?" Her voice rose in sharp outrage. "Good grief. Does he actually believe that I've been carrying the torch for you and you alone for six whole months?"

He winced at the derisive tone. "Not exactly. He thinks that after that blowup in the Pacific Rim Club, you got saddled with a certain, uh, reputation."

"I see. The Ice Princess thing?"

"Hayden implied that the title may have scared off a few of your date prospects."

She gave a short, ladylike snort. "Do you really think I'd want to date any man who got scared off that easily?"

He studied the arrogant tilt of her chin and smiled. He had definitely been wrong about the ice part, he thought, but not about the rest of it. There was something innately regal about her.

"No," he said.

"Look, we're getting a little off track here. We were talking about Vicky and Dawson Holland."

"I need to know," Jack said simply.

"What, exactly, do you need to know?"

"Was it the fallout from that scene at the club that put a damper on your social life?"

She exhaled deeply. "Brace yourself, Jack. Believe it or not, there were one or two men who worked up the nerve to ask me out after you announced to the world that I was frigid. What's more, I got the distinct impression that they were interested in more than just a friendly chat about what the Fed will do with interest rates."

He forced himself to ignore the sarcasm. He drew his finger across her bare nape. "So why haven't you been dating?"

"I've been busy." She turned slowly around to face him at last. There was steely determination in her eyes. "About Vicky Bellamy—"

He knew that he had pushed her as far as she was willing to be pushed. Reluctantly he dropped his hand to his side. "If you won't talk about packing your bags and heading back to Seattle—"

"I won't even discuss it," she said crisply. "I'm not going anywhere. You need me, Jack."

He looked at her and felt everything inside him focus one hundred percent on her. He put his hands very carefully around her neck. He used his thumbs to tip up her chin.

"I won't argue with that," he whispered.

Something in her eyes softened and deepened. "What a relief." She raised her mouth for his kiss.

This time they made it upstairs to his bed before he got her out of her jeans.

LATER, AFTER SHE had fallen asleep beside him, he lay back against the pillow, one arm behind his head, and silently asked the other question, the one he had not asked earlier.

Do you need me?

DAWSON PICKED UP the two balloon glasses and handed one to Vicky. "It's time for another assault from our stalker."

"I don't think it's working," Vicky said. "Everyone has concluded that the whole stalking thing is just a PR stunt. Even the masseuse at the spa asked me yesterday if it wasn't just a publicity gimmick."

"It's your fault. You're not acting sufficiently terrorized when he strikes."

Vicky swirled the liquor in the glass. "Maybe it is my fault. But I want to call it off. At least until the festival is over. Please, Dawson. This is an important week for me. I want to enjoy it."

He hesitated and then decided to relent. "You're right. This is your big week. I suppose we can cancel our stalker for a while."

She gave him a glowing smile. "You are so good to me, Dawson."

He looked at her. She was wearing the white peignoir tonight, the one that made her look like an innocent acolyte from some medieval cloistered retreat. She knew how much he liked this game, he thought. Hell, she knew everything there was to know about his sexual tastes. She had studied him; devoted herself to learning what pleased him in bed. She could have been the perfect mistress. Instead, she was the perfect wife. His wife. Every man he knew envied him. Every man who saw Vicky wanted her. But as long as he could afford her, she was his.

So why *did* he need the other women? he wondered. What

was he looking for when he spent himself inside those face-less, nameless bodies? None of them could hold a candle to Vicky. If he tried to explain his problem to a shrink, the guy would think he really was nuts.

Vicky smiled as she sank down onto her knees in front of him.

The fabric of her white gown settled around her in grace-ful folds, brushing the tips of his shoes. She looked up at him from beneath her lashes, a novice kneeling at the feet of her chosen instructor, eager to learn the mysteries only he could impart.

He felt himself grow hard. It was as if she worked some magical spell on him. He did not have to do anything. She always did all the work. She was the aggressor, even when they played the acolyte game. How many men would kill to be in his place?

She put her fingertips on his knees and opened his legs. His robe fell open. She leaned forward, lips parted.

A short time later, on the brink of abandoning himself to the white-hot climax, he opened his eyes for a split second. He looked down at the top of Vicky's golden head and had a revelation. Suddenly he knew why he still needed the other women.

He sought them out because he needed reassurance. From time to time he needed to confirm his own manhood in the oldest, most fundamental way. He needed to prove to him-self that he was still the one in control.

Because when he was with Vicky he knew that he was not in control. Like some exquisitely trained geisha, she gave him everything and at the same time she gave him nothing of herself. He could own her, but he could not truly possess her.

She was smart. He was a little worried that she might be even smarter than he was. But lately what disturbed him the most was that she was always in complete command of herself. She never drank too much, never ate to excess, never truly surrendered to the pleasures of sex. He was almost certain now that she was frigid.

As far as he could tell, she had no weaknesses other than her desire to act in films, and even when it came to that she drew the line. Acting was important to her, but not so important that she would have been willing to sacrifice everything for an acting career. Perhaps that was why she had never made it in Hollywood.

The blinding truth hit him.

Sometimes she scared the hell out of him.

ELIZABETH STOOD ON the sidewalk outside a small shop that featured expensive handmade jewelry and pretended to study the display of one-of-a-kind necklaces behind the window. But her attention was on the faint reflection of Vicky Bellamy, who was walking into a clothing boutique on the opposite side of the street.

Tailing someone was proving to be a lot more boring in real life than it looked in the movies, Elizabeth thought. Either that, or Vicky just had a lot of dull stuff on her schedule today.

She couldn't complain, though. It had been her idea to follow Vicky around this morning. Jack had warned her that it would be a waste of time. He had remained at the house to make phone calls to Milo Ingersoll and to Larry. When she had left him he had been deep into a conversation with his brother. The topic had been Dawson Holland's recent business activities.

Jack had looked up from the phone and frowned when he noticed that she was heading for the door.

He'd put one hand over the receiver and said, "Don't do anything stupid."

She'd made a face and walked outside to her car.

Finding Vicky in town had been easy enough. Elizabeth had consulted the festival schedule, noted an actor's workshop that featured her quarry on a panel, and simply waited.

When the panel had concluded, Vicky had promptly gone shopping. An hour had passed and she was still cruising through the trendy boutiques and shops that lined the main street of Mirror Springs.

The small downtown district was crowded with festival-goers who were taking a break from screenings and workshops, but it was not difficult to keep track of Vicky. Dressed in a winter white turtleneck, flowing, wide-legged white trousers, and a long sweep of dashing white coat, she stood out like a beacon amid the sea of black and denim. Not just wanting to be noticed, Elizabeth thought. Needing it. Craving it. Living the part of Victoria Bellamy, Actress.

Or just making it easy for someone to follow her?

She was so intent on Vicky that she did not sense the presence of the large, burly man who had moved into her personal space until he spoke.

"Lizzie? Hey, talk about luck, huh? I was just about to drive out to your place."

She started at the sound of the too-familiar voice. Her gaze snapped from Vicky's reflection to that of the man standing beside her. At the sight of him she felt a small sigh unfurl within her.

Her brother-in-law always reminded her of a good-natured, eager-to-please St. Bernard. There was something refreshingly innocent and endearing about him. It was almost impossible to resist his friendly, engagingly unhandsome face. His red hair and cheerful blue eyes gave him a look of honesty and sincerity that she knew was utterly genuine.

He was actually quite brilliant. Grand schemes and plans

bubbled forth from him in a seemingly endless fountain of cleverness. On top of everything else, he was an utterly devoted husband and a proud father of three.

Too bad he was such a screwup, she thought fondly. The downside of Merrick was that something inevitably went wrong whenever he tried to implement his great ideas. In the years since he had married her sister, Rowena, he'd had at least a dozen jobs, tried three times to start his own business, and lost a lot of money in the stock market.

Definitely a screwup, but he was family. That made him her screwup.

After her initial jerk of surprise, a fatalistic sense of resignation went through her.

"What are you doing here, Merrick?"

"Kind of obvious, isn't it?" He smiled his slightly canted smile, the one that curved a little more on the right than it did on the left and made his eyes crinkle slightly. "I came here to find you, Lizzie. Since when are you into this film noir stuff, by the way?"

"I don't believe this." She swung all the way around to face him. "You *followed* me to Mirror Springs?"

"Just got here." He scrubbed his face with his hand. "Been a long trip. Caught a red-eye to Denver and then had to rent a car and drive that damned mountain road. I thought I'd stop for some coffee here in town before I looked up the address of the place where you're staying. Lucky I spotted you when I left the café. I was just on my way back to my car when I saw you standing here."

She tightened her hands into fists inside the front pockets of her down coat. "How did you get my address here in Mirror Springs?"

"Called Louise. She gave it to me."

"I'll have to speak to Louise."

"What the heck's going on, Lizzie?" Merrick cocked his head. "You've been avoiding me for the past month. You didn't return any of my calls. Then I arrive in Seattle and find out you've left town to attend a film festival, of all things. And what's all this about you being here with some guy named Fairfax?"

Elizabeth sorted through the flood of questions and picked the one that had the simplest answer. "I am here with Jack Fairfax."

Merrick's red brows came together in a troubled frown. "I didn't know you were seeing anyone special these days."

"You and I haven't talked a lot lately, Merrick. We've both been busy."

"Who is he?"

"Fairfax? Among other things, he's the CEO of Excalibur Advanced Materials Research. The Aurora Fund has a heavy investment in the company."

Merrick's eyes widened in alarm. "You're sleeping with a client?"

She ground her teeth. "I prefer not to use the phrase 'sleeping with a client.' Sounds tacky."

"Geez, I'm sorry, Lizzie. It's just that that kind of thing's not your style. Sort of a shock to hear that you're, uh, fooling around with a client."

"He's not exactly a client. Well, technically speaking, he is, I guess." She angled her chin. "I prefer to think of him as a business partner."

"Sure, sure, call him whatever you want. So what's the deal? Is this serious? Rowena's going to have a million questions when I tell her."

"Merrick, I really don't want to talk about this. My personal life is my own affair. Tell me what you want and then you can leave."

He looked crushed. "You make it sound like I only come to see you when I want something."

"We do seem to have our most intimate chats when you're looking for someone to back one of your projects."

"That's not the way it is, and you know it," he said earnestly. "We're family, Lizzie."

"I know, I know." She smiled ruefully. He was right. They were family. "What is it this time? I better warn you I'm not putting another dime into frozen methane hydrate technology. You can get methane out of the back end of a cow a lot cheaper than you can by drilling through the ocean floor."

Merrick looked briefly distracted. A familiar light appeared in his blue eyes. "Methane hydrates are the fuel of the future, Lizzie. An enormous natural gas resource. That company I invested in was just a little ahead of its time, that's all. Sometime in the next five years someone will make that drilling technology financially viable."

"I think I can wait."

"Actually, that wasn't why I tracked you down," he said quickly. "I want to talk to you about this computer security lock idea I've got. It's a completely new approach. Mechanical instead of a software design, see? What's more, it's perfect for the new light-based technology."

"Excuse me, Merrick." She stood on tiptoe to peer over his broad shoulder. "You're standing in my way."

She spotted Vicky emerging from the doorway of the clothing boutique. Sunlight glinted on the actress's dark glasses as she turned and walked along the sidewalk to a white Porsche parked at the curb.

"I've got a business plan this time, Lizzie," Merrick continued. "I've also talked to some computer guys. Real hackers and crackers. They say my idea looks good. But I need some backing—"

"I'm a little busy at the moment, Merrick."

"I'll lay it on the line." He drew himself up. "We both know my track record is not real good. I've got nowhere else to turn. You're my only hope."

"Uh-huh." Elizabeth started to edge around him. "Call me when I get back to Seattle, okay?"

Down the street Vicky got into her white Porsche and pulled away from the curb.

"Damn," Elizabeth muttered.

"Lizzie?" Merrick frowned. "Is something wrong?"

Elizabeth contemplated running back to where she had parked her own car and following the other woman. But that did not sound promising. Vicky was probably on her way home.

So much for her budding career as a private eye, Elizabeth thought. Resigned to the inevitable, she turned back to Merrick.

"All right." She started along the sidewalk. "Let's go someplace and talk."

Relief erased the incipient concern on Merrick's face in an instant. His boundless optimism snapped back into place. His eyes brightened with excitement as he fell into step beside her. Elizabeth suppressed another sigh. She knew that look. He was sure everything was going to be all right now. She would come to his aid with the Aurora Fund and he would rush recklessly forward with his blue-sky dreams.

"All I need this time is a small commitment from the Fund," Merrick assured her. "Seed money. Just enough to get the attention of some other potential investors. You know how it is. Money follows money. Once other people know that the Aurora Fund is in on the deal, they'll want a piece of the action. The idea is great. Guaranteed return on your investment. But it will take a little time to get it up and running."

"That's what you said the last time."

"I know. But this time things are going to work for me, Lizzie. I can feel it."

"That's what you said the last time," Elizabeth repeated. But she said it under her breath.

MERRICK LOOKED UP with a frown when the man's shadow fell across the fender of the car. "Do I know you?"

"The name's Hayden Shaw." Hayden smiled at him. "I saw you talking to Elizabeth Cabot a few minutes ago."

Merrick removed his hand from the car door handle and turned around with a quizzical expression. "You know Lizzie?"

"I'm in business in Seattle. We're both members of the same club. You a friend of hers, too?"

"I'm her brother-in-law. Married her sister, Rowena." Merrick stuck out his hand. "Name's Merrick. Merrick Grenville."

Hayden's smile widened slowly as he shook hands. "What a coincidence. Are you here for the festival?"

"This film thing?" Merrick grimaced. "No. I just came in for the day to see Lizzie. Gotta get back to Phoenix tonight."

"If you can spare fifteen minutes, I'd like to buy you a cup of coffee."

"Thanks, but I'm in kind of a hurry. Long drive back to the airport."

"This won't take long." Hayden clapped a hand on his shoulder. "I think you'll want to hear what I have to say."

"What's this all about?"

"It's about your sister-in-law's relationship with Jack Fairfax."

Merrick frowned. "You know the guy?"

"Yes," Hayden said. "I know him very well. And there are a few things I think you should know about him, too."

CHAPTER EIGHTEEN

JACK SAW ELIZABETH THE MOMENT THAT SHE walked into the restaurant. He glanced at his watch and frowned. She had kept him waiting twenty minutes for lunch. She was never late.

Almost never.

"What happened?" He got out of the booth and took her coat. "Get lost following Vicky Bellamy around town?"

"Shush." Elizabeth scowled as she sat down on the other side of the table. "For heaven's sake, lower your voice."

"Sorry."

"You think I'm wasting my time watching her, don't you?"

"Uh-huh. I'm going to learn a lot more from Larry than you will playing private eye. So why are you late?"

"Not because of Vicky. My brother-in-law, Merrick, showed up out of the blue."

Merrick Grenville. The brother-in-law who had lost his job when Morgan had swallowed up Galloway. Damn. He did not need this particular complication, Jack thought. Not now.

"Grenville came all the way here just to see you?" he asked warily.

"He wanted to talk business." She opened her menu with a

tense, jerky little motion. "I spent an hour and a half with him. He left a few minutes ago. Said he had a plane to catch."

"What did he want?"

Her jaw tightened. She did not look up from the menu. "It was just a personal conversation. Family stuff."

"In other words, he wanted money."

"Like I said, it was a personal conversation," she said tightly.

He reached out and removed her menu from her fingers. It wasn't easy. She tried to hang on to it. When she was finally forced to release it and meet his eyes, he did not like the mix of emotions he saw in her face.

"Did you tell him about me?" he asked bluntly.

"He knows I'm staying with you, yes."

"Don't play games with me, Elizabeth. Did you tell him that I was the consultant behind the Galloway takeover?"

She reached across the table, seized the menu, and yanked it back out of his hand. "The subject did not arise." She bent over the list of appetizers as though seeking divine portents.

"In other words, you didn't tell him. He doesn't know you're sleeping with the man who took Galloway apart."

She did not look up from the menu. "I didn't think it was any of his business."

"Why didn't you tell him about me?"

"I think I'll have a salad," she said. "I'm not very hungry for some reason."

He leaned partway across the table. "Why didn't you tell him about me?"

She closed the menu. Her Ice Princess mask was firmly in place. "Because I knew it would upset him and I was not in the mood for a scene. Now, can we please change the subject? Did you have any luck talking to Larry?"

"You're afraid to tell him about us, aren't you? You think he'll conclude that I'm using you."

Anger flared in her eyes, melting the ice in a flash of blue-green fire. "I told you, I want to change the subject."

"How long do you think you can keep our relationship a secret from your family?"

"I wouldn't exactly call what we have a relationship."

"What would you call it?"

She narrowed her eyes. "At the moment, I suppose it could be classified as a business fling."

"Business fling, huh?" Anger shafted through him. "How would you define 'business fling'?"

"Gosh, I'd say it looks pretty much like any other kind of fling to me. Limited in both scope and duration."

"You think that what we have going between us will burn itself out so quickly that you'll never have to explain me to your family? Is that your big plan?"

"We don't have time for this," she said through her teeth. "We've both got another priority, remember? What did you find out from Larry?"

He wanted to argue. He wanted to make her admit that what they had together was not limited in scope or duration. He wanted to force her to tell her family about him.

But one look at the stubborn determination in her eyes and he knew he would get nowhere today. The waiter arrived to take their order. Jack sat back, took a deep breath, and concentrated on the problem of Soft Focus.

When the waiter disappeared, Jack met Elizabeth's eyes across the table. "Larry had some more background data on Holland's business dealings. The guy's had his financial ups and downs in the past, but that's not unusual for a high roller. The most interesting piece of news is that he's chalked up some big losses in the past year. Took a huge position in an international hedge fund that went belly-up."

Elizabeth looked thoughtful. "That is interesting. I wonder if he plans to use Soft Focus to recover."

"Maybe. But to do that, he'd have to take it out of the country." Jack reached for a chunk of the focaccia bread that the waiter had left on the table.

"I suppose it goes without saying that there's been no sign of Tyler Page?"

"No. The little worm seems to have vanished from the face of the earth."

The waiter returned with the salad Niçoise that Elizabeth had ordered and a plate of grilled salmon. Jack picked up his fork. He got one bite of the salmon before he saw Elizabeth stiffen. Her gaze went to a point just behind his shoulder. Her mouth parted on a soft, wordless exclamation.

Adrenaline pumped. He put down his fork. "What is it? Do you see Page?"

"No, I—" She broke off. "Jack, wait, don't get up."

But he was already on his feet, turning to see who it was she had spotted in the crowded restaurant.

He stepped straight into a swinging fist. He had about half a second to see it and turn away in an arc that harmonized with the direction of the moving fist. The result was that the blow clipped him on the side of the jaw and slid off into thin air. But he had been caught off balance. He lurched to the side and came up hard against the end of the booth.

"Merrick!" Elizabeth sounded both furious and horrified. "What do you think you're doing?"

Elizabeth knew the guy, Jack realized. Wonderful. Instinct warned him not to defend himself. He would come off looking like the aggressor, and women always took a dim view of that kind of thing. He reached out, grabbed the back of the seat, and made a show of trying to steady himself.

A startled hush had fallen. Every eye in the restaurant was directed at the three of them.

Great. Another restaurant; another scene. Somehow, Jack thought, he just knew Elizabeth was going to blame him again even though he had made no move to retaliate to the unprovoked attack. He took in the sight of the large, red-headed, red-faced man who loomed in front of him. Merrick was breathing heavily, fists clenched. Jack glanced past him and saw Hayden hovering at the entrance of the restaurant.

Hayden caught his eye, gave him an icy smile, and flipped a one-fingered salute. Then he turned and walked outside.

"What the hell do you think you're doing with my sister-in-law?" Merrick demanded in a voice that shook with right-eous indignation.

Jack cautiously touched his jaw while he contemplated the various possible answers to the question. "Funny you should ask. I was just telling Elizabeth that she really ought to introduce me to her family."

"I already know who you are, Fairfax. You're the bastard who took down Galloway."

Elizabeth was on her feet. "Merrick, please. Don't say another word."

"Do you know who this is, Lizzie?"

"I know who he is," she got out in a half-strangled voice. "We are in the middle of a restaurant, and everyone is star-ing at us. I do not want to hear another word from either of you. Is that clear?"

"Sure clear to me," Jack said.

Merrick pressed his lips tightly together and watched Jack as though he were a snake that might strike at any instant.

Jack cautiously checked his teeth with his tongue. Everything seemed solidly in place. He didn't taste any blood. His lucky day.

Elizabeth opened her purse, removed a handful of cash, and tossed it down on the table. Then she hitched the strap of her purse up onto her shoulder and looked at each man in turn.

"You will both follow me out of here and you will not speak until we are outside." She started toward the door without a backward glance.

Jack looked at Merrick. "After you."

Merrick hesitated, and then he turned with an awkward motion and stalked out of the restaurant in Elizabeth's sizzling wake.

Heads swiveled to follow the trio. Elizabeth and Merrick went through the front doors without looking at the hostess, who stood at her post, clutching a stack of menus as though they were bibles she could use to ward off vampires and demons.

Jack took pity on her.

"Don't worry," he said as he went past the stunned woman. "It's a family trait. You get used to it after a while."

He went out the door and saw Elizabeth and Merrick standing on the sidewalk. He caught the tail end of the low-voiced quarrel.

"Shaw told me the whole story," Merrick said. The words were muffled and tight with fury. "How Fairfax seduced you into backing Excalibur and then humiliated you in front of half of Seattle."

"It wasn't exactly *half* of Seattle," Elizabeth said stiffly.

Jack glanced at her. "If that's your idea of setting the record straight, I think I'd better handle this myself."

They both turned to glare at him.

Jack sighed. "Why don't you go back to the house, Elizabeth? Merrick and I will take a walk down by the river and sort this out."

"Oh, no, you don't," Elizabeth said. "I am not about to leave the two of you alone. I will not tolerate any more stupid, macho, chest-beating scenes."

"Coming from the lady who poured a full pitcher of ice water over my head and called me an egg-sucking son of a bitch in front of *half* of Seattle, that's almost funny," Jack said.

Elizabeth glowered at him. "I am not going to let the two of you go off alone together."

"I give you my word we won't kill each other." Jack opened her car door. "Get in."

"I have absolutely no intention of leaving."

"This is something Merrick and I need to discuss alone," Jack said patiently. "Your presence will only complicate the issue."

A flicker of uncertainty appeared in her eyes. She glanced at the stone-faced Merrick. He said nothing.

"I don't think this is a good idea," Elizabeth insisted.

"Trust me," Jack said softly.

She hesitated a couple of seconds and then got behind the wheel. She took out her sunglasses, put them on, and sat there, frowning at him.

"Drive carefully," Jack said. "You're a little upset, so pay attention to the road, okay?"

"I am perfectly capable of driving safely."

"Glad to hear it." He shut the car door and stood back.

She shoved the key into the ignition and pulled away from the curb with only the slightest screech of burning rubber.

Jack looked at Merrick. "Let's go for a walk."

ELIZABETH TOSSED THE keys down onto the hall table and slammed the door closed. It was all she could do not to scream with frustration. What else could possibly go wrong?

She stalked into the kitchen, grabbed the kettle, and turned on the faucet. It was as if some malign force was determined to jinx every attempt to recover the crystal. Or maybe the force was just bent on screwing up her relationship with Jack. Either way, the result was the same. She was no closer to getting her hands on Tyler Page and the crystal, and no closer to resolving the thorny questions embedded in her affair with Jack.

Why had Merrick chosen this week, of all times, to show up asking for money? It was her own fault, she thought. She should have returned his phone calls before she left Seattle. She groaned as she set the kettle on the stove. Aunt Sybil would have told her that that's what she got for trying to avoid a problem.

The phone rang just as she was pouring the boiling water over the loose green tea in the pot. She reached for the kitchen extension with her free hand.

"Hello?"

"I'm calling for Jack Fairfax." The voice was low, urgent, male. "Tell him it's important."

She heard voices in the background. They sounded like they were coming from a sound track. "Who is this?"

"Just get him, will you? I gotta talk to him. He's expecting my call. It's a business thing, y'know?"

Intuition kicked in. "Is this Leonard Ledger, by any chance?"

There was a short pause on the other end of the line.

"I gotta talk to Fairfax."

"Jack isn't here right now. Can I take a message?"

"Uh, no. No, I gotta talk to him myself. I'll try his cell phone."

"I think I hear his car in the drive," Elizabeth said smoothly. "Do you want to hold on, Mr. Ledger?"

"Yeah, sure," he said automatically. "I'll hold on."

She smiled as he confirmed his identity. Who said she couldn't play the role of the private eye. "Sorry, Mr. Ledger. It wasn't his car, after all."

"Damn. Okay, I'll try his cell phone."

There was a sharp click in her ear as Leonard hung up. She replaced the receiver and studied the teapot for a long moment. After she thought she had given Leonard enough time to make his call, she poured a cup of tea and started to reach for the phone again. It rang just before she touched it.

She answered quickly, expecting to hear Jack's voice.

"Hello?"

"I'm sorry about that scene in the restaurant," Hayden Shaw said quietly. "Just wanted you to know there was nothing personal in it."

"Nothing personal?" She heard her voice rise in renewed fury. "It was one hundred percent personal. What is it with you and Jack, anyway? You're not a stupid man. I can't believe you're going to let this ridiculous vendetta ruin your life."

"You don't understand, Elizabeth."

"Damn right." She hung up the phone.

"SHAW TOLD ME about what you did to Lizzie." Merrick stood at the edge of the river and gazed out over the tumbling water. "How you lied to her to get her to renew the funding for Excalibur. You seduced her to get what you wanted. You used her. Humiliated her. I oughta beat the crap out of you."

"I didn't lie to her," Jack said. "And what happened between us six months ago wasn't a seduction. It was the start of a serious relationship."

Merrick shot him a look of angry disbelief. "A serious relationship?"

"I admit things have been a little rocky from time to time, but we're still together." He thought about the monthly board meetings. "We've been seeing each other on a regular basis."

"Bullshit. You're using her. She hasn't had a serious relationship since she broke up with Garth Galloway."

An ominous cloud of gloom settled around Jack like a fog. "Garth Galloway? As in Camille Galloway's son? The chief financial officer at Galloway?"

"Yeah." Merrick shoved his hands into his coat pockets. "Elizabeth was engaged to him."

"Engaged. To Camille Galloway's son." He was caught in some sort of doom loop, Jack thought. Every time he made some progress, he was faced with another disaster. "Figures."

Merrick scowled. "What do you mean?"

"Forget it. Why did she break up with Galloway?"

Merrick sighed. "She told everyone that the stress of the hostile takeover put too much strain on their relationship. And it was true, as far as it went. After you demolished her company, Camille blamed Garth for leaving the firm financially vulnerable. Garth blamed everyone in sight for his failure. He got angry, and then he got depressed, and then he started sleeping with someone else."

"I see." Jack looked at the fast-moving water. "I didn't know that Galloway was engaged to Elizabeth."

Merrick gave him a derisive look. "Would it have made a difference?"

He hesitated, thought about Larry, and then shook his head. "No."

"I didn't think so. In the end, she confronted Garth with his infidelity and broke off the engagement." Merrick paused a grim beat. "Garth then told her that the only reason he had gotten engaged to her in the first place was because his mother had wanted the match. Camille liked the idea of having the Aurora Fund in the family, you see. She thought that it would make a nice, ongoing financial cushion for her company."

Jack felt his insides turn cold. "In other words, Galloway wanted to marry her for her money."

"He wanted to use her," Merrick said evenly. "The same way you did. But I'll give Garth Galloway credit for one thing. He didn't humiliate her in a public scene in front of her friends and colleagues."

"Do you think she loved him?"

"Well, sure." Merrick frowned. "I mean, she was engaged to him, right?"

"If you say so."

"Of course she was in love with him." Merrick hunkered deeper into his coat. "She got over him eventually, but it was hard on her for a while. And then you come along a second time and screw up her life all over again."

"Believe it or not, I didn't mean to screw it up this time."

Merrick gave him a dark look. "So what's the deal between you two?"

"I've been trying to figure that one out for six months."

"Come up with any answers?"

"No."

"Well, let me help you get some context here," Merrick said. "It's real simple. You need the backing of the Aurora Fund to keep Excalibur going, so you're sleeping with the lady who writes the checks. What's going to happen when you no longer need her money?"

"Beats me," Jack admitted. What would he do when he no longer had that tenuous link with her?

"I don't get it. This whole thing just doesn't make sense."
Merrick eyed him for a few tense seconds. "There's something else going on here. What is it?"

"Nothing that concerns you."

"Like hell. She's family. I've got a right to know—"

The cell phone rang, silencing Merrick. Grateful for the
interruption, Jack quickly removed the small instrument
from his jacket pocket.

"Fairfax here."

"This is Leonard Ledger. You know that guy you were
looking for? Tyler Page?"

Jack stilled. "I'm listening."

"I think I've got a lead on him."

"Where is he?"

"I can't talk now. Come to my hotel room tonight, okay?
Make it around eleven-thirty. I gotta go to some screenings,
and then I gotta have drinks with some people who are interested in investing in my film."

"Ledger, if you expect me to shell out hard cash for your
next project, you'd better come across now—"

"You never told me this guy was trouble." A whining note
infused Leonard's words. "I can't afford to piss off certain
people, y'know? I gotta be real careful here."

"Listen, Ledger—"

"Room three-oh-five. The Mirror Springs Resort. Eleven-
thirty. Don't bother coming around earlier. I won't be here."

The phone went dead.

"I DON'T LIKE this, Lizzie." Merrick shoved his fingers
through his hair and slanted a suspicious look at Jack. "I
don't like leaving you here alone with him."

Jack, occupied with making coffee in the kitchen, did not
look up from his task.

Elizabeth summoned up a reassuring smile for Merrick. "Don't worry about me. I can take care of myself."

Jack did pause briefly at that comment. He glanced at Merrick. "My advice is to listen to her. She's an adult. She's smart. She knows what she's doing. She's also real stubborn. Take it from me."

Merrick stabbed his fingers through his hair again. "There's something about this whole damn situation that doesn't ring true."

"If I tell you the truth, will you give me your word that you'll keep your mouth shut?" Elizabeth asked him.

Jack shot her a quick, warning glare. "Elizabeth—"

"It's okay, Jack," she said quietly. "I trusted you earlier when you said you wanted to talk privately to Merrick. Now you'll just have to trust me."

Jack subsided, but he did not look thrilled.

"I knew it," Merrick turned eagerly back to Elizabeth. "Something is going on. What is it?"

"What do you think it is?" Elizabeth smiled blandly. "It's business, of course."

Relief flashed across Merrick's face. "That makes more sense. I knew that you were way too smart to fall for another jerk."

Elizabeth was very careful not to look at Jack. "I appreciate your faith in my intelligence, Merrick."

"But what the hell kind of business are you doing here in Mirror Springs? Don't tell me it's got something to do with the film festival."

"Indirectly," Elizabeth said smoothly. "We're trying to put together a deal with someone who is attending the festival. He wanted to spend the week here. We wanted to get together with him, so we're here, too."

"Huh." Merrick's brow puckered slightly. "If it's business,

why did Shaw give me that song and dance about the two of you being involved in an affair?"

"Hayden Shaw is pursuing the same prospect we are," Elizabeth said. "He's got his own reasons for wanting to put a spanner in the works."

Merrick slanted another suspicious glance at Jack. "So how come you and Fairfax are both staying here together?"

"There's a severe shortage of accommodations in town." It occurred to Elizabeth that she'd had to make this excuse a lot lately, first to Louise and now to Merrick. "When Jack arrived he was told his reservation had been lost. He didn't have a place to stay. I let him share this place. There's plenty of room."

Merrick eyed the twin sleeping lofts. "Not a lot of privacy."

"We're careful," Jack said from the kitchen.

Merrick frowned at him and then turned back to Elizabeth. "What kind of deal are you two putting together that involves both Excalibur and the Aurora Fund? Licensing agreement?"

"Something like that," Elizabeth said. "I really can't tell you any more than that. Lot of money involved. If we close the deal, the Aurora Fund stands to make a huge return on its investment."

"I see." Merrick was definitely wavering now.

Elizabeth decided to take advantage of his growing uncertainty. She looked pointedly at her watch. "It's getting late, Merrick. You've got a long drive ahead of you if you're going to make your plane. Rowena will be waiting."

A pang of anxiety lit Merrick's eyes. "I know."

"I'll walk you out to the car," she said gently.

She crossed the room and opened the front door. Cold, crisp air wafted into the room. Merrick looked at the open door and then at Jack.

"Business, huh?" he said, obviously wanting to be convinced.

"You heard Elizabeth." Jack flicked the switch on the coffee machine and lounged back against the edge of the counter. "Business."

"No other reason she'd be here with you," Merrick muttered.

"Right," Jack said without any inflection. "There's no other reason why she'd be here with me."

Merrick turned slowly and walked through the door past Elizabeth.

She followed him out onto the deck, closed the door, and went down the steps beside him to where his car was parked in the drive. She could feel the uneasy tension in him and was touched.

"It's all right, Merrick. Everything's under control." Mentally she crossed her fingers.

"If you say so." He stopped beside the car and looked at her. "You'll call me if you need me?"

She held her blowing hair out of her eyes. "I'll call you if I need you."

"Rowena and I are here for you, Lizzie. Always. You know that."

"I know." She put her arms around him and hugged him tightly. He was solid as a rock and, as long as you didn't look at the financial aspect, just as dependable. He would always be a dreamer, filled with plans and ideas that would probably never quite work out the way he had envisioned, but she knew that if she ever needed him, he would be there. Just as she knew that her sister would always be there.

He hugged her back, a big, brotherly, bearlike embrace. Then he patted her on the shoulder with one broad hand and opened the car door. He wedged himself in behind the wheel and looked up at her.

"I'll send a revised copy of my business plan to your office."

She sighed. "Thanks. I'll get to it as soon as I get home."

Optimism glowed in his eyes. "Thanks. I'll tell Rowena everything's all set."

Elizabeth reminded herself that some things were more important than making money. Family was one of those things.

"I'll call you next week," Merrick promised.

He closed the car door, put the vehicle in gear, and drove down the drive to the tree-lined road.

Elizabeth watched until the car disappeared. After a while she turned to find Jack standing in the open doorway behind her.

"You're going to give him the money, aren't you?" he asked neutrally.

"Probably." She started up the steps. "Don't worry about it, Jack. It's not your problem. The Fund has a special account for family loans. Aunt Sybil was very farsighted."

"You're not doing him any favors. He'll never learn how to handle his business affairs if you keep bailing him out."

She brushed past him. "Like I said, it's not your problem."

He followed her back into the house, closed the door, and stood in front of it as though he would block the exit if she tried to make a run for it.

"I didn't know you were engaged to Garth Galloway," he said.

She opened the refrigerator. "Would it have made any difference?"

There was a long silence behind her. She finally glanced at him.

"Your brother-in-law asked me the same question."

She raised one brow. "Well?"

He did not reply.

"Didn't think so," she said.

She walked behind the granite counter and opened the refrigerator. "What do you say we have a sandwich? We never did get to eat lunch today."

"Elizabeth, I didn't even know you when the Galloway deal went down."

"No, but you knew there were a lot of innocent people who were going to get hurt."

His jaw tightened. "It happens in business. You know that."

She looked out the window as she took some feta cheese out of the refrigerator. There was some yellow in the trees on the hillsides, she noticed. The aspens were starting to turn color. In a short while they would ignite the mountains in a blaze of gold.

"Damn it, Elizabeth—"

"Speaking of business," she said, picking up a knife, "why don't we talk about ours? It certainly beats raking up old history. Tell me, what do you think Leonard Ledger meant when he told you that he did not want to make certain people mad?"

"I don't know." Jack abandoned his guard post in front of the door and came to stand on the other side of the counter. He picked up his unfinished coffee. "That's one of the questions I want him to answer tonight. Elizabeth, about your brother-in-law—"

"I'm sorry he hit you this afternoon." She rinsed off the tomato under running water. "It's not like him at all. He's really a gentle man. He must have been extremely upset. Are you okay?"

Jack hesitated. She held her breath.

But Jack must have realized that he was fighting a losing skirmish. He was too good a strategist not to know when to retreat.

"Don't worry, I'm not going to sue," he said.

"That's a relief." She smiled very brightly. "I'm not sure the Aurora Fund's insurance would cover that kind of lawsuit. You might bankrupt us."

Jack watched her over the rim of his cup. "Wouldn't want to do that."

"Of course not." She started to slice a plump, red tomato. "The Fund wouldn't be of much use to you or Merrick if it got wiped out in a lawsuit, would it?"

Jack was silent for a long moment.

"No," he said eventually. "It wouldn't."

Elizabeth saw the drop of blood before she felt the sting. "Damn."

"What happened?"

"Nicked my finger with the knife."

He set down his cup and walked around the end of the counter. He turned on the faucet and grasped her wrist.

"I read about a situation like this once," he said, holding her injured finger under the cold running water.

"What kind of situation?"

"You know, princess pricks finger. Drop of blood appears. She falls under a spell. Gets awakened by a kiss from a frog."

"A frog? Not a prince?"

"Don't you know anything about fairy tales?" Jack turned off the faucet. "The frog doesn't turn into a prince until after she kisses him back."

CHAPTER NINETEEN

"WHAT D'YA MEAN, HE DIED OF NATURAL *causes? You murdered the guy, Verna. You shot him down in cold blood."*

"If you knew Joey the way I knew Joey, you'd know that getting himself murdered was the most natural thing in the world that coulda happened to him. Besides, it beat the alternative."

"Yeah? What was the alternative?"

"I coulda married him. But my better nature prevailed."

"Better nature?"

"I don't believe in torture. Not even for guys like Joey."

The black-and-white images faded to black on the screen and the credits for *Natural Causes* began to roll. Leonard Ledger's name appeared as director. A smattering of applause broke out in the crowded theater.

Elizabeth leaned toward Jack, who was sitting next to her in the balcony. "It looked like the whole movie was shot in a kitchen. I could swear that section of the tunnel wall where Joey gets it was a refrigerator door."

"Got to give Ledger credit for being able to work within a limited budget," Jack said as the lights came up.

Elizabeth's eye was caught briefly by an elegantly gilded figure that projected outward from a stately column. The Silver Empire Theater was a beautifully restored Victorian treasure. According to the brochure she had read, it had originally been built as an opera house. No expense had been spared. It was adorned with red velvet seats, crimson curtains, chandeliers, and elaborate giltwork.

It had been constructed in the late eighteen hundreds when silver and gold had flowed in bright, shiny rivers out of the Colorado mountains. Newly rich miners had competed to show off their wealth and hastily acquired culture by investing in such emblems of civilization as opera houses, theaters, and spas. Privately, Elizabeth thought that the grand Silver Empire looked a little odd here in the middle of a town that had once been a mining camp and was now a ski resort, but she had to admit that the theater did have a certain charm.

Jack appeared to be oblivious to his ornate surroundings. He shifted forward in his seat and rested both arms on the balcony railing. She realized that he was studying the crowd streaming out of the seats below, a hunter waiting for prey to break cover. He was searching for Ledger's face. It had been his idea to try to locate the filmmaker at the screening of *Natural Causes* and follow him back to his room at the Mirror Springs Resort. His inability to get Ledger on the phone had made Jack increasingly restless all evening.

She was just as eager to find out what Ledger had to say, Elizabeth thought. But for the past two hours, she had been aware of a gathering sense of deep unease that she could not explain away. It was Jack's fault, she told herself. The dark anticipation in him was indeed affecting her nerves.

She was starting to wonder exactly what he would do if he did find Tyler Page. How could he force the other man to turn over Soft Focus? Threats? Violence? Jack could be intimidating when he chose. He would be quite capable of scaring Dr. Page to death.

"It's eleven o'clock," she reminded him quietly. "Only another half hour to go. It doesn't matter if you don't see Ledger here. We'll catch up with him soon enough."

"I don't like the way he's set this up." Jack continued to scrutinize the crowd down below. "A little too melodramatic for my taste."

"He's a filmmaker who makes movies in his kitchen. What do you expect?" Elizabeth got to her feet and collected her coat. "Come on, let's go. By the time we get the car, drive to the resort, park, and find his room, it will be eleven-thirty."

"You're right." Jack did not take his eyes off the crowd below as he stood. "Let's get out of here."

They joined the tide of people on the red-carpeted staircase that led down to the lobby. Elizabeth caught a fleeting glimpse of Vicky Bellamy and Dawson Holland, but neither appeared to notice her or Jack.

A number of filmgoers milled around outside on the sidewalk, waiting for the midnight performance of another festival entry, a low-budget picture titled *Truth Kills*. Snatches of film-speak floated in the air.

". . . like, total mastery of the language of film, man, you know?"

". . . The guy's a master with a camera, especially hand-held work. Can frame a perfect shot on the fly."

". . . got a fabulous script, but so far, no backers . . ."

". . . completely misinterpreted the symbolism of the gut-
ter scene . . ."

The theater crowd thinned quickly just beyond the brilliant marquee lights. But as she and Jack walked through the
parking lot Elizabeth saw another oasis of bright light and a
small cluster of people gathered around it. An air of concentrated activity surrounded the scene.

"They're making a film over there," Elizabeth said. "Must
be one of the groups in the contest."

"They'd better not have blocked the exit with their equipment," Jack replied, barely looking up. "I'm not going to
miss that meeting with Ledger just because somebody has
decided to shoot a movie in the parking lot."

Elizabeth studied the scene more closely. "The exit is
clear. They're working in the space next to it. Must be a murder mystery. See, there's a body on the ground."

"Every film we've seen since we got here has had a dead
body in it." Jack dug his keys out of his pocket. "Murder
seems to be a staple of the genre."

"Of course it is. Haven't you learned anything this week?
Noir is all about the dark underbelly of modern life. It's a
reflection of urban decadence and moral ambiguity. It came
so naturally to American filmmakers in the forties that they
didn't even realize they were creating a genre. The French
had to come up with the name for it."

"Don't start." Jack opened the car door and bundled her
inside. "I am not in the mood for another lecture on film noir."

"I can tell."

Jack closed the door, walked around the car, and got
behind the wheel. He pulled out of the parking space with
smooth, economical skill and pointed the vehicle toward the
exit.

Elizabeth lowered her window to watch the filmmaking

going on at the far end of the lot. There was a figure sprawled on the pavement. Two actors dressed in black masks stood over the "body." One held a length of metal pipe. The other grasped an extremely realistic-looking pistol. A man with a handheld camera hovered over the scene. A woman fussed with what appeared to be sound equipment.

"Okay, people," a paunchy man in a billed cap shouted. "Let's do it again. This time I want the beating to go on a little longer before Calvin pulls the trigger. This is the guy who supposedly double-crossed his partner and slept with his wife, remember? We're talking revenge here. Let me feel it."

Jack drove out onto the street. Elizabeth sat back and raised the window.

"Kind of chilly out here to be making movies," she observed.

"From what I can tell, these independent film people don't let anything get in the way of making movies."

Elizabeth thought about that. "There's something rather endearing about artists who are so passionate about their art."

"You call that art?"

She smiled. "Given that you are about to sign on as a producer for something called *Dark Moon Rising,* I would think that you'd take a more open-minded approach to the subject."

"I've seen enough here this week to know that filmmaking is a business, not an art."

"Hah. I'll bet you'll take an entirely different attitude when you see your own name in the credits."

"I doubt it, but tell me, Elizabeth, will you attend the premiere of my film with me?"

For some reason the invitation caught her off guard. Probably because it implied a future for the two of them, she thought. She hadn't realized that Jack had been thinking that far ahead. She certainly had been trying to avoid the subject.

She cleared her throat. "It, uh, generally takes quite a while to make a film and get it screened. Even a little independent film. Leonard probably won't get his movie premiered until the next neo noir festival. That's a whole year from now."

"Right." Jack slowed for the turn into the Mirror Springs Resort parking lot. "So is it a date?"

He was serious, she thought. He was talking about a date next year. As if he expected them to still be involved in a relationship twelve months from now. She noticed that she was breathing shallowly, the way she did when she was tense or anxious. Or scared. Or excited.

"We'll see," she said quietly.

He parked the car in a slot and ripped the keys out of the ignition with sharp, controlled motion. "I love it when you're so decisive."

"Okay, okay, it's a date." Exasperated, she yanked hard on the door handle. "If you actually do produce a film, I'll attend the premiere with you."

"Be nice to me," he said in a voice that was heavily shaded with wicked innuendo, "and maybe I'll let you have a walk-on."

"Does this offer involve a casting couch?"

His eyes gleamed. "It sure does."

"Let's go see Ledger." She opened her car door quickly and leaped out.

Jack climbed out from behind the wheel and joined her. Together they walked toward the lights of the resort lobby. A young man in a red shirt, black bow tie, and black trousers opened the door.

The lobby was nearly deserted except for the front-desk staff. Jack did not stop to use the house phone to call Ledger. He headed straight for the elevators. She had to quicken her pace to keep up with him.

He said nothing as they rode the elevator to the third floor and stepped out into the hushed corridor. Elizabeth could feel his anticipation. Adrenaline was flowing through her veins, too, but the sensation made her deeply uneasy. She should have been excited about the prospect of getting a lead on Tyler Page, she thought. Instead, she was aware of a gathering sense of dread.

"Do you think he's found Page for us?" she asked as they went down the hall to room 305.

"He'd better have something useful. Ledger won't get a dime out of me if I find out he's wasted my time with some vague story about having seen Page around town."

They came to a halt in front of room 305. Elizabeth heard the faint sound of a television set emanating from inside. Jack raised his hand to knock.

Elizabeth glanced down and saw the card key sticking out of the slot. "Jack, wait."

He followed her gaze and frowned when he saw the key. "Why in hell would he leave it in the door?"

"It happens sometimes." Elizabeth swallowed. "If a person has other things on his mind, he might forget about the key in the lock."

"Huh." Jack knocked three times, very quietly, very deliberately.

There was no response.

Elizabeth felt the unease twist more tightly in the pit of her stomach. "I don't like this."

"No kidding." Jack slid the key in and out of the slot in a single, smooth motion, unlocking the door. "I was just thinking the same thing."

He opened the door and pushed it inward. The only light came from the flickering images on the television screen. Elizabeth braced herself, although she did not know what she was tensing against. She tried not to think of all the films she had seen in which the hero and heroine keep a midnight appointment only to discover that the person they were going to meet had been murdered moments before they arrived.

The television set was louder now. A video. She recognized the dialogue immediately. Leonard Ledger's *Natural Causes.*

"*. . . I trusted you, Verna.*"

"*Big mistake. I'm attracted to men with brains. I could never fall for a guy who was dumb enough to trust me.*"

It was obvious from where she stood that the room was empty. Elizabeth breathed a small sigh of relief. Then she glanced at the bathroom door. It stood ajar. The interior of the smaller room was dark.

Jack flipped the switch on the wall. "Ledger? Are you here?"

The only response came from the television set. Elizabeth stared at the bathroom door. Jack met her eyes. Then he took a step forward, reached around the edge of the doorjamb, and turned on the light inside the small room. He eased the door inward, revealing the tub, commode, and basin.

Empty. Elizabeth exhaled deeply.

"What's the matter?" Jack gave her a humorless smile. "Expecting a body in the tub?"

"Weren't you?"

"The possibility crossed my mind. We've obviously seen one too many movies in the past few days." He opened a nearby closet. There were no clothes hanging inside. No body, either.

Elizabeth took a closer look inside the bath. There were some wet towels on the floor but none of the usual male travel accoutrements. No razor, toothpaste, or condoms.

She walked farther into the main room and watched Jack open a drawer beside the bed.

"Anything inside?" she asked.

"No." Jack straightened. His face was grim. "The bastard's gone. Packed up and left. Took off so fast, he forgot his key in the lock."

"The question is, why?"

"I can think of one very likely reason." Jack studied the room with brooding eyes. "Someone else offered him more money than I did."

". . . You set me up, Verna."

The voices on the small screen were annoying. Elizabeth glanced around for the clicker and saw it lying on the bed next to a videotape box. She picked up the small instrument and silenced the TV. Then she took a closer look at the plastic tape container.

"He left this behind." She plucked the box off the bed and saw that there was a tape inside. She removed it and glanced at the hand-scrawled title. *"Betrayal."*

Jack put out his hand. "Let me see that."

She gave it to him. He took it and went toward the armoire that housed the hotel room's entertainment equipment.

"What are you doing?" she asked.

"What does it look like I'm doing? I'm going to play the tape."

"For heaven's sake, why?"

"This is the only thing left in the room, and it was left in plain sight."

She stared at him as he removed the previous tape and fed the tape into the slot. "You think Leonard Ledger wanted you to find that tape?"

"It seems like a reasonable conclusion under the circumstances."

Jack punched a button. There was a soft, mechanical whir. New black-and-white images appeared on the television screen.

The scene was grainy and obviously shot by an amateur, but Elizabeth had no trouble making out the setting. She was looking at the door of a hotel room. It appeared to be an inexpensive establishment. Portions of the carpeted hall were visible. As she watched, she saw a maid push a cart past the closed door and disappear.

Another figure walked into view. Hayden Shaw.

Elizabeth's sense of foreboding went ballistic. Her stomach was a solid knot of tension now. She watched Hayden remove a card key from his pocket, open the hotel-room door, and vanish inside.

"Jack, what's going on here?"

"I don't know yet." Jack did not take his eyes off the screen. "But the plot is starting to look interesting."

Another man bustled into camera range. He was short with a round face and a nervous air. The top of his head was completely bald. What hair he had left was too long and tied in a straggly ponytail. Gold, wire-rimmed glasses gleamed on his face. He wore a baggy black linen jacket and pants and a lot of gold chains. He clutched a briefcase.

Jack whistled softly. "Tyler Page."

Elizabeth watched Page knock twice. The door opened almost immediately. Page disappeared inside.

"That bastard," Jack said very quietly. "I knew he was in this somewhere."

"Page? But we already guessed that he was involved."

"I'm talking about Hayden." Jack gazed enigmatically at the screen. "I knew that he hated me. Just didn't realize how much."

Elizabeth did not know what to say in the face of such overwhelming evidence of betrayal. She could only imagine what it would feel like to find out that your own blood kin would do something like this to you. She touched Jack's arm. He did not seem to notice.

Nothing else happened on the screen for a while. But the camera never wavered. Elizabeth wondered if the photographer had hung around to catch the two men leaving the hotel.

Another minute or two passed. Elizabeth glanced back toward the door.

"Someone could walk in on us at any minute, Jack. Why don't we take the tape back to the house and finish watching it there?"

"You're right." He started to walk toward the television to retrieve the tape.

But just as he reached out to punch the button, a third person walked into view on the film.

At first Elizabeth did not recognize herself.

And then she did, and the floor seemed to fall away beneath her feet. Her hands suddenly felt as if she'd plunged them into ice water. The tingling was so sharp, it hurt.

She almost stopped breathing altogether when she saw herself walk to the hotel room door and knock twice.

No. Impossible.

On the small screen the hotel door opened. Elizabeth watched herself enter the room where Hayden Shaw and Tyler Page waited.

The video ended with shocking suddenness.

She remembered the title. *Betrayal*.

"IT WON'T BE much longer now," she said in that warm, husky voice that sent exciting little chills down his spine. "Then we can be together. Think of it, Tyler. Paris. Rome. Madrid. The world will be ours."

"Yes." Tyler Page held the phone to his ear with one hand. He used his other hand to dig more potato chips out of the bag.

The house was dark. The only light in the room came from the video playing on the television screen.

He munched chips and watched Bette Davis in *The Letter*. *So good when she's bad*.

"Tyler?"

"I'm here, Angel Face."

On screen Davis, in the role of Leslie Crosbie, shot her lover in a jealous rage.

"We must not see each other until this is finished. You understand that."

"I understand," he said.

"It's hard on both of us."

"Yes," he said. "Very hard." And it was also becoming a bit boring. He felt as if he'd been sitting here alone in this house forever.

"Goodbye, my darling."

"*Farewell, My Lovely*." He hung up the phone and stared at the screen. He knew what would happen. Leslie Crosbie would go free in court, but she would die in the end. The Production Code had to be satisfied. She had to pay for her crime.

He wondered if he would eventually have to pay for his crime, too.

He reached into the bag for another potato chip.

He thought about Angel Face. He had sacrificed everything for her. He had exchanged all that he had once held dear for the woman who held him in thrall. When it was finished, there would be no going back.

No Going Back. A shudder went through him.

No Going Back.

Deep down inside he knew that he was already starting to miss his pleasant routine at the lab. Life had been so simple there. People tolerated his little idiosyncrasies. They left him alone with his work. He also missed the peace and quiet of his little house. At home no one pestered him about dishes in the sink or crumbs on the carpet. He could leave his dirty laundry on the floor for weeks if he wanted.

But *she* didn't approve of that kind of behavior. When this was over and they were finally able to be together, he would have to become Cary Grant for her. Debonair, articulate, clever, and above all, fastidiously neat. It was a daunting thought.

It would be worth it, he assured himself. She was his *Gilda,* his *Laura, The Woman in the Window, The Lady in the Lake.*

But sometimes she scared the hell out of him. Maybe that was why he'd bought the gun a few weeks ago.

ELIZABETH COULD NO longer bear the silence. She was choking on it. She jerked her gaze away from the view of the narrow, winding road and looked at Jack. He seemed wholly absorbed in his driving. It was as if getting back to the house they shared was the only thing that mattered.

He had said nothing since they had left the resort. Not one bloody word. On the other hand, she reminded herself, neither had she.

The shock was only now beginning to ebb. A rush of

clean, hot anger was sweeping in to take its place. She could deal with this now. She *would* deal with it.

"What are you thinking?" she asked.

Jack frowned, as if he had forgotten that she was sitting there beside him. He turned briefly toward her and then returned his attention to the twisting pavement ahead.

"I was thinking about that video we found," he said.

"What, precisely, were you thinking about it?"

"Mostly I was wondering who planted it there in Ledger's room for us to find."

She folded her arms tightly beneath her breasts and stared at the trees. "Someone who wanted you to think that Hayden, Tyler Page, and I all conspired to steal Soft Focus."

"Believe it or not, I had figured out that much." He slowed for a sharp turn. Halfway through it, he accelerated smoothly. "The question is, who would want me to have that information, and why now?"

"The information is false," she said very evenly.

"Sure it is. But that only makes the list of people who might have planted the video in Ledger's room longer than it would have been if the tape was for real."

For a split second she did not think she had heard him right.

She turned as far as the seat belt would allow. "Wait a second. Are you telling me that you don't believe what you saw on that videotape?"

"Give me a break." He kept his eyes on the road, but his mouth twisted in cold amusement. "We are surrounded by several hundred professional filmmakers and video experts of all kinds. In addition, there are upwards of a couple thousand serious film buffs in the immediate vicinity of Mirror Springs, any one of whom probably knows how to fake a piece of videotape. Of course I don't believe what I saw on the tape."

The great, icy monster that had sunk its claws into her insides released its grip so suddenly, she was surprised she did not take flight. Okay, so he had dismissed the evidence on the video on technical grounds. So what? He had refused to believe it. That was the important thing.

"I see." She could not think of anything else to say.

He gave her a quick, searching look. "Are you okay?"

"I'm great," she said softly. "Fine and dandy."

"When we get back to the house, I'm going to call Larry again. He's had enough time to come up with more information."

"I'll call Louise, too."

"Maybe if we get it all down on paper and take a look at it, we might come up with a new angle—" He broke off on a half-muttered groan of resignation and took his foot off the accelerator. "Damn. Not another one. We don't have time for this."

"What's wrong?" Elizabeth asked. Then she followed his gaze and saw the bright lights and the van that partially blocked the thin ribbon of pavement.

The door on the driver's side of the van was flung wide. In the glare of the beams a motionless figure could be seen draped across the steering wheel. Blood gleamed. There seemed to be a lot of it.

Equipment was scattered around the edge of the scene. Elizabeth saw two light stands anchored by sandbags. Only one of the lights was switched on. There were also some cables and a generator.

A man with a camera balanced on his shoulder moved about restlessly, apparently lining up his shot. He had his back to her, but when he stepped briefly into the circle of light she saw that he was dressed in a black denim, waist-length jacket and black jeans. He had a billed cap pulled down low over his averted face. The half-circle of shiny metal that decorated the heels of his chunky black boots glinted when he moved.

"Another body, another movie." Jack sounded irritated. He braked to a stop.

"They're probably involved in the contest," Elizabeth said.

"They've got a hell of a nerve blocking the public road like this."

"Be fair, Jack." Fair? Heck, she could be downright generous tonight. Jack hadn't believed the video in Ledger's hotel room. Life was good. "I'm sure they weren't expecting any traffic on this stretch. Not at this hour of the night."

"Kind of a small crew." Jack undid his seat belt and opened the door. "I only see two people."

He climbed out of the car and walked toward the van.

Elizabeth opened her own door and got out.

"How much longer are you going to be?" Jack asked as he drew closer to the van.

The photographer did not turn around. He stayed hunched over his camera, concentrating on lining up the shot of the bloody scene inside the van. "Gonna be a while. Mind cutting your headlights? They're messing up the shot."

"Sorry," Jack said. "We can wait a few minutes, but that's all. We're in a hurry."

"Screw you, we're makin' a movie here." The man gestured toward the sandbagged light stands and the carefully positioned van. "Took us an hour to set up this shot."

"If you just shift that one light stand," Jack suggested, "I can get around the van."

A ripple of unease trickled through Elizabeth. "Let them get their shot, Jack," she said urgently. "We can wait a few more minutes."

He paused and stared back at her. In the glare of the headlights, she could see his alert, questioning look.

"Please," she said tightly. "Come back to the car. We don't want to get in the way of their art, do we?"

He hesitated, but to her profound relief, he asked no questions. "No, sure wouldn't want to get in the way of art," he said.

At that moment, the actor draped over the wheel stirred and raised his head. His features were hidden behind the mask of phony blood that covered his head and face.

"Hey, a woman," he called out cheerfully. "We can use her in the shot. How about it? Wanna be in pictures, lady?"

Elizabeth opened her mouth to tell him that she was not interested in taking up an acting career. But she stopped when she saw that the photographer had set down his camera. He took a step toward the light stand.

"Touch my equipment and I'll have you arrested," he yelled at Jack.

Jack gazed back over his shoulder. "I'm not going to touch your stuff. We'll give you a few minutes to finish the shot."

"We're gonna finish this, all right." He broke into a run, charging toward Jack. "Come on, Benny."

Benny scrambled out of the van and started after his pal.

"Jack," Elizabeth screamed. "Behind you."

Jack had already whirled around to face the two men rushing toward him.

The cameraman reached Jack and swung a fist in a short, brutal arc. Jack sidestepped the punch. The artfully bloodied actor grabbed his arm and pulled him off balance.

Jack went easily to the ground. Too easily, Elizabeth realized. He took the actor with him. The other man hit the pavement hard. Jack landed on top.

"Hold him." The cameraman danced agitatedly around the pair. "Hold him, goddammit."

Elizabeth ran toward the van.

"Stay back," Jack shouted at her.

She kept moving toward her goal. She got her first good look at the cameraman's face when she went past him. She saw that the bill of his cap and the deep shadows had concealed the ski mask he wore.

The cameraman lashed out at Jack with a booted foot. Jack rolled off the actor, who took the blow in his ribs.

"Shit," the actor screamed, clutching at his side. "Shit."

Elizabeth saw that Jack was back on his feet, closing with the cameraman. She reached the nearest light stand and seized the spindly metal upright.

"My lights," the actor shouted. He sounded more alarmed now than he had when he took the kick that had been meant for Jack. "Don't touch my lights."

She yanked at the metal stand. The light fixture mounted on top wobbled and crashed to the ground, exploding on contact with the pavement. A length of metal came free in her hand. She swung it in a wide arc as she turned back to the mêlée.

The actor screamed, an agonized, keening sound that echoed forever.

"My lights."

Elizabeth ignored him. She saw Jack turn aside from a heavy blow that glanced off his shoulder. He stuck out a foot, grabbed the cameraman's wrist, and tugged.

The cameraman flew forward, landing on his belly with a hoarse grunt. Jack started toward him.

The actor was screaming curses at Elizabeth. She turned and saw him lunge toward her. She swung the light stand again, catching him on his arm.

"Put down my stuff, you bitch."

He tried to grab the length of metal out of her hands. She skittered backward, wielding the upright as if it were a long sword.

"Don't touch her," Jack shouted at the actor.

He turned away from the cameraman and launched himself at the actor.

The cameraman lurched to his feet. Apparently concluding that he'd had enough, he dashed for the driver's side of the van.

"Wait for me, goddammit." Abandoning the attempt to recover the light stand, the actor halted in midcourse, whirled around, and barreled toward the passenger side of the van.

Jack grabbed him as he shot past.

"No, no, *no*." The actor's artificially bloodied features crumpled in grotesque despair. He did not even struggle in Jack's grasp.

The van's engine roared to life. The headlights flashed. Wheels screeched on the pavement. The vehicle careened off into the night, rear doors clanging.

"Bastard." The actor sagged. "Lousy, stinking bastard."

A stark silence descended on the scene. Elizabeth stood frozen on the white line. She looked at Jack.

"Are you all right?" he asked tersely.

"Yes." She realized she still held the length of metal. It was quivering in her grasp. Very carefully she carried it to the side of the road and set it down. "Yes, I'm all right. What about you?"

"I'm fine." He looked at his captive. "You want to tell me

what the hell that was all about? Or shall I just go ahead and call the cops."

"Huh?" The actor squinted through his mask of fake blood. "Cops?"

"That was the next thing on my to-do list," Jack said.

"But he said there wouldn't be any cops." The actor sounded aggrieved now. "He said this was one of those white-collar crime gigs. He said nobody ever called the cops if things went wrong."

"What, exactly, went wrong?" Jack asked.

The actor looked sullen. "I dunno. Ollie offered me five hundred cash if I would give him a hand tonight. Now look what's happened. The light's ruined. It'll cost a hell of a lot more than five hundred to replace."

Elizabeth walked slowly forward. "What's Ollie's last name?"

"Dunno. He just goes by Ollie."

"What's he do for a living?" Jack asked.

"He's a stuntman. Got kicked outta the big studios for drinking on the job."

Elizabeth stopped next to Jack. "What's your name?" she asked gently.

"Benny. Benny Cooper." Benny searched her face. "It was just supposed to be a warnin', see? That's all. We were just supposed to rough him up a little and tell him to pack his bags and get outta town."

"That's it?" Jack asked. "That was the whole message? Leave town?"

"Yeah." Benny heaved a deep sigh. "But it all went wrong. Ollie said nobody would call the cops if it did."

Jack smiled coldly. "This is your lucky day, Benny. Ollie was right."

• • •

FIFTEEN MINUTES LATER Jack parked the car in the drive and cut the ignition. Elizabeth made no move to get out. She sat gazing blankly through the windshield.

"Another warning," she said. "Do you think this one was also from Vicky Bellamy and Dawson Holland?"

"Maybe." Jack did not open his door either. He sat beside her, staring pensively at the front door.

"Maybe we should have called the cops, Jack."

"If we do," he said very neutrally, "this whole thing will blow up in our faces. Everyone involved will disappear. We can probably kiss off any chance of finding Tyler Page or the crystal."

"True."

"Not much the police could do about what happened tonight, anyway," he continued in a judicious tone. "Except let us file a report."

"By the time we did that and got an officer out to investigate, it's highly unlikely that there would be any evidence left anyway."

"True," he agreed.

They sat in silence for a few more minutes.

"Amazing how two intelligent people like us can sit here in the middle of the night and rationalize not going to the police in what is obviously a clear-cut case of assault," Elizabeth said eventually.

Jack opened the car door. "We didn't get to be hotshot CEOs for nothing."

CHAPTER TWENTY

ELIZABETH PULLED UP THE COLLAR OF HER white robe, opened the glass slider, and stepped out into the night. The well-chilled air made her catch her breath. Words like *clean* and *fresh* and *invigorating* took on new meaning at this altitude, she thought.

She looked toward the hot tub. There was enough moonlight for her to see Jack. He reclined on one of the benches, arms stretched out along the curved sides of the tub. The water swirled around his chest. His head was back, his eyes closed.

"Are you sure you're all right?" she asked.

"Yeah." He opened his eyes and looked at her. "Thanks to you. Nice trick with the lights. Certainly got Benny's attention. We were lucky."

"How's that?"

"Ollie and Benny are obviously just a couple of small-time guys connected to the small-time film business, not professional rent-a-thugs." Jack touched his ribs.

"You're sure you don't want to go to the emergency room?"

He grunted in disgust. "I'm sure."

"Thank goodness you've studied the martial arts."

"My father signed me up for lessons when I was eight years old. Larry said that he got signed up at about that age, too. I wouldn't be surprised if Hayden was also sent off to a martial arts instructor at the age of eight. Dad tended to do things in a very methodical way. I've kept up with my instruction over the years. For the exercise. Never actually used the moves for real until tonight."

"I wonder if Hayden is getting any warnings," Elizabeth mused.

"That," Jack said slowly, "is an excellent question. There is, of course, another possibility."

"What?"

"He may be the one who sent those two after me tonight. Maybe he's got his own plan to cut down the competition."

"Don't look now, but your paranoia is showing."

"Huh."

"Jack, pay attention. Read my lips. If you don't believe that scene of me walking into the hotel room to meet with Tyler Page, you can't take the scene of Hayden going into that room seriously, either."

Jack closed his eyes and leaned his head back against the edge of the tub again. "The fact that you're not involved doesn't mean that Hayden isn't."

"You're letting your personal feelings get in the way of sound logic. If Hayden was involved in a conspiracy with Tyler Page, why would he hang around the Mirror Springs Resort? He'd take Soft Focus and catch the next flight to Amsterdam or Berlin or the Middle East."

"Revenge is no fun if your target doesn't know you pulled it off."

"Hayden had nothing to do with the theft." She sat down on the edge of the tub and dangled her bare feet in the warm water. "He's here for the same reason we are. The auction."

"You can't be certain of that," Jack said.

"Yes, I can. On the day he arrived, and again the other night at The Mirror, while you were carrying out high-level negotiations in the men's room, he suggested that I use the Aurora Fund to back him instead of you when the bidding started."

Jack slitted his eyes. "Son of a bitch. Why didn't you tell me?"

She shrugged. "I didn't want to add any more fuel to the fire that's already burning between you two."

"Son of a bitch," Jack said again. "You should have told me."

"I made an executive decision."

"Damn it, Elizabeth—"

"The point is," she said firmly, "he wouldn't have approached me like that if he wasn't here for the auction. I'm telling you, he didn't steal the specimen. He's here to bid on it."

Jack looked as though he wanted to argue the point, but he changed tactics instead. "Last Tuesday night, the night Hayden took you to dinner and told you he'd heard the rumors about Soft Focus, did he tell you *how* he'd gotten the news?"

"To tell you the truth, I was so stunned by the possibility that Soft Focus was gone that I'm not sure I picked up all the details." She summoned up a mental image of her dinner with Hayden. "But now that I think about it, I'm almost certain he just said something about having received an anonymous phone call."

"Not exactly original. I'm surprised he didn't come up with something a little more high-tech, like a mysterious E-mail message or a fax."

Elizabeth shrugged. "Actually, when you stop and think about it, a call from a pay phone is still the simplest, surest way of delivering a message that you want the recipient to get. And it's easy enough to disguise a voice."

"Yeah."

She looked at him. "Earlier this evening you suggested that we sit down with everything we've got and try to put the pieces together. I think that's a good idea."

"So do I. But not tonight. I need some sleep before I tackle that project."

"Me, too."

He settled deeper into the water. "Are you going to just sit there twiddling your toes in the water, or are you going to get into the tub?"

"Would you answer a question before I decide?"

"As long as it does not involve extensive use of logic or rational thinking. I'm not at my best at the moment."

"It's a simple question." She paused to gather her nerve. "Earlier, before we ran into those two thugs on the road, you said that you didn't buy the video of me joining Hayden and Tyler Page in that hotel. You said you didn't put any credence in it because it could have been faked by any number of people."

"So?"

"But you were not so quick to dismiss the possibility that Hayden and Page might have gotten together to conspire in that hotel room."

"So?" he said again.

This was getting painful, Elizabeth thought. But she could not stop now. "So I was just wondering why you found it easy to throw out the evidence against me?"

"The only motive you would have for arranging the theft of Soft Focus would be revenge."

It was her turn, she realized. "So?"

"Elaborate, carefully plotted revenge involving coconspirators and extensive cover-ups and a lot of outright lies is not your style."

"Oh." She pondered that briefly. "What is my style?"

He opened his eyes and gave her a fleeting grin that showed some of his excellent teeth. "Toe-to-toe and to the point is your style. Ice water in my face in a fancy restaurant is your style. Calling me an egg-sucking SOB in front of a hundred people is your style."

She groaned. "I'm never going to live that down, am I?"

"Not if I have anything to say about it."

"Do you think my style of revenge is sort of boring and predictable?"

"Nothing about you is boring."

"But predictable?" she pressed.

"Only in the most attractive way," he assured her.

"I suppose I'll have to be satisfied with that." She studied him closely. In the darkness it was impossible to see beneath the surface of the foaming water. "Are you wearing a swimsuit this time?"

"Funny you should mention that."

"You're not wearing one, are you?"

"When it comes to some things, I, too, have a tendency to be predictable."

"But never boring," she said softly.

She untied the sash of her robe and let the garment fall from her shoulders. When the cold air wrapped itself around her bare skin she sucked in her breath and quickly slipped into the hot water.

Jack smiled slowly as she sat down beside him on the submerged bench. "You've given up wearing swimsuits in hot tubs, I see."

She put a hand on his bare thigh. "I wouldn't want to become too predictable."

She traced a slow, circular pattern slowly up the inside of his leg.

He captured her hand and raised it above the surface to his mouth. He watched her through half-closed eyes as he kissed her wet fingers. She saw the dark hunger in him, and her insides were suddenly hotter than the water in the tub.

He bit gently down on her thumb, then nibbled a bit on her knuckles. She sighed softly and settled closer against him. Very deliberately he drew her palm back beneath the churning water and curved her fingers around him.

He was fully aroused, taut and hard. Gently she tightened her grasp. A shudder went through him.

"The most predictable thing around here is my response to you," he whispered against her lips. "Just like the sunrise."

She opened her mouth for him. He drank deep. After a time she decided to try his own tactic against him. She sank her teeth into his lower lip. He endured the gentle assault for a moment and then groaned, muttered something unintelligible, and pulled her across his legs. He kissed her deeply, with a thoroughness that sent delicious little shock waves through her.

She twisted against him and stroked him slowly, digging her nails gently into his damp shoulders. Beneath her hip she could feel his fierce reaction to her touch. He was straining against her thigh.

His hand slid down her spine to the cleft of her buttocks, and then his fingers were between her legs. When he prodded her gently open with his thumb and forefinger, a surge of exultant energy zapped through her. The liquid heat welled up inside. Irresistible. Unstoppable. Too late she realized the climax had taken her by surprise.

"*Jack.*"

"Don't fight it." He kissed her throat and forged deeper. "There's plenty more where it's coming from."

The strident jangle of an alarm bell cut into a dream of endless hallways and crisscrossing corridors that ended in blank walls.

The alarm was unnecessary, an annoying distraction that only made everything worse.

She did not need the shrill ringing to warn her of the danger. She was all too well aware that they were both in jeopardy. She had to concentrate. She had to think clearly, logically. How was she supposed to do that with that bloody bell going off in her ear?

Elizabeth came awake abruptly, blinked at the dull sheen of a cloudy sky visible through the windows. She groped for the telephone, found it, got it to her ear.

"Hello?"

"My, my, someone woke up on the wrong side of the bed this morning," Louise said cheerfully.

"Save the cutesy stuff, Louise. I'm not in the mood." She felt Jack slide one leg between her calves and tighten his arm around her. *Get a grip. It was just a dream.* "What have you got for me?"

"I'm not sure yet," Louise admitted. "Probably nothing. But I talked to a couple of people who know some people who have covered the film festival circuit for years. There are film festivals everywhere these days. Used to be just places like Cannes and Santa Fe, but now every town that's got a theater holds a festival."

"Could you get to the point, Louise?"

"Sure. Point is Dawson Holland has hung on the fringes

of the film crowd for years. Likes to sleep with aspiring actresses. Still does, even though he's married again."

"What?" Elizabeth sat up very quickly against the pillows. "He sleeps around, even though he's married to Vicky Bellamy?"

"Yep. But no one special. Different woman every time. What can I say? The guy likes to get laid. But he doesn't seem to get serious about any of the ladies who engage his affections for an evening of fun and frolic. Faithful in his fashion, you could say."

"To Vicky?"

"For the past eighteen months, at any rate," Louise agreed.

"They've only been married for a year and a half?"

"Uh-huh."

"Hmm." Elizabeth wondered if Vicky knew or cared about the other women. "Anything else on Holland?"

"Uh-huh." Louise paused for effect. "He was married twice before he met Vicky Bellamy."

"I know that much. Not all that unusual, especially in his crowd."

"Ah, but do you know that he's a widower twice over?" Louise said softly.

Elizabeth saw that Jack was watching her intently. He had caught the drift of the conversation.

"Natural causes?" Elizabeth asked carefully.

"Nope. Car accidents. The first wife was killed nearly twenty years ago. The second one went off a cliff eight years ago. And here's the really interesting part. Holland inherited a lot of money both times. The first wife left him several thousand shares of high-tech stock that coincidentally took a huge jump in the months just before she died."

"What about the second wife?"

"Oddly enough," Louise said dryly, "he had taken out a very large insurance policy on her shortly before her death."

Elizabeth tightened her grip on the phone. "Was there an investigation?"

"Sure. According to my source, the insurance company sent out an investigator, but he couldn't prove anything. The company paid off."

Elizabeth went cold. "Is Vicky rich in her own right?"

"Nope. I checked. No family money. Seems to have lived by her wits, as they used to say in the old days, for most of her life. I couldn't dig up too much on her, but there was no indication that she had money of her own." Louise shuffled through some more notes. "But it might be interesting to see whether or not Dawson Holland has taken out an insurance policy on her."

"Creepy thought," Elizabeth said.

"Dawson Holland appears to be a professional creep."

"And maybe something worse, if you're right about the two dead wives."

"Like I said, there was no proof in either case. But my source tells me that there's probably more than coincidence involved." Louise paused. "I think that's all I've got for now. Want me to keep digging?"

"Yes." Elizabeth drummed her fingers absently against Jack's shoulder. "Call me right away if you find anything else."

"Will do." Louise paused. "So how's it going with the egg-sucking son of a bitch?"

Elizabeth felt herself turn very warm. She stared intently out the window, avoiding Jack's eyes. "Fine. Just fine."

"He's there, isn't he? Right there in bed with you."

"I've got to run, Louise."

"I hesitate to inquire, but my old journalistic instincts demand to know." Louise cleared her throat. "Is there anything extra special about doing it with an experienced eggsucker?"

Elizabeth hastily slammed down the phone.

Jack gave her a politely inquiring look. "Well?"

"Do you think Larry could use his computer to find out whether or not Dawson Holland has taken out an insurance policy on Vicky Bellamy?"

"Probably." He propped himself on his elbow. "What have you got?"

"A very nasty feeling."

TWO AND A half hours later, Jack put down the phone and looked at her. There was a cool, calculating expression on his hard face.

Elizabeth picked up her coffee. "What did Larry say?"

"He said that your hunch was right." Jack walked behind the counter and helped himself to coffee. "Dawson Holland took out a very large policy on Vicky about four months ago."

A shiver ran through her. "Did he confirm that the deaths of Holland's first two wives were suspicious?"

"There's nothing in the records to indicate that the first death was anything other than an accident." Jack took a swallow of coffee. "And the insurance company did pay off on the second death. Officially there's no indication of foul play, but . . ."

"I'm listening."

"But in the months before each death," Jack continued softly, "Holland had experienced severe financial losses. The first time he was able to recover because of the stock he inherited from his wife. The insurance policy on Mrs. Holland Number Two pulled him out of the red the second time."

Elizabeth met his eyes. "The last time Larry called he said that Holland had experienced some serious money problems in the past few months, didn't he? Something about taking a big hit in a hedge fund?"

"Yes." Jack's brows rose. "What are you thinking?"

She paused a moment longer to contemplate the idea that had just occurred to her.

"I'm thinking," she said, "that one good warning deserves another."

CHAPTER TWENTY-ONE

VICKY WATCHED DAWSON IN THE MIRROR AS he walked out of the bathroom. The effects of his last face-lift were wearing off, she noticed. He was getting soft around the jawline. He was still slender, but no amount of time spent with his personal trainer could give him the hard, fit body of a younger man again. The slackness of age was overtaking him rapidly.

She wondered what the other women saw in him. After all, he was never with any of them long enough for them to get their hands on his money. Did they really fall for his vague promises? Were they silly enough to believe that he could get them into films?

She couldn't blame them. She had believed him for a while back at the beginning, but she knew the truth now. When she had first met him, Dawson had had the money to make himself a player, but he'd had no real interest in the Hollywood game. He stayed strictly on the fringes of the film business because it gave him access to starlets and pretty little wannabes who could make him feel young. But she knew now that he would never risk serious money on a major film.

And lately there wasn't as much serious money to risk.

She did not know all the details. Dawson was very secretive about his assets, but she was no fool. She knew that he was in trouble. She was fairly certain he would recover. He seemed to have the Midas touch, after all. But in the meantime, she suspected that he was getting by on his charm and his track record.

But even after he had recouped his finances, she knew there would be nothing more for her than a series of small-time roles in low-budget films like *Fast Company*. Perhaps she had known the truth all along. She usually prided herself on her realistic approach to life, but she had to admit she was guilty of deluding herself when it came to her desire to act.

What the hell, everyone was entitled to a weakness.

Dawson's was pretty, brainless women. She was amused by the great lengths he took to conceal his meaningless affairs from her. She found it oddly touching in a perverse sort of way. He was no doubt afraid that she would leave him if she found out about the others.

She could hardly assure him that he had nothing to fear on that front. To do so would be to give up much of her power over him. And power was the only true currency in a relationship. She had learned that lesson long ago.

"Tomorrow night's the big night, my dear." Dawson adjusted the collar of his black silk shirt in front of the other mirror. "Excited?"

"A little."

He smiled at her. "Relax. I know you're going to win."

"Do you really think so?"

"No question about it." He chuckled as he turned away from the mirror. "I'm afraid that *Fast Company* won't win Best Neo Noir Festival Film, but the judges can't possibly overlook your performance in it. You were fantastic."

"Thanks to you."

She rose from the dressing-table chair and went to the closet. It gave her an excuse not to have to look at his soft, smiling face.

She hated it when he smiled the way he was smiling now. It struck her as a paternal smile. The sort of smile her father had given her on the mornings after the nights he had come to her bedroom. A smile founded on lies and secrets that could not stand the light of day. It was a smile that had long ago frozen her to the bone. She knew that she would never thaw.

She took down an ice-pale blouse and a pair of pale blue trousers, concentrating very hard so that the image of her father's smiling face was no longer superimposed on Dawson's blandly handsome features. It took an effort, but she managed.

"What are your plans for the day?" Dawson asked with idle, husbandly interest.

"I thought I'd go to the spa. I feel like a massage and a soak in one of the pools." She turned around and gave him her brightest smile. "Dawson, about tomorrow night—"

"There is no doubt but that you'll win, my dear."

She gave him an amused glance. "Don't tell me that you've bribed the judges."

"There was no need," he said gallantly. "They would have to be incredibly dense not to see how good you are in *Fast Company*. Going to wear the white and silver gown?"

"Yes."

"Excellent. You look wonderful in it."

She hesitated. "Dawson, you did tell Ollie that the stalker stunts are finished, didn't you? I don't want him splashing paint on me tomorrow night, of all nights."

"Of course I told him, my dear." Dawson smiled. "Publicity is all well and good, but I certainly wouldn't allow him to ruin your big night."

"I appreciate that." She relaxed, went to him, and kissed him lightly, provocatively on the mouth.

She was a good actress, she thought. Too bad no one else knew just how very good she was.

She was good enough, for example, to conceal the fact that she sometimes saw the ghost of her father's features on Dawson's face when they had sex. It was the reason why she always went out of her way to be the seducer rather than the seduced. As long as she was in control of the game, she held the power.

And power was everything—the only thing that guaranteed survival.

JACK STUDIED THE neatly organized items on Dawson Holland's desk. A plump pen trimmed with tiny bands of gold was positioned to the side of an old-fashioned, leather-bound writing pad. A laptop computer and a two-line telephone completed the simple work scene.

He had kept his plans to search the Holland home to himself. He'd had a feeling that Elizabeth would have fretted if she'd known what he intended to do. He didn't have any great hopes of turning up a fabulous clue, especially now that he had discovered that he couldn't get anything off the computer, but he was short on options. He had no intention of cooling his heels until Tyler Page chose to conduct the auction.

He eyed the laptop in frustration. He had already attempted to download at least a portion of the contents onto a floppy disk, but he'd quickly discovered that the machine was password protected. Unfortunately, he hadn't been able to bring Larry along to deal with little snags like that.

He was reaching for one of the desk-drawer pulls when he heard the car in the drive.

Fifteen minutes ago he had watched from the depths of the nearby woods as Vicky and Dawson had both left the house in separate vehicles. Perhaps one of them had forgotten something and turned around to get it.

He heard the vehicle stop.

Not good. He was pretty sure he could deal with the cops, but he did not relish the prospect of trying to explain to Elizabeth how he'd come to get arrested for breaking and entering.

He crossed to the bank of windows that formed the south wall of the bedroom and looked down through a crack in the blinds. A well-worn pickup stood in the driveway. Not Vicky's white Porsche or Holland's high-end SUV.

As he watched, a middle-aged woman got out of the truck. She hurried toward the side door, keys in her hand. The housekeeper, Jack thought.

He breathed a small sigh of relief.

Then he heard her enter the too-quiet house. A moment later, she was on the stairs.

Damn.

He swept the room with a quick glance. None of the obvious hiding places appealed. The closets and the bathroom were too risky. There wasn't enough space under the bed.

It would have to be the deck. There was no way down to the ground, but he had noticed a storage locker under the eaves. With luck the housekeeper was not coming upstairs to retrieve an item from the locker.

He grasped the handle of the glass slider and pulled the door open. Cautiously he stepped out onto the deck and shut the door again.

He went to the storage locker. The door was latched but not padlocked. He opened it cautiously and peered inside. A hose lay coiled on the floor. Next to it was a folded chaise longue and a watering can. There was room enough for him.

He slid into the locker and closed the door. The shadows closed around him. He stood listening intently.

The housekeeper did not stay long. A short time later, the pickup trundled off down the drive.

He opened the locker door and started to move out onto the deck. The edge of his running shoe brushed up against an object.

He glanced down and saw three small cans of paint stacked neatly next to the hose.

Red paint.

ELIZABETH PAUSED BESIDE the padded lounger. "Mind if I join you?"

Vicky Bellamy, fresh from a massage and swathed in a turban and a thick, white robe, opened her eyes. If she was surprised to see Elizabeth standing over her, she did not show it.

"Be my guest."

"Thanks." Elizabeth set down the fruit smoothie she had bought from the spa's refreshment bar and took the lounger next to Vicky's.

She glanced quickly around to make certain that no one else was within hearing distance. Fortunately, the array of tiled, hot spring-fed pools were quiet at this hour. There was only a handful of people in the elegantly restored spa. Most were wrapped in robes, as she and Vicky were. A few were seated on the steps in the deep tubs. Attendants in white uniforms bustled back and forth between the various therapy rooms, offering several kinds of massage, mud wraps, and facials.

"The other night outside The Mirror, I got the distinct impression that you were trying to give me a warning," Elizabeth said. "Was I right?"

Vicky closed her eyes. "You can take it any way you like."

"Fine. I'm going to go with my intuition. You were trying to warn me off. Which means that you know who I am."

"You're the head of the Aurora Fund."

"And you're married to Dawson Holland," Elizabeth said quietly.

"What does my husband have to do with this?"

"I think he's here for the same reason that Jack and I are here. Maybe you're also here for the same purpose. We've all come to Mirror Springs to attend an auction."

"I have no idea what you're talking about. I'm here for the film festival."

"You know," Elizabeth said, "some men just aren't good at marriage. I hear that Dawson Holland is one of those men."

Vicky opened her eyes at last. She fixed Elizabeth with an assessing, catlike gaze. "I know that he was married twice before he met me, if that's what you mean. I know that he has affairs. I don't have a problem with those facts. And they're certainly none of your business."

"Did you know that both of his wives died in car accidents and that Dawson came into a lot of money on each occasion? Were you aware that the insurance company was suspicious of the second death? Did you know that Dawson took out a very large insurance policy on you a few months ago?"

Vicky's beautiful face was an enigmatic mask. "Why are you telling me this?"

"Like I said, you gave me a warning. I thought I'd return the favor. I'll admit that my warning isn't nearly as clever and subtle as yours was, but then, I don't have a script. I'm ad-libbing."

Vicky studied her for a long moment. Then she smiled coldly. "You're sleeping with Jack Fairfax."

"Is that important?"

"Not to me." Vicky closed her eyes again. "But it does make me question your judgment as well as your motive for giving me your little warning about Dawson. I know what Fairfax did to you, you see. Dawson told me how he suckered you into giving him the financial backing he needed to salvage that little company he's running back in Seattle."

"Dawson knows about what happened in Seattle?"

Vicky smiled. She did not open her eyes. "Apparently it's common knowledge in certain circles."

Elizabeth watched a bather go down the steps into one of the wide, chin-deep pools of hot, crystal-clear springwater. The faint odor of the mineral-rich waters filled the large, colonnaded chamber. Soft dripping and splashing sounds echoed gently against the white and blue tiled walls.

"Is that why you gave me your warning the other night?" she asked eventually. "Do you feel sorry for me because you think I've let myself fall for a man who is taking cold-blooded advantage of me?"

"Naïveté can be quite charming, Elizabeth. But it comes with a very high price tag."

CHAPTER TWENTY-TWO

IT TOOK THREE TRIES BEFORE HE COULD MAKE the card key work in the slot. He finally got into the darkened hotel room. He went straight to the minibar. When he removed the miniature bottle of scotch he noted with disgust that his hands were still shaking.

"Shit."

He could still feel the unpleasant prickles created by the slowly evaporating adrenaline. His insides were ice cold. He felt light-headed.

It had been close. So damn close that he knew he would probably have nightmares for a while. In his head, he could still hear the sucking rush of air as the car swept past only inches away. If he hadn't glanced back over his shoulder at that precise instant . . .

If he hadn't reacted with blind instinct; if he hadn't relied on the reflexes the martial arts training had given him . . .

He did not want to think about what had almost happened, but he could not get the images out of his mind. The windows of the steel-colored rental car had been tinted. He had not been able to see the driver's face. But that did not matter.

He knew who drove a steel-gray rental car here in Mirror Springs.

He downed the scotch and went to the window. He stared into the thickly wooded river canyon while he waited for the liquor to melt the ice in his gut.

His mother had been right. His half brother detested him. But until tonight, Hayden thought, he hadn't realized that Jack hated him enough to try to kill him.

"I CAN'T BELIEVE it." Elizabeth stormed across the landing that separated her sleeping loft from Jack's. "Are you totally nuts? You went to their house? Searched their *bedroom*?"

"What can I say?" He opened the closet and took out a fresh shirt. "Seemed like a good idea at the time."

She stared at him, momentarily speechless with shock and outrage. Under any other circumstance she would have enjoyed watching him change clothes. She had never seen another man who looked so interesting without a shirt. But the shock of hearing that he had spent the afternoon committing an act of breaking and entering while she had been at the spa with Vicky overwhelmed everything else, including the sight of his bare chest.

"You could have been arrested," she blurted.

"I doubt it." He shrugged into the shirt and started to fasten the buttons. "Holland doesn't want the police dragged into this any more than we do."

"You can't be certain of that." She realized she had begun to wave her hands in the air. Never a good sign. "Jack, you ran a terrible risk."

"Take it easy. No harm done."

"Is that so? Well, if it wasn't such a risk, why didn't you tell me what you planned to do before you did it?"

He glanced at her as he rolled up the cuffs of his shirt. "Because I knew you'd have a fit."

"I've got a right to have a fit. Good grief, when I think of what might have happened. And it was all for nothing. Absolutely nothing."

"Not entirely." He managed to look offended. "I told you, I found some red paint."

"Big deal," she shot back. "We already suspected that the red-paint stalker routine was a publicity hoax. It's not connected to the theft."

"Maybe. Maybe not."

She folded her arms and glared at him. "What's that supposed to mean?"

"I'm not sure," he admitted. "But it occurs to me that if Dawson Holland is thinking about getting rid of wife number three, making her the victim of a stalker might be one way to handle the problem."

Elizabeth swallowed. "You're right. It would certainly make a change from car accidents."

"Yes, it would." Jack walked toward her. "What did Vicky say when you told her about Dawson's history of bad luck with wives?"

"She was cool about it." Elizabeth turned away. "I got the impression that she thinks I'm not real bright when it comes to men."

Jack came up behind her. His hands closed over her shoulders. "She said that because you're with me?"

She cleared her throat. "Something along those lines, yes."

"What about you, Elizabeth?" His voice was very even, completely without inflection. "Do you still think I made a fool out of you six months ago? That I used you?"

She gazed straight ahead, very conscious of the weight

and heat of his hands. "This isn't a good time for this kind of discussion."

"Did you love Garth Galloway?"

"Garth?" Stunned by the unexpected question, she stepped quickly out from under his hands and whirled around. "What in the world does he have to do with any of this?"

"Your brother-in-law said you loved Galloway but that you found out after the takeover that he had only asked you to marry him in order to please his mother. Merrick told me that Camille Galloway wanted the Aurora Fund in the family."

Elizabeth groaned. "Merrick talks too much."

"Is it true?"

"Does it matter?"

"Yes," Jack said. "It matters."

She eyed him suspiciously. "Why?"

"Because it makes me wonder just how badly you got hurt by what happened two years ago and how much you blame me for it." His gaze was intent and steady. "It makes me wonder if you think Vicky's right about you being not too bright because you're sleeping with me. It makes me wonder if—"

The muted rumble of his cell phone sounded, cutting off the rest of his words. An impatient expression flashed in his eyes. Then he reached for the phone lying on the end table.

"Fairfax here," he said brusquely, his gaze still on Elizabeth's face.

His expression turned to stone as he listened to whoever was speaking on the other end of the connection. He said nothing at all in response. A few seconds later, he ended the call and just stood there, looking at her.

A rush of anxiety swept through Elizabeth. "What's wrong?"

"That was Hayden." Jack drew a long breath. "He thinks I

tried to kill him sometime late this afternoon. From what I can gather, someone almost succeeded in running him down with a car at about the time I was returning from the Holland place."

"THIS IS A waste of time," Jack said as he followed Elizabeth off the elevator.

"Quit whining." She led the way down the hotel corridor to Hayden's room. "You've already made your position clear. But I still say we've got nothing to lose."

She came to a halt in front of Hayden's door and knocked. Behind her, Jack loomed, grim-featured.

Hayden opened the door. He looked surly and resentful. But Elizabeth got the impression he had been in that mood before he realized who was standing in the hall.

He gave Jack a disgusted look and then pointedly ignored him. He studied Elizabeth.

"What are you doing here?" he asked.

Elizabeth caught the scent of alcohol on his breath. He'd been drinking, she realized, but he was not yet drunk.

"I think it's time the three of us talked," she said.

"I'm more than willing to talk to you," Hayden drawled, "under the right circumstances. But I haven't got a damn thing to say to Jack."

Elizabeth flattened a hand on the door and pushed firmly inward. "Unless you like being played for a sucker, I think you'll want to cooperate with us."

Hayden fell back, scowling. "What's this about being played for a sucker?"

"Someone's playing some unpleasant games," Elizabeth said. "You aren't the only victim."

She walked into the room. Jack followed without a word and closed the door.

"Sit down," Elizabeth said to both men. "Try to deal with this as adults. Hayden, we need some answers from you."

Hayden sprawled in the chair and looked mutinous. "I don't see why I should tell you a damned thing about what I know or how I came to know it."

Jack said nothing. He just stood gazing stoically out the window.

Elizabeth sighed. This was even harder than she had imagined. She could only give thanks that none of her family relationships had taken this terrible turn. She made a mental note to transfer a nice, fat sum from the Aurora Fund into Merrick's account the moment she arrived back in Seattle. It was worth every penny to know that, whatever else happened, she had family she could depend on in a crunch.

"Someone is handing out warnings," she said to Hayden. "It sounds like you got one earlier today. We got one last night."

"What are you talking about?" Hayden muttered.

"Two thugs waylaid us on the road and tried to beat up your brother."

"Half brother," Hayden said automatically. "And I don't believe a word of it. He looks fine to me."

"It's the truth," Elizabeth snapped. "You may not trust Jack, but I think you know that you can trust me."

"Yeah? How do I know that?"

Elizabeth just looked at him. He had the grace to turn a dull red. She noticed a room-service tray in the corner. There was a large pot of coffee and some sandwiches on it. She found a clean cup on top of the minibar and crossed the small space to help herself to the coffee.

"We think that someone who is here in Mirror Springs for the auction has decided to try to scare off some of the competition," Jack said from the window.

"Someone such as yourself, maybe?" Hayden's jaw tightened. "I'm surprised you used a car, Jack. Next time try a gun. Hit-and-run with a car usually leaves some trace evidence."

"If you really think I tried to run you down," Jack said, "go to the cops."

"With what?" Hayden growled. "I can't prove a damn thing, and you know it. But I saw the car. Silver gray. Just like that rental you're driving."

"There must be a couple of hundred silver-gray rentals in town this week."

"Stop it." Elizabeth slammed down her cup. "I will not tolerate these stupid accusations. Jack had nothing to do with whatever almost happened to you this afternoon, Hayden."

"Is that so?" Hayden gave her a politely inquisitive look. "Were you with him all afternoon? Can you vouch for his whereabouts at approximately four o'clock?"

Jack turned his head and gazed at her with laconic amusement. She knew exactly what he was thinking. She had been on her way home from the spa at four o'clock. He had not been with her. He had been driving back from Holland's house.

"Jack was not with me," she admitted quietly. "But I know that he would never do what you've suggested."

"How can you be so damned sure of that, given what he did to you?" Hayden asked.

"What are you? Crazy?" She looked at him, amazed at how deep his bitterness had gone. "Grow up. Jack might be a little ruthless when it comes to business, but—"

"A *little* ruthless." Hayden uttered a short, sharp laugh. "That's a joke, and you know it. Look what he did to Galloway. Hell, look what he did to you six months ago. I can't believe you've bought his line of bull. You always struck me as smart, Elizabeth. At the very least, I would have thought that you were intelligent enough to learn from your mistakes."

"And I think you're too smart to let the anger and bitterness of the past blind you to the facts," she retorted. "No, I didn't like what Jack did at Galloway, but at least I now know why he did it. He was trying to get justice for your brother Larry. Given the same set of circumstances, I might have done something similar."

Jack gave her a quick, surprised look over his shoulder. But he said nothing.

"I'm not sure what that says about you," Hayden drawled. "I heard you were engaged to Garth Galloway and that the stress of the hostile takeover wrecked your relationship. Didn't that mean anything to you?"

"Garth wasn't exactly a paragon of honor and manly virtue. He only wanted to marry me to help his mother get her hands on the Aurora Fund," she said.

Hayden snorted. "I'll bet Jack told you that."

"No," she said quietly. "Garth told me that himself. He was very, very clear on that point."

A short, awkward silence fell. Hayden's mouth was a grim line.

"Sorry," he said after a while. "I know how it feels to have someone lie to you like that. And how it feels to fall for the lie hook, line, and sinker. I really thought that Gillian— Hell, never mind. It doesn't matter now."

"You're right," Elizabeth said. "It doesn't matter now. What matters is that you stop blaming Jack for everything that's ever gone wrong in your life and start dealing with reality. We've got a problem here. It could be a lot more serious than any of us first thought."

Hayden eyed her morosely. "What's more serious than almost getting killed in a hit-and-run accident?"

Jack finally turned away from the window. "Actually getting killed in a hit-and-run accident."

Hayden blinked. "What's that supposed to mean? Are you threatening me?"

"No," Jack said quietly, "I'm not threatening you. I'm telling you that there's an outside chance that this situation could turn dangerous. Elizabeth and I think that Dawson Holland is here for the auction. If that's true, we've all got to watch our backs. Some people are convinced, for example, that he might have arranged the murder of his first two wives in order to collect on an inheritance and some insurance."

"Dawson Holland?" Hayden stared at him in disbelief. "The guy who's involved in all this film stuff? Where the hell did you get the idea that he's here because of Soft Focus?"

"His wife gave me the idea," Elizabeth said.

Hayden frowned. "She actually mentioned the specimen and the auction?"

"Well, no, but she sort of implied that it might be a good idea if I got the heck out of Dodge. And last night, after we were stopped on the road, one of the thugs admitted that he had been hired to, quote, 'deliver a message.'"

"This is bullshit." Hayden levered himself up out of his chair. "Pure bullshit."

"In addition to the warnings," Jack said coolly, "there is a possibility that the trashing of the Excalibur lab might be connected to the theft."

"Hard to see how," Hayden said.

"The Vanguard of Tomorrow crowd doesn't want to claim responsibility. They've certainly been eager enough to take credit for their vandalism in the past. So we have to wonder if there could be another reason for the break-in. Given that it occurred within hours after Soft Focus disappeared, I think we can assume that it might have been done in an attempt to distract attention from the theft."

Hayden scowled. "You're starting to sound like some kind of conspiracy nut." But he appeared reluctantly thoughtful now.

"And there is one other outstanding matter that has not been resolved to our satisfaction," Elizabeth said very quietly. "A man is dead."

That got Hayden's attention. "What the hell are you talking about?"

"A lab tech named Ryan Kendle was murdered the night the lab was trashed," Jack said. "The cops think that he was killed in a drug deal. But it turns out he was working at Excalibur under an assumed identity."

"Probably because he was involved in the drug scene," Hayden muttered with exaggerated patience. "Maybe he had a history with the law. You know it's not uncommon for someone to fake a résumé."

"A few details maybe, but not an entire identity."

"It happens."

Jack shrugged. "Yeah. It happens. And I admit there is no direct connection between Kendle and Tyler Page. Kendle didn't even work in the same lab. But I don't like the coincidence."

Elizabeth went to stand behind the nearest chair. She gripped the back with both hands. "The point here is that it's possible this thing is escalating beyond the normal parameters of high-tech, white-collar crime. In which case it would behoove all three of us to stick together."

Hayden threw a sour look at Jack. "Forget it. I offered you a deal, Elizabeth, but it sure as hell doesn't extend to Jack."

"I'm not interested in going into partnership with you,

either," Jack said. "But you're here. That means you're involved. Tell us what you know about this mess, Hayden."

Hayden hesitated and then shrugged. "Even if I felt like helping you out, which I don't, I couldn't. I don't know anything useful. I'm here because I got a phone call inviting me to an auction. That's it."

"Has anyone contacted you since you arrived?" Elizabeth asked sharply.

"Once. The night I got here. I was told that I would get a call just before the auction was scheduled. That was all." Hayden's mouth thinned. "Until someone tried to run me down tonight, that is."

"It wasn't me," Jack said. "But I will give you a warning, Hayden. If, by some bizarre chance, you do get your hands on that specimen, I'll tie you up in court for years even if I have to pay for it out of my own pocket. You'll never be able to use the technology in your own labs."

Hayden gave him a beatific smile. "Jack, Jack, you just don't get it. I don't give a damn about Soft Focus. All I care about is keeping it out of your hands long enough to kill the deal you've set up with Veltran."

Elizabeth frowned. "You know about the Veltran presentation?"

Jack took a step toward him. "Who told you?"

"The same person who called to invite me to the auction," Hayden said. "Guess he wanted to make sure I'd have a good incentive to take part in the bidding. Timing is everything here, isn't it? If you don't get Soft Focus back by the presentation date, you might as well scrub the whole project."

"Tyler Page." Jack glanced at Elizabeth. "He's the only one who could have known about the timing of the Veltran presentation."

"We've known all along that he was the thief," Elizabeth

said. "Nothing new there." She looked at Hayden. "One more thing. Did you ever meet with Tyler Page in a hotel room?"

"Hell, no, I've never met the guy anywhere. Didn't even know he existed until I got that phone call telling me that a specimen of a crash-research project at Excalibur had disappeared."

Elizabeth traded glances with Jack. He shrugged but did not say anything.

She looked at Hayden. "Think about what you're doing here. If you keep us from making the Veltran presentation, it won't be just Jack who gets hurt. Excalibur will go down the tubes, too. A lot of innocent people will be put out of work. A family heritage will be destroyed."

"You know what they say about making omelets," Hayden murmured. "Gotta break a few eggs."

"What a perfectly disgusting thing to say." Elizabeth picked up her purse. "Jack was right. You're so obsessed with your need for revenge that you're willing to do something stupid and vicious. And you've got the nerve to accuse your brother of being ruthless."

"How the hell can you defend him after the way he screwed you over not once, but twice," Hayden demanded.

"My differences with Jack stem from the Galloway takeover," she said tightly. "I didn't like what happened two years ago and I didn't like the way he handled it. But I can understand his motive."

"To make a nice profit," Hayden drawled.

Elizabeth threw her hands into the air, beyond exasperated now. "I told you, he did it for your brother Larry's sake."

Hayden's expression tightened again. "You might be willing to buy that story, but I'm not."

"Why don't you pick up the phone and ask Larry for the truth?" Elizabeth suggested through her teeth. She looked at Jack. "I've had enough of this. Let's get out of here."

"Whatever you say." He followed her to the door.

Neither of them looked back at Hayden as they went out into the hall. They waited for the elevator in silence. When the cab arrived, Elizabeth stepped inside. Jack followed.

She gazed determinedly at the closed doors. "That was my fault."

"Your fault?"

"That scene with Hayden. I'm sorry about it. I honestly thought I could talk some sense into him. I didn't realize he would be so . . . so rigid."

"Told you so."

"Yes. You did mention it once or twice."

Jack exhaled slowly. "He hates me, Elizabeth."

"I agree that something is eating him up inside and he's projecting it outward, focusing those feelings on you. But I don't think he really hates you."

"Has anyone ever told you that your naïveté is quite charming at times?"

"Vicky mentioned it this afternoon. She seemed to think it was an unfortunate character flaw."

Jack smiled slowly. He caught her chin on the edge of his hand and leaned down to kiss her briefly, a quick, hard, hungry kiss that left her slightly breathless. She gazed at him, wide-eyed.

"What was that for?" she asked.

"For championing my honor and my integrity back there in that hotel room."

She flushed. "Don't be ridiculous. We both know you didn't try to scare off Hayden by nearly running him down this afternoon."

"I know it." Jack's eyes gleamed. "But how can you be so certain? You weren't with me."

"That kind of thing just isn't your style," she said brusquely. "You might confront him. You *did* confront him, in fact. But you wouldn't use scare tactics, especially not the kind that could result in physical injury or . . . or worse."

"Not my style, hmm?"

"What's so funny?" she demanded.

"Nothing. It's just that I recall saying something very similar to you after we watched that video."

Silence fell again. Elizabeth said nothing as they walked through the lobby and out into the resort parking lot. She waited until she was in the car and Jack was behind the wheel.

"About Garth Galloway," she said quietly.

He paused, his hand on the ignition. He glanced her way, his eyes concealed behind his sunglasses. "What about him?"

She gazed straight ahead at the row of parked cars in front of her. "For the record, Garth and I had begun to have problems before you launched your assault on Galloway. I suspected that he, well, it's not important now."

"You knew that he was seeing someone else?"

"Yes." She cleared her throat. "What I'm trying to say is that the engagement would have ended even if the takeover had never occurred. I delayed the inevitable because I didn't want to abandon Garth and Camille while they were under siege. It just didn't seem right, somehow. They were old friends of the family. I had known them both for so long, you see."

Jack folded his hands on top of the steering wheel and stared out over the hood of the car. "You didn't answer my question. Did you love him?"

"Whatever it was I felt for Garth, it was founded on lies

and errors in judgment. My judgment. As Vicky Bellamy once told me, nothing is ever quite what it seems in the movies or in real life."

He turned with unexpected speed, whipping around in the seat, catching her by the shoulders, hauling her toward him. "Don't give me that bullshit. *Did you love him?*"

She went very still, hardly daring to breathe. "Back at the beginning? Yes, I loved him. Is that what you wanted to hear?"

His jaw tightened. She could see her own reflection in the lenses of his glasses.

"No," he said. "It's not what I wanted to hear. But I had to know the truth."

"Stop it," she ordered gently.

"What?"

She touched his taut jaw with her fingertips. "Garth killed my love for him before you came on the scene, Jack. You've got some things to answer for because of what you did to Galloway, but wrecking my engagement is not on the list. You don't have to assume responsibility for destroying the great love of my life, okay?"

"Was it the great love of your life?"

"No." She hesitated. "It was nice while I thought that it was real. But looking back, it never was great."

He did not move for a long moment, just sat there studying her intently from behind the shield of his sunglasses.

"I told you once that if I had to do the Galloway deal again, I would," he said, as if he wanted to be certain she understood.

"I know. Because of your brother Larry."

He looked as if he wanted to say something else but changed his mind. He bent his head and kissed her instead.

It was a different kind of kiss, unlike any of the others she had received from him. There was a deeply buried hunger in it, not for sex, she realized, but for something else. Something more. Absolution?

Whatever it was, she sensed the need and could not resist the appeal. She put her arms on his shoulders and kissed him back, not with the fire and passion that his kisses usually induced in her, but softly, gently. Offering him the forgiveness he seemed to be searching for in the embrace.

He wrapped her close against him and held her very tightly. It was a long time before he released her, turned the key in the ignition, and drove out of the parking lot.

He said nothing, but she saw the grim, unyielding plane of his jaw and she knew a sense of failure. He had not gotten whatever it was he had wanted from her.

If it wasn't forgiveness he had been seeking, what had he been searching for in that kiss?

SHORTLY BEFORE EIGHT the following evening, Elizabeth took her seat in the first row of the balcony and watched the festivalgoers arrive for the awards ceremony. It had been her idea to attend this evening. She was convinced that Tyler Page would want to be here to see if his film or Vicky Bellamy won an award. Jack had agreed that it was possible Page would break cover for the event.

She glanced at him as he took the aisle seat beside her. He wore an expensively cut, deceptively casual jacket, black pullover, and black trousers. His attire was similar to that of a number of other men pouring into the theater, but unlike the majority of them, he looked as if he really did wield power and control. It wasn't a question of money or industry influence, she thought. It was that impression of self-mastery that radiated from him. That was what made him both dangerous and compelling.

She was still wondering what she had misunderstood
about the kiss in the resort parking lot yesterday. One thing
was for certain: She was not about to ask for explanations.
Jack had made it obvious that his only concern was his mis-
sion to find Tyler Page.

She studied his hard profile as the other ticket-holders
streamed down the aisles to their seats. During the drive to
the Silver Empire Theater this evening, he had been silent.
He had handled the car and the narrow, winding road with
his usual flawless precision and control, but she had sensed
the cold determination in him. She had known that the scene
with Hayden had disturbed him, but she was somewhat surprised by the return of this chilling reserve.

Just like the old days, she thought. She had seen a lot of
this attitude during the past six months.

"Are you going to stay in this mood all evening?" she
asked pleasantly.

"Depends."

"On what?"

"On whether or not Tyler Page shows up."

"It wasn't wondering if Page would show that turned you
surly tonight," she reminded him. "It was that conversation
with Hayden last night. Want to talk about it?"

He frowned and turned briefly to look at her. She was startled to see a flash of surprise in his eyes.

"No," he said.

She sighed. "That is so typical."

He slanted her a brief, derisive glance. "Of the male of the
species?"

"No, of you, in particular. You always act like this when
things don't go just the way you planned them."

"Like what?"

"Like *this*." Bright little flashes of crimson danced before her eyes. Her nails. He had her waving her hands again. She checked the telltale movement and quickly folded her fingers neatly in her lap. "You go all distant and cold and watchful. It makes it difficult to carry on a meaningful conversation."

"Really? I hadn't realized that we were involved in a meaningful conversation."

Anger sparked through her. She covered it with a steely smile. "You know, a shrink could have a field day analyzing the relationship between you and your brother."

"I doubt if any therapist would touch our case."

"Why not?"

Jack's smile was devoid of all amusement. "Because neither Hayden nor I would ever pay anyone real money to analyze us. And I can't see any therapist worth his or her salt doing the job for free. Can you?"

"No. Especially if he or she knew that the clients weren't interested in the results."

THE FILM CLIP from *Fast Company,* the audience was told, was a scene that took place three-quarters of the way through the movie. The dramatic lighting gave Vicky Bellamy's spider-woman character a luminous glow. It wasn't Rita Hayworth in *Gilda,* or Lauren Bacall in *The Big Sleep,* Elizabeth thought, but it wasn't bad.

Unfortunately, the dialogue wasn't *Casablanca,* either.

> *"But I didn't kill him. Eden, for God's sake, you've got to tell the cops the truth."*
> *"I make it a habit to never tell the truth, Harry. I believe in living a simple life, and the truth always seems to complicate things."*

Under cover of the enthusiastic clapping that followed the clip, Jack leaned toward Elizabeth.

"We're wasting our time. He's not here. I've checked every damn seat in the house."

"I don't understand it," she whispered. "How could he stay away? He might not have expected *Fast Company* to win Best Picture at the festival, but what about Vicky?"

"I told you that you were putting too much stock in the theory that Page is a victim of passion."

"I still think he's here somewhere," she insisted.

"The ceremony is almost over. Only Best Actress and Best Film left. If Page is here, he'll probably try to leave just before the houselights come up."

"Then it's time for my fallback plan," Elizabeth said briskly. "Ready?"

Jack hesitated, then reluctantly got to his feet. Elizabeth collected her coat and followed him up the darkened aisle. A moment later they emerged into the plush, red and gold upstairs lobby. It was empty except for a couple of idling ushers and the waiter lounging behind the wine bar.

"You're sure you want to do this?" Jack asked.

"It's not like we have a lot of other options," she reminded him.

"All right. You take this exit. I'll take the other one."

He turned to the left, as though he intended to go to the men's room. Elizabeth hurried in the opposite direction toward the women's room.

Once in the dimly lit hall she kept going past the door marked "Ladies," all the way to the emergency exit. She was relieved to see that it was not equipped with an alarm.

She glanced over her shoulder to make certain that no one was watching her. Then she opened the door. Unlike the lush Victorian lobby, the stairwell was starkly utilitarian. The harsh, fluorescent lighting revealed a set of concrete steps. She grasped the handrail and went quickly down to a door marked "Exit." When she pushed it open, the brisk night air swirled around her.

Outside she huddled into her coat and walked swiftly down the alley toward the back of the theater. When she got there she saw a small parking area. Jack stepped briefly into the weak yellow glare of the single streetlamp that illuminated the rear of the theater. He raised a hand to let her know that he had seen her. Then he moved back into the shadows on the opposite side of the building.

She pulled up the collar of her coat and prepared to wait. The plan was simple enough, she reminded herself. She would watch the emergency exits on this side of the theater. Jack would watch the exits on the other side. Between the two of them they would be able to see anyone leaving via one of the side doors.

Jack had bought into the scheme with something less than enthusiasm, and only after she had pointed out that they would be within easy hailing distance of each other. He considered the vigil a waste of time.

Minutes ticked past at a relentlessly slow pace. Elizabeth scrunched deeper into her coat and clenched her gloved hands inside her pockets. Eventually the dull, muted thunder of applause broke out inside the theater. The Best Actress Award. She wondered if Vicky had won.

Next up would be Best Picture.

A few minutes later, muffled applause again echoed through the old theater building. Elizabeth tensed in expectation and peered into the alley. If Tyler Page had attended the ceremony, he would no doubt try to leave quickly and quietly now that it was over. With any luck, by a side entrance. She watched the alley door, waiting for it to open.

There was another rumble of applause inside the theater. The ceremony was over. Still the alley door did not open. Frustration rose inside her. She had been so sure of her analysis of Page's motivation. The man had done what he'd done for love of Vicky Bellamy, his femme fatale. How could he bring himself to miss his lover's big night?

People were leaving the theater now. She heard laughter and conversation from the vicinity of the front entrance. But the emergency exit door on her side of the building did not budge.

She sensed Jack and turned to see him coming toward her. With his coat collar up and his face hidden, he looked like Humphrey Bogart in *The Maltese Falcon*.

"Give up?" he asked.

"Not yet. Maybe he decided to wait until the theater is empty. He could be hiding in the men's room or a utility closet." She took one hand out of her pocket and made a shooing motion. "Go back to your post."

"Face it, he didn't show."

"I still think—" She broke off as the roar of a motorcycle engine split the darkness behind her.

She and Jack both turned quickly toward the sound. A single headlight beam pierced the night. Elizabeth realized that the motorcycle was racing along a service road behind the theater. As they watched, it turned into the small parking lot where she and Jack stood.

"What the hell?" Jack took her arm and hauled her deeper into the darkness near the wall. "Don't move," he said in her ear.

She obeyed, standing very still in the circle of his arm.

The motorcycle flashed past the pool of shadows where they waited. The driver did not appear to notice them. He drove down the narrow alley on the right side of the building toward the entrance of the theater. The vehicle was not moving at a great speed, but the engine was revved to a loud, full-throated roar.

Once the motorcycle had gone safely past them, Elizabeth felt Jack release his hold on her. Together they stepped out into the alley to watch the bike zoom toward the street.

When the cyclist passed beneath the yellow bulb above the exit door, Elizabeth caught her breath. The pale light glinted malevolently on a black helmet that effectively concealed the driver's face. Metal studs gleamed on a black leather jacket and, very briefly, on the metal trim that decorated a familiar-looking black leather boot.

"Jack." She grabbed his arm and tugged him forward in the wake of the cycle. "It's the other guy who tried to beat you up the other night. Ollie, the one that got away in the van."

"How do you know?"

"His boots. Come on. Something's going to happen, and I bet it's going to involve Vicky."

He did not argue. Together they ran down the alley in pursuit of the motorcycle. Elizabeth silently cursed her high heels.

The cycle had reached the brightly lit front entrance of the theater. It slowed. Elizabeth saw the driver raise one hand. He was holding something in his gloved fist. A cylinder-shaped object.

At that moment Vicky Bellamy appeared. Her white and silver gown glowed in the brilliant marquee lights. Dawson was a short distance behind her, smiling proudly. He paused to speak to a man in a dark coat.

The driver of the motorcycle made a throwing motion with his arm. A stream of liquid arced through the air.

"Whore. Scarlet woman. Jezebel."

Vicky screamed, a high, cresting shriek of mingled anger and fear, as the red paint splashed across her gown.

"For God's sake, somebody stop him," Dawson shouted.

As if there were anything that anyone could do, Elizabeth thought. It had all happened too fast. The driver gunned the motorcycle's engine and careened off into the night. The crowd of theatergoers gazed, dumbfounded, after him.

Elizabeth limped to a halt beside Jack, breathing hard.

Vicky's voice rose to a theatrical wail above the murmurs and exclamations. "Dawson, look what he did. Why does he hate me? Why does he call me those terrible names?"

Dawson put his arm around her shoulders in an unmistakable protective movement. "I'm going to talk to the police again, my dear. There must be something they can do. Whoever he is, he's sick and he's dangerous. I'm afraid he's growing bolder."

JACK TOOK THE cognac bottle down out of the cupboard. He watched Elizabeth kick off her sadly scuffed high heels and flop lightly down on the sofa in front of the fire. The skirt of her slim black gown rode high on her thigh. It occurred to him that she had very pretty feet— elegantly arched and incredibly sexy, especially when sheathed in a pair of black hose.

And to think he'd never considered himself a foot man.

He heard a sharp clink and winced when he realized he'd struck the edge of one glass with the neck of the cognac bottle. *Clumsy.*

Out of the unholy mix of murky emotions that had been screwing up his thought processes lately, at last emerged one he knew that he could comprehend. It glowed like a homing beacon. Bright, obvious, riveting. That was the nice thing about sex. It wasn't complicated.

He allowed his eye to follow the long line of Elizabeth's neatly curved legs to the point where her thighs disappeared beneath the hem of her dress. He felt his blood heat.

She scowled at him as he finished pouring the cognac into two glasses. He remembered that she had berated him earlier for being in a surly mood. So much for sex not being complicated. He groaned softly. With Elizabeth, everything was complicated.

"There was something strange about what happened outside the theater tonight," she announced.

"There's something strange about this whole damn setup." He picked up the glasses and walked around the corner of the granite counter. "I feel like we're in one of those films where everything keeps turning out wrong and the characters get sucked deeper and deeper into a quagmire of disaster."

"I know what you mean." Her eyes traveled to the bound script lying on the coffee table. "Sort of like the plot for *Fast Company*. But I meant that there was something weird about Vicky's reaction tonight."

He stopped beside the sofa and handed her one of the glasses. "Why do you say that? Looked like a pretty straightforward publicity gimmick to me. Beautiful star victim of crazed fan."

"Her initial scream sounded genuine."

"She's an actress, remember?"

Elizabeth turned the glass of cognac in her hands, studying it. "The scream sounded for real. But a few seconds later, she sounded like an actress again. *Why does he hate me? Why does he do these things to me?* Kind of phony. And Dawson sounded even phonier when he talked about going to the cops again because the stalker was getting bolder."

Jack snorted. "I think it's a good bet that Holland has not gone to the police about the so-called stalker. If he had, good old Ollie would have been out of a job by now. He's not smart enough or fast enough to avoid getting caught."

"And if everyone's right about the stalker incidents being a publicity gimmick, Dawson wouldn't want to have the police looking too closely into the incidents anyway. But that's not my point."

Jack noticed that her brows were etched in a frown of deep concern. "You're worried that the stalker thing is part of Dawson's plan to get rid of a third wife, aren't you?"

Elizabeth twisted restlessly on the sofa. "It's just that I got the impression that Vicky wasn't expecting to have red paint thrown at her tonight. I wonder why not. After all, she must be involved in the planning of the stalker incidents. They'd have to be choreographed ahead of time, wouldn't they?"

"If you were after maximum publicity, yes."

"You know what?" She met his eyes across the top of the cognac glass. "I think something went wrong tonight. Vicky recovered fast, but I'd be willing to bet that she didn't expect the stalker to strike."

Jack thought back to the scene at the theater entrance. Holland folded protectively around his wife, warning everyone in earshot that the stalker was getting bolder. "Dawson expected it."

"Yes."

They looked at each other for a long moment. Jack exhaled slowly.

"You've warned Vicky. There's nothing more that you can do. And we could be wrong about Holland."

"I know." She sat up on the edge of the sofa and put the cognac glass down on the table. "There's something else that's worrying me. I still think that Tyler Page is madly, passionately in love with his femme fatale. What's going to happen when he discovers that Vicky doesn't intend to run off with him after the auction of Soft Focus? Because I sure can't see her throwing away everything for poor Dr. Page."

Jack groaned. "Please don't tell me that you're starting to worry about that little bastard. He's the one who created this mess, remember?"

Elizabeth's expression grew more troubled. "He's obviously a man of intense passions. Something tells me that he won't take Vicky's rejection well. Not after he's sacrificed so much for her. He could make himself . . . difficult."

"How?" Jack asked dryly. "By going to the cops? Not a chance. Like everyone else involved in this thing, he's not about to drag the police into it. He could end up in jail if this deal goes public."

"I can't help but think of Page as a victim of passion."

"Victim? The little shit stole Soft Focus." Jack set his glass down very forcefully on the mantel and left it there. He started across the room toward Elizabeth. "If you're going to feel sorry for anyone, feel sorry for us. If we don't find him and that damned crystal, Excalibur will go out of business, my professional reputation will be in the toilet, and the Aurora Fund will lose a hell of a lot of money."

"I'm very aware of the business and financial implications," she said stiffly. "That's not the issue."

"The hell it's not." He reached down, closed his hands around her shoulders, and pulled her to her feet. "This is no time to lose sight of the main objective."

"I know."

The anxiety in her eyes irritated him. "Do me a favor. Don't go all soft and sentimental about Tyler Page— or Vicky Bellamy, either, for that matter. Both of them can take care of themselves. They don't deserve your sympathy. You know something?"

"What?"

"You've got a bad habit of feeling sorry for people. Page, Vicky, your brother-in-law, Camille Galloway. Hayden. Hell, yesterday afternoon in the parking lot you felt sorry for me. Where does the list stop?"

Her chin came up fast. "It stops with you." She turned away from him with a sharp, angry movement. "I can see where you got the idea that I'm the world's easiest pushover. After all, I'm sleeping with you, aren't I?"

He stiffened. "That's got nothing to do with this."

"It has everything to do with it." She spun around, eyes alight with anger. "You think I'm a wimp or an idiot, or both."

"Damn it to hell, that's not true and you know it. *I just don't want to be on your feel-sorry-for list.*"

She blinked. For an instant he thought she was going to throw something at him. Then, quite suddenly, the fires of battle faded. He was not sure he liked the closed, speculative expression that took their place any better. Fires of battle he understood. This look was much more complicated and therefore much more dangerous.

She folded her arms. "If you don't think I'm a wimp or an idiot, what do you think?"

His blood chilled. What had gone wrong? He was losing control of the situation again. Why in hell did this kind of thing always happen whenever he tried to talk to her about something other than business? He groped for a way to get the conversation back on track.

"You once asked me what I would do if I failed to recover the crystal for Excalibur," he said.

"You told me that you would liquidate the company for the Ingersolls and track down Tyler Page."

"Right. I'm real clear on those two points. But what about us?"

She went very still in front of the fire. "Are you asking me if I'm interested in continuing our affair after whatever happens"—she waved a hand— "happens?"

"Yes." He watched her, aware that inside he was coiled so tightly he was afraid he might snap. "That's what I'm asking."

She did not take her eyes off the flames. "Don't you think it's a little too soon to be making any long-range decisions in that direction?"

Shit. Now what the hell was he supposed to say? He tried to plow forward, afraid that he was sinking deeper with each step. "What I think is that we're both attracted to each other. We've fought it for six months."

Her mouth twitched. "We haven't exactly been fighting it this past week."

"You've got to admit that what we've been doing for the past few days is pretty convincing evidence that we wasted a hell of a lot of time during the past six months."

She put one hand on the mantel. Her lipstick-red nails glowed like rubies in the flickering light. "You know something? I've been thinking about what's been happening between us since Soft Focus disappeared."

Hope ignited in him. He took a step toward her and then stopped. "Me too."

She contemplated him thoughtfully. "We've been thrown together under a highly abnormal set of circumstances. We're both under a lot of stress this week. We're two single, healthy people forced to share the same space. We're united in a mutual goal."

"I'm probably going to hate myself for asking, but just where are you going with this?"

She began to tap her nails against the mantel. "I'm saying that, what with everything that's happened during the past few days, it's quite possible that we have both experienced an artificial sense of bonding."

"Is that what you call it? Bonding?"

She pursed her lips. "It seems obvious to me that sex may be our bodies' natural way of relieving the tension in what is, after all, a highly unnatural situation."

"There is nothing unnatural about it." His jaw tensed. "Or artificial, either, for that matter."

"I don't think we should read too much into what's been going on between us during the past few days."

"You're calling this a one-week stand?"

"What else can we call it?" She swung around to face him. "Don't you understand? We won't really know how we feel about each other until we're back in Seattle. We need to try having a normal relationship before we can decide what this is all about. It's possible that what's happened between us here in Mirror Springs is just one of those things."

The fierceness that had been gnawing at his insides all evening welled up once more. He took another step toward her. "I already know that I want us to continue sleeping together after we return to whatever passes for a normal life back in Seattle."

"I think we should go very slowly here. Neither of us should put pressure on the other."

"Why the hell not?"

She eyed him with an unreadable expression. "Well, for one thing, I've got a rather poor track record when it comes to choosing the right man."

"I knew it. You don't trust your feelings for me." He smiled slowly. "Who would have thought that the Ice Princess would be such a coward?"

Anger flared in her eyes. "Don't you dare call me a coward just because I want to make sure that this whole affair amounts to something more than a one-week stand."

He gathered her into his arms. "What are you afraid of, Elizabeth?"

"I'm not afraid of anything." She put her hands on his shoulders, holding herself away from him. "I just don't intend to make any more mistakes where you're concerned."

"For six months we've been stuck together like a couple of staples in a jammed stapler."

"Oh, that's a romantic image."

He ignored her. "Now we're sleeping together, which, for my money, is a lot more comfortable. What's wrong with this picture?"

"Nothing, as far as this week goes," she shot back. "It's comfortable, all right. But I refuse to be pushed into making a sweeping decision about what will happen when this business with Soft Focus is finished. I don't want to go too far out on a limb."

"When are you going to realize that we've already gone too far out on this branch? You can't turn back now any more than I can."

She opened her mouth. He realized she was going to continue to argue. He also knew that he was out of words. He kissed her quickly, swallowing her indignant protest with a kiss.

She made a muffled, exasperated sound.

"Okay, okay," he muttered against her mouth. "No commitments beyond this week. I'll take what I can get and shut up."

She tilted her head back against his arm. "Will you really? Shut up about it, I mean?"

"It might be a one-week stand, but it's the best week I've

had in six months, even if I have lost my client's only tangible business asset and very possibly my own career." He lowered the zipper of her gown to her waist. "Which only goes to show how miserable the last six months have been."

"A COUPLE OF jammed staples?" she mumbled a long time later.

"I'm a CEO, not a scriptwriter."

CHAPTER TWENTY-THREE

SHE STILL DIDN'T TRUST HIM. OR MAYBE SHE just didn't trust herself. Either way, the result was the same. He had a problem.

Jack punched up the pillow behind his head so that he could study the dull glow of a cloudy mountain dawn. Beside him, Elizabeth slept soundly, the sweet, lush curve of her derriere settled against his hip. He had called her a coward, but he knew the truth. The tension between them was all his fault, not hers. He had really pissed in his chili six months ago.

The bottom line was that he'd gotten exactly what he'd told himself he wanted: a second chance with Elizabeth in his bed.

Be careful what you wish for . . .

She was willing to have an affair, or at least a one-week fling, but she was not about to commit to anything more. Not yet, at any rate. He had a sudden vision of finding himself back in Seattle and discovering that she intended to see other men while she waited to find out exactly how she felt about him.

The bleak mood that had crowded in on him during those rare hours when he had not been working during the past six months threatened to settle on him again. But this time he could not escape to the dojo. This time his problem was lying right here beside him.

Somehow he had to make her see that what they had was worth working on—worth a commitment.

He tried to step back mentally and view the situation the way he would any other kind of business problem. He needed a strategy. He was usually pretty good at strategies.

The phone rang, cutting into his swirling thoughts. It was the house phone, he realized. Not his cell phone. Elizabeth stirred beside him as he groped for the receiver.

"Fairfax here."

"I'm calling for Elizabeth Cabot."

For a split second he didn't recognize the low, sultry voice. Then it hit him. He sat up suddenly. "Vicky Bellamy?"

There was a slight pause before she said, "May I please speak with Elizabeth?"

"Sure. Right." He shook Elizabeth gently. "For you."

She opened her eyes and yawned. "Who is it?"

He put his hand over the mouthpiece. "Vicky Bellamy."

She snatched the phone from him.

"This is Elizabeth."

Jack listened intently to the silence while Elizabeth listened to Vicky. He saw her expression change from surprise to cool and shuttered.

"I can handle it," she said crisply. "I'm really not as naïve as everyone seems to think. Why did you call?"

More silence.

"I understand." Elizabeth turned toward Jack. "I can promise you that he won't."

Another pause.

"Yes, of course. I'll be there." Elizabeth gave the phone back to Jack.

He tossed it down onto the end table. "What did she want?"

Elizabeth sat up amid the tumbled sheets and wrapped her arms around her updrawn knees. "She wants to talk. Privately. She doesn't want Dawson to find out that she's meeting with me."

Anticipation pumped through him. "How the hell is she going to arrange that?"

"She's got it all figured out," Elizabeth said thoughtfully. "I got the impression that she spent a lot of time planning this before she called me. I wonder why."

"Should be interesting." Energized by the new turn of events, he threw back the covers and got to his feet. Then he remembered something. "What did she say to you when you first took the phone?"

"Hmm?" Elizabeth sounded distracted as she reached for her robe.

"Your answer was 'I can handle it.' What was the question?"

"Nothing important." Elizabeth tied the sash. She did not look back at him as she walked toward the bathroom. "She just asked me if I knew what I was doing sleeping with you."

She disappeared into the bathroom. Jack looked at the closed door for a long moment. *I can handle it.*

THE ONLY LIGHTS in the empty interior of the Silver Empire Theater were the dimly glowing fixtures located at the ends of the aisles. The details of the ornate ceiling were lost in the darkness overhead. The rows of velvet seats marched down the sloping floor, a regiment of hulking, headless robots frozen in formation. Steeped in the thick gloom, the heavy crimson curtains appeared as dark as midnight. The thick folds of velvet were drawn closed across the stage, concealing the screen.

"It's a different world when there's no crowd and nothing happening on the screen, isn't it?" Vicky said from somewhere in the darkness.

Elizabeth, poised at the top of one aisle, started slightly at the sound of the other woman's voice. She peered into the depths of the theater, willing her eyes to adjust quickly to the dim light.

"Just isn't the same without the smell of popcorn," she said.

"That can be faked, too, just like everything else in the movies." Vicky rose languidly from an end seat. The pale, smoke-colored pantsuit she wore gave her a ghostly look. "Remember what I told you, Elizabeth. In the movies and in life, things are seldom what they seem."

"It's the same way with business." Elizabeth started slowly down the aisle. "But I assume you didn't ask me to meet you here just to trade philosophical observations on our respective careers."

"No, I didn't." Vicky smiled slightly. "I understand that the Aurora Fund has an old tradition of underwriting business ventures launched by women."

"The Fund has branched out in recent years, but you're right. Aunt Sybil started it with the goal of helping entrepreneurial women get financial backing when they couldn't secure it from other sources." Elizabeth halted when she was two rows away from Vicky. "Did you call me because you want to request funding for a business venture?"

"Something along those lines, yes. I'm changing careers. I'm getting out of the film business."

"I have to say, I'm surprised."

"It's time to move on. I know that better than anyone.

Whatever chance I had came and went years ago. I'm too old for Hollywood now, and I've decided I've had enough of the independent film industry."

"You're just going to walk away from your acting?"

"Not bloody likely." Vicky gave a short, harsh laugh. "I've acted all my life. It's the only thing I know how to do. But I won't be doing it in front of a camera anymore. *Fast Company* will be my last film."

"I see. And you want the Aurora Fund to underwrite your new career?"

"Not entirely. Just some of the initial start-up expenses. I've always known this day might come." Vicky hesitated. "I just didn't expect it to come quite so soon. I thought I'd have a little more time."

A chill went through Elizabeth. She tried and failed to read Vicky's face in the darkness. "What are you going to do?"

"I'm going to disappear."

Elizabeth felt her jaw unhinge. "Disappear? For heaven's sake, why?"

"It's time." Vicky gazed out over the rows of velvet seats. "In the old days they used to call women like me adventuresses, you know."

"I've heard the term."

"It was a euphemism, of course. What people really meant was that we used sex to get what we wanted. They said that we lured men into our webs and manipulated them as if they were stupid, mindless creatures who thought only with their balls."

"Femme fatales."

"Yes. Nice work if you can get it, hmm?" Vicky's eyes were ice cold. "But I can tell you from experience that it isn't as easy as it sounds. For starters, you have to be able to act big time. I mean, you've got to be *good*. Academy Award good."

Elizabeth nodded. "I can see where it would be difficult to live a lie twenty-four hours a day."

"The hard part is not letting your so-called victim know that what you really want to do is run into the bathroom and throw up every time you have sex with him."

"Yes, I can see that would put a strain on a relationship. You were saying something about disappearing."

"I've got good survival instincts," Vicky said. "For the past few months they've been telling me that it was time to move on. I should have done it by now, and I would have if it hadn't been for *Fast Company*. I knew it would be my last film. I wanted to see how it would go over in the independent film circuit. But after last night, I knew I couldn't wait any longer. I've pushed my luck as far as it will go."

"Last night? You mean the red paint incident after the awards ceremony? I thought that was just a publicity stunt. Are you telling me that the stalker is for real?"

"The stalker thing was Dawson's idea. He thought it would help grab some publicity for me during the festival. But last night's assault was not on my schedule. I have a feeling that there may be more incidents like that. One of them will go too far."

"My God." Elizabeth stared at her. "Do you think some nutcase has decided to stalk you for real?"

"Nutcase." Vicky sounded briefly amused. "I wonder if—" She broke off with a shrug. "Doesn't matter, I guess."

"What's going on here, Vicky?"

Vicky seemed to collect herself. She was abruptly all business. "Dawson handles my publicity. As I said, he came up with the stalker concept. He scripted all the incidents. Hired an out-of-work stuntman to carry them out."

"A hulking type named Ollie. Wears black leather boots with metal trim on the heels, right?"

"You know about him?" Vicky's eyes narrowed.

"We had a run-in with him and his pal on the road the other night. They said they had been sent to deliver a warning. We figured it came from Dawson."

"And you ignored it." Vicky chuckled. "Ollie told Dawson that the warning had been delivered. But obviously that was not the whole story. Not if you managed to learn his name. Dawson would not be pleased if he knew that there had been a screwup."

"You said last night's stalker incident was not on your schedule?"

Vicky's full mouth tightened. "Dawson arranged the assault, as usual. But he didn't bother to tell me about it until afterward."

"Why not?"

"He claims that I was getting blasé about the stalker. He said that my reactions were not believable. He thought my acting would improve if I was taken by surprise."

Elizabeth grimaced. "Some surprise. I can imagine how you must have felt when that jerk threw the paint."

"I like to think I rose to the occasion," Vicky said dryly. "But I was furious with Dawson for not warning me. He had promised me that there wouldn't be any more incidents. It was only later that I thought about what you said to me the other day in the spa. I did some checking, and now I'm starting to wonder if Dawson has rewritten the script. Maybe given it a different ending."

Elizabeth drew a deep breath. "Holland did take out a policy on you, didn't he?"

"Yes." Vicky's voice was clipped and emotionless. "A business policy. Taken out by the Holland Group. But Dawson is the Holland Group. After you and I spoke, I went on the Internet. Did some research. Found out that you were right about the deaths of his first two wives. There were rumors and questions, even though Dawson was never officially under suspicion."

"And after last night, you no longer trust him, is that it?"

Vicky laughed softly, harshly. "I don't trust any man. Professional suicide for an adventuress. "

"I suppose so."

"I've made my decision. I'm getting out. But it's not going to be simple. Lately Dawson has been acting increasingly possessive. He rarely lets me out of his sight. Right now, for instance, he thinks I'm in the spa. It was the only excuse I could come up with that would allow me to get away from him long enough to see you in private."

"What do you want from me?"

"I'm going to make you a business proposition," Vicky said. "Think of it as an application to the Aurora Fund."

"I'm listening."

"I've got some information to sell."

Elizabeth held her breath. "What kind of information?"

"Call it deep background concerning the provenance of a certain item that is scheduled to go up for auction soon."

Elizabeth reminded herself to breathe. "Go ahead."

Vicky gave her a cool, knowing look. "I'll tell you everything I know about Dawson's other business here in Mirror Springs. I admit it's not a lot. But you and your friend, Jack Fairfax, might find some of it helpful. At the very least, you won't be going into the auction unprepared."

"You think we should be prepared?"

Vicky smiled grimly. "If you plan to go up against Dawson Holland, yes, I think you should be prepared. I don't know what it is that's being auctioned off, but I can tell you that Dawson will do whatever is necessary to get his hands on it."

"Because he needs the money?"

"Not the money. He needs the item itself, whatever it is, to get himself out of some very deep manure."

One could never have too much information before one went into a business negotiation, Elizabeth told herself. "How much do you want from the Aurora Fund to finance your midcourse career change?"

"Don't worry, I'm not going to soak you." Vicky's mouth twisted. "I've got enough in ready cash in my purse to get to Florida. But I'll need a little help after that."

"Good grief, you're planning to leave the *country*?"

"I've learned a lot in my career as an adventuress," Vicky said. "One of the things I've learned is how and where to purchase a new identity. But it will cost me."

"You think it's necessary to hide under a different identity?"

Vicky closed her eyes for a few seconds. Then she opened them and looked straight at Elizabeth. "Let's just say that as long as that insurance policy exists, I'd rather not have Dawson find me."

"I see your point. You want the Aurora Fund to help you finance this new identity, is that it?"

"Think of it as an investment."

Elizabeth pondered the offer for all of two seconds. It really was a no-brainer. "Okay, it's a deal. Tell me what you know about Dawson's business here in Mirror Springs."

"Mostly what I know is that he's desperate," Vicky said bluntly. "And that makes him dangerous. Several months ago he scammed a rather unpleasant group of offshore investors. These are not the kind of people who take you to court to get their money back, if you see what I mean."

Elizabeth shivered. "I see."

"Dawson has never discussed the situation with me, and I've certainly never let him know that I'm aware of his problems. But I think he bought some time for himself by promising to turn over something very valuable in the high-tech field. And I'm almost positive that whatever is going down is supposed to be concluded here in Mirror Springs this week."

"Speaking of warnings," Elizabeth said, "can I assume that the ones Ollie was supposed to deliver to Jack and Hayden came from Dawson, not you?"

"I certainly didn't send Ollie out to deliver any warnings to anyone."

"What about the videotape in Leonard Ledger's hotel room?"

Vicky looked mildly curious. "What videotape?"

"Never mind." That must have come from Dawson, too. An attempt to sow dissension among his competitors. "What do you know about Tyler Page?"

"Other than the fact that he loves film, very little." Vicky met her eyes. "But I do know that Dawson has been looking for him since we got here."

Elizabeth tensed. "Has he found him?"

"No. I assume that Page is the one who stole this piece of high-tech hardware that everyone seems to want?"

"Yes." Elizabeth frowned. "Are you telling me that Holland didn't ask you to seduce Page into stealing it?"

Vicky laughed. She sounded genuinely amused for the first time. "No. I told you, Dawson did not involve me in this thing. I met Page on the set a few times, but all we talked about was *Fast Company.* That was the extent of my relationship with him."

"Is there any possibility that he thinks he stole Soft Focus for your sake?"

"If you're asking me if he had a crush on me, the answer is no."

"You're sure?"

Vicky looked amused. "Trust me, Elizabeth, I know when a man is interested and when he's not. Page was not."

"Damn." So much for her theory about Vicky's being Tyler Page's femme fatale. "Does the name Ryan Kendle mean anything to you?"

"No." Vicky paused. "Should it?"

"I don't know," Elizabeth admitted. "Do you know anything about the trashing of an Excalibur lab?"

"No."

"Guess that's about it," Elizabeth said. "When do you want your money and how do you want it?"

"I've written down the number of a bank account in Florida, and the amount I'll require. Have the money wired into it as soon as you've heard that I've disappeared."

Elizabeth stared at her as she took a folded piece of paper from Vicky. "There's going to be an announcement?"

Vicky chuckled. "I certainly hope so. Pay attention. When you hear about it, just remember what I told you, nothing is ever what it seems in the movies."

"All right." Elizabeth hesitated. "Just one more question."

"Make it quick. I've got to get back to the spa."

"Why did you try to warn me off that night outside the club?"

"Once every decade or so I get this irrational, overwhelming impulse to do a good deed. Just for the hell of it."

"Thoughtful of you," Elizabeth said.

"I should have saved my energy this time. You didn't take advantage of my gentle hint to go back to Seattle, did you? Maybe next decade I'll resist the impulse."

"SHE'S AN ACTRESS, Elizabeth," Jack said. "What makes you think Holland didn't tell her to feed you that entire story?"

Elizabeth shot him a quelling look, silently warning him to keep his voice down.

Not that there was much chance anyone had overheard him, she assured herself. There was only a handful of people browsing through the display of classic film posters in the gallery, and most of them were at the far end of the long room.

She turned back to study the framed poster on the wall in front of her. The creases where it had once been machine folded were still visible. The title, *The Woman in the Window,* was written in lurid yellow script under an image of the stars, Edward G. Robinson and Joan Bennett.

A single glance at the array of noir artwork displayed for sale made it obvious that bright, shrieking yellow ink had been extremely popular with the artists who had produced the posters and lobby cards used to hype the old films. The other dominant colors were bloodred, midnight blue, and black. The heavily saturated hues together with the gritty, suspenseful images combined to give the classic posters their unique look. Guns, dangerous-looking women, and men with 1940s-era hats pulled down low over their cold eyes figured as the most prominent motifs. The prices on the little placards next to the framed pictures indicated that they were pricey collectibles.

Ten minutes after leaving the theater, Elizabeth had found Jack waiting for her in an espresso bar. She had hurriedly dragged him into the gallery to tell him about the interview with Vicky. He had listened, but it was clear he was not entirely convinced.

She glared at him, exasperated. "Why would Dawson tell Vicky to give me so many details about his business dealings? From the sound of it, he's coloring outside the lines."

"Just another tactic designed to try to scare us off," Jack

said patiently. "All this stuff about dangerous offshore investors who are threatening his life, et cetera, et cetera, is a little hard to take."

"What about Vicky's plans to disappear?"

"Probably a scam to con some money out of you."

"She was telling the truth, Jack. I could feel it."

He frowned. "Look, all I'm saying is that we can't trust Vicky Bellamy any further than we can trust Dawson Holland. She's the kind of woman who's always got an angle. From what you've just told me, I'd say she's trying to make a little extra cash for herself on the side."

Elizabeth nibbled on her lower lip. "You really think she's trying to scam me?"

"Uh-huh." Jack turned his attention back to Robert Mitchum's grim, world-weary face in a poster for *Out of the Past*. "That's exactly what I think."

"I don't know." Elizabeth moved on to the image of Rita Hayworth posed in sultry invitation against a yellow backdrop in a title card for *The Lady from Shanghai*. "I think she's planning to split."

"She's planning to separate you from some of your money."

"Don't be so negative. Everything she told me about the stalker incidents and those warnings you and Hayden got from Ollie adds up, doesn't it?"

"So what? She and Dawson have probably guessed that we've already figured most of that stuff out for ourselves. And even if she is on the level, you'll notice that she didn't give you any hard information that we can use to find Tyler Page and the crystal."

"That's because she doesn't know where they are." Elizabeth drummed her fingers on the strap of her shoulder bag. "There's only one thing that doesn't quite fit."

"Your idea that she was Page's femme fatale?"

"Yes." Elizabeth gazed at a framed lobby card for *The Big Sleep*. The chemistry between Bogart and Bacall was unmistakable, even in a simple ad for the film. "I was so sure—"

"Look on the bright side," Jack said. "If I'm right about not being able to trust her, your theory that she seduced Page into stealing the crystal remains intact."

"But I do believe her. Which means that there was no woman involved in this, after all." She thought about the report that Ryan Kendle had been overheard arguing with a woman shortly before his death. "Scratch the Kendle connection."

"It was always a damn weak link anyway," Jack reminded her. "The police were sure from the start that he was killed in a drug deal. But I have a hunch that the trashing of the lab is a solid connection. Page probably thought he could muddy the waters that way, just in case I did go to the cops."

"Vicky didn't know anything about that, either."

"Why am I not surprised?"

Elizabeth gazed pensively at Veronica Lake in *This Gun for Hire*. The uneasiness she had been feeling ever since she had left the theater was getting worse. "Well, one thing's for certain. We should get some answers soon."

"What do you mean?"

"If Vicky suddenly disappears, we'll know that she was telling us the truth about her own plans to make a new life for herself."

"Financed by the Aurora Fund," Jack said dryly. "Now, that I can believe."

"Why would you buy that part of her story?"

"Because according to Larry, Holland is really on the rocks again financially. Even if she wasn't afraid that he might be thinking of cashing in the insurance policy he has on her, Vicky would be looking for greener pastures."

THE DISTANT, MUFFLED sound of thunder brought Elizabeth awake with a suddenness that left her tingling from head to toe. She sat straight up in bed and blinked at the gray dawn scene outside the window. It took a few seconds for her dream-drenched brain to register the fact that there was no storm.

Jack was already out of bed, padding toward the windows.

"What is it?" she asked.

"Sounded like an explosion of some kind. I can't see anything from this angle." He turned, stepped into a pair of khakis, and headed for the stairs.

Elizabeth scrambled out of bed, seized her robe, and hurried after him. She caught up with him as he opened the downstairs slider and stepped out onto the deck. She winced as her bare feet came in contact with the cold, dew-dampened wood.

"There." Jack pointed toward a plume of smoke that rose skyward in the distance.

She strained to see it. "What on earth?"

"I'm not sure, but from the looks of it, I'd say a car just went off the road into the canyon. It must have gone up in flames. Now the scrub is on fire."

"Oh, my God," she whispered.

Sirens sounded in the distance.

Jack put his arm around her. Together they watched the smoke spiral upward into the dawn.

Elizabeth felt the prickle of tiny goose bumps on her arms. She hugged herself to chase away the chill. It didn't work.

"You okay?" Jack asked quietly.

"Yes." But the prickling sensation did not vanish.

After a while they turned silently and went back indoors. The house was so cold that Jack switched on the gas fire.

AN HOUR LATER, showered and dressed, Elizabeth paused in the act of slicing some bananas for breakfast and turned on the radio to catch the local news. The local announcer, probably more accustomed to giving ski-condition reports, sounded shaken.

> "... *The brush fire caused by the explosion was brought under control almost immediately. Chief Gresham stated that the victim had apparently been thrown from the car and had been swept downstream. A search is under way, but the authorities warn that it will not be easy, given the force of the water in that section of the canyon.*
>
> *"The vehicle has been identified as a white Porsche registered to Victoria Bellamy. Ms. Bellamy has reportedly been stalked in recent weeks by a ..."*

Elizabeth snapped off the radio and sat down hard on one of the counter stools. She stared blankly at the knife in her hand.

"*Jack.*"

"Right here." He came down the stairs, buttoning his shirt. His hair was still damp from the shower. "What's wrong?"

"I just heard the news. The car that went into the canyon is Vicky's Porsche. There's a search under way for her body. They think she was thrown into the river."

He halted on the last step. "Are you sure?"

"I'm sure."

"Interesting." He crossed the room and took the stool

beside her. "You think she really did it? Pulled off a disappearing act?"

"Either that or Holland killed her," Elizabeth said. "Maybe she waited too long. She said she knew that she had been pushing her luck."

Jack looked thoughtful. "I don't think he killed her."

"Why not? It's the same kind of accident that happened to his first two wives."

"Which is why I don't think he's responsible. Holland is smart. He has to know that, given the questions raised by the insurance company last time, there would be a lot of suspicion centered on him if a third wife died under similar circumstances. The last thing he wants right now is to have the police hanging around asking questions about Vicky's death."

Elizabeth's spirits lifted. "You're right. He doesn't want them in the way while he's trying to find Soft Focus."

"There's another point, too. If he had murdered her, he would probably have made it look like an assault by the stalker. Everything was in place for that kind of ending to the story. All he needed to do was throw a little red paint on the car."

"There was no mention of red paint in the newscast." Elizabeth was feeling almost euphoric with relief now. "Jack, you're brilliant."

He smiled faintly. "Your good buddy, Vicky, may have done us a very big favor on her way out the door."

"What do you mean?"

"If she did arrange her own accident, she picked the one surefire way of making certain that Dawson would fall under immediate suspicion. If he's dealing with the cops right now, he's going to have a hard time attending an illegal auction."

"She told me to remember that nothing is ever what it

seems in the movies or in real life." Elizabeth smiled. She hopped down off the stool and grabbed the phone. "Excuse me, gotta make a call to Louise."

Jack swung slowly around on the stool, watching her as she punched out the number. "You're going to transfer the money into that account in Miami, aren't you?"

"Yes, I am."

"Damn. I was afraid of that. It's a scam, Elizabeth."

"It's a bargain. And a deal's a deal." She eyed him as she waited for Louise to answer the phone. "I would think that you, of all people, would understand that, Jack. You're the one who wouldn't let me out of the Excalibur contract, remember? Not even after I poured ice water all over you in front of God and everyone in the Pacific Rim Club."

CHAPTER TWENTY-FOUR

"SHE TOOK EXCELLENT CARE OF HER BODY, I'LL say that for her." The masseuse bore down on Elizabeth's shoulders with the heels of her strong hands. "Most people come in here hoping that a soak in the hot pools and a massage will instantly bring back muscle tone and energy. They walk out the door and head straight back to their recliners and their remotes. But not Ms. Bellamy. She worked out every day and watched her diet."

The masseuse poured more warm oil on her hands. Elizabeth stifled a groan as the woman went to work on her lower back. She had made the appointment at the spa with the idea of picking up some local gossip. But shortly after stretching out on the table, she had decided that she really did need the massage. She had certainly been somewhat tense lately.

"Were you her regular masseuse?" Elizabeth asked.

"Yes. She always asked for me when she was in town." The woman sighed. "Hard to believe she's dead."

"Maybe she's not dead," Elizabeth said cautiously. "I hear that they still haven't found the body."

"It can take a while to recover a body that gets washed downriver. "

"A terrible accident."

"Well, now." The masseuse lowered her voice to a confidential tone as she began a vigorous kneading motion. "My friend, Ethel, works as a dispatcher at the station. She says that Chief Gresham isn't so sure it was an accident."

"Good heavens." Elizabeth exhaled sharply as the masseuse intensified the pressure. "Do they think the stalker got her?"

"Between you and me, there wasn't any stalker. Ms. Bellamy told me that in confidence one day. Said it was just a publicity stunt. Chief Gresham is no fool. Ethel says he guessed that it was just a PR thing. Holland never filed a complaint."

"What does Chief Gresham think happened?"

"I couldn't say for sure." The masseuse pummeled Elizabeth's buttocks. "But Ethel says he's looking for Dawson Holland as we speak. Wants to ask him a few questions. Apparently Holland's first two wives died in similar accidents."

Elizabeth sagged beneath pounding fists. She buried her face in the little opening provided in the massage table and tried to breathe. "What do you mean, Gresham's looking for Holland? Everyone knows where he lives here in Mirror Springs."

"Didn't you hear? Dawson Holland's housekeeper, Mary Beth, says that Chief Gresham went to the house early this morning to notify Holland of his wife's death. When he went back a couple of hours later to ask him some questions, the place was empty. Looked like Dawson had packed up all of his personal stuff and left town."

FORTY-FIVE MINUTES later, Elizabeth slithered languidly into the espresso shop booth and smiled benignly at

Jack. She set the pot of herbal tea and the cup she had picked up at the counter in front of her.

"What's the matter with you?" he asked. "You're glowing a weird pink color."

"Just finished my massage and a soak in the hot spring pools at the spa. You know, I really ought to do that kind of stuff more often. Very relaxing. And informative."

He glanced at the tea as she poured some into the cup. "There's no caffeine in that."

"Nope. Don't want any. It would spoil the afterglow."

He settled back into his seat. "What did you learn?"

"For starters, Dawson Holland has disappeared. Chief Gresham has notified the authorities between here and Denver to watch for his car."

"Yeah, I got that much just sitting here waiting for you. In fact, I'm a step ahead of the spa gossip. The kid at the counter says it's all over town that a man who fits Holland's description got on a plane in Denver late this morning."

"Why are the local cops suddenly so concerned? Gresham jumped on this kind of quick, didn't he?"

Jack smiled faintly. "Word has it that someone phoned in a tip to the police shortly after Vicky's Porsche went off the road. Suggested that the authorities should ask Holland where he was when the accident occurred and take a look at how his previous two wives died."

"I'll bet it was Vicky," Elizabeth said.

"I'll bet you're right."

Elizabeth sipped her herbal blend. "Did Larry get a chance to check that account in Miami?"

"I talked to him just before you got here. So far the money is still sitting there."

"She probably took an indirect route to Miami to hide her

tracks. Lots of layovers. Weather en route. Could be several reasons why she hasn't picked up her money yet."

He hesitated, not wanting to destroy her bubble of confidence. "There's another reason why Vicky might not have collected her money. She might be dead."

Some of Elizabeth's warm, rosy glow dimmed. "If that's true, we'll have to talk to the cops. Tell them what we know."

He thought about that for a moment and then shook his head. "Maybe. But not yet. Chief Gresham is already looking for Holland. Let's give Vicky a few more hours to pick up her money and get out of the country."

Elizabeth looked at him over the rim of her cup. "Any way you look at this, one thing's for sure. With Holland gone, the auction is going to be a very small event. Unless there's someone in the picture we don't know about yet, Tyler Page is left with only two bidders. You and Hayden."

THE PHONE RANG at seven-fifteen that evening. Hayden jumped at the sound. He was mildly surprised to realize that night had fallen. He had been sitting in the dark for some time now. Ever since he had finished talking to Larry.

"Hello?"

"The auction will take place at nine o'clock tonight. I will give you the address. No late bidders will be seated."

The click of the hangup was painful in his ear. Hayden slowly lowered the phone. He sat in the gloom of the hotel room for a few more minutes, thinking. Then he picked up the phone again and punched out a number.

THE CELL PHONE sounded just as Jack eased the car into a parking slot in the lot across the street from the Silver Empire Theater. Elizabeth whipped around in the seat, her eyes wide with excitement.

"Jack?"

"Take it easy." He switched off the engine and reached for the phone. "Could be anyone. A lot of people have this number." He spoke into the instrument. "This is Fairfax."

"I just got my summons to the auction," Hayden said.

Jack tightened one hand on the wheel and looked at the bright lights of the Silver Empire. The world premiere of *Fast Company* was scheduled to begin at eight-thirty. Elizabeth had insisted on arriving early to watch for Tyler Page.

"Why are you telling me?" Jack asked.

Hayden did not answer that. "Did you get the call?"

"No."

"Place out on Loop Road, about thirty minutes away. Nine o'clock."

"One more time. Why are you telling me this?"

"Wouldn't want you to miss the auction. Not every day a man gets a chance to buy back his own property."

Hayden hung up.

Jack slowly lowered the phone. Elizabeth watched him from the other side of the car.

"What's going on?" she asked.

"Hayden got the call from Page. The auction's scheduled for nine this evening. A place out on Loop Road. About a thirty-minute drive, Hayden said."

"So why haven't you gotten a call?"

"Beats me. Can't hold much of an auction without bidders to drive up the price." Absently he tapped the cell phone against the backseat. He studied the bright lights of the theater marquee. "*Fast Company* starts in half an hour."

"Yes, I know. Forget about my plan to watch for Page. Obviously he won't be in the audience. He'll be conducting the auction."

Jack turned his head to look at her. "Doesn't it strike you

as strange that, after everything he put into it, Tyler Page would be willing to miss the premiere of his film?"

For a second or two, Elizabeth said nothing. Then her eyes widened. "What are you thinking?" she asked.

"That maybe you were right all along. Maybe there is a femme fatale in this script."

HAYDEN OPENED THE door, saw Jack and Elizabeth standing in the hall, and glowered. "What the hell is this all about?"

"Just thought we'd stop by and pick you up for the auction," Jack said. "We're both going to the same place. Might as well use one car. Think of it as a little brotherly togetherness after all these years."

"Screw you."

"Actually, I think we are both about to get royally screwed," Jack said. "Want to talk about an alternative?"

Hayden turned away, but not before Elizabeth glimpsed the weary pain in his eyes.

"No," he said.

"You're not real good with the big-picture thing, are you?" Jack asked. "How the hell did you ever get to be a big-time CEO?"

"Is this conversation going anywhere? If not, I've got plans for the evening."

"Yeah, I know, you're going to attend an auction."

"As a matter of fact, I thought I'd take in a film instead."

Elizabeth stared at him. "What do you mean?"

"I've decided not to bid on Soft Focus." Hayden threw himself down into one of the chairs and looked at Jack with hooded eyes. "It's all yours, brother. Good luck. Not that you should have too much trouble getting it. With Holland and me both out of the running, I doubt you'll face any competition."

Jack closed the door very deliberately. "What made you decide to take yourself out of the bidding?"

Elizabeth smiled slowly. "You called Larry, didn't you? Got the other side of the story."

Hayden gave a massively indifferent shrug. "Odds are, the specimen won't work, anyway. Might as well save my money."

Jack glanced at Elizabeth and then turned to Hayden. "What is this?"

"Hayden is telling you, in his own fashion, that he's changed his mind. He's not going to go after Soft Focus in order to get a little revenge."

Jack looked at Hayden as if he were some odd, new carbon life-form that had just stepped off a spaceship.

Hayden gave another elaborate shrug. "Like I said, Soft Focus probably isn't worth what it would cost me to keep it out of your hands. And it's not like I can use the damn thing myself. Hell, I'm still not real clear on what it's supposed to be able to do. Page, or whoever called me, never went into technical details."

Elizabeth gave him an approving smile. "It's all right, Hayden. You don't have to play Mr. Tough Guy. We all know you're doing this because you've come to realize that taking your revenge against Jack won't change the past. He's not to blame for what happened between your parents. You know he's innocent."

Hayden grunted. "There's nothing innocent about Jack. But you're right. Screwing with his business reputation won't change anything. I'm going home in the morning. I've wasted enough time here in Mirror Springs."

Jack eyed him thoughtfully. "I think someone is going to be very disappointed if you don't show up at the auction tonight."

"Tyler Page?" Hayden gave a short, humorless laugh. "My advice is, don't give him a dime for Soft Focus. Beat it out of the creep. He stole it from you in the first place, didn't he?"

"I don't think Tyler Page is the one who will be waiting for you out on Loop Road," Jack said. He took his cell phone out of his pocket.

Elizabeth glanced at him. "What are you doing?"

"I think it's time we called in the cops."

THE ISOLATED CABIN off Loop Road was a single-room, one-story log structure. It had the neglected look of a house that has been abandoned for years. In the headlights, Jack could see that the railing on the steps that led to the front door had been broken long ago. Weeds grew wildly in a yard.

A stone fireplace formed one wall, but there was no sign of a fire or any other kind of warmth or light visible through the single front window.

"This is the old Kramer place," Chief Gresham said as he got out of his patrol car. "No one's used it in years." He flicked on his flashlight and gave Jack and Hayden a sour look. "I don't see anyone around. Are you sure about this?"

"No," Jack admitted. He shoved his hands into the pockets of his jacket and looked at the unlit house. "But I couldn't think of any other explanation that fit the facts."

"You should have contacted the authorities right at the start of this thing," Gresham muttered. He started toward the front steps. "Damn corporate suits. Always think you can handle things better than the cops."

Jack looked at Hayden and Elizabeth as they got out of the car beside him. Elizabeth shrugged. Hayden raised his brows but said nothing.

They trekked behind Gresham to the front door. The

police chief was a small, wiry man with an aura of competence and command. He might be a small-town cop, Jack thought, but he knew his business.

Gresham had not been thrilled when he had been summoned from home to listen to Jack's version of recent events. But he had not wasted any time taking charge of the situation, either.

Gresham knocked on the front door of the cottage with the butt of the flashlight.

There was no response.

Jack stood with Hayden and Elizabeth. They watched Gresham knock a second time.

"I still think you figured this wrong," Hayden said quietly.

"I hope I did," Jack said.

Gresham gave up knocking and went to the grimy window. He aimed the flashlight into the darkened interior.

"Well, hell," Gresham said softly. "I did not need this."

He went back to the door and turned the knob. The door swung inward. The beam of Gresham's flashlight sliced into the small, dark room.

The light glanced across an outflung hand that lay, palm up, on the floor. Then it skimmed over blond hair that had been stained red with blood. The smell of death was heavy in the air. The woman's forehead had been partially destroyed by the bullet, but there was no doubt about her identity.

Elizabeth gave a muffled cry, put her hand to her mouth, and turned quickly away from the gory scene. Jack put his arm around her shoulders.

"Oh, Christ." Hayden sounded as if he was about to be ill. "It's Gillian. You were right, Jack."

"Not exactly." Jack tried to breathe through his mouth as he stared at the body on the floor. "She wasn't supposed to be dead."

CHAPTER TWENTY-FIVE

A LONG TIME LATER, HAYDEN SLOUCHED INTO the booth at the back of the Mirror Springs Resort bar and wrapped his hands around a glass of scotch. "Page probably made that call. He intended for me to be found standing over the body when you arrived, Jack. It would have been perfect. Angry husband kills wife because she's giving him trouble over divorce settlement. He'd have been in the clear."

"Well—" Jack began, looking thoughtful.

"Damn," Hayden interrupted fervently. "If you hadn't come to my room tonight and made me listen to your screwy theory, I'd have been trying to talk my way out of a murder rap tonight."

Jack shook his head. "You had already changed your mind about attending the auction, remember?"

Hayden grimaced. "Yeah, but that was a real last-minute thing. Who could have known?"

Elizabeth shook her head. "Either way, I don't think Tyler Page set it up to make you look guilty. If he really did kill her, as Gresham and everyone else seems to think, he did it in a fit of passion. Probably because he found out that

Gillian never intended to run off with him after she conducted her auction."

Jack looked at her. "You're a real die-hard romantic, aren't you?"

"I keep telling you that Page is a man of passion, not a cold-blooded strategist," she said.

"Whatever he is, he's probably a long way from Mirror Springs by now. But, unlike Holland, who got away, I have a hunch the authorities will find Page fast. He doesn't have the skills and the know-how that it takes to hide from the police for long."

Hayden turned to Jack. "How did you figure out that Gillian was the one who had orchestrated the theft and set up the auction?"

"It was Elizabeth who insisted all along that there was a woman in this somewhere," Jack said.

"I thought at first that it was Vicky Bellamy." Elizabeth sipped her mineral water. "But I changed my mind. I had pretty much abandoned the whole femme fatale concept when Jack came up with his own variation on it tonight."

Jack looked at Hayden. "Tyler Page is not the organized type. But whoever had planned the theft and made Page disappear here in Mirror Springs was good at organizational details. For a while I thought Dawson Holland might have been more than just another bidder."

"You thought he had used Vicky to seduce Page and convince him to steal the specimen? Set up the auction?" Hayden asked.

Jack nodded. "Like I told Gresham, Holland had had plenty of contact with Page over the past few months. And according to Larry, he had motive. But it didn't quite fit. Holland was too savvy and too well connected to want to

waste time trying to sell Soft Focus here in the States. I figured if he actually had it in his possession, he'd take off for
Europe, where the sky would be the limit at an auction."

"And then Vicky more or less confirmed that she thought
Holland was here in Mirror Springs for business reasons,"
Elizabeth said. "She told me that she thought he was planning to get hold of something of a high-tech nature that he
could turn over to a consortium of foreign investors."

"Which meant that he was just another bidder," Jack
said. "That didn't leave a lot of candidates for the job of
organizing Tyler Page and setting up an auction. Tonight
when you called me to tell me that you had been given
directions for the auction and that it was going to take place
during the premiere of *Fast Company,* I started thinking.
Finally."

"About Gillian?" Hayden asked.

Jack nodded. "She fit Elizabeth's theories as well as mine.
A femme fatale who, through her father, was connected to
the high-tech scene. She was smart enough to have picked
up the rumors of Soft Focus and understand the potential.
She would have known how to go about getting a spy into
Excalibur—"

"Ryan Kendle?" Hayden asked. "I heard you tell Gresham about him."

"Kendle probably identified Page as the one person who
could most easily steal the crystal. Gillian researched Page,
discovered his weakness for filmmaking, and went after
him."

"But why did she fixate on stealing Soft Focus?" Hayden
asked. "Taking it hurt you, not me."

"You still don't get it, do you?" Elizabeth said quietly.

"Get what?"

"No one will ever be able to prove it now," Jack said. "But

Elizabeth and I think that the reason you got the call first tonight was because Gillian intended to kill you."

"Oh, Christ." Comprehension lit Hayden's eyes.

"Jack would have been called later," Elizabeth said. "Because she planned for him to be the one the cops found standing over the body with the smoking gun."

Hayden stared at her. "I knew she hated me because I wanted out of the marriage and Daddy was not happy about that."

"And she hated me because I had also refused to be the son-in-law Daddy wanted," Jack said.

Hayden rubbed his temples. "So she planned to kill me and let you take the rap."

"Can't you see the headlines? 'Long-Standing Feud Between Two Brothers Ends in Murder.'" Elizabeth snapped her fingers. "Just like that, she gets revenge on both of you. One is dead and one goes to jail for murder."

Hayden gave a visible shudder and took another swallow of scotch. "I realized shortly after I married her that she had some serious problems. It got a little scary, to tell you the truth. But even after I filed for divorce I didn't realize that she was capable of murder."

"A real femme fatale," Elizabeth said. "The genuine article."

Hayden winced. "I hate to admit it, but you did try to warn me about her, Jack."

Jack said nothing.

"Gillian used Tyler Page," Elizabeth said softly. "Treated him like a pawn, as if he had no strong passions or emotions."

"And in the end, he killed her," Hayden said.

ELIZABETH GLANCED BACK over her shoulder as she went through the front door of the house. "Did you realize that Gillian was crazy?"

"No." Jack walked across the room and switched on the gas fire. "I just knew that there was a screw loose somewhere and that it had to do with Daddy Ringstead."

Elizabeth hung her coat in the closet. "How did you end your relationship with her?"

"I thought I'd handled it fairly well. Made it clear that I could never fill her father's shoes at Ring, Inc. Pointed out that I was just a small-time consultant who would never amount to much, et cetera, et cetera. I thought she came to the conclusion that she could do much better than me. And as it happened, Hayden started sniffing around at about that time. He reinforced the idea that I had limited ambitions and prospects."

"She concluded that he would make a better husband to take home to Daddy, is that it?"

"That's it." Jack sank into a chair in front of the hearth and stretched out his legs. "When I realized that Hayden was actually serious about marrying her I told him he might want to think about it some more. But that only pushed him faster toward the altar."

"Human nature. Weird."

"Yeah. Just look at you and me. Talk about a weird relationship."

Elizabeth sat down across from him. "But never dull."

"No." He smiled faintly. "Never dull."

Silence fell. Elizabeth listened to the flames crackling on the hearth for a while. Then she reached up to remove the clip in her hair.

"We both need sleep," she said. "We should go to bed."

Jack watched her hair tumble around her shoulders. "I know."

Elizabeth turned to watch the flames leap. "It's over, isn't it?"

"It's in the hands of the cops now." Jack scrubbed his face with one hand. "Gresham was right. Should have called in the authorities back at the beginning."

"Think they'll catch up with Page before the Veltran presentation?"

"Maybe." He hesitated. "But even if they do find him, it won't do Excalibur any good. The crystal will probably get taken into custody as evidence. Could be months before we get it back. By then, the company will be in bankruptcy."

She hesitated. Then she decided to take the plunge. "I've been thinking."

"What about?"

"Your future."

He smiled faintly. "I won't starve, you know."

"I know. You can take care of yourself." She looked at him. "But would you consider a position in management with the Aurora Fund?"

"You're offering me a job?"

"Well, yes. I guess so."

"Working for you?" he said very carefully.

"Why not? You'd fit in very well."

"The Aurora Fund is a two-person operation. You and your assistant, Louise. Just how would I fit in?"

"You have experience in analyzing small start-up and troubled companies," she said quickly. "You would be terrific at assessing candidates for funding. Or we could even add on a whole new department. In addition to funding new ventures, we could offer start-up and management consulting expertise to our clients."

"Me taking orders from you," he said thoughtfully. "An interesting concept."

She began to grow irritated. "What's the matter? Don't you think you can deal with taking orders from me?"

"Hmm."

Pride twisted inside her. "If you aren't interested, just say so."

He propped his elbows on the arms of the chair and steepled his fingers. "What I'm interested in is something a little more permanent."

She glared at him. "The Aurora Fund is very permanent. It's much stronger now than it was when I took charge. Regardless of what happens with Soft Focus, it will turn a profit this quarter."

"Lucky you," he said.

"Jack—"

He met her eyes. "I wasn't talking about a permanent job. I was talking about marriage."

She stopped breathing for a few seconds. "Marriage?"

"I'm a lot more interested in marrying you than I am in working for you."

She swallowed. Then she swallowed again. "I thought we decided that we needed time," she finally managed to get out in a strangled voice. "We agreed that we wouldn't rush things."

"That was your idea, not mine. I've known what I've wanted for six months."

She gazed into his gleaming eyes. "You have?"

He shoved himself up out of the chair, walked to the sofa, and scooped her up in his arms. "Yes."

"But—"

"Tell you what," he said as he started for the stairs with her in his arms. "When you work up enough guts to take a chance on marrying me, I'll let you know whether or not I'm willing to risk working for you."

"That's a ludicrous bargain, and you know it." She

clutched at his shoulders. "For heaven's sake, put me down. You've been through a ton of stress tonight. You must be exhausted. You're in no shape to carry me up a flight of steps."

"Watch me."

"This is no time to show me how macho you are."

"It's not like I've got anything better to do." He reached the landing and turned right into his sleeping loft. "We were both headed for bed anyway."

"You're not going to solve anything with sex, you know."

"Maybe not, but you have to admit that it does help keep us both entertained while we wait to see what you decide."

"I'm trying to have a serious discussion here."

"Sex is more fun."

He walked to the bed and opened his arms. Elizabeth tumbled down onto the quilt. She pushed her hair out of her eyes, looked up, and saw that he already had his shirt off.

"Are you serious about marriage?" she whispered.

"Uh-huh." He unfastened his belt buckle.

She watched with growing fascination as he finished undressing. His erection was full and hard and heavy. She felt the familiar excitement uncoil within her when he put one knee on the bed.

He came down on top of her, caging her within his arms.

"But I'm also very, very serious about sex," he said.

"I can see that," she whispered. She put her arms around him and pulled him down on top of her, relieved to be able to escape into the passion that flared so easily between them.

But she knew, even as he eased himself between her thighs and crushed her into the bedding, that it was only a temporary reprieve.

Marriage?

To Jack?

A LONG TIME later, Jack rolled onto his back and hooked an arm around her. "There is another item on the agenda tonight. In the interests of unbridled honesty, there is one more thing you should know about me before you tell me that you'll marry me."

She groaned and raised herself up on her elbow. "Must I brace myself?"

"Maybe. I just thought that I ought to clear up a small misunderstanding under which you have been laboring for the past week."

Her eyes widened. "Don't tell me, let me guess. You are actually independently wealthy, and even if we don't find Soft Focus and even if your professional reputation goes down the toilet, it's okay because you are secretly filthy rich."

"There wasn't any misunderstanding on that point," he said dryly. "I am not secretly filthy rich."

"Oh. Well, in that case, what was it you lied about that first night here in Mirror Springs?"

"I prefer to think of it not as a lie but rather as a slight bit of judicious misdirection," he said.

"About?"

"About the problem with those reservations I told you I had at the Mirror Springs Resort."

She flattened her hand on his chest. "Okay, I've braced myself for the worst."

He settled himself more comfortably against the pillows and regarded her through half-closed eyes.

"The strings I mentioned, the ones I pulled to get a room, didn't exactly break," he said. "My booking was on file when I got to the resort. I told the front-desk clerk that I didn't want the room. He gave it to the person in line behind me, who was profoundly grateful because he had arrived without a reservation."

She drummed her fingers on his chest. "Then you showed up on my doorstep, gave me that tale of woe about not having a place to stay, and begged me to take you in."

He frowned. "I don't recall begging."

"Darn close."

"Darn close," he agreed. "Looking back, I took a hell of a risk. I shouldn't have canceled the reservation until I knew for sure I could talk my way in here."

She pursed her lips and appeared to ponder that admission. "Holding on to the reservation until you knew for sure that I'd fall for your line would definitely have been the savvy, street-smart CEO kind of thing to do."

"Don't know why I didn't think of it," Jack mused.

She stopped drumming her fingers and gave him a smug smile. "I know why."

"Yeah?" He wrapped his hand around the back of her head. "Why?"

She cleared her throat. "It has come to my attention in recent months that you are, at heart, an old-fashioned romantic, Jack Fairfax. A regular Don Quixote."

His hand stilled in her hair. He stared at her, too astonished to speak for an instant. Then he started to laugh.

He laughed so hard, he considered the fact that he did not fall out of bed a near miracle. When he finally recovered, he summed up his opinion of her observation in a single word.

"Bullshit," he said.

"It's true." She appeared unperturbed by his incredulous reaction to her announcement. "You are a knight in somewhat tarnished armor. That's why you feel obliged to atone for some of the damage you think your father did. It's why you consult for small, troubled companies that can't afford you. It's why you never insist on a golden parachute before you sign on to a contract with a firm that is facing disaster. It's why you prefer to work for closely held businesses that have a personal history and a family legacy instead of big, soulless corporations."

He grinned. "Let me get this straight. You think it was this wildly romantic streak of mine that convinced me to take my chances with you that first night here in Mirror Springs?"

"Absolutely. It's the only thing that could possibly explain your taking such a ridiculous risk."

"Huh."

"And that," she announced, "is why I've decided to accept your proposal of marriage."

Some type of rare and extremely precious energy burst through him. If he could bottle it, he would be the richest man in the world, he thought. Then again, it was right there inside him, rushing through his veins, making him lightheaded, creating all sorts of new sensations for him to savor. He didn't need to sell the joy to get rich. He already owned it.

"I'll let you in on a little secret." She bent her head and brushed her mouth across his. "I think it was just as wildly romantic of me to take you in."

"Yeah? Why?"

She smiled. "Because even as I held the door open for you and invited you inside, I was almost certain that you were lying through your teeth."

A tide of heat flooded his veins. Not sexual arousal, he realized, although that was probably somewhere in the mix; something else. Something infinitely more satisfying. She'd taken him in even though she'd suspected that he had given her a line about the hotel room.

He put his other hand into her hair and gently tightened his fingers. "Apparently, I'm not the only closet romantic here. I do love you, you know."

"I love you, too." She started to kiss him and then paused, her gaze growing abruptly thoughtful.

"What?"

"It brings up that old problem, doesn't it?"

"It's up, but it's not that old, and I honestly don't consider it a problem."

"Stop grinning like that." She sat up slowly amid the rumpled sheets. "This is serious. I think."

He put both of his hands behind his own head. "I'm listening."

"All that talk about your little game with the hotel reservations makes me wonder just where Tyler Page stayed while he was here in Mirror Springs. Gresham said that it looked as if Gillian drove in from Denver for the day, remember?"

"Go on."

"But we've assumed all along that Page was here in Mirror Springs. We thought he'd want to be as close to the festival as possible."

"Maybe we assumed wrong."

Elizabeth's eyes gleamed. "Maybe we didn't."

Jack sat up slowly. "What are you getting at?"

"We all agree that Page is not good with the details of daily life. The details of a fake identity are even trickier to handle."

"Gillian must have taken care of that end of things for him."

Elizabeth tightened her hand in the sheet. "The first day I saw Hayden I asked him how he managed to get a room at the resort. He told me that he knew the general manager and had pulled a few strings. He said it very casually, more or less in passing. It's possible that he met the manager somewhere else."

"High-ranking hotel personnel frequently get transferred from one property to another on a regular basis," Jack said slowly.

"But it's also possible that Hayden met him right here in Mirror Springs. Which would mean that this wasn't his first visit."

"It's a popular ski resort in the winter. Hayden skis." Jack paused. "So does Gillian."

"Jack, what if—"

"Hang on." Jack grabbed the phone off the end table. Then he rummaged in the drawer for the small Mirror Springs phone book. "We can put an end to this one way or the other with a call."

He found the resort number and punched it in. Hayden came on the line after several rings. He sounded half asleep and groggy.

"How much more scotch did you drink after Elizabeth and I left?" Jack asked.

"If you think that you can start playing big brother after all these years, forget it. Besides, I had a right. It was a rough night."

"I can't argue with you there," Jack said. "You can go back to sleep in a minute. Right after you answer a question."

Hayden groaned. "Just because you saved my life, don't get the idea that you can call me up in the middle of the night anytime you feel like it. My newfound brotherly gratitude only goes so far."

"Hayden, pay attention here. You told Elizabeth that you got that room there at the resort because you knew the manager."

"Douglas Finley. Nice guy. So what?"

"Have you stayed at the resort in the past?"

"No."

"Damn." Jack's sense of anticipation went flat, but he caught Elizabeth's eye and decided to push a little more. "How did you get to know Finley?"

"To tell you the truth, I don't really know him. At least not personally. I used my ex-in-laws' name to pull some strings with him."

"Finley knows Gillian's family?"

"Yeah. But he didn't know about the divorce. Probably wouldn't have given me the room if he had known about it. Can I ask where in hell this is going? I need my sleep. I got a call from Gillian's father earlier. Ringstead's on his way back from Zurich. A family lawyer is on his way here tonight. I'm going to have to deal with both of them tomorrow."

"Stick with me for a little longer," Jack said. "Are you telling me that Gillian's family vacations in this area?"

"Not her immediate family. But one of her cousins has a place a few miles out of town. Gillian and I used it once or twice."

Jack was amazed that the phone didn't crack in his hand. "Her cousin has a place here?"

"Yeah. But what with the divorce and all, I'm persona non grata with the Ringsteads these days. Figured there was no point asking for the key to the cabin, so I tried my luck here at the resort instead."

CHAPTER TWENTY-SIX

THE HOUSE WAS INVISIBLE FROM THE ROAD, impossible to see until Jack reached the end of the long access lane and turned the corner. Elizabeth sat forward, watching as the headlights splashed across a large, sprawling structure. The windows were dark. There was no car parked in the drive.

"If Page was staying here, he's long gone." Jack switched off the engine and picked up the flashlight. "But maybe we'll find something that will tell us where he's headed."

Elizabeth gave him an uneasy glance as she opened her door. "Chief Gresham is not going to be thrilled when he finds out we came here without consulting with him."

"What with Vicky's car crash and Gillian's murder, Gresham has enough on his hands at the moment. Besides, this is probably just another wild-goose chase. If we turn up anything useful, we'll call him."

"Sure." She slid out, closed the door, and buttoned her long down coat. She gave him a knowing look over the roof of the car. "Right after we set out after Page ourselves."

"If Page is in Europe, there's nothing Gresham can do anyway. But there might be something we could do if we catch up with him before he figures out how to unload Soft Focus in the foreign market."

She shook her head as she followed him toward the house. "That's one of the things I admire about you, Jack. You never give up."

"Giving up is not usually a viable strategic maneuver." He pulled on a pair of leather gloves. "Let's face it, finding a missing lab specimen is not a high priority for Chief Gresham. He's after a couple of murderers. Excalibur's stolen property is low on his list right now. We're the only ones with a vested interest in getting that damned crystal back before the Veltran presentation."

"You don't need to remind me." She took her gloves out of the pocket of her coat and put them on. Then she hurried up the steps to the rear deck and watched Jack test the locks on the door and the nearby windows.

"There's a name for this," she said.

"Breaking and entering." Jack continued around the corner of the deck. "Not our first time. You should be getting used to it by now."

"When we went through Page's house in Seattle, we had a key and a semi-legitimate-sounding excuse. This could be a little trickier to explain."

"I'll deal with it if necessary."

"Spoken like a real CEO."

"A good CEO can talk his way out of anything."

"Or into anything," Elizabeth said. But she said it very quietly.

She tried to ignore the hot-cold feeling in her hands as she trailed after Jack. He was halfway around the wide deck that encircled the big house.

She followed him around the corner and saw that the entire front wall of both stories was a mass of floor-to-ceiling windows. Anyone standing inside would have an expansive view of the mountain. But from where she stood on the deck the dark glass appeared as an impenetrable barrier.

Jack started toward the nearest sliding glass door. Elizabeth cast her own small flashlight around the deck. The beam of light grazed a large, professional-size stainless-steel outdoor grill, two chaise longues, a table, and a hot tub.

"Looks like hot tubs are big here in Mirror Springs," she said. "Everyone's got one."

"After our recent experience I've decided I've got a keen interest in them myself. I'm thinking of installing one when we get home." Jack moved to the next door.

"You live in a condo."

"We could put it in at your place. How about that balcony outside your bedroom?"

She frowned. "How do you know that there's a deck outside my bedroom?"

"I can see it from my front window."

"Not without a pair of binoculars, you can't."

He did not respond to that.

"Jack, were you spying on me during the past six months?"

"I couldn't get a clear view," he assured her. "There were some bushes in the way. You know, you should probably tell your gardener to cut back some of the shrubbery on that balcony. Getting a little overgrown, don't you think?"

She groaned, not sure whether to be outraged or flattered. She was about to tell him where he could stick the excess shrubbery when she noticed that the lid of the outdoor grill was open. An array of cooking implements was scattered across a greasy steel counter that extended out from the side.

"I think someone used the grill recently. Look at all the utensils and the mess on the counter. I wonder if—" She broke off, staring at the dark shape that projected around the edge of the hot tub. Her first thought was that someone had left a shoe out on the deck.

A man's shoe.

Then she saw that the shoe was connected to a pant leg. "Oh, my God. *Jack*."

He crossed the deck in three long strides and halted beside her. He aimed his own light toward the side of the tub. "Damn."

He walked toward the edge of the small pool, never taking the beam off the shoe.

"Please, God," Elizabeth whispered. "Not another one."

She went slowly forward, wanting to look away from the shoe but unable to do so. It was as if she were under the influence of a terrible compulsion.

She came to a halt next to the large grill, put out a hand, and gripped the counter extension to steady herself. Her fingers brushed against the handle of a long, unwashed cooking fork.

The hot tub was uncovered, but it was not running. The motor was silent, the interior lights off. The surface of the water was still.

Jack walked around the edge of the circular pool and aimed the flashlight at what appeared at first to be a pile of rumpled clothing.

Elizabeth saw a thin, bony-fingered hand. Then she saw the blood that still oozed from the head wound. She was grateful that the man's face was turned away from her. Something glinted at the edge of the light. A stylish, stainless-steel cocktail shaker lay on the deck next to a chair leg. The shaker's lid had been removed, she noticed. The dead man must have been caught in the act of mixing himself a martini.

"Dear heaven." She lowered the light. The beam shined across a dark metal object on the deck. "Jack—?"

He glanced at the gun that had apparently fallen from the man's hand. "I see it."

When she glanced back at the body she noticed the wide, dark stain that had spread out from beneath the head. It could have been water that had splashed out of the uncovered hot tub, but she knew that it wasn't. Her stomach lurched.

She watched, mesmerized, as Jack crouched and felt for a pulse at the throat.

"It's Page, isn't it?" she whispered.

"Yes." Jack stood and started to reach into the pocket of his jacket for his cell phone. "He never made it out of town."

"He must have shot himself after he killed Gillian. Lover's remorse. The poor man. She truly was his femme fatale."

A dark figure moved out of the shadows beneath an awning. A third flashlight winked on. Elizabeth felt a scream rise in her throat. But nothing happened, because she could not seem to get her breath.

"Not suicide, I'm afraid," Dawson Holland said. "The stupid little bastard refused to hand over Soft Focus. He kept saying that Gillian had *betrayed* him and that he would never give me the crystal. He actually had the nerve to pull a gun on me. I had to kill him."

"Why are you still hanging around?" Jack's voice was stunningly even. He did not rise from his crouched position near the body. "Coming on top of Gillian's death and a missing wife, another murder is going to be a little tough to explain, isn't it?"

"I have no intention of sticking around long enough to explain anything to anyone."

"You killed Gillian," Elizabeth whispered. "It wasn't Tyler Page, after all."

"The bitch went crazy on me. Kept ranting on and on about getting revenge." Dawson swung the flashlight beam directly into Elizabeth's eyes.

She staggered back as if he had used a laser. She stumbled against the grill and fumbled wildly to catch her balance. The implements on the counter clattered and clanged. A heavy pan crashed to the deck. It bounced twice and then went still. Jack never took his eyes off her, but he said nothing.

Dawson Holland smiled and swung the light back toward Jack. "I think she's nervous."

"You're enough to make any intelligent person nervous," Elizabeth said.

"And you are an intelligent person, are you not? Do you know, there is something very exciting about clever women. I find them fascinating, especially when they are also beautiful. But in the end, one can never trust them. They always have their own agendas, and that makes them dangerous."

"Speaking of dangerous," Jack said casually, "you've had a real run of bad luck lately, haven't you? First Vicky splits before you can murder her for the insurance money, and then Gillian turns out to be more obsessed with her revenge than with the business of selling Soft Focus abroad."

"Gillian screwed up the whole deal." Dawson's face worked in fury. "She wasn't interested in the money. She only wanted her silly revenge. She used me."

Elizabeth watched him as if he were a cobra. "How did you meet her?"

"She attended a film festival in Sedona a few months ago. Sought me out. Introduced herself. She'd done her research. Knew who I was and that I might be interested in an offshore business venture."

"She needed someone who could give Tyler Page what he wanted so badly," Elizabeth said. "A film he could claim to have produced."

Dawson's mouth thinned. "As I said, she used me. At first it seemed like an ideal partnership. I needed Soft Focus to get some people off my back, and I was preparing to cash in on Vicky's insurance policy anyway. I thought I could kill a couple of birds with one stone here in Mirror Springs."

"But in the end Gillian didn't cooperate, did she?" Jack said.

"The crazy woman hid herself and Page, too. I couldn't find either of them. " Dawson's voice rose. "And then you and Shaw showed up. I tried to scare you off, but neither of you budged. Then you sent Ledger out to ask questions about Page, and I had to buy him off."

"Where did you get that video?"

Dawson grimaced. "Gillian had it made weeks ago. Just in case, she said. She wanted to make certain that, if anything went wrong, the evidence would point toward someone else. She was willing to give me a copy, so I took it and kept it. Just in case."

"The authorities think you're on your way to Amsterdam," Elizabeth said.

"I had to pretend to disappear after Vicky staged her accident. I bought the ticket for Amsterdam at the airport this morning. But then I rented a car and drove back here. I had Shaw's hotel room bugged. I knew when he got the call from Gillian. I got to the location first and confronted her."

"She told you where she had hidden Page?" Jack asked.

"The crazy bitch was so excited about her plans for vengeance finally coming to a head that she laughed in my face and told me I could have Soft Focus. She even told me where she'd stashed Page."

"So you shot her dead and came here," Elizabeth whispered.

"Page was about to leave." Dawson grimaced. "The fool was going to try to sneak into the theater tonight to watch the screening of *Fast Company,* if you can believe it. A fortune at stake, and he wants to go see his movie."

"You came here to force Page to hand over Soft Focus, and he refused because he guessed that Gillian had betrayed him with you," Elizabeth said. "And he was right."

In the backwash of the flashlight, Dawson's face was a shadowed mask of fury. "The idiot kept saying that Soft Focus was right in front of my eyes but that I would never find it."

"You figured you could find it, though, didn't you?" Jack gave him a humorless smile. "How long have you been searching for it?"

"I've spent the past few hours tearing the goddamned house apart." Dawson's voice throbbed with frustrated rage. "I even searched the hot tub. Page taunted me. I really believed him when he said it was somewhere in plain sight."

"But you've run out of time, haven't you?" Jack said. "Even if the cops don't find you, your offshore business associates will. How far do you think you'll get?"

"All I have to do is get off this damned mountain." Dawson's cheek twitched nervously. "Once I'm out of Mirror Springs, I'll be in the clear. I have a new ID. All I have to do is disappear for a while."

"The cops will catch you before you get off this mountain," Elizabeth said.

"I don't think so." Dawson smiled coldly. "But just in case, I'm going to have a hostage with me. Insurance, you understand. I've always been a big believer in insurance."

Elizabeth sucked in her breath. "If you think I'm going to go with you—"

"That is exactly what I think." Dawson motioned with the hand that held the flashlight. "Come over here. Quickly."

"What about Soft Focus?" Jack asked. "Are you going to give up on it?"

"One learns to cut one's losses, Fairfax." Dawson made another gesture with the flashlight. "Come here now, Elizabeth. Or I will shoot Fairfax."

He meant it, she thought. Holland would not hesitate to kill again. She walked slowly toward him.

"Quickly, my dear. Fairfax is correct in one regard. Time has run out on me." When she was no more than a step away from him, he took the gun off Jack and aimed it at her instead. "Excellent. Now, then, Fairfax. One move and I will kill her without a second's hesitation and take my chances. Is that clear?"

"Yes," Jack said softly. "It's clear."

"My car is parked on a side road not far from here." Dawson kept the gun trained on Elizabeth, but he did not take his gaze off Jack as he issued instructions. "Move. Slowly, Elizabeth."

She did not budge. "You're going to kill Jack as soon as I start toward the car, aren't you?"

He smiled approvingly. "You really are an intelligent woman, my dear. Under other circumstances we might have done very well together."

"Not for long," she said.

"No, not for long. Now, move, or you will have to watch him die, and somehow I do not think you would like that."

She looked at Jack. He was still crouched beside the body, a good two yards from the gun that Page had dropped.

"Jack?"

"It's okay, Elizabeth. Do what you have to do." Jack paused for a heartbeat. "But do it quick, okay?"

"Right." She turned as if to walk back around the deck.

Dawson continued to point the gun at her head, but his attention was on Jack.

The handle of the cooking fork that she had swiped off the grill and shoved under her sleeve a moment earlier was in her fingers. She pulled the implement free of her sleeve.

She felt Dawson's weight shift. He took the gun off her and started to swing the barrel toward Jack.

There was no time to aim the fork. She plunged it wildly toward Dawson. She felt the tines tear through the fabric of his trousers, felt the sickening resistance of flesh and muscle.

Holland convulsed in pain and fury. He screamed.

"Bitch."

The pistol roared, deafening her. Light sparked. Dawson's flashlight hit the deck and rolled. She felt rather than saw the collision as Jack slammed into Dawson. The two men struck the deck with enough force to send a shudder through the wooden supports.

Elizabeth scrambled madly out of the way. She tripped and reeled back against the railing. She swung around.

A bloody apparition rose from the shadows of the hot tub. Tyler Page sat up slowly. He swept out a hand, groping blindly. His fingers closed around the gun. He seized it and pointed it toward the struggling men. His arm shook wildly.

"You stole her away from me," he gasped in a quivering voice. "She betrayed me with you."

"Jack," Elizabeth yelled. "Get out of the way."

Jack glanced up, saw Page, and assessed the situation in a single glance. He rolled free of Holland and threw himself headlong out of range.

"Don't do it," he yelled. "It's okay, he's—"

But it was too late. There was another crash and a flash of light, and then Holland went utterly limp on the deck.

"Angel Face," Tyler whispered. "My beautiful Angel Face."

He fell back and lay still once more.

A stark silence descended.

"Elizabeth?"

"I'm okay." She stared at Tyler Page. "I thought he was dead."

"No, unconscious. Holland's bullet got him on the side of the head." Jack went down beside Dawson and felt for a pulse. "Holland's still alive, too. Got your cell phone?"

"Yes." Grateful for the distraction, she pulled the little phone out of her coat pocket and concentrated hard on punching in the emergency number.

It seemed an eternity before the emergency operator came on the line and Elizabeth gave her the details of the situation.

When she finished the call, she saw that Jack had moved back to the hot tub. As she watched, he bent down to scoop up the silvery container that had fallen on the deck.

She walked slowly toward him. In the distance she heard the first keening wail of a siren.

"What are you doing with that cocktail shaker?"

"It's not a cocktail shaker." He aimed the flashlight at the object. "It's a sort of high-tech thermos. Designed in the Excalibur lab specifically to transport Soft Focus."

She stared at it, suddenly riveted. "It's empty. Do you think Page threw the crystal into the woods to spite Holland?"

"Next to *Fast Company,* the development of the crystal was Page's only major accomplishment in life. I don't think he would have destroyed it." Jack gazed thoughtfully into the hot tub. "He told Holland that it was right in front of his eyes. Maybe he was telling the truth."

Jack went to the control panel and flipped a switch. The underwater lights came on inside the tub.

Elizabeth peered over the edge. "You think he tossed it in there? But Holland said he looked in the tub." The submerged lighting provided a clear view of the interior. There was nothing under the water except the benches.

"Holland was no high-tech wizard. Gillian probably told him they were going to steal a crystal, so he naturally assumed that Soft Focus would look like a chunk of quartz." Jack upended the thermos and unscrewed a small section. "And it does. Sort of. When it's not in a state of suspension, that is."

Elizabeth suddenly understood. "Of course. It's a new type of colloidal crystal, isn't it? Page transported it in the thermos because the particles are suspended in a liquid."

"Only under certain conditions. Soft Focus has several unique properties."

The sirens were closer now. Elizabeth glanced out across the valley. She caught a glimpse of flashing lights on Loop Road.

"You've got maybe ten minutes at most," she said. "Once they're here this whole house will become a crime scene. They won't let you tear the place up to search for Soft Focus."

"If I'm right, I won't need ten minutes."

Jack had the bottom of the container off now. A small plastic envelope fell into his hand. He opened it and tossed the contents into the hot tub.

"What's that?" Elizabeth demanded.

"The catalyst. Unlike true colloidal crystals, Soft Focus needs this stuff to make the particles clump together in a semisolid form. It won't take long. If Page dumped the specimen into this tub, it will take shape fast."

Elizabeth watched intently. At first she saw nothing. Then she caught a glint of what looked like a shard of blue-green glass on one of the benches.

"There it is." Satisfaction laced Jack's voice. He rolled up the sleeve of his shirt. "Just another couple of minutes and we'll have the whole damn thing."

The chunk of crystal grew swiftly beneath the water as the tiny particles floating invisibly in the pool reacted to the attractive force induced by the catalyst.

The sirens were very loud now. The first car had turned into the access road that led to the house.

"That looks about right." Jack plunged his bare arm into the water and scooped the crystal off the bench.

He held it cradled in his palm for a moment and aimed the flashlight beam into its heart.

Elizabeth caught her breath. It was like looking into the depths of an impossibly brilliant diamond. Soft Focus glowed with blue-green fire. It pulsed and sparkled and glittered.

"It's spectacular," she whispered.

"And it's ours."

The sirens cut off abruptly. Car doors slammed. Footsteps sounded on the rear deck.

Jack closed his fingers around Soft Focus and dropped it very casually into his pocket.

"If the question should arise," he said, "the crystal Page took was a mock-up, a decoy version of the actual crystal. Luckily, the real one is safe in the Excalibur labs."

"You think that story will work?"

"Like I said, a good CEO can talk his way through anything."

CHAPTER TWENTY-SEVEN

TYLER PAGE WAS A TRAGIC FIGURE IN THE hospital bed. His head was swathed in bandages. An IV line hung from a nearby stand, the contents dripping into his veins. His bent glasses sat askew on his nose. He looked up at Jack with sad resignation.

"I know it's too late to apologize, Mr. Fairfax. Nevertheless, I would like to tell you how sorry I am about this entire affair. I don't know what came over me."

Elizabeth saw the derisive look in Jack's eyes and quickly moved closer to the bed. "Jack understands, Dr. Page. You were a victim of passion. For a time you lost your bearings. These things happen."

Jack raised his eyes to the ceiling.

Tyler switched his glum gaze to Elizabeth. "She was so beautiful. Beautiful women like her never notice men like me. But she did. She made me feel brilliant and important and dashing. When I was with her I was Bogart and Mitchum and Grant, all rolled into one."

"Gillian used you," Jack said bluntly.

Elizabeth frowned at him from the other side of the bed. "There's no need to belabor the point."

"I know she used me," Tyler said. "But by the time I understood that she had convinced me to steal Soft Focus for her own purposes, not so that we could run off to a tropical island together, it was too late. The whole thing became a nightmare. I couldn't see any way out."

"Did you ever think of picking up the phone and giving me a call?" Jack asked without any evidence of sympathy.

"Jack," Elizabeth said quietly. She infused her tone with a strong note of warning, but she got the distinct impression that he was not paying attention.

"I felt helpless," Tyler explained. "Trapped in her web. Do you know, when Chief Gresham told me that Gillian was dead, I felt a terrible sense of relief. It was as if the scales had fallen away from my eyes. I was finally free of her clutches. Looking back, I can see what a coward I was."

"You are certainly no coward," Elizabeth said firmly. "You stood up to Dawson Holland, even though he tried to murder you. That was a very brave thing to do. Incredibly heroic, in fact."

Jack raised his brows but said nothing.

Tyler looked at her with fragile hope. "Do you really think so, Ms. Cabot?"

"Yes, and so does everyone else." Elizabeth pinned Jack with a bristling expression. "Isn't that right, Jack?"

"Yeah, sure," Jack said. Then his mouth curved slightly. "As a matter of fact, it was. Defying Dawson Holland took balls, Tyler."

Tyler blushed. "Thank you, sir. Is Mr. Holland . . . ?"

"Dead?" Jack nodded. "An hour ago. In surgery."

"I see." Tyler looked as if he was trying to square his shoulders against the pillows. "I suppose I shall have to stand trial for that, as well."

"Don't think so," Jack said easily. "Gresham is convinced

that it was a pretty clear-cut case of self-defense. Holland was trying to kill us, remember."

Elizabeth met Jack's eyes across the white-sheeted bed. Neither of them had seen any reason to point out to Gresham that Jack had already subdued Holland when Tyler surfaced briefly from his unconscious state and fired the fatal shot. Details, Jack had said. Unimportant details.

"The chief is not happy with any of us," Jack continued, "but no one is going to jail."

Tyler blinked owlishly. "But surely I must pay for my crime."

"Excalibur is not pressing charges," Elizabeth said.

Tyler blinked again. "I don't understand. I stole the result of a valuable research project. I'm a thief."

"Excalibur has decided to overlook the incident," Jack said smoothly. "Especially in light of the fact that the item you took was merely a mock-up of the original, which has been in safekeeping at Excalibur the entire time."

Tyler's mouth dropped open. "But—"

"New security measure that was installed last month," Jack said. "Milo and I were the only ones who knew about it."

"But—"

"I ought to know, don't you think?" Jack gave him a cool look, heavy with meaning. "I *am* the CEO of the company."

Tyler brightened as understanding dawned. "I'm very glad to hear that, sir. That was . . . extremely clever and far-sighted of you, Mr. Fairfax."

"Yes, it was, wasn't it?"

"I can't tell you how delighted I am to know that there will be no long-term ill effects on Excalibur from my actions. It's a fine company. The Ingersolls have always treated me well. I shall miss them."

"Not for long," Jack said. "You're expected to report

back for work in the lab as soon as you're released from the hospital."

Tyler stared at him. "You want me to return to Excalibur?"

Elizabeth smiled. "The company needs you, Dr. Page. You're the only one who truly understood the theoretical work that Patricia Ingersoll did on colloidal crystals. The firm would be lost without you."

"Lost." Tyler looked dazed. "Without me."

"Absolutely." Elizabeth looked at Jack. "Isn't that right?"

"Damn right," Jack said. "Absolutely lost."

"I hadn't realized—" Tyler broke off, a look of wonder in his eyes. "Nobody's ever been lost without me before, you see."

THE TENSION IN Excalibur's executive suite was so thick, Elizabeth was amazed that she could breathe the air. She glanced around at the anxious faces of the other members of the Excalibur board of directors. The various Ingersolls were scattered about the office. Some slumped in chairs. Some gulped coffee. Some paced. All had gone from a state of euphoric excitement to one of deep despair.

Elizabeth couldn't blame them. The presentation to Grady Veltran and his people had begun three hours ago. Thus far no one had emerged from the lab to give a report. With every passing moment, disaster seemed more imminent.

"Something's gone wrong." Angela came to a halt in front of the window. "If Soft Focus had worked as Page promised it would, we'd have heard something by now. We might as well face the facts. We're ruined."

"Everything Patricia worked for all those years," Milo's uncle, Ivo, muttered. "Down the drain."

Angela looked grim. "I knew we shouldn't have let Jack

concentrate all of our resources on a single project. I told you it was a mistake. I told all of you. Remember?"

Milo's aunt glared. "It's not as if we had any choice," Dolores retorted. "This company was going under. Jack was our only hope."

Elizabeth turned away from the window. "Calm down, everyone. If there had been a problem in the lab, I'm sure the Veltran people would have left by now. They're still here. I can see the limos in the parking lot. That means there's still hope."

"It's over," Ivo moaned. "Nothing left but liquidation. We should have done it months ago."

The door opened before Elizabeth could respond. Everyone turned to watch Milo walk somberly into the room. Jack was a pace behind him. Both men were stone-faced.

Milo came to a halt and faced his relatives. For a second he showed no emotion whatsoever.

Then he broke into a huge, boyish grin. He let out a whoop that rattled the windows and punched the air with his fist. "*Yes*. The sucker worked. Just like Tyler Page said it would. The demonstration went perfectly. Tell 'em, Jack."

Jack met Elizabeth's eyes across the room. His smile was slow and satisfied. Not unlike the way he smiled when he made love to her, she thought.

"Well?" she prompted.

"We were delayed getting back here because Grady Veltran insisted on signing a preliminary licensing agreement before we even got out of the lab," Jack said. "We had to wait until the lawyers could get everyone's signature."

"Hot damn." Ivo shot to his feet. "Hot damn. You did it."

"Jack did it." Milo grinned and pounded Jack on the back. "He pulled it off."

"*We* did it." Jack clapped his shoulder. "You were cool during the demo, Milo. Nerves of steel."

Milo could not seem to stop grinning.

"I don't believe it," Angela whispered, hope and relief lighting her eyes. "It worked?"

"Perfectly." After a quick glance at Jack, who was leaning very casually, arms folded, against the edge of his desk, Milo cleared his throat.

Elizabeth watched the younger man assume a cloak of composure that bore a startling resemblance to Jack's own enigmatic air of executive cool. She hid a smile. Milo was learning fast. Then again, he was taking lessons from a master.

"Aunt Patricia's theories concerning the fundamental nature of colloidal crystals were right," Milo said. "Tyler Page was right when he said he could make them work. Hell, we're *all* right." He nodded toward Jack. "Thanks to you and the Aurora Fund, Excalibur is set to be a major player in the next generation of light-based computer technology."

Elizabeth went to a cupboard, opened it, and removed the two silver buckets she had placed there nearly three hours earlier. Each held a bottle of champagne. The ice in each bucket had long since melted.

"I think this calls for a celebration," she said. She looked at Jack and Milo. "Will you two gentlemen do the honors?"

"Oh, wow," Milo said, cool slipping away as quickly as it had come. "Champagne."

"Great idea." Jack straightened from the desk and walked across the room to pick up one of the bottles. He looked at Elizabeth as he went to work on the cork. "I take it you never had any doubts?"

She smiled. "None at all."

"What a coincidence," he said softly. "Neither did I."

She looked into his eyes and saw the intense happiness there. She knew that he saw the same expression mirrored in hers. Both of them knew that it had nothing to do with Soft Focus.

The cork came out of the bottle with a very satisfactory pop. It hit the ceiling. Everyone laughed with delight.

Milo held up a brimming glass. "Here's to Soft Focus. And while we're doing toasts, I'd like to be the first to propose another. 'To Jack and Elizabeth. May they live happily ever after.' "

CHAPTER TWENTY-EIGHT

SHE WAS LATE.

She saw him waiting for her the moment she walked into the Pacific Rim Club restaurant. He was seated in the exact same booth in which he had waited for her on the day after their ill-fated first night together. Not a coincidence, she thought. She smiled to herself.

Hugo, the maître d', hurried over to greet her. "Ah, you're here, Miss Cabot. Mr. Fairfax has already arrived."

"So I see."

Hugo escorted her to the booth. Elizabeth sensed several heads turn en route. She caught glimpses of smiles and knew that she was not the only one who was experiencing a mild case of déjà vu. This was the first time that she had met Jack for lunch here since their spectacular scene.

She saw the gleam of amusement in his eyes and knew that he was enjoying watching her walk the elegant gauntlet. When she reached the table, he got to his feet and brushed her mouth in an unmistakably possessive kiss.

"You're late," he said.

She ignored him to smile at Hugo. "Thank you."

"Of course, Miss Cabot." Hugo beamed. "Please allow me

to offer my sincerest congratulations on your engagement. We look forward to holding the reception here on Friday."

"We're both looking forward to the party, too," Elizabeth said.

Hugo smiled again and retreated.

Elizabeth refused to acknowledge any of the sidelong looks from the other diners. She set her purse down on the cushion and slipped into the booth. Jack sat down across from her.

"You're probably wondering why I called this meeting," he said.

She glanced meaningfully around the room. "I assumed it was to make a point."

He grinned. "Okay, I admit I couldn't resist replaying this particular scene in front of this particular audience. I wanted to get it right."

"You're doing very well so far. At least I haven't poured ice water over you."

"Things are definitely looking up," he agreed.

She helped herself to a bread stick. "By the way, we got an engagement present from Vicky."

"No kidding? What did she send?"

"An autographed poster of *Fast Company*. I'm going to get it framed for my office."

"I saw Page this morning. He was excited. Seems that the film has been picked up for foreign distribution and is going to be available on video. It'll never make any money, of course, but at least it's out there." Jack leaned back in the booth and fixed her with a steady gaze. "Want to order first, or shall we get right down to business?"

"You're starting to scare me, Jack." She reached for the menu. "What's this all about?"

"While we were in Mirror Springs you offered me a business proposition."

"You never got back to me on the offer, as I recall."

"I've been doing a lot of thinking."

She slowly lowered the menu. "Are you serious? You want to go to work for the Aurora Fund?"

"Not exactly. But something you said at the time you made your offer stuck with me."

"What was that?"

"You pointed out that the goals of the Fund and the goals of Fairfax Consulting are very similar. You search out small companies that need venture capital. I specialize in turning around small companies that are in serious trouble. Why not join forces and offer a package deal?"

She smiled. "Sounds like a winning combination to me. But I've got to say, I'm a little surprised. I thought that the idea of taking orders from me was more than you could handle."

"It is." He sat forward and clasped his hands on the table. He looked directly into her eyes. "I love you more than I have ever loved anyone else in my life, but I don't intend to work for you. Nothing personal. It's just that I don't take orders well. However, I have another arrangement in mind."

"I knew it. There's a catch."

"Not a catch, an alternative. I'm proposing a joint venture. Fairfax Consulting and the Aurora Fund will maintain their individual business identities, but they will form a partnership to handle certain selected projects."

"Hmm." The muted buzzing of her cell phone interrupted her contemplation of his suggestion. She opened her purse, reached inside, and withdrew the small instrument. "This is Elizabeth."

"Lizzie?" Merrick's ever-cheerful voice boomed in her ear. "I've been trying to get hold of you all week. Did you get a chance to take a look at my business plan?"

She stifled a small groan. "I did glance at it, but I've been a little busy lately, Merrick. What with the arrangements for the engagement party and all, I haven't—"

"I know, I know. Congratulations, by the way. But getting back to my plan. This is the big one, Lizzie. I can feel it in my bones."

"As I said, I haven't gone through the plan in detail, Merrick." She saw a glint appear in Jack's eyes. She had not discussed Merrick's business plan with him, and she was pretty sure that he could guess why she had not done so. His obvious disapproval irritated her, so she spoke rashly. "But I trust your instincts. I'll have the funds transferred into your account immediately."

"Hey, Lizzie, that's terrific." Merrick's enthusiasm was, as usual, contagious. "Fantastic. You won't regret it. Things are going to work this time. You'll see."

"Give me that phone." Jack reached across the table and deftly removed it from her fingers.

She glared at him. "What do you think you're doing?"

He paid no attention to her fuming. "Merrick? Jack Fairfax here. Yeah, yeah, I know how lucky I am. Now, about your business plan. The Aurora Fund and Fairfax Consulting are setting up a joint venture. If you take the funding, you also take the consulting."

Elizabeth felt her jaw drop. She tried to grab the phone out of his hand. "Jack, wait, we haven't really discussed this yet."

He held the phone out of reach and continued to speak to Merrick. "I'll be working with Elizabeth, not for her. No, we haven't signed the papers yet."

"We haven't even talked about the details." Elizabeth stood up and tried again to swipe the phone away from him. "For all you know, I've changed my mind."

Jack angled his head to indicate the three business executives seated in the booth across the aisle. She glanced at them and saw that they were watching her with keen expectation.

"I agree," Jack said. "A good matchup of skills and market niches. Thanks, I thought it was a pretty good idea myself."

Blushing furiously, Elizabeth subsided back into her seat with ill grace. She tapped one red nail pointedly on the table as Jack concluded the call.

"It's a deal," he said finally. "I'll be in touch."

He handed the phone back to Elizabeth. "There you go, our first joint-venture client."

She glowered at him. "That was a little premature, don't you think? Something tells me that if that's an example of the way you do business, this joint venture of ours is not going to be as easy and smooth as you seem to believe."

"Are you reneging on your offer?"

"My original offer," she reminded him very evenly, "involved you working for the Aurora Fund. Not a joint venture."

"You're just ticked because I won't agree to an organizational chart that has me taking orders from you."

She started to argue, hesitated, and then reluctantly succumbed to the laughter that was fizzing inside. "Dang. It was such a lovely fantasy."

He grinned. "You want a good fantasy? Wait until tonight. I bought a book on massage. And if that doesn't work, I think I can come up with something else that will entertain you. What's more, it won't be a fantasy, either. Guaranteed."

She felt herself grow warm in the glow of love that she saw in his eyes. This was the real thing, she thought. This was the love that would last a lifetime. She knew that as surely as she knew that the sun would rise.

"What are you thinking?" he asked.

"Just that we lucked out."

"We sure did." He smiled. "We got the happy ending."

And don't miss

LOST AND FOUND

The exciting new novel by Jayne Ann Krentz

Coming soon in hardcover from G. P. Putnam's Sons!

THE RANKS OF MEDIEVAL WARRIORS, FOREVER frozen in their steel carapaces, loomed behind him in the shadows. Mack Easton's face was as unreadable as that of any of the helmed figures standing guard on the other side of the office window. There was something about Easton that made him appear locked in time, too, Cady thought. A quality of stillness, perhaps. You had to look twice to see him there in the shadows. If it hadn't been for the glow of the computer screen reflecting off the strong, fierce planes of his face and glinting on the lenses of his glasses, he would have been invisible.

Not a youthful face, she thought. Definitely mature. But not *too* mature. Thirty-nine or possibly forty. A good age. An interesting age. At least it looked interesting on Mack Easton.

The weird thing was that, even though she had never been able to imagine an exact image of him with only the telephone connection to go on, now that she was actually face-to-face with him she could see that he fit the voice perfectly. Take the serious, dark-rimmed glasses, for example. Never in a million years would she have thought to add that touch if she had been asked to draw a picture of him based on their long-distance conversations. But when he had removed them from his pocket a few minutes ago and put them on she had decided they looked absolutely right on him.

"We have a photograph," he said. "It was found in the museum's archives."

Museum was not the word she would have used to dignify Military World, she thought. What was she doing here? She must have been temporarily out of her mind last night when she took Easton's call. She was at home in hushed galleries, art research libraries, and the cluttered back rooms of prestigious auction salons. She mingled with connoisseurs and educated collectors.

Military World, with its low-budget reproductions of arms and armor from various wars was very much as she had envisioned it; tacky. Then again, maybe that was just her personal bias showing. She had never been overly fond of armor. To her it symbolized all that was brutish and primitive in human nature. The fact that the artisans of the past had devoted enormous talent and craftsmanship to its design and decoration struck her as bizarre.

The office in which they sat belonged to the two owners of Military World, a pair that went by the names of Notch and Dewey. They hovered anxiously in the shadows, having surrendered the single desk to Easton and his laptop computer.

Mack occupied the space behind the desk as if he owned it. She got the impression that was the way it was with any place he happened to inhabit at any particular moment. Something that just sort of happened to him; something he took for granted.

She wished that she could get a better look at his eyes but the reflection on his glasses concealed them as effectively as the steel helms hid the features of the armored figures beyond the windows.

He pushed the photograph toward her across the battered desk and reached out to switch on the small desk lamp. She watched, unwillingly fascinated, as the beam fell on one large, powerful-looking hand. No wedding ring, she noticed. Not that you could be sure a man was unmarried just because he didn't happen to wear a ring.

With an effort she tore her gaze away from his hand and focused on the photo. It featured a horse and rider garbed in flamboyantly styled armor that looked as if it had been designed for a video game or dreamed up by an artist for the cover of a science fiction fantasy novel. She recognized it as a fairly accurate reproduction of the elaborately embellished armor crafted during the Renaissance. Such impractical styles had never been intended for the battlefield. They had been created for the sole purpose of making the wearer look good in ceremonies, festivals, and parades.

"Fifteenth century, judging from the helm and breast plate," she said. "Italian in style." *In style* was a polite way of saying *reproduction*.

"I'm aware of that, Miss Briggs," Easton said with icy patience. "But if you look closely, you can see a portion of another display behind the horse's, uh, rear."

She took a closer look. Sure enough, if she looked past the tail of the fake horse she could just make out the dimly lit image of a standing figure garbed in heavily decorated steel.

"Half-armor," she murmured. It was always good policy to impress the client, even if you weren't particularly interested in the job. Word of mouth was important. "In the style of the Northern Italian armorers of the sixteenth century. Looks like part of a garniture meant for jousting at the barriers. Suits of armor from this era often consisted of dozens of supplementary and interchangeable pieces that allowed the set to be modified for specific uses. Sort of like a modern all-in-one tool kit."

"It's the helm that we're interested in here," Mach said.

She peered at it. The bad lighting made it difficult to see much detail. "What about it?"

"It's the only piece that was stolen."

She looked up. "Is there a better photo around?"

One of the two men who hovered near the far end of the desk, the individual who went by the name Dewey, edged closer with a crablike movement.

"Lucky to have that one," he said, sounding apologetic.

She could only guess at Dewey's age. His face was a worn and weathered map that could have belonged to a man of fifty or seventy. He was dressed in military surplus complete with camouflage fatigues, battered boots and a wide leather belt. His graying hair was caught in a scruffy ponytail secured with a rubber band. She would not have been surprised to learn that he commuted to and from work on a very large motorcycle.

It was hard to imagine that he was representative of Lost and Found's typical clientele. How in the world had he and his partner managed to find the very-hard-to-find Mack Easton? More to the point, why had Mack agreed to help them? Surely he was too expensive for this pair. If he wasn't, she certainly was.

"I was going for a shot of the fifteenth-century display," Dewey explained. "We had just finished setting it up, you see. This was maybe two years back, right Notch?"

The other man nodded vigorously. "Right."

Dewey returned his attention to Cady. "I wanted to get a picture for our album. Lucked out and accidentally got a bit of the other exhibit in the shot."

"Never would have guessed that the helmet on the sixteenth-century suit was the real thing." Notch spread his hands. "Like, who knew, man?"

Cady cleared her throat. "How did it come into the, uh, museum's collection?"

"I found it right after we bought Military World from old man Belford. He had it stashed away in the back room. I polished it up and added it to the rest of the outfit. Seemed to match, y'know?"

"I see." She tapped one finger against the photo while she considered her options. As much as she wanted to take on another assignment for Lost and Found, she had a reputation to maintain. One had to draw the line somewhere. She did not trace reproductions.

Surreptitiously she glanced at her watch. She might be able to catch the one o'clock flight if she left Military World within the next forty-five minutes. She could be home in time for dinner.

She turned back to Easton. Something in the way he was watching her told her that he had noticed her checking the time. She summoned up what she hoped was an expression of professional interest. "What did the insurance people say when you notified them about the theft?"

Notch and Dewey exchanged uneasy looks.

Mack did not move. "There's a slight problem with the insurance situation."

She sighed. "In other words, the helm was uninsured?"

Notch made an awkward sound deep in his throat. "Things have been a little rough lately, financially speaking. Dewey and me had to economize and make some cutbacks, y'know? Sort of let some of the insurance go."

"Not that the insurance company would have covered the helm for anything like its true value, anyway," Dewey said quickly. "If we'd had coverage, it would have been for a reproduction, not the real thing on account of we didn't know it was genuine, if you see what I mean."

"I don't want to be rude," Cady said gently, "but what makes you think the helm is a genuine sixteenth-century piece?"

Dewey and Notch stared at her, open-mouthed.

"You're supposed to be an expert," Dewey said. "Can't you tell from looking at it?"

She made a bid for patience. "This is only a photograph. There is no way I or anyone else can use it to determine whether or not the helm is genuine."

Notch looked stricken. "But Mack here said that you knew your stuff."

"Old armor is very popular right now," she explained. "A lot of the well-heeled early retirees in the software industry are collecting it like mad. Guess it reminds them of all those sword-and-sorcery video and computer games they love to play. Prices are going through the roof. Unfortunately, antique armor is fairly easy to fake. Bury a piece of steel in the ground with some acidic substance for a while and, presto, you get aged armor."

Notch bristled. "Are you sayin' our helmet is a forgery?"

"I'm saying that is an extremely likely possibility." Cady spread her hands. "Even the experts get burned a lot when it comes to armor. And the business of creating counterfeits isn't exactly new. A lot of the best reproductions of antique armor were made in the nineteenth century. By now, the steel has taken on the patina of genuine age and can easily pass for the real thing."

"I still say our helmet is the real thing," Notch declared.

Cady slanted a quick, searching glance at Mack. He

moved his head in the smallest of negatives. He was staying out of the argument; letting her handle the clients.

Summoning up her best professional expression, she turned back to Notch and Dewey. "Why are you convinced that the helm is genuine when every other piece in your collection is a reproduction?"

"Simple." Dewey rocked triumphantly on his heels and looked shrewd. "Someone stole it."

PENGUIN PUTNAM INC.
Online

Your Internet gateway to a virtual environment with
hundreds of entertaining and enlightening books
from Penguin Putnam Inc.

*While you're there, get the latest buzz on
the best authors and books around—*

Tom Clancy, Patricia Cornwell, W.E.B. Griffin,
Nora Roberts, William Gibson, Robin Cook,
Brian Jacques, Catherine Coulter, Stephen King,
Jacquelyn Mitchard, and many more!

**Penguin Putnam Online is located at
http://www.penguinputnam.com**

PENGUIN PUTNAM NEWS

Every month you'll get an inside look at our upcoming books and new features on our site. This is an
ongoing effort to provide you with the most
up-to-date information about
our books and authors.

**Subscribe to Penguin Putnam News at
http://www.penguinputnam.com/ClubPPI**